- 2017

W9-CFQ-479

THE ADVENTURES OF
SUPERHERO GIRL™

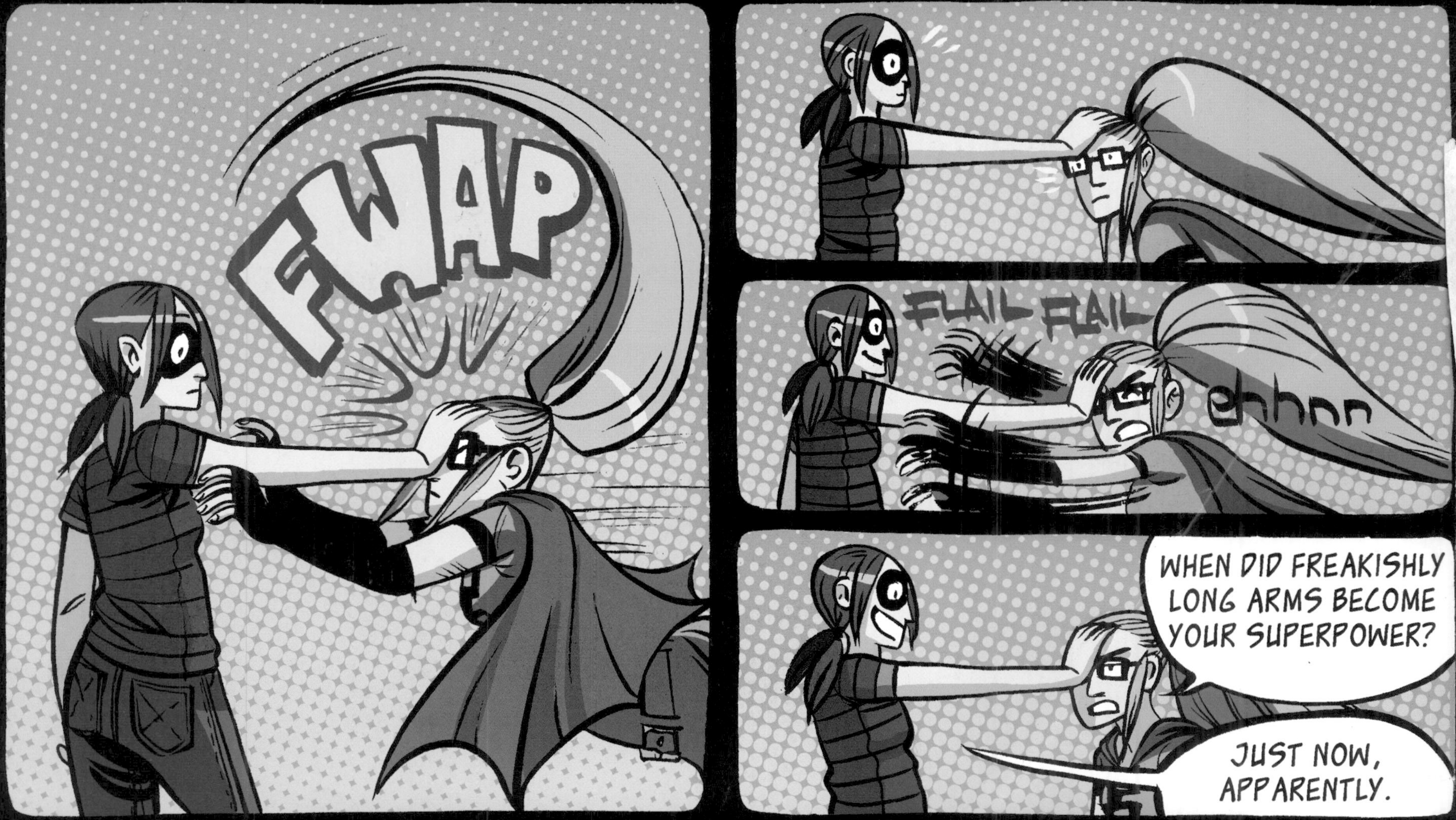
FWAP
FLAIL FLAIL
ehhnn
WHEN DID FREAKISHLY LONG ARMS BECOME YOUR SUPERPOWER?
JUST NOW, APPARENTLY.

THE ADVENTURES OF SUPERHERO GIRL™

EXPANDED EDITION

WRITTEN AND DRAWN BY

FAITH ERIN HICKS

COLORS BY CRIS PETER

INTRODUCTION BY KURT BUSIEK

DARK HORSE BOOKS

PRESIDENT AND PUBLISHER
MIKE RICHARDSON

EXPANDED EDITION EDITOR
DANIEL CHABON

FIRST EDITION EDITOR
JAY (RACHEL) EDIDIN

ASSISTANT EDITORS
JEMIAH JEFFERSON, RACHEL ROBERTS

DESIGNER
ETHAN KIMBERLING

DIGITAL ART TECHNICIAN
CHRISTINA McKENZIE

THE ADVENTURES OF SUPERHERO GIRL (EXPANDED EDITION)

Published by Dark Horse Books
A division of Dark Horse Comics, Inc.
10956 SE Main Street
Milwaukie, OR 97222

DarkHorse.com
AdventuresOfSuperheroGirl.com

Second edition: June 2017
ISBN 978-1-50670-336-7

10 9 8 7 6 5 4 3 2 1
Printed in China

THE ADVENTURES OF (da da DA!) SUPERHERO GIRL

INTRODUCTION

I don't know Faith Erin Hicks, really, aside from the occasional Twitter exchange, or the comment threads on her online strips. And not even that, when I started reading *Superhero Girl*.

No, I came to her work in the old-fashioned way: By looking for good comics for my daughters to read.

Sydney and Katie had gone bananas over Raina Telgemeier's *Smile*, and, no fool I, I went looking for books like it—books that would hook them as hard as comics had hooked me when I was young. I'm a dad; I love comics; and I like to share what I love with my family, so off I went. One of the books I found was Faith's *The War at Ellsmere*, which everyone liked, and that led us to *Superhero Girl*, the online (and later in print) *Friends with Boys*, and the current *Nothing Can Possibly Go Wrong* . . .

And one of the great rewards in looking for cool stuff your daughters will like is that you find new stuff you like, too. It's win-win.

I've liked all of Faith's stuff, and I'm eager for every new page of hers that hits the web or the bookshelves. Her work has charm, energy, emotion, accessibility, and a wonderful sense of humanity. But for all that I'm kind of indiscriminate in liking it—she could adapt the minutes of an Ottawa city council meeting, and I'd want to read it—there's a special place in my heart for *Superhero Girl*

I'm a superhero fan; I'm a superhero writer; I'm immersed in the genre. Wallowing in it; overthinking it; fat packed with trivia so arcane I can send other superhero obsessives scrambling to *Wikipedia* and Google to find out what the hell I'm talking about. And it's easy, when you're that deep in things, to miss the forest not just for the trees, but for the bark on the trees and the bugs on the bark and the patterns on the wings of the bugs on the . .

You get the idea.

So I started reading *Superhero Girl* because I'd bought *The War at Ellsmere* and liked it, and my first reaction was, "Cool. A really good superhero parody!"

As time went on, and I read more of it, I realized I was wrong about that.

Not about the "really good" part—*Superhero Girl* is a terrific strip, full of all the great drawing and engaging charm Faith brings to her work. And it's funny. If you've read it before, you know this. If you haven't read it yet, you will. Bear with a Monocle alone would make the strip a winner, but from

Spectacle Girl's origin to Superhero Girl's archnemesis Shaun, to Kevin (arrgh, Kevin!), to King Ninja—it's as funny as they come.

It's just not really a parody, is it?

Like I said, steeped in superheroes as I am, it's easy to lose sight of the important stuff, and when you're surrounded by continuity concerns and massive crossovers and often overly grim, overpopulated superhero worlds full of complex and contradictory histories of fictional metals and incomprehensible rules of time travel, it's easy to assume that a funny superhero strip must be a parody of the "real" stuff.

But while Faith is obviously having fun playing with the trappings of the superhero genre, that's not what the strip is really about. Spoofing superheroes isn't the point. She's simply using the genre—genre, as a set of trappings, structures, tropes, whatever gives us a framework in which to tell stories about universal things—to talk about something else.

Superhero Girl is about life. It's about being a younger sister, about being a broke roommate, about needing a job, being underappreciated, getting sick, feeling out of place at parties, being annoyed by people carping when you're doing your best—all wrapped up in the package of being a young superhero in a small-market city where you're pursuing your dreams but don't seem to be getting anywhere.

That's not parody. There may be elements of parody on the surface, but really, that's rich, human storytelling. It's telling the truth through humor, and using the trappings of the superhero genre to universalize it, to turn it into something symbolic, so we can all identify with it, maybe more than we could if SG was a paralegal or a barista or a surgical intern. The superhero stuff is the context, the package, and the humanity and emotion and the humor found in it are the content. The story.

And that's way more about telling a story that connects with readers honestly than a million dimensional wars and fussery about the properties of made-up metals.

The Adventures of Superhero Girl is a superhero story. A funny, human look at how we deal with the craziness of life and dreams and struggle, all dressed up in a cape and a mask and the joy of leaping over tall buildings and biffing some monster clear over the horizon. It's fun. It's charming. It's clever. But above all, it's truthful, funny, and warm.

Or at least, that's the reason why I love *Superhero Girl*. You're going to have your own reason, and it may be completely different from the perspective of a steeped-in-genre, overanalyzing industry professional. But whatever it is, I'm sure you're going to like it, and like me, you're going to hope this is just the first volume of many.

And in case you're wondering: Sydney and Katie haven't read all that much *Superhero Girl*. They come at comics in a different way from their dad—they like graphic novels and collected editions, they're not that into traditionally formatted comic strips, and they've never really latched on to superheroes the way I have. But they like funny comics, they like comics where girls get to be the lead character, and they like comics they can relate to, the ones that are more about people than about cosmic wars. When this book comes out, as a book they can curl up on the couch and spend time with, they'll be all over it.

And that'll be one more thing I get to share with my family.

I hope you'll have as much fun sharing it with yours.

KURT BUSIEK
OCTOBER 2012

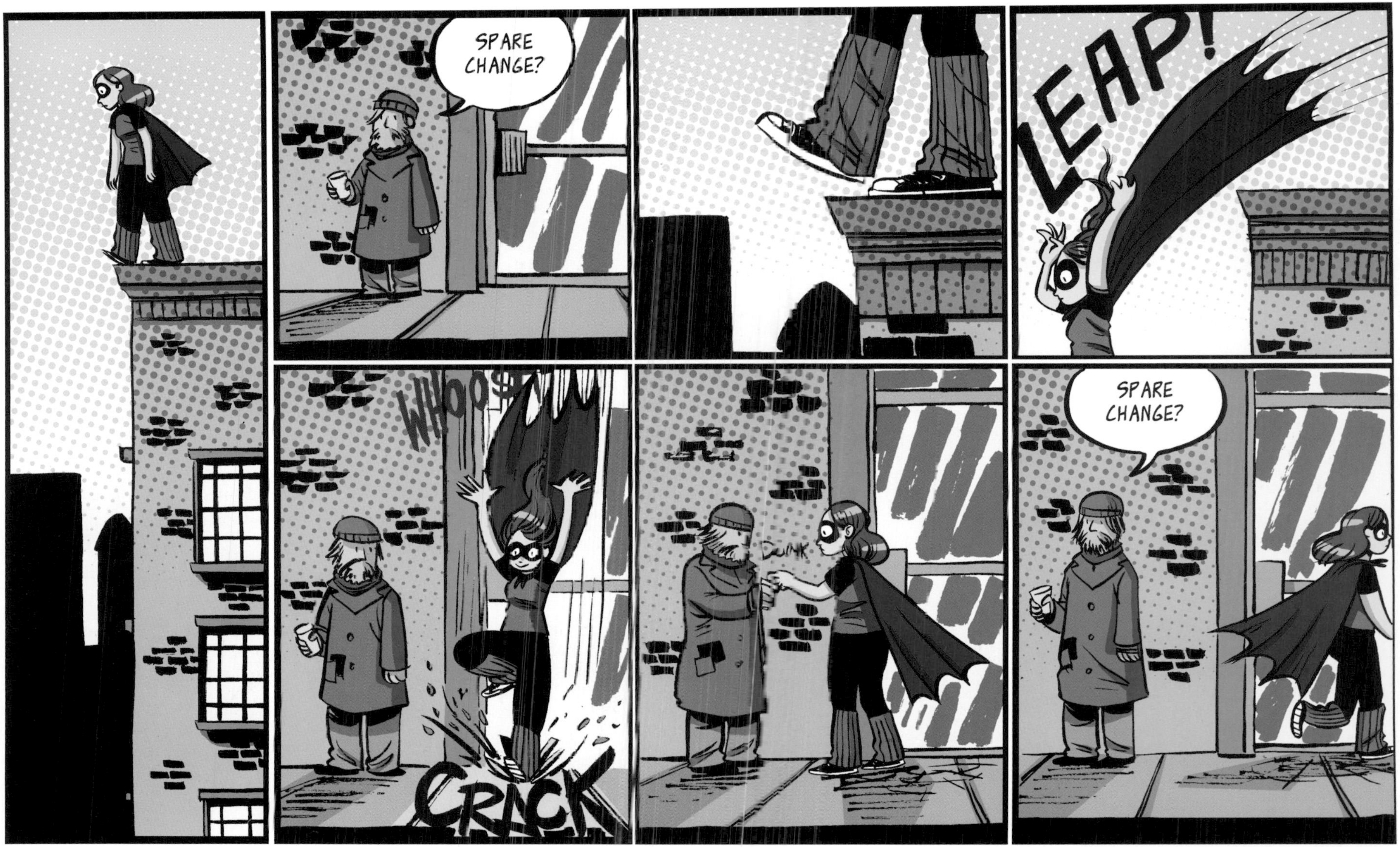
SPARE CHANGE?
LEAP!
WHOOS
CRICK
CLINK
SPARE CHANGE?

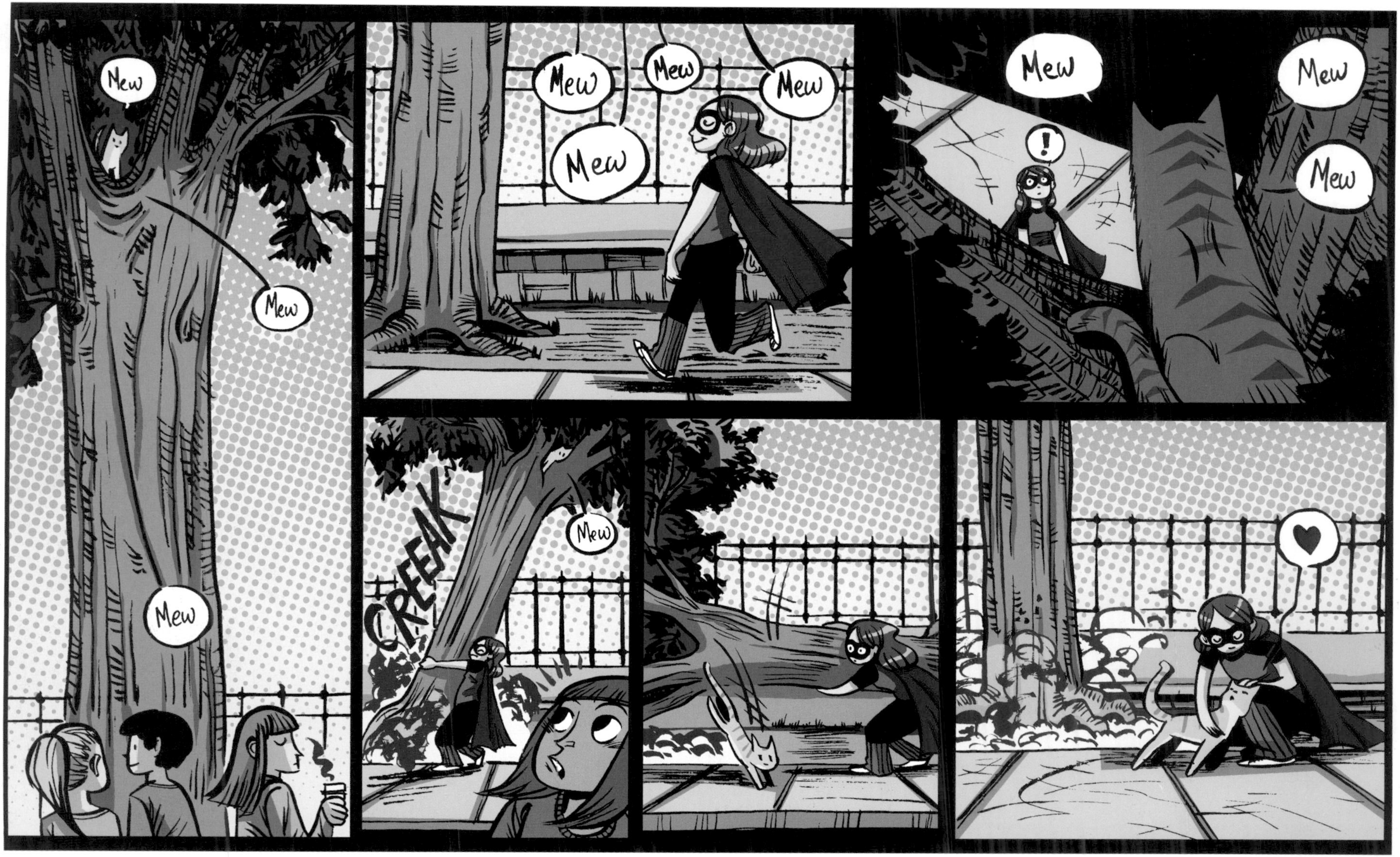

Mew
Mew
Mew
Mew
Mew
Mew
Mew
Mew
!
Mew
Mew
CREEAK
Mew

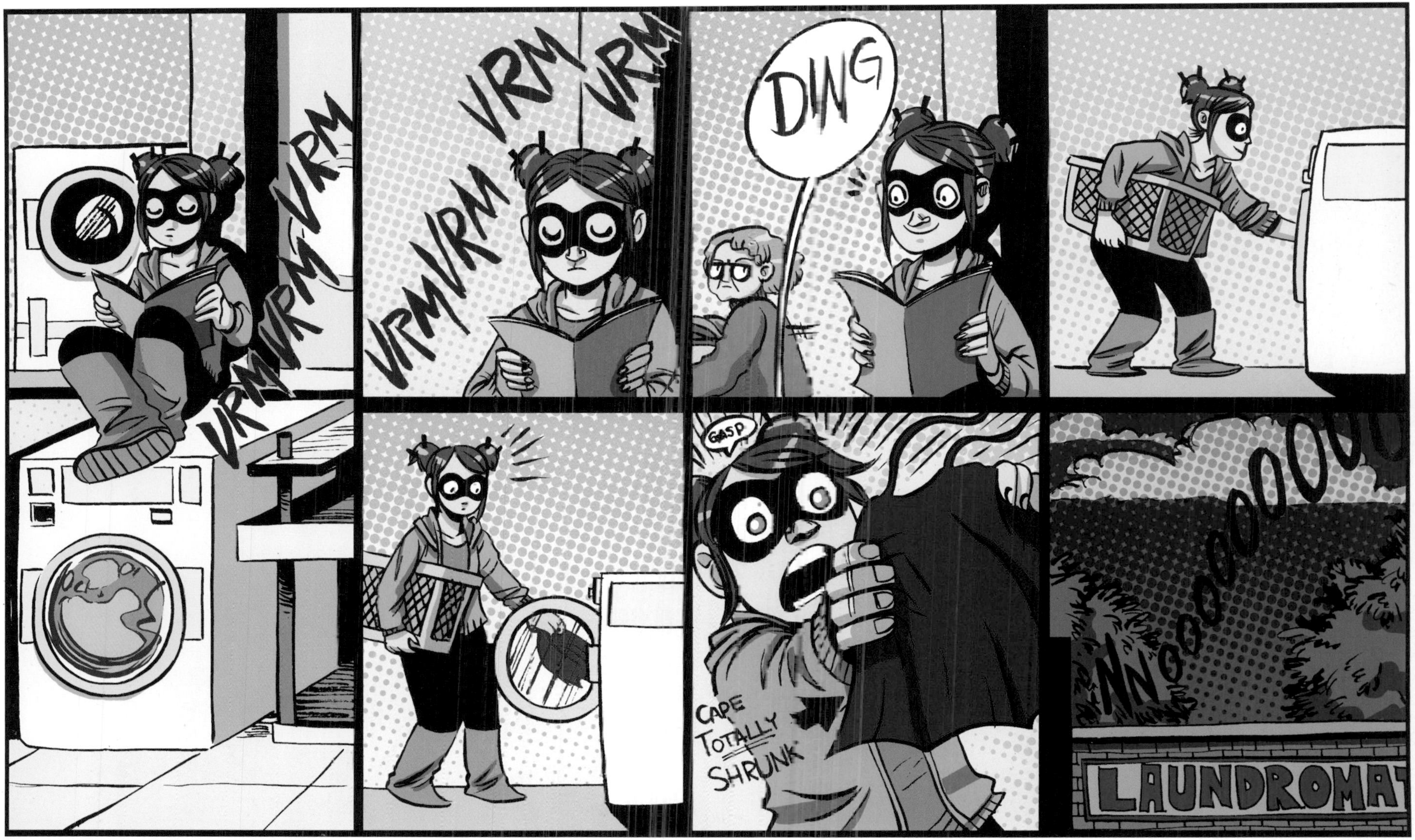
VRMVRMVRMVRM
VRMVRMVRMVRM
DING
GASP
CAPE TOTALLY SHRUNK
NNOOOOOOOOO
LAUNDROMAT

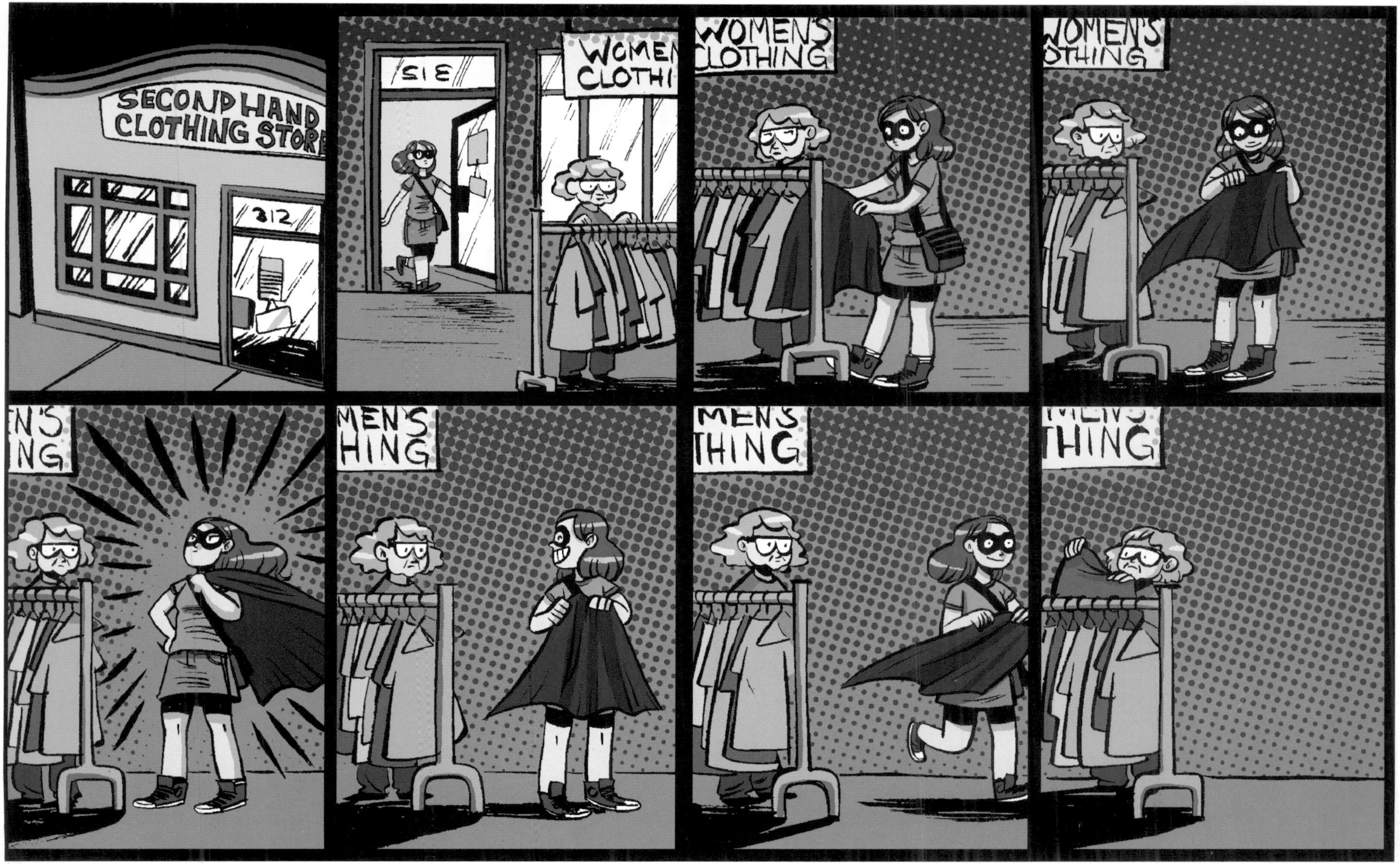
SECONDHAND
CLOTHING STORE
312
WOMEN'S
CLOTHING

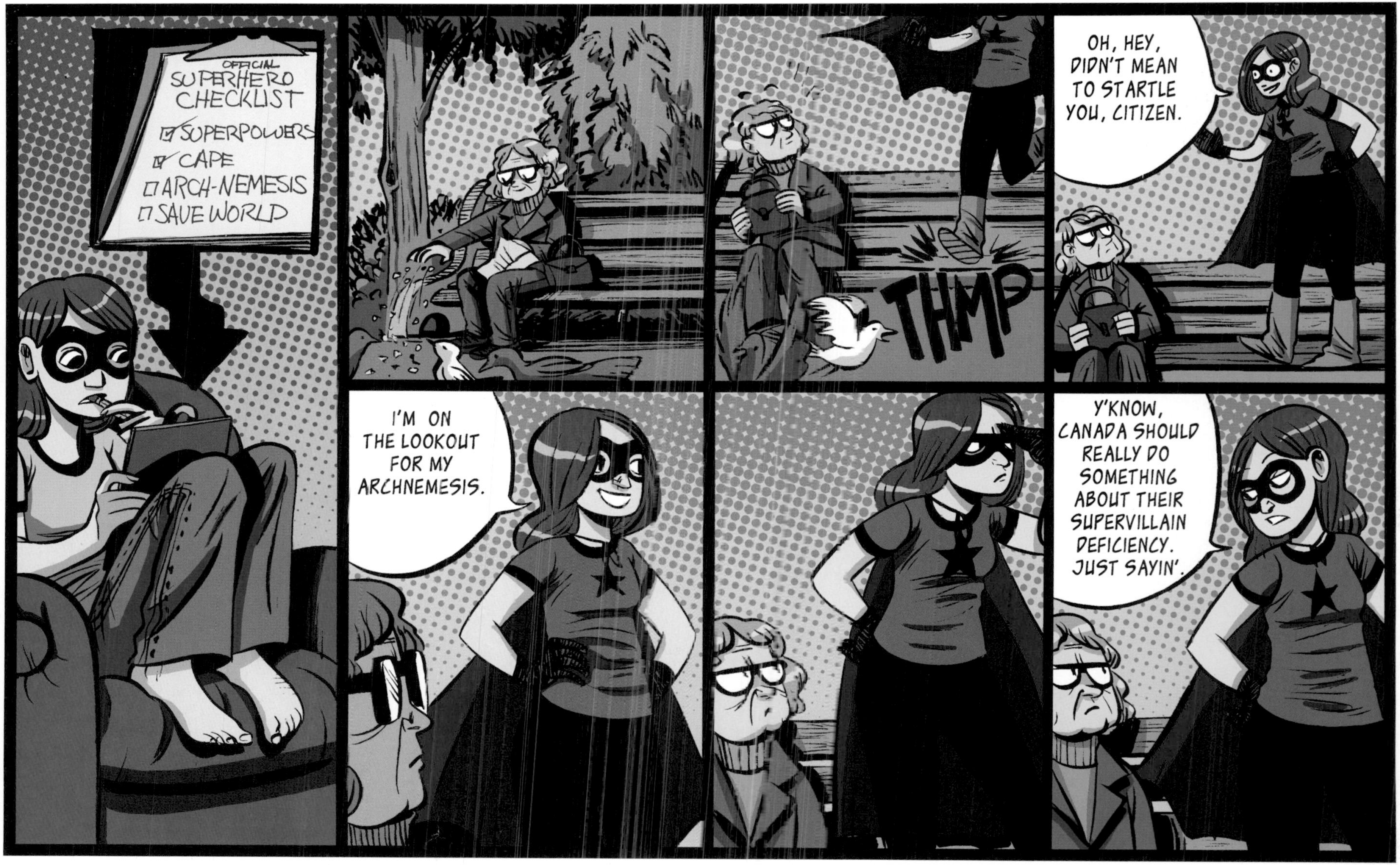

OFFICIAL SUPERHERO CHECKLIST
☑ SUPERPOWERS
☑ CAPE
☐ ARCH-NEMESIS
☐ SAVE WORLD
THMP
OH, HEY, DIDN'T MEAN TO STARTLE YOU, CITIZEN.
I'M ON THE LOOKOUT FOR MY ARCHNEMESIS.
Y'KNOW, CANADA SHOULD REALLY DO SOMETHING ABOUT THEIR SUPERVILLAIN DEFICIENCY. JUST SAYIN'.

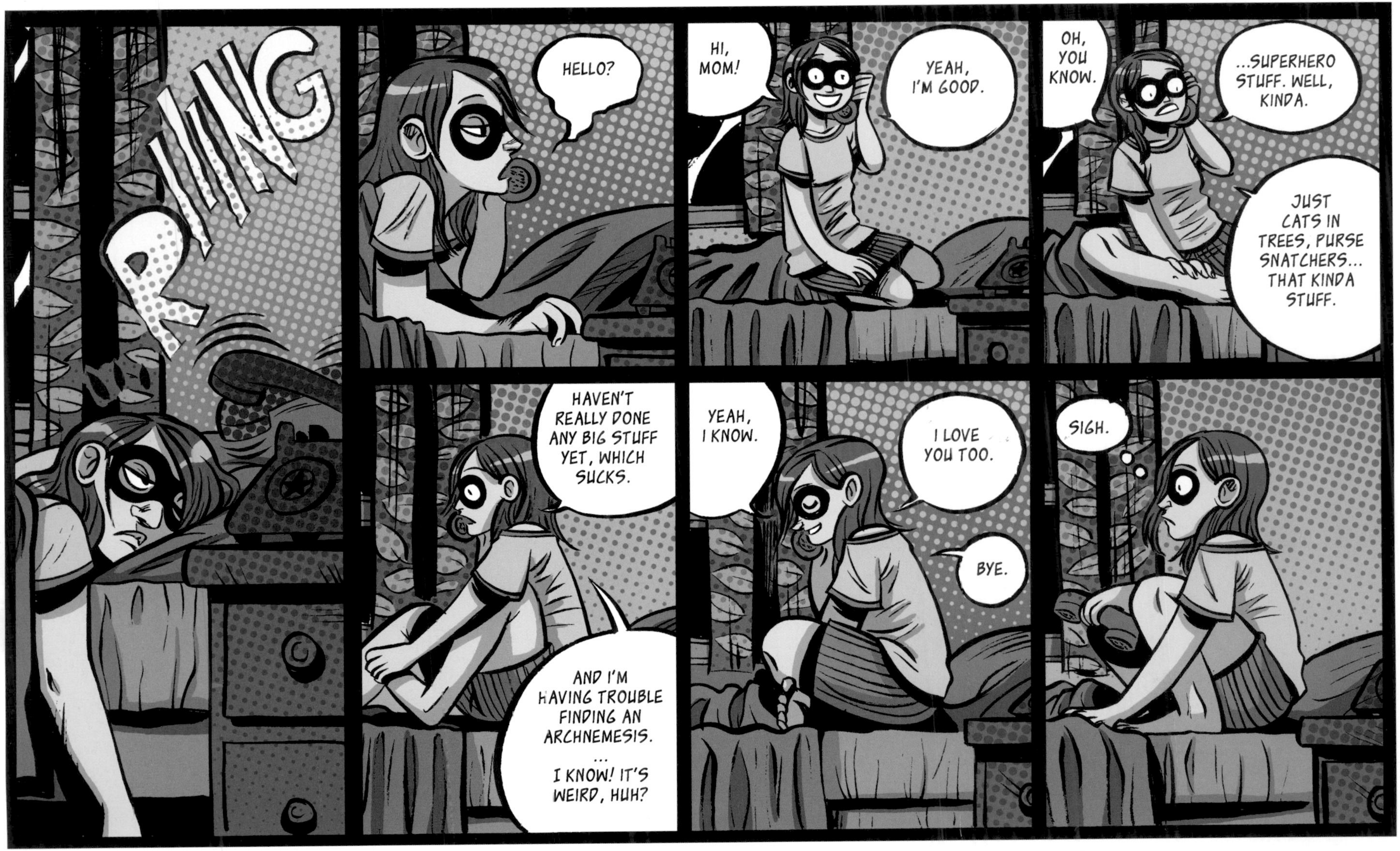
RRING
HELLO?
HI, MOM!
YEAH, I'M GOOD.
OH, YOU KNOW.
...SUPERHERO STUFF. WELL, KINDA.
JUST CATS IN TREES, PURSE SNATCHERS... THAT KINDA STUFF.
HAVEN'T REALLY DONE ANY BIG STUFF YET, WHICH SUCKS.
AND I'M HAVING TROUBLE FINDING AN ARCHNEMESIS. ... I KNOW! IT'S WEIRD, HUH?
YEAH, I KNOW.
I LOVE YOU TOO.
BYE.
SIGH.

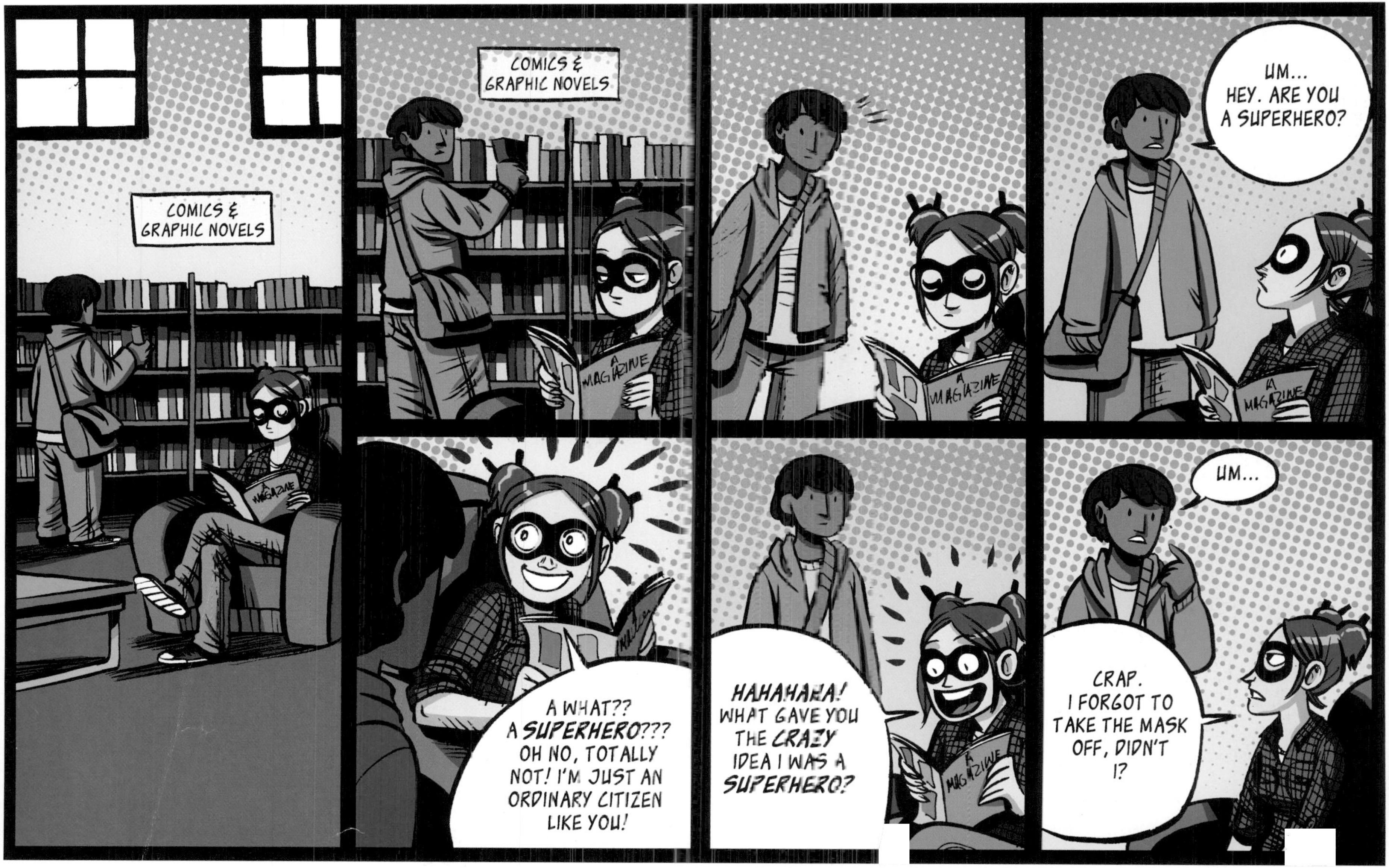
COMICS & GRAPHIC NOVELS
COMICS & GRAPHIC NOVELS
A MAGAZINE
UM... HEY. ARE YOU A SUPERHERO?
A WHAT?? A SUPERHERO??? OH NO, TOTALLY NOT! I'M JUST AN ORDINARY CITIZEN LIKE YOU!
HAHAHAHA! WHAT GAVE YOU THE CRAZY IDEA I WAS A SUPERHERO?
UM...
CRAP. I FORGOT TO TAKE THE MASK OFF, DIDN'T I?

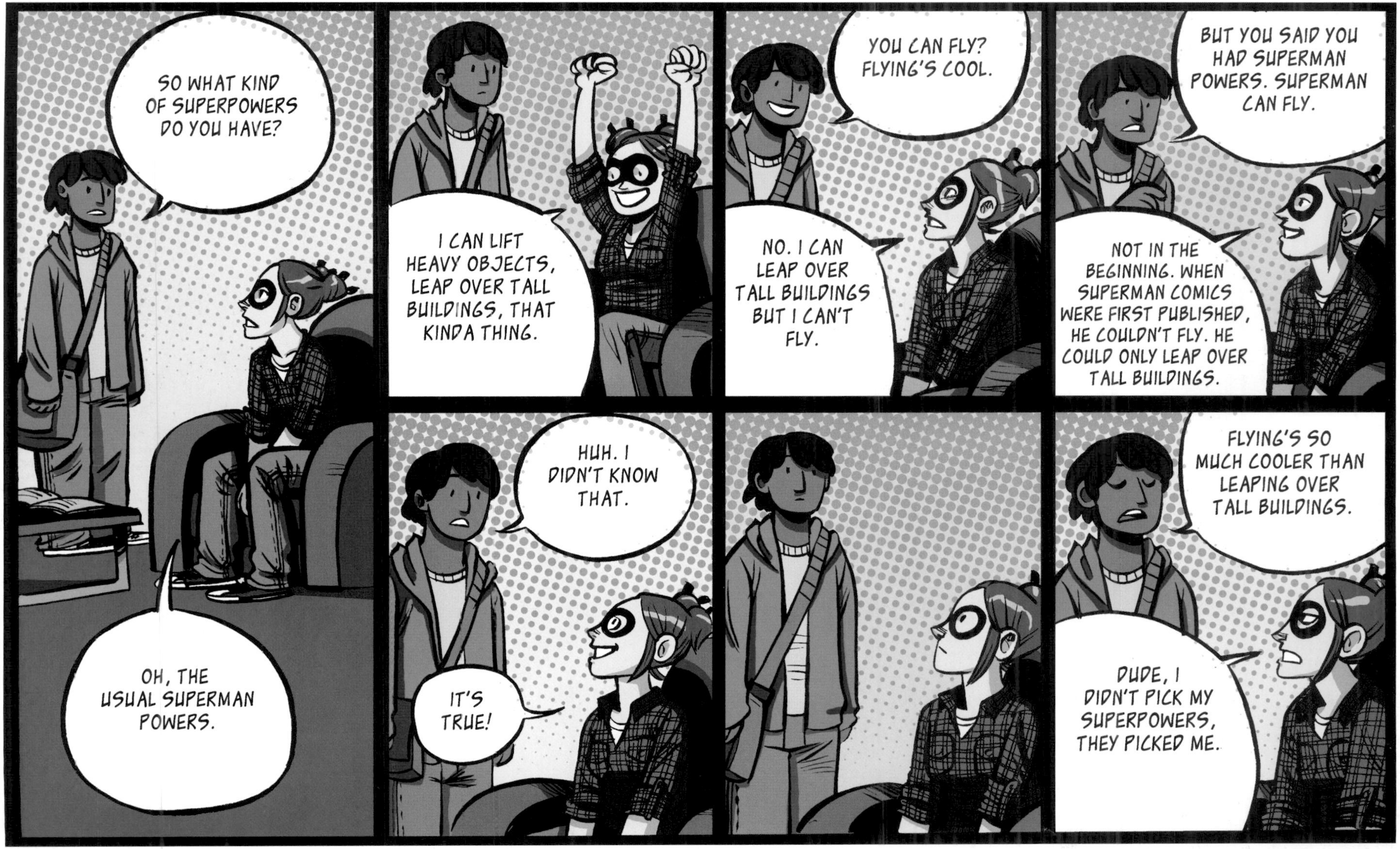
SO WHAT KIND OF SUPERPOWERS DO YOU HAVE?
OH, THE USUAL SUPERMAN POWERS.
I CAN LIFT HEAVY OBJECTS, LEAP OVER TALL BUILDINGS, THAT KINDA THING.
YOU CAN FLY? FLYING'S COOL.
NO. I CAN LEAP OVER TALL BUILDINGS BUT I CAN'T FLY.
BUT YOU SAID YOU HAD SUPERMAN POWERS. SUPERMAN CAN FLY.
NOT IN THE BEGINNING. WHEN SUPERMAN COMICS WERE FIRST PUBLISHED, HE COULDN'T FLY. HE COULD ONLY LEAP OVER TALL BUILDINGS.
HUH. I DIDN'T KNOW THAT.
IT'S TRUE!
FLYING'S SO MUCH COOLER THAN LEAPING OVER TALL BUILDINGS.
DUDE, I DIDN'T PICK MY SUPERPOWERS, THEY PICKED ME.

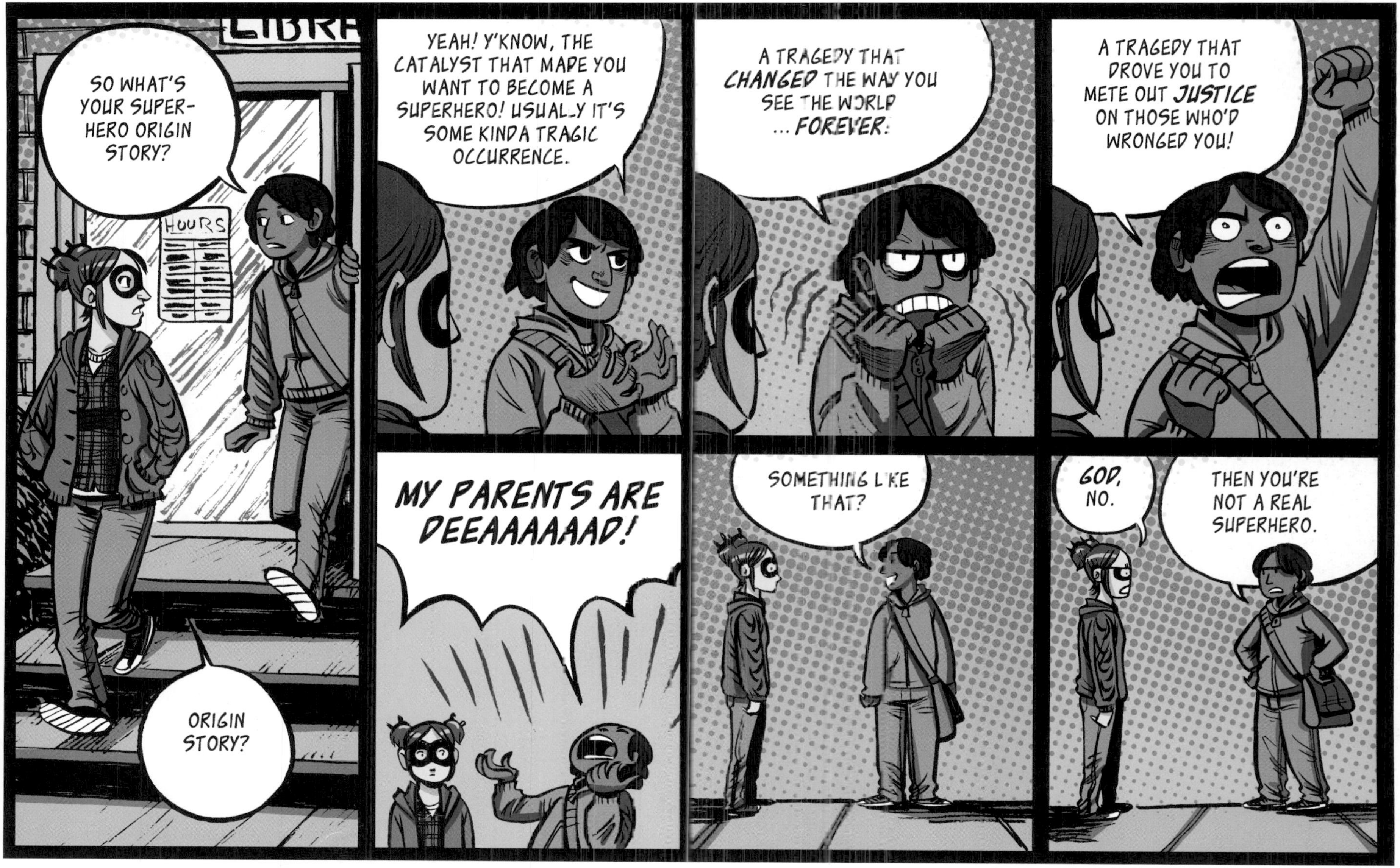
LIBRA
SO WHAT'S YOUR SUPER-HERO ORIGIN STORY?
HOURS
ORIGIN STORY?
YEAH! Y'KNOW, THE CATALYST THAT MADE YOU WANT TO BECOME A SUPERHERO! USUALLY IT'S SOME KINDA TRAGIC OCCURRENCE.
A TRAGEDY THAT CHANGED THE WAY YOU SEE THE WORLD ... FOREVER!
A TRAGEDY THAT DROVE YOU TO METE OUT JUSTICE ON THOSE WHO'D WRONGED YOU!
MY PARENTS ARE DEEAAAAAAAD!
SOMETHING LIKE THAT?
GOD, NO.
THEN YOU'RE NOT A REAL SUPERHERO.

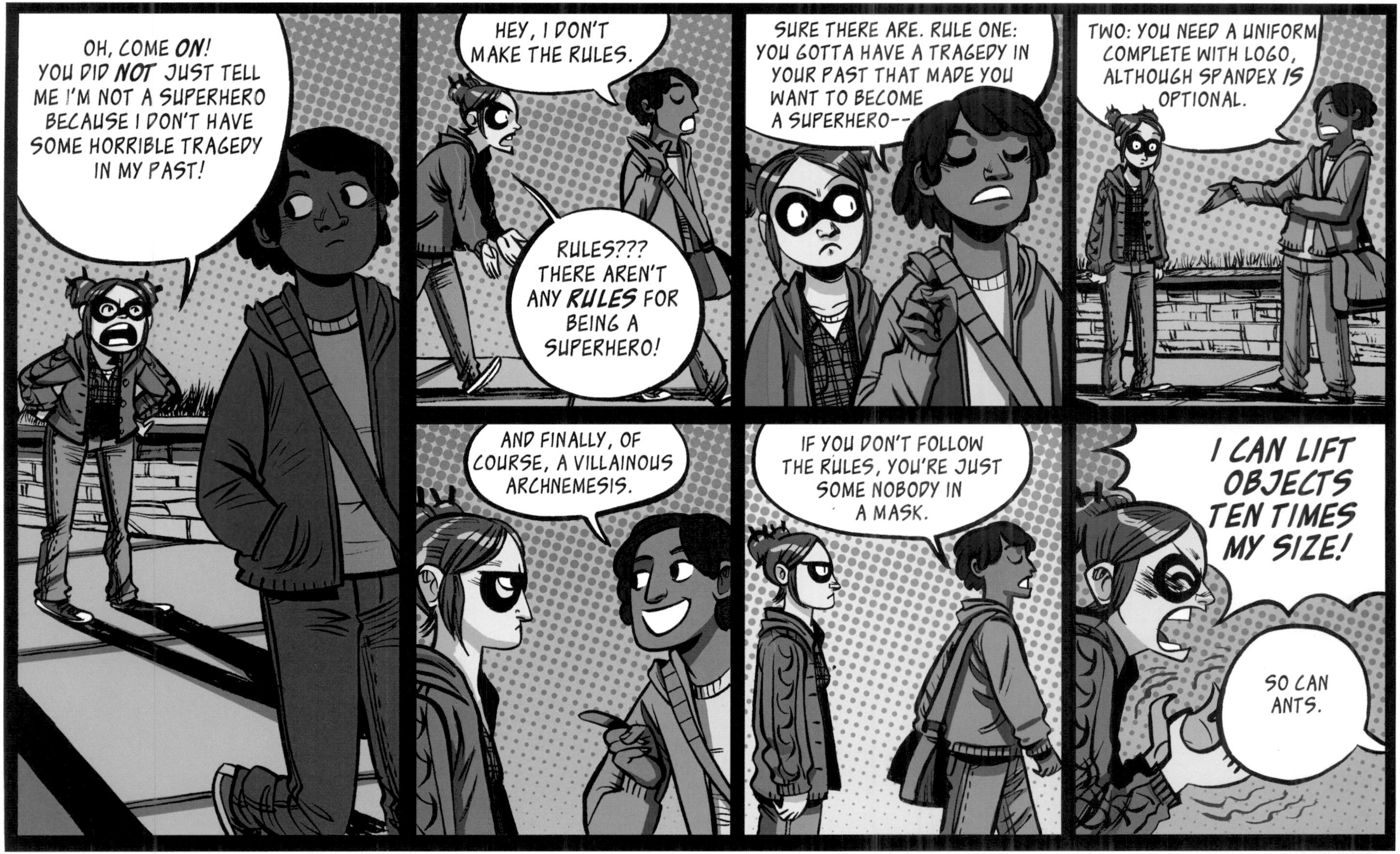
OH, COME ON! YOU DID NOT JUST TELL ME I'M NOT A SUPERHERO BECAUSE I DON'T HAVE SOME HORRIBLE TRAGEDY IN MY PAST!
HEY, I DON'T MAKE THE RULES.
RULES??? THERE AREN'T ANY RULES FOR BEING A SUPERHERO!
SURE THERE ARE. RULE ONE: YOU GOTTA HAVE A TRAGEDY IN YOUR PAST THAT MADE YOU WANT TO BECOME A SUPERHERO--
TWO: YOU NEED A UNIFORM COMPLETE WITH LOGO, ALTHOUGH SPANDEX IS OPTIONAL.
AND FINALLY, OF COURSE, A VILLAINOUS ARCHNEMESIS.
IF YOU DON'T FOLLOW THE RULES, YOU'RE JUST SOME NOBODY IN A MASK.
I CAN LIFT OBJECTS TEN TIMES MY SIZE!
SO CAN ANTS.

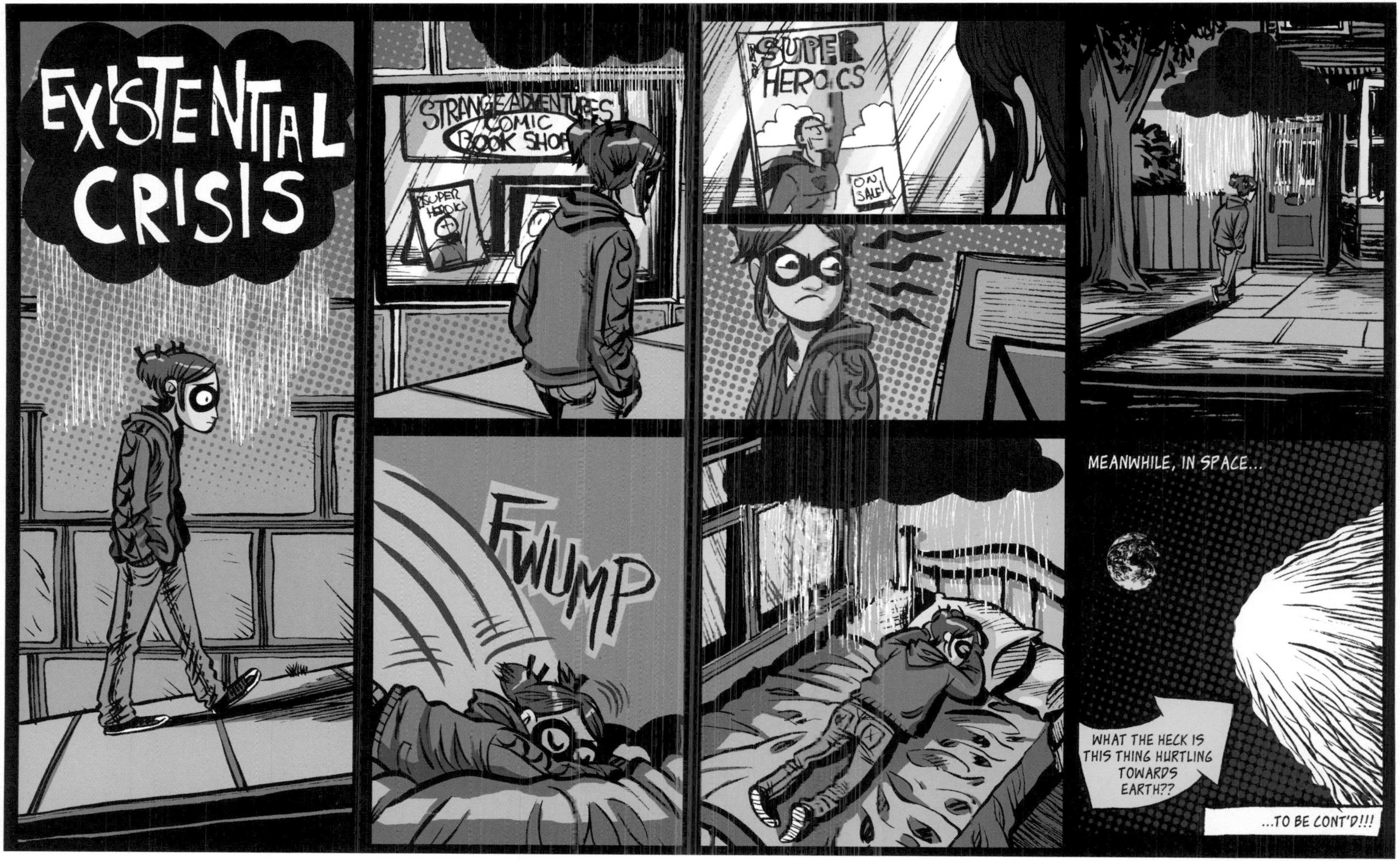
EXISTENTIAL CRISIS
STRANGE ADVENTURES
COMIC BOOK SHOP
SUPER HEROICS
SUPER HEROICS
ON SALE!
FWUMP
MEANWHILE, IN SPACE...
WHAT THE HECK IS THIS THING HURTLING TOWARDS EARTH??
...TO BE CONT'D!!!

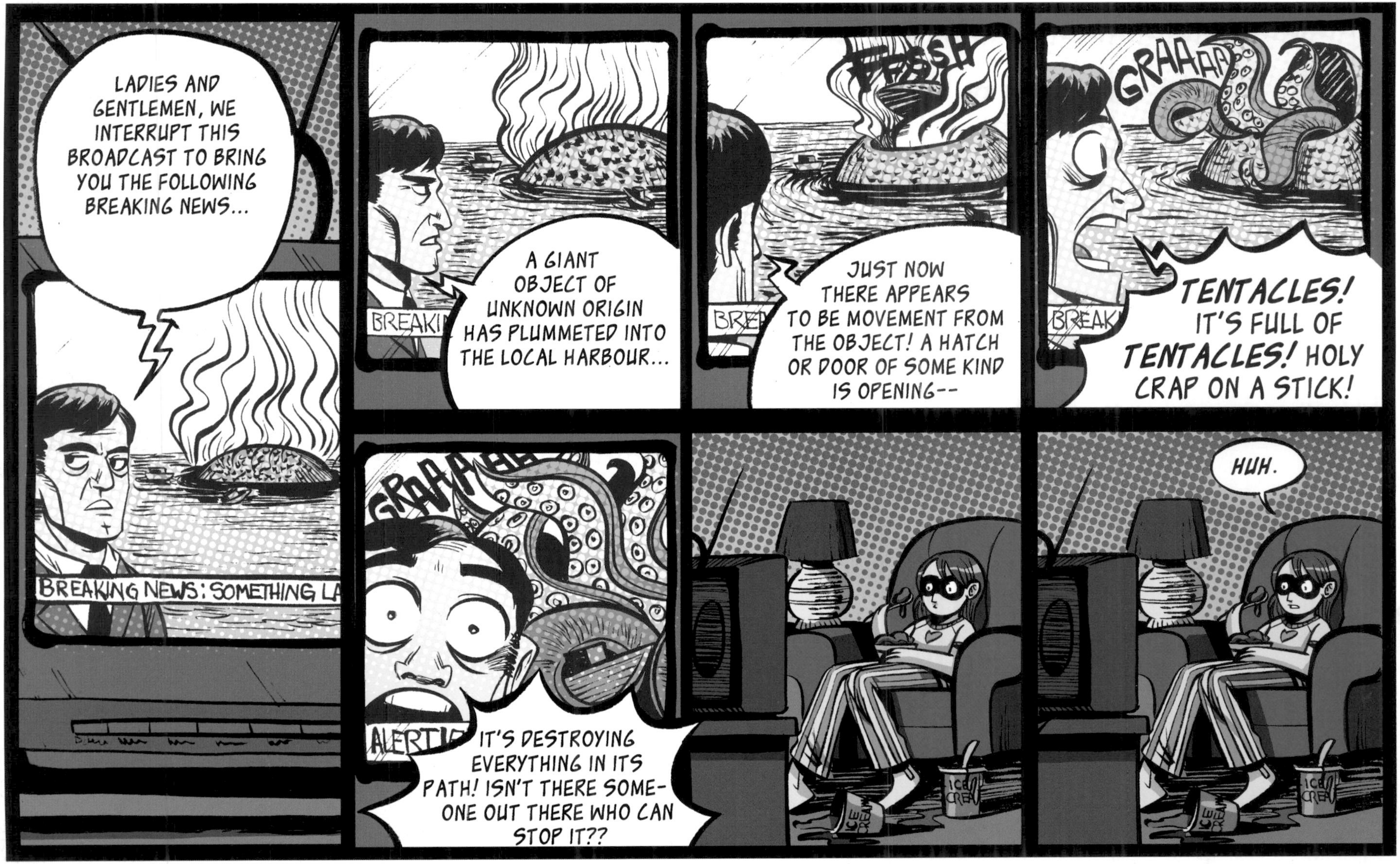
LADIES AND GENTLEMEN, WE INTERRUPT THIS BROADCAST TO BRING YOU THE FOLLOWING BREAKING NEWS...
BREAKING NEWS: SOMETHING LA
A GIANT OBJECT OF UNKNOWN ORIGIN HAS PLUMMETED INTO THE LOCAL HARBOUR...
BREAKI
JUST NOW THERE APPEARS TO BE MOVEMENT FROM THE OBJECT! A HATCH OR DOOR OF SOME KIND IS OPENING--
BRE
GRAAAA
TENTACLES! IT'S FULL OF TENTACLES! HOLY CRAP ON A STICK!
BREAK
GRAAAA
ALERT!
IT'S DESTROYING EVERYTHING IN ITS PATH! ISN'T THERE SOME-ONE OUT THERE WHO CAN STOP IT??
ICE CREAM
HUH.

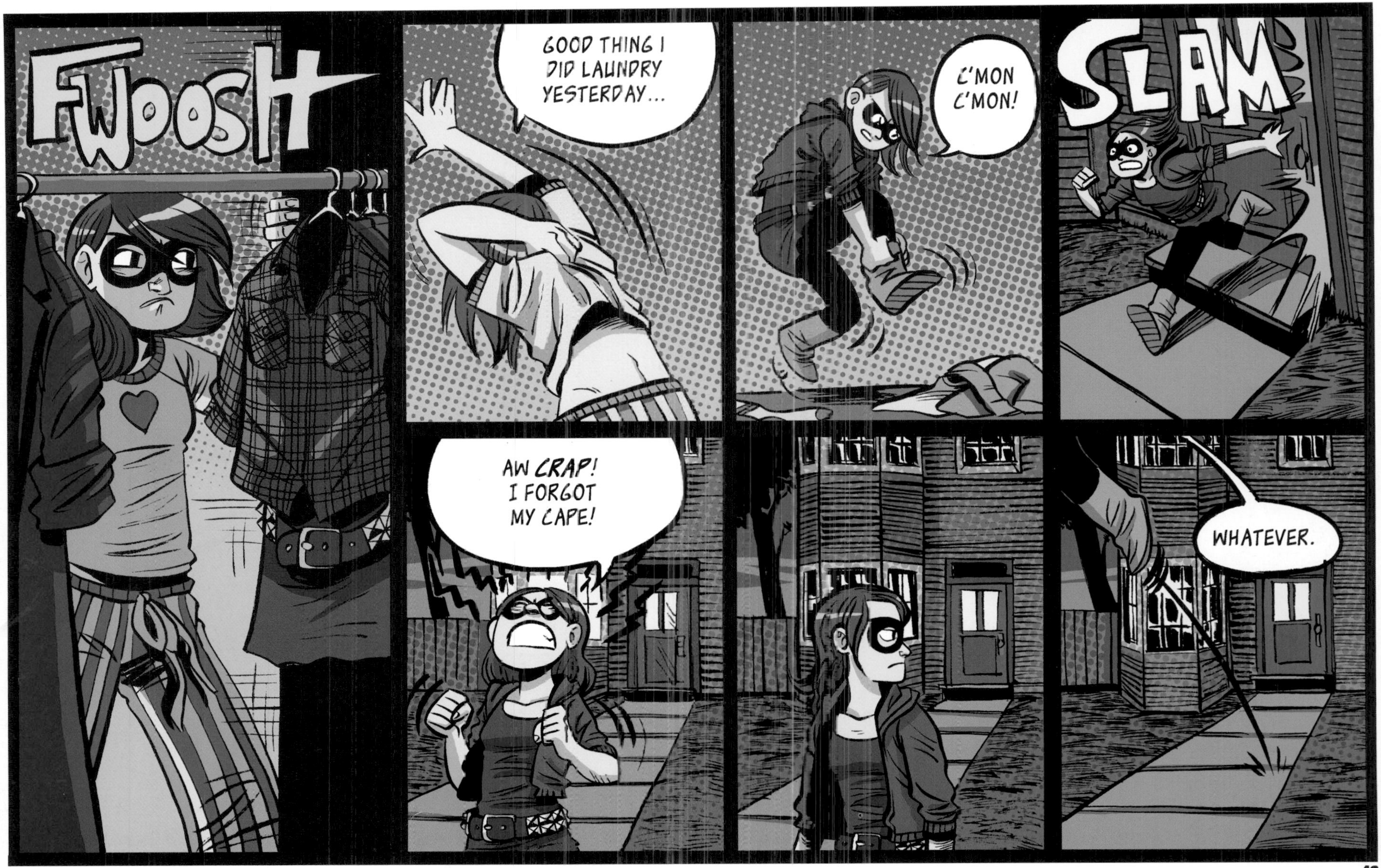
FWOOSH
GOOD THING I DID LAUNDRY YESTERDAY...
C'MON C'MON!
SLAM
AW CRAP! I FORGOT MY CAPE!
WHATEVER.

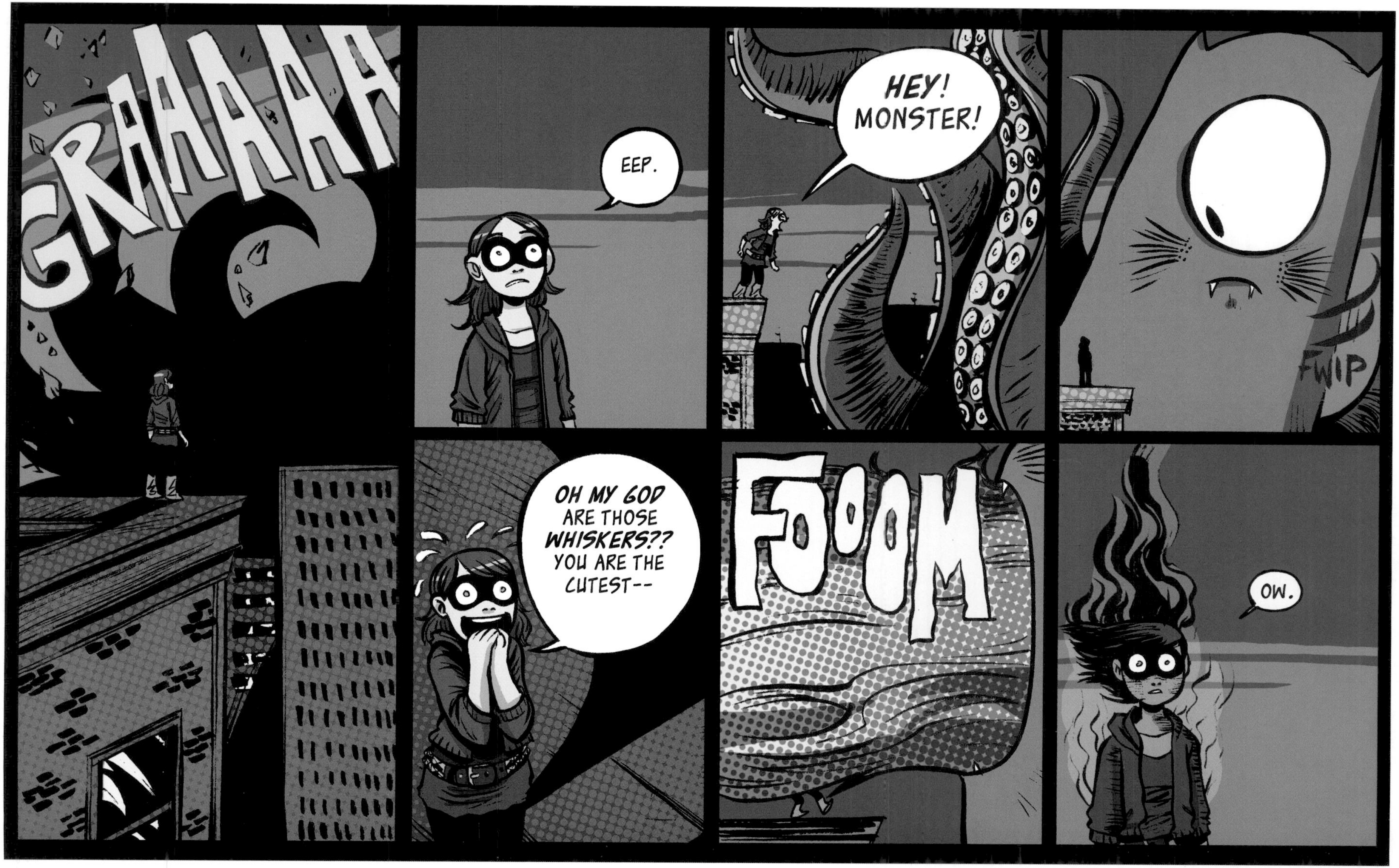
GRAAAAAH
EEP.
HEY! MONSTER!
FWIP
OH MY GOD ARE THOSE WHISKERS?? YOU ARE THE CUTEST--
FOOOM
OW.

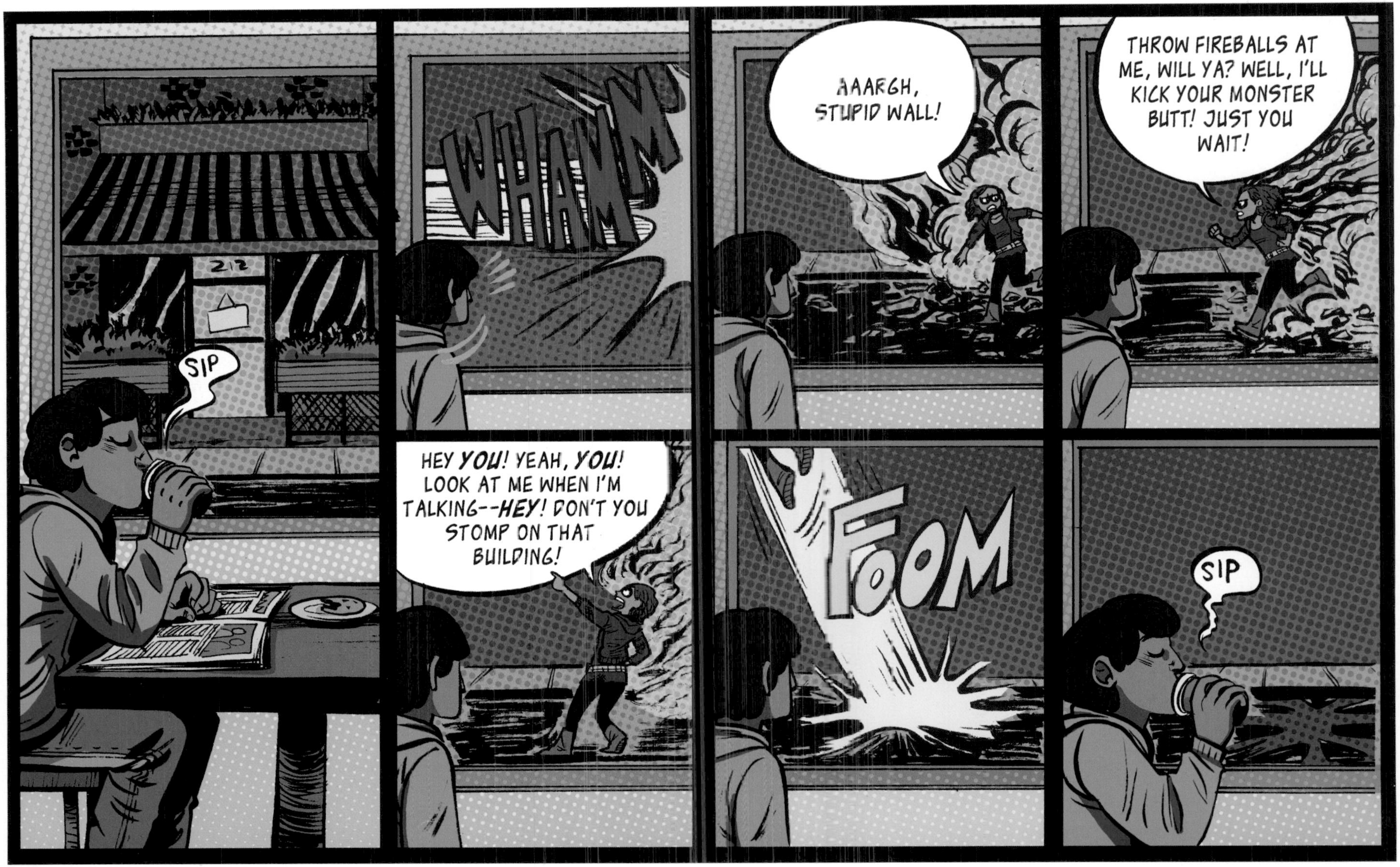

SIP
WHAMM
AAARGH, STUPID WALL!
THROW FIREBALLS AT ME, WILL YA? WELL, I'LL KICK YOUR MONSTER BUTT! JUST YOU WAIT!
HEY *YOU*! YEAH, *YOU*! LOOK AT ME WHEN I'M TALKING--*HEY*! DON'T YOU STOMP ON THAT BUILDING!
FOOM
SIP

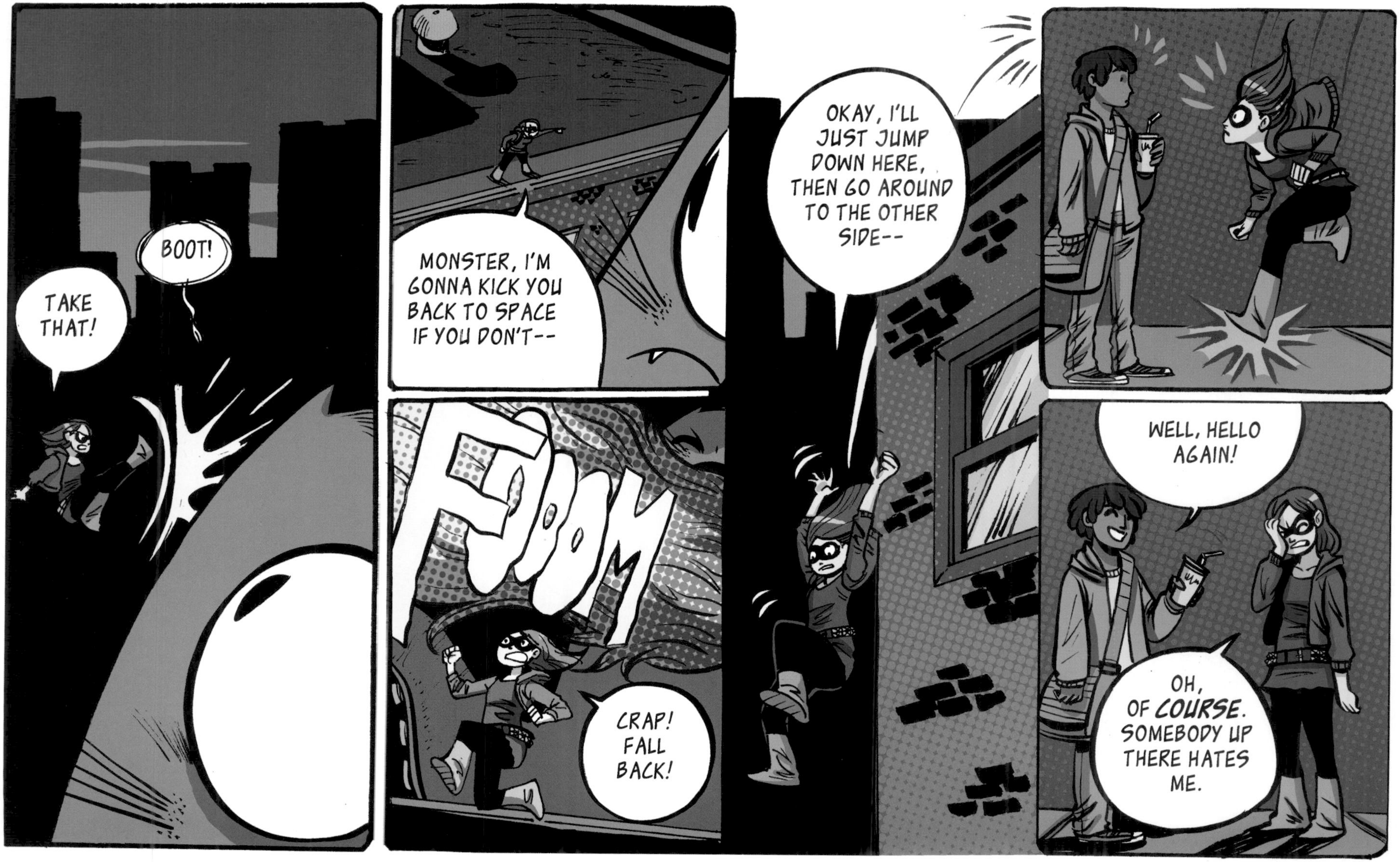
BOOT!
TAKE THAT!
MONSTER, I'M GONNA KICK YOU BACK TO SPACE IF YOU DON'T--
FOOOM
CRAP! FALL BACK!
OKAY, I'LL JUST JUMP DOWN HERE, THEN GO AROUND TO THE OTHER SIDE--
WELL, HELLO AGAIN!
OH, OF *COURSE*. SOMEBODY UP THERE HATES ME.

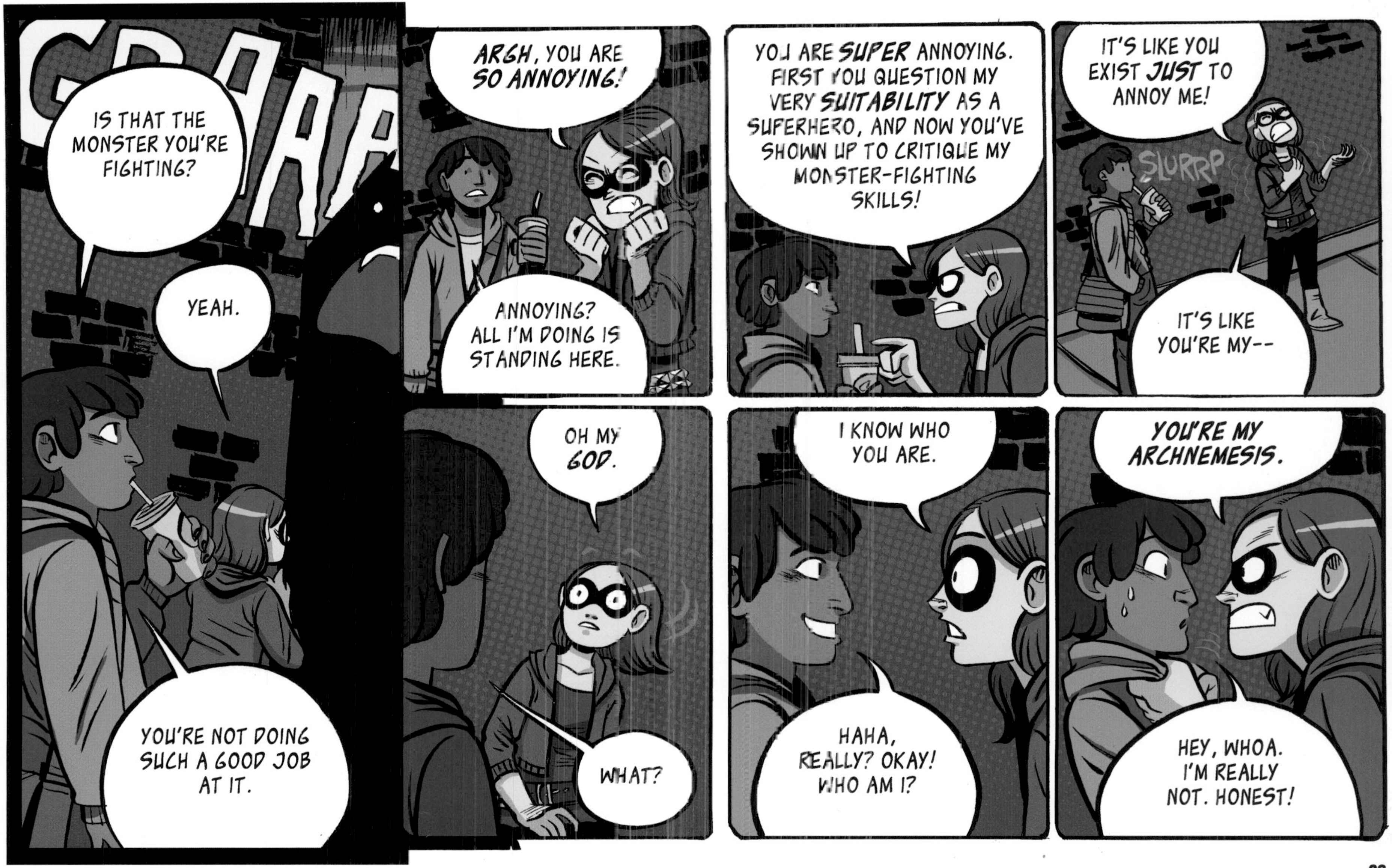
GRAAA
IS THAT THE MONSTER YOU'RE FIGHTING?
YEAH.
YOU'RE NOT DOING SUCH A GOOD JOB AT IT.
ARGH, YOU ARE SO ANNOYING!
ANNOYING? ALL I'M DOING IS STANDING HERE.
YOU ARE SUPER ANNOYING. FIRST YOU QUESTION MY VERY SUITABILITY AS A SUPERHERO, AND NOW YOU'VE SHOWN UP TO CRITIQUE MY MONSTER-FIGHTING SKILLS!
IT'S LIKE YOU EXIST JUST TO ANNOY ME!
SLURRP
IT'S LIKE YOU'RE MY--
OH MY GOD.
WHAT?
I KNOW WHO YOU ARE.
HAHA, REALLY? OKAY! WHO AM I?
YOU'RE MY ARCHNEMESIS.
HEY, WHOA. I'M REALLY NOT. HONEST!

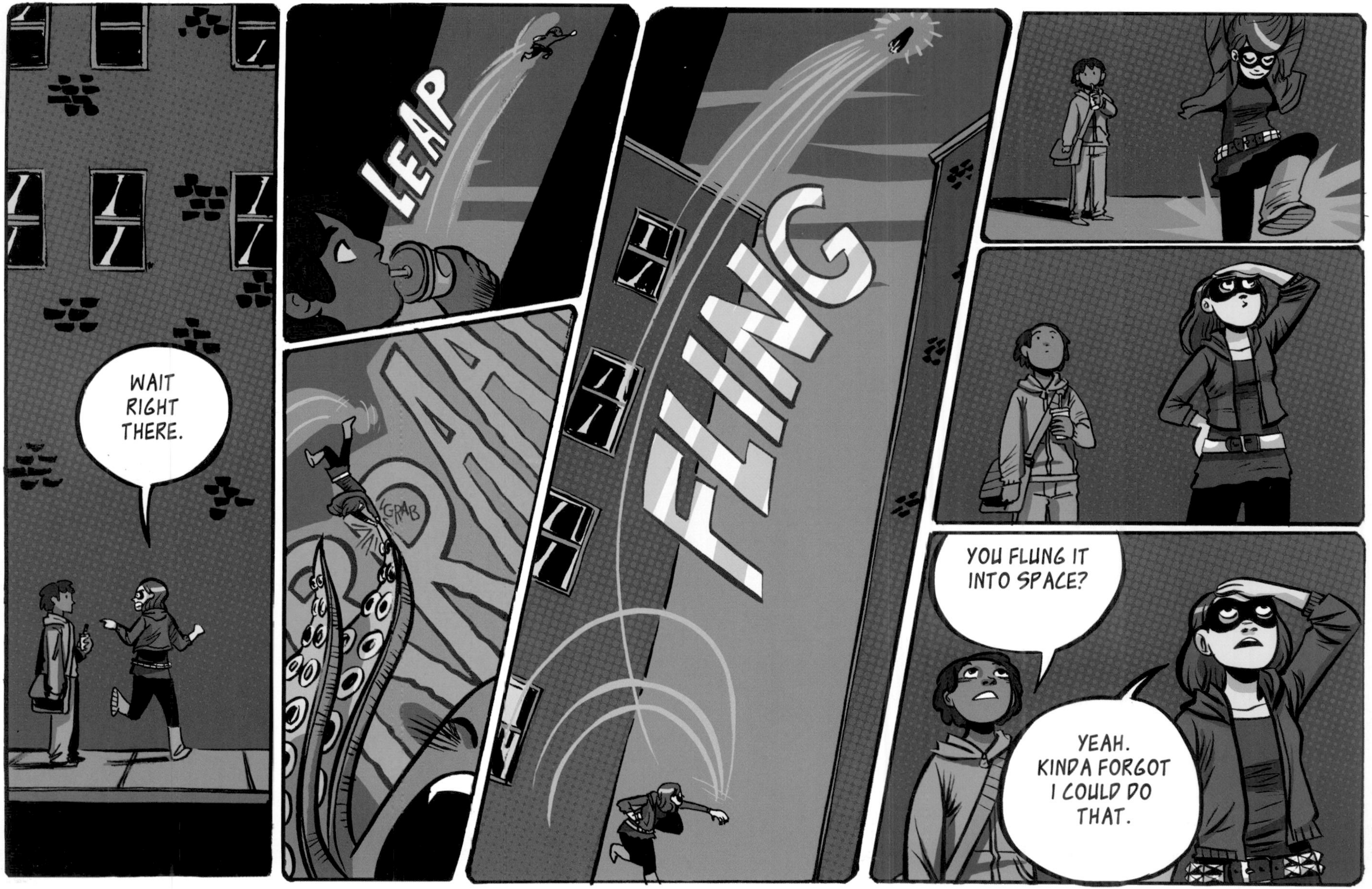
WAIT RIGHT THERE.
LEAP
GRAB
FLING
YOU FLUNG IT INTO SPACE?
YEAH. KINDA FORGOT I COULD DO THAT.

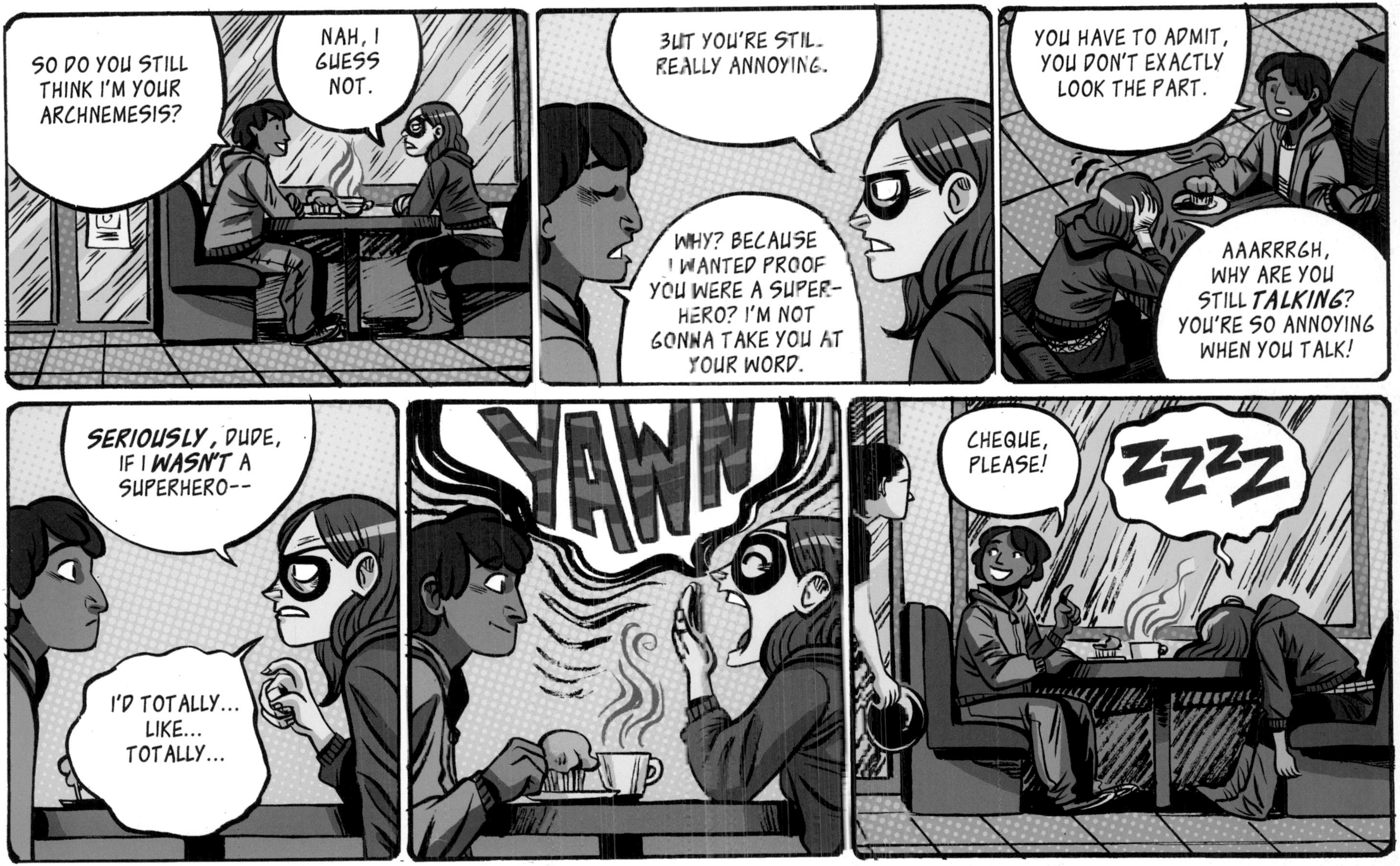

SO DO YOU STILL THINK I'M YOUR ARCHNEMESIS?
NAH, I GUESS NOT.
BUT YOU'RE STILL REALLY ANNOYING.
WHY? BECAUSE I WANTED PROOF YOU WERE A SUPER-HERO? I'M NOT GONNA TAKE YOU AT YOUR WORD.
YOU HAVE TO ADMIT, YOU DON'T EXACTLY LOOK THE PART.
AAARRRGH, WHY ARE YOU STILL *TALKING*? YOU'RE SO ANNOYING WHEN YOU TALK!
SERIOUSLY, DUDE, IF I **WASN'T** A SUPERHERO--
I'D TOTALLY... LIKE... TOTALLY...
YAWN
CHEQUE, PLEASE!
ZZZZ

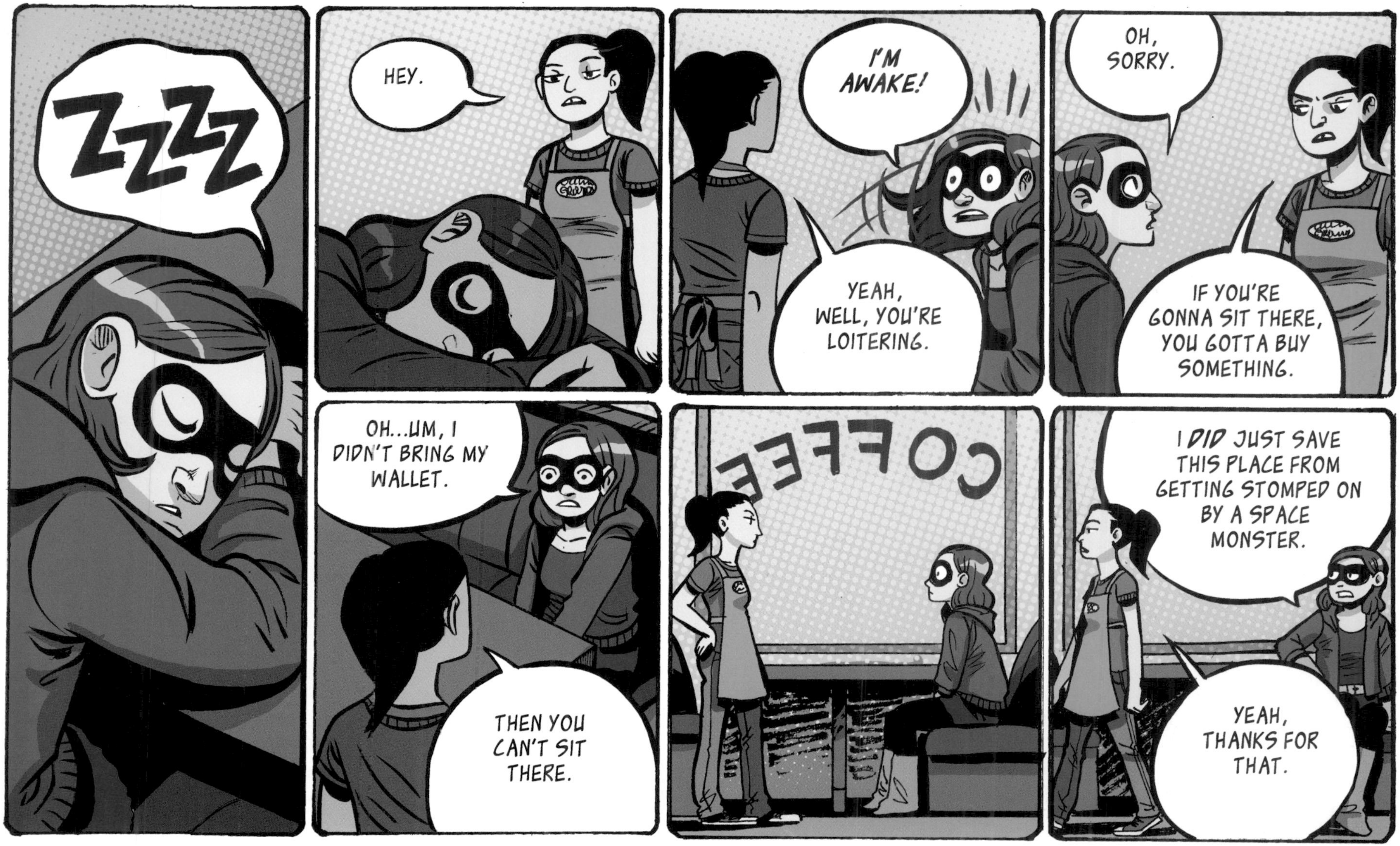
ZZZZ
HEY.
I'M AWAKE!
YEAH, WELL, YOU'RE LOITERING.
OH, SORRY.
IF YOU'RE GONNA SIT THERE, YOU GOTTA BUY SOMETHING.
OH...UM, I DIDN'T BRING MY WALLET.
THEN YOU CAN'T SIT THERE.
COFFEE
I DID JUST SAVE THIS PLACE FROM GETTING STOMPED ON BY A SPACE MONSTER.
YEAH, THANKS FOR THAT.

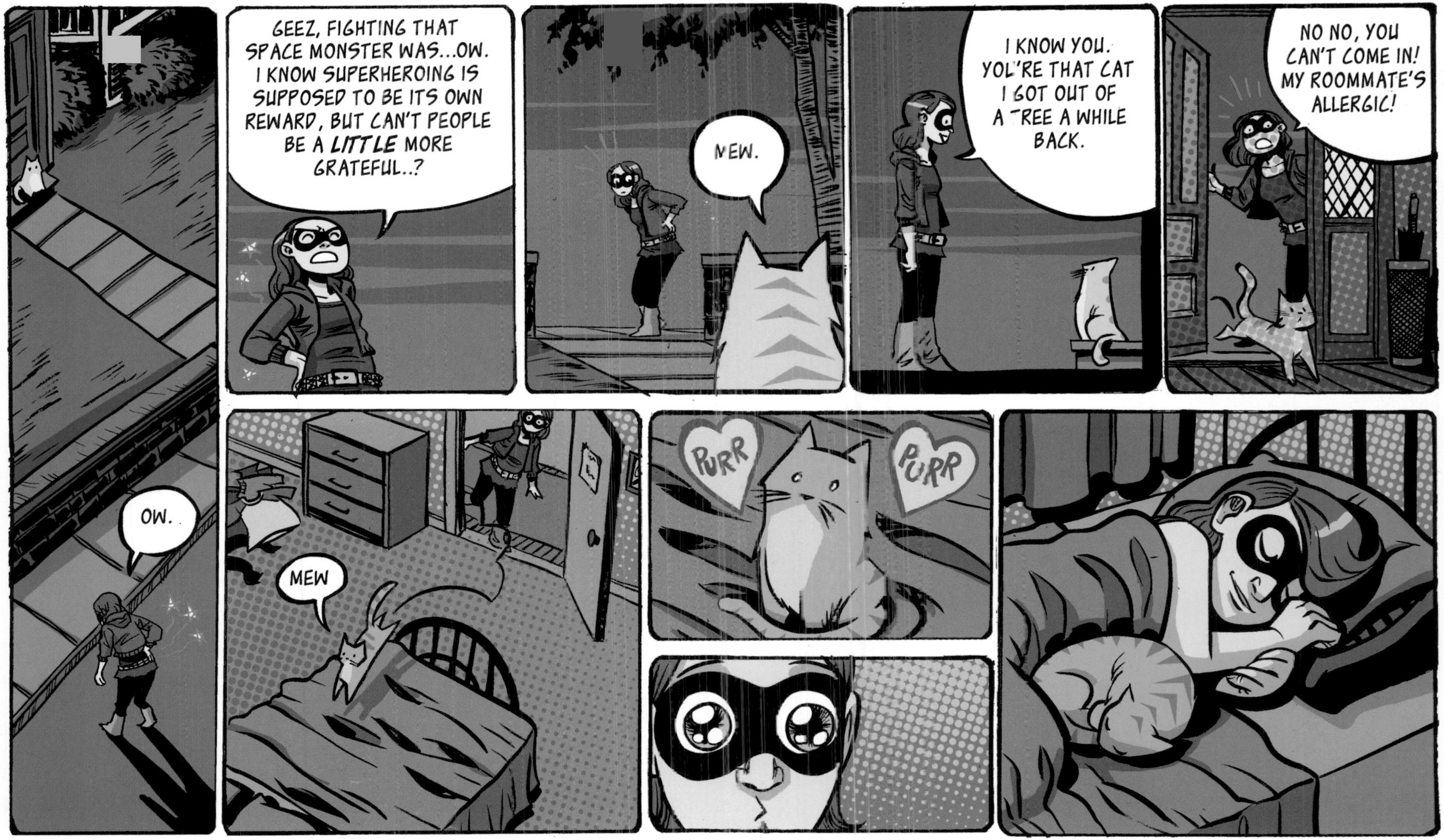
OW.
GEEZ, FIGHTING THAT SPACE MONSTER WAS...OW. I KNOW SUPERHEROING IS SUPPOSED TO BE ITS OWN REWARD, BUT CAN'T PEOPLE BE A *LITTLE* MORE GRATEFUL..?
MEW.
I KNOW YOU. YOU'RE THAT CAT I GOT OUT OF A TREE A WHILE BACK.
NO NO, YOU CAN'T COME IN! MY ROOMMATE'S ALLERGIC!
MEW
PURR
PURR

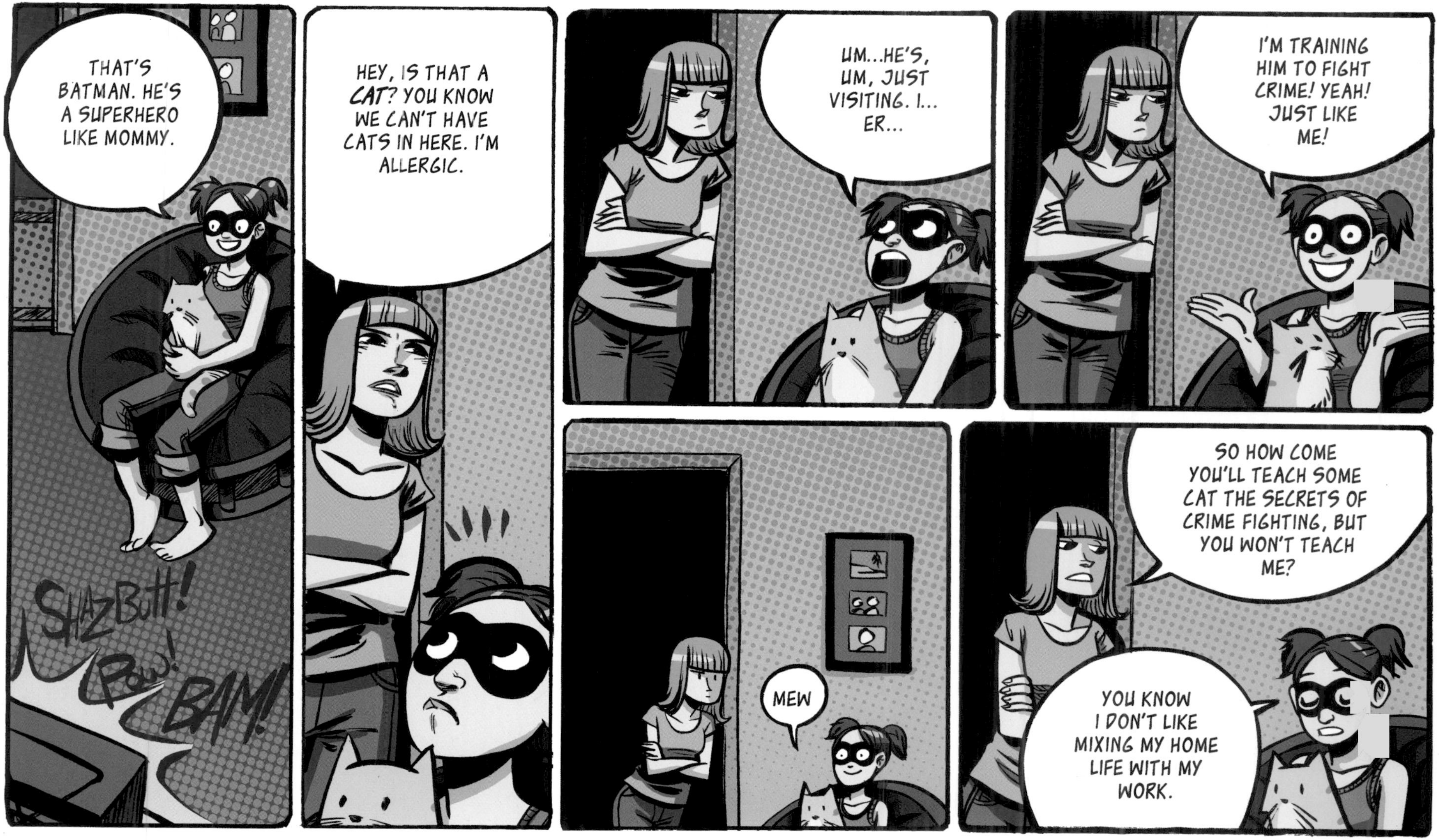
THAT'S BATMAN. HE'S A SUPERHERO LIKE MOMMY.
SHAZBUTT!
POW!
BAM!
HEY, IS THAT A CAT? YOU KNOW WE CAN'T HAVE CATS IN HERE. I'M ALLERGIC.
UM...HE'S, UM, JUST VISITING. I... ER...
I'M TRAINING HIM TO FIGHT CRIME! YEAH! JUST LIKE ME!
MEW
SO HOW COME YOU'LL TEACH SOME CAT THE SECRETS OF CRIME FIGHTING, BUT YOU WON'T TEACH ME?
YOU KNOW I DON'T LIKE MIXING MY HOME LIFE WITH MY WORK.

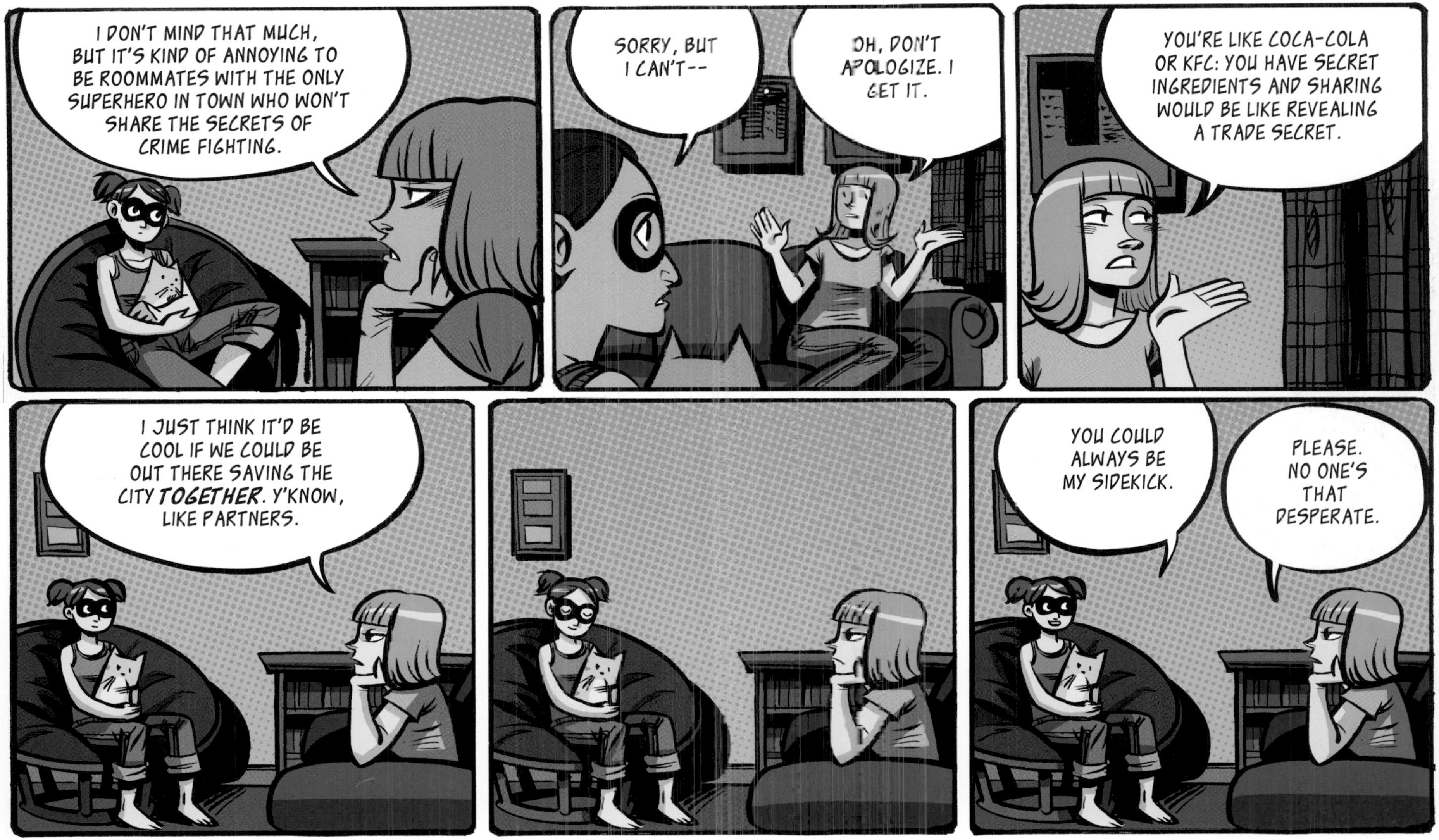
I DON'T MIND THAT MUCH, BUT IT'S KIND OF ANNOYING TO BE ROOMMATES WITH THE ONLY SUPERHERO IN TOWN WHO WON'T SHARE THE SECRETS OF CRIME FIGHTING.
SORRY, BUT I CAN'T--
OH, DON'T APOLOGIZE. I GET IT.
YOU'RE LIKE COCA-COLA OR KFC: YOU HAVE SECRET INGREDIENTS AND SHARING WOULD BE LIKE REVEALING A TRADE SECRET.
I JUST THINK IT'D BE COOL IF WE COULD BE OUT THERE SAVING THE CITY *TOGETHER*. Y'KNOW, LIKE PARTNERS.
YOU COULD ALWAYS BE MY SIDEKICK.
PLEASE. NO ONE'S THAT DESPERATE.

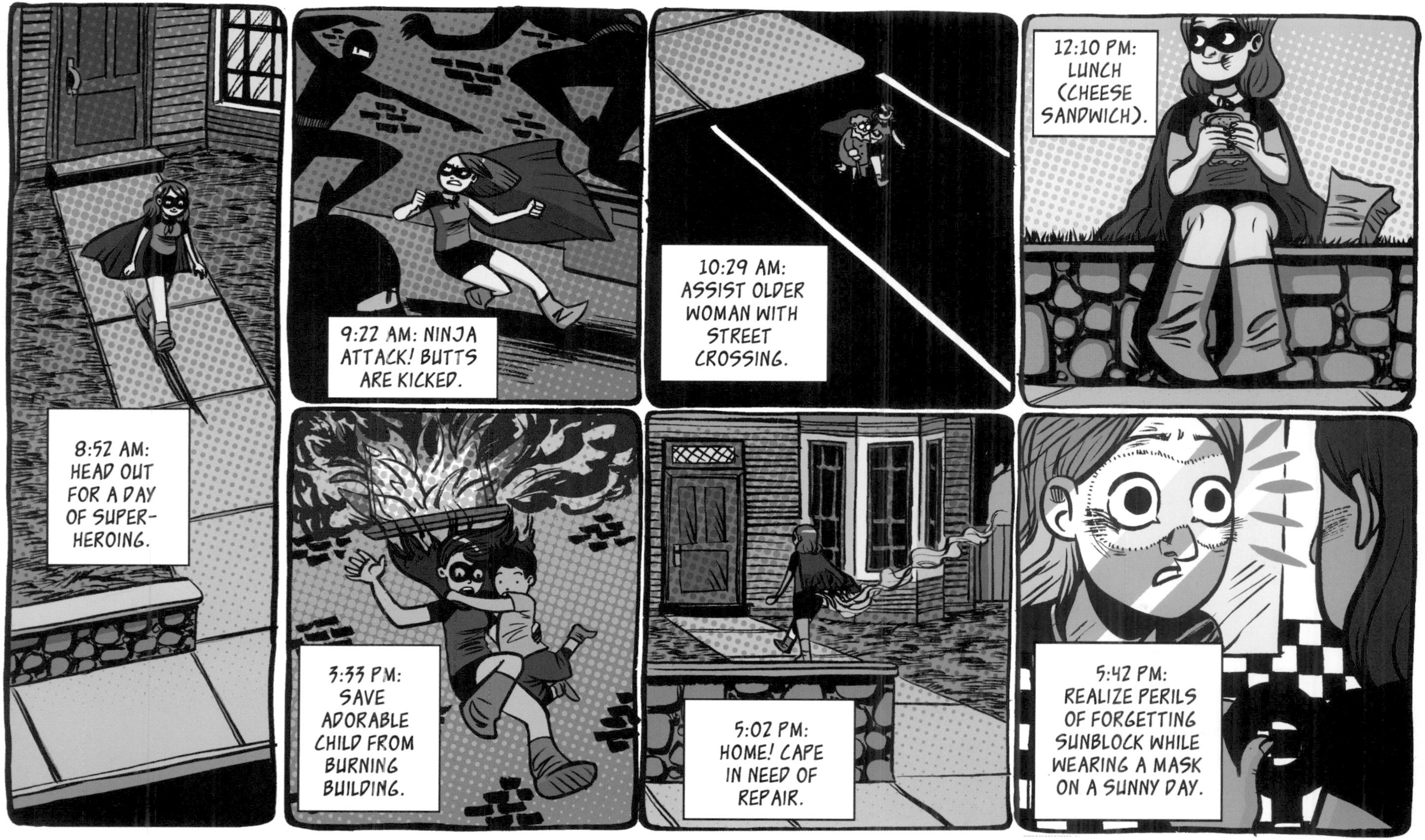

8:52 AM: HEAD OUT FOR A DAY OF SUPER-HEROING.
9:22 AM: NINJA ATTACK! BUTTS ARE KICKED.
10:29 AM: ASSIST OLDER WOMAN WITH STREET CROSSING.
12:10 PM: LUNCH (CHEESE SANDWICH).
3:33 PM: SAVE ADORABLE CHILD FROM BURNING BUILDING.
5:02 PM: HOME! CAPE IN NEED OF REPAIR.
5:42 PM: REALIZE PERILS OF FORGETTING SUNBLOCK WHILE WEARING A MASK ON A SUNNY DAY.

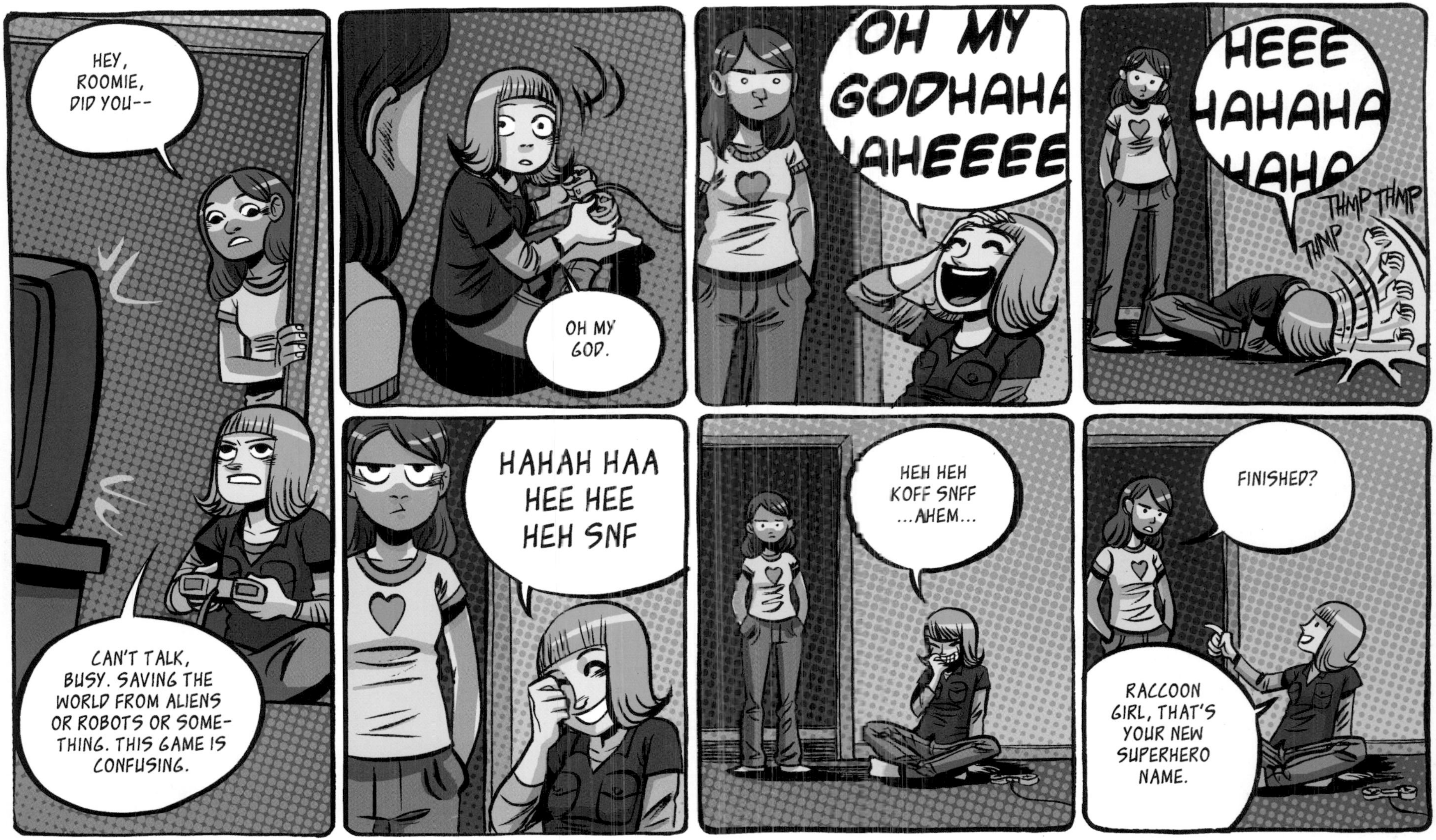
HEY, ROOMIE, DID YOU--
CAN'T TALK, BUSY. SAVING THE WORLD FROM ALIENS OR ROBOTS OR SOME-THING. THIS GAME IS CONFUSING.
OH MY GOD.
OH MY GODHAHAHAHEEEEE
HEEE HAHAHA HAHA
THMP THMP THMP
HAHAH HAA HEE HEE HEH SNF
HEH HEH KOFF SNFF ...AHEM...
FINISHED?
RACCOON GIRL, THAT'S YOUR NEW SUPERHERO NAME.

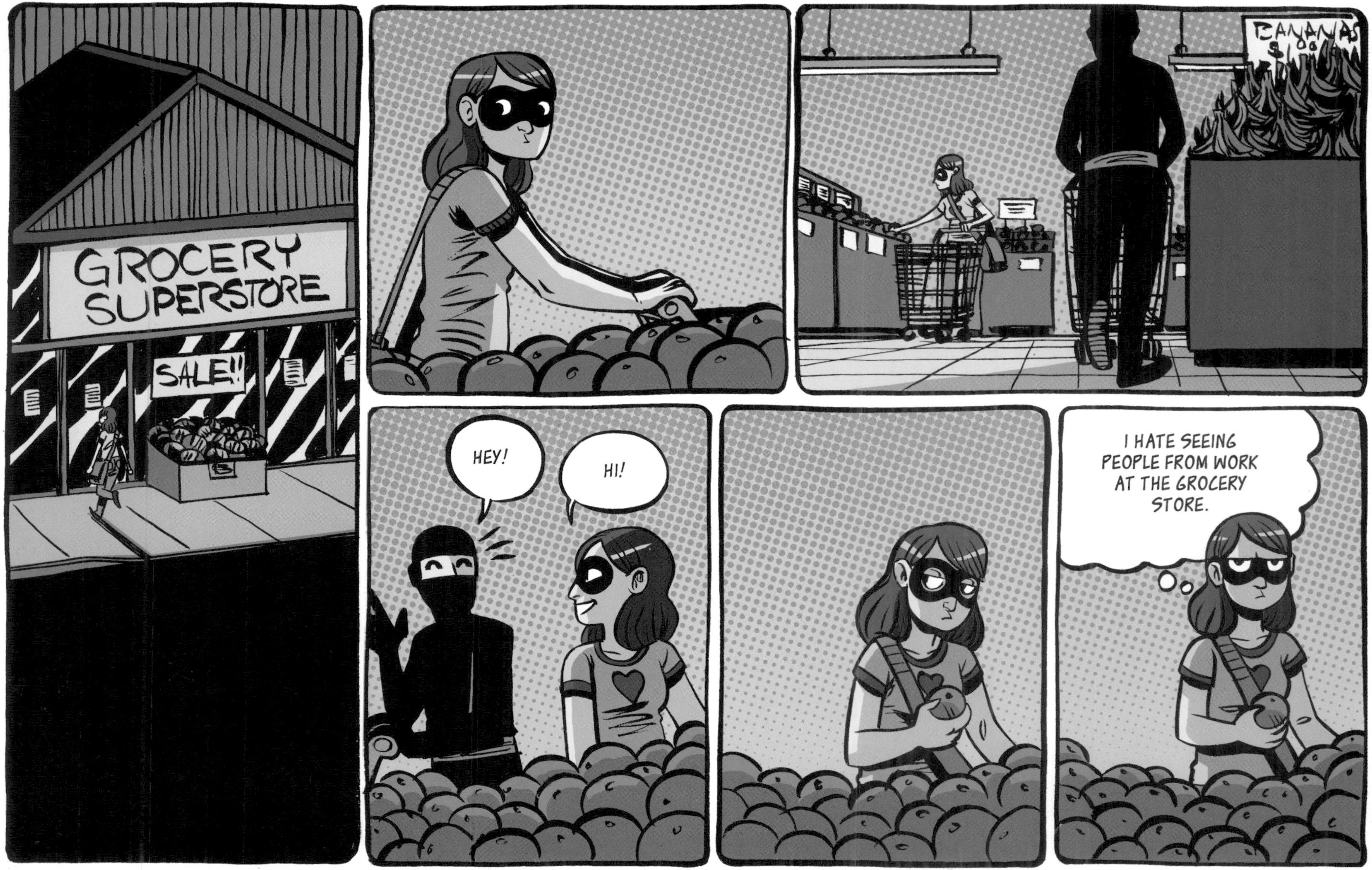
GROCERY SUPERSTORE
SALE!!
BANANAS
HEY!
HI!
I HATE SEEING PEOPLE FROM WORK AT THE GROCERY STORE.

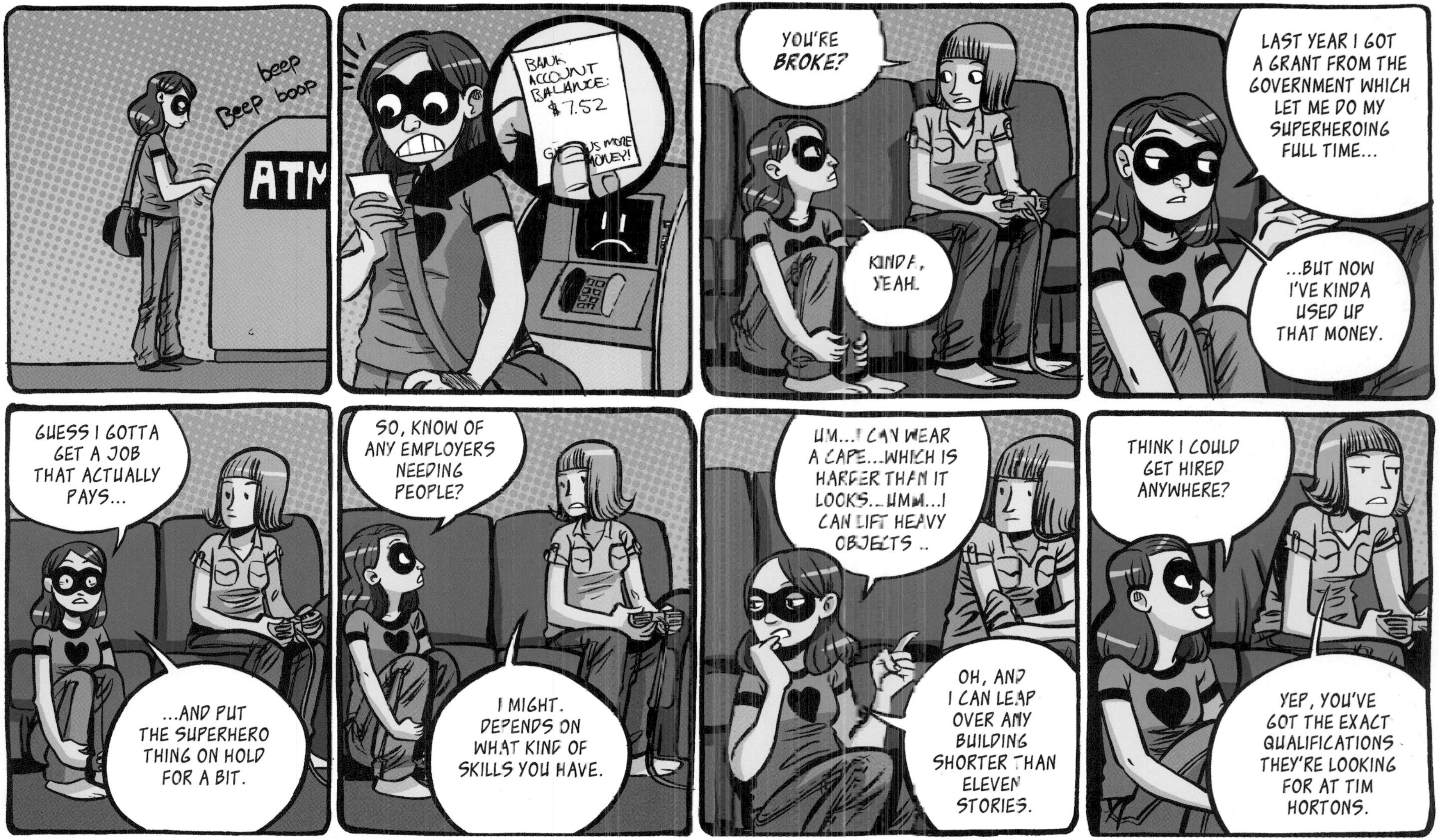

beep
Beep boop
ATM
BANK ACCOUNT BALANCE: $7.52
US MORE MONEY!
YOU'RE BROKE?
KINDA, YEAH.
LAST YEAR I GOT A GRANT FROM THE GOVERNMENT WHICH LET ME DO MY SUPERHEROING FULL TIME...
...BUT NOW I'VE KINDA USED UP THAT MONEY.
GUESS I GOTTA GET A JOB THAT ACTUALLY PAYS...
...AND PUT THE SUPERHERO THING ON HOLD FOR A BIT.
SO, KNOW OF ANY EMPLOYERS NEEDING PEOPLE?
I MIGHT. DEPENDS ON WHAT KIND OF SKILLS YOU HAVE.
UM...I CAN WEAR A CAPE...WHICH IS HARDER THAN IT LOOKS...UMM...I CAN LIFT HEAVY OBJECTS...
OH, AND I CAN LEAP OVER ANY BUILDING SHORTER THAN ELEVEN STORIES.
THINK I COULD GET HIRED ANYWHERE?
YEP, YOU'VE GOT THE EXACT QUALIFICATIONS THEY'RE LOOKING FOR AT TIM HORTONS.

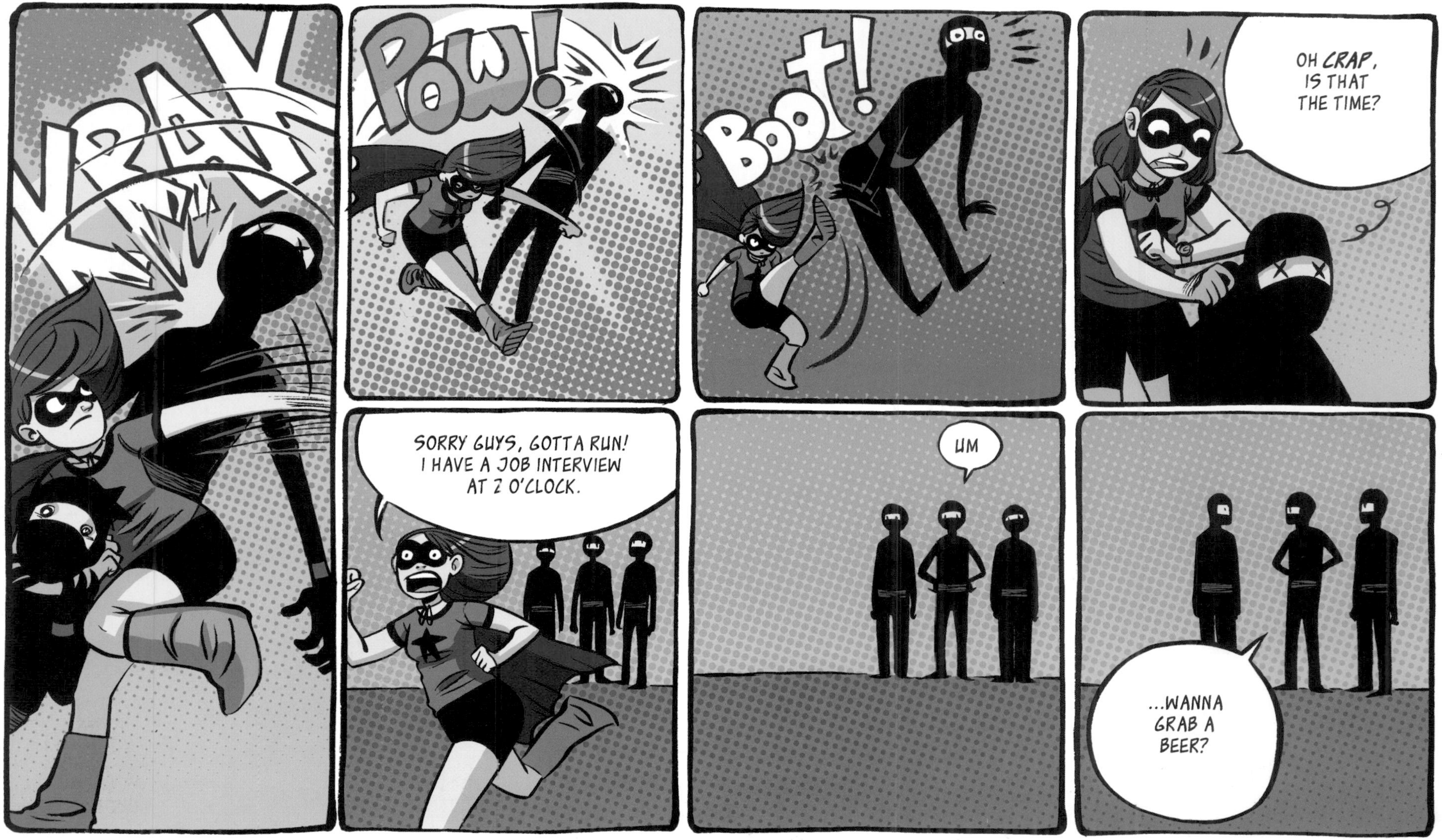
KRAK!
POW!
BOOT!
OH CRAP, IS THAT THE TIME?
SORRY GUYS, GOTTA RUN! I HAVE A JOB INTERVIEW AT 2 O'CLOCK.
UM
...WANNA GRAB A BEER?

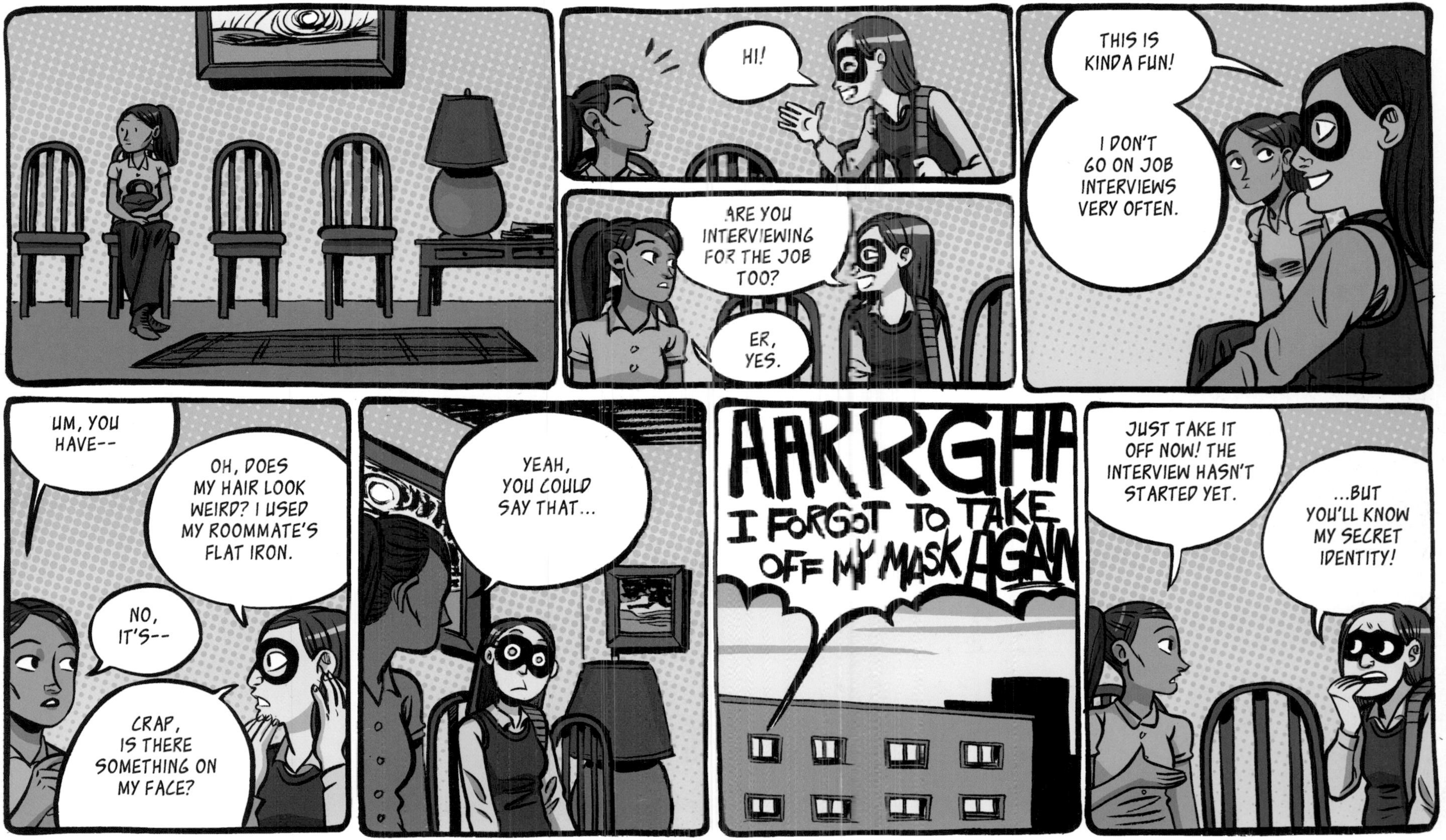
HI!
ARE YOU INTERVIEWING FOR THE JOB TOO?
ER, YES.
THIS IS KINDA FUN!
I DON'T GO ON JOB INTERVIEWS VERY OFTEN.
UM, YOU HAVE--
OH, DOES MY HAIR LOOK WEIRD? I USED MY ROOMMATE'S FLAT IRON.
NO, IT'S--
CRAP, IS THERE SOMETHING ON MY FACE?
YEAH, YOU COULD SAY THAT...
AARRGHH
I FORGOT TO TAKE OFF MY MASK AGAIN
JUST TAKE IT OFF NOW! THE INTERVIEW HASN'T STARTED YET.
...BUT YOU'LL KNOW MY SECRET IDENTITY!

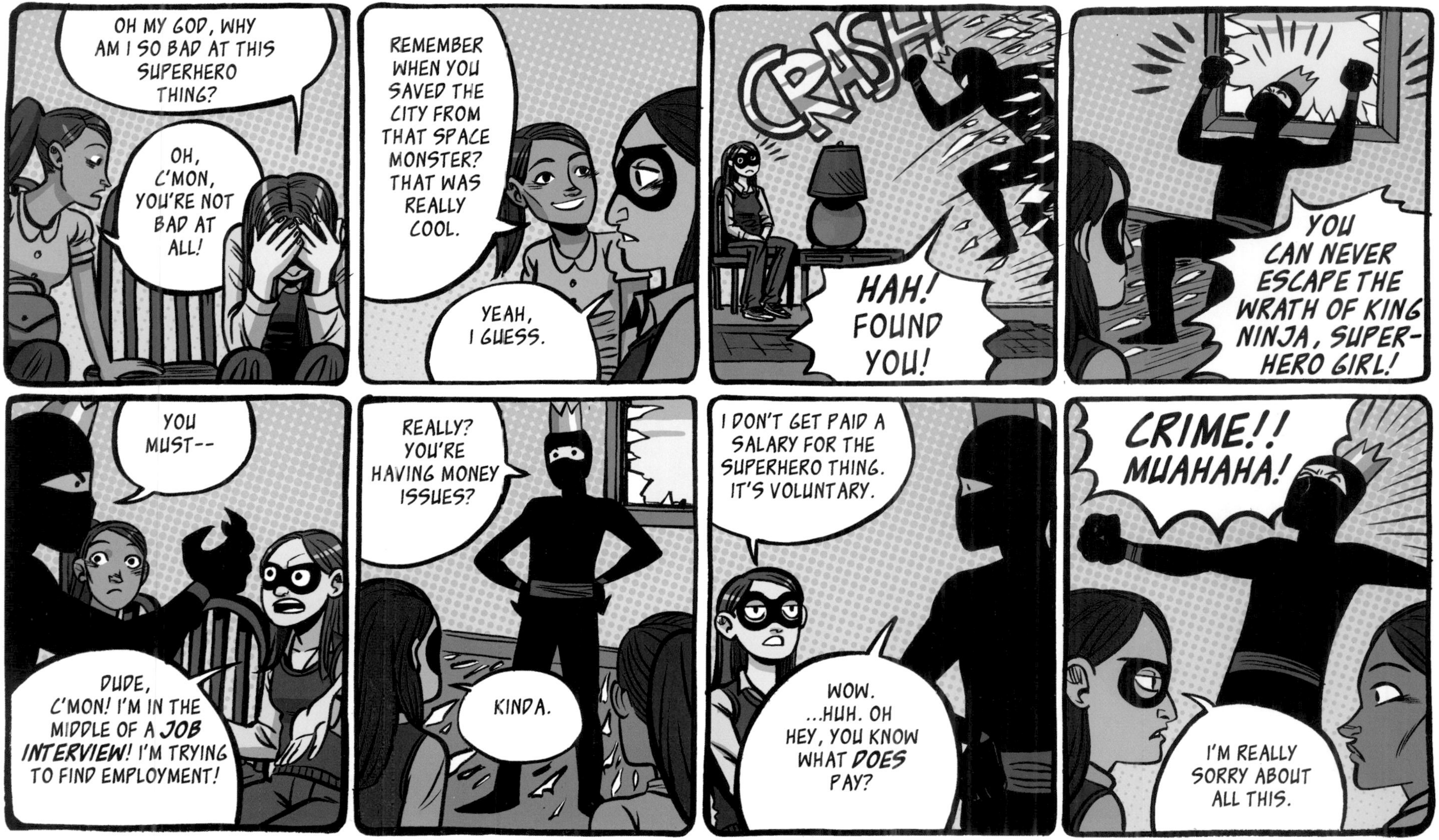
OH MY GOD, WHY AM I SO BAD AT THIS SUPERHERO THING?
OH, C'MON, YOU'RE NOT BAD AT ALL!
REMEMBER WHEN YOU SAVED THE CITY FROM THAT SPACE MONSTER? THAT WAS REALLY COOL.
YEAH, I GUESS.
CRASH
HAH! FOUND YOU!
YOU CAN NEVER ESCAPE THE WRATH OF KING NINJA, SUPER-HERO GIRL!
YOU MUST--
DUDE, C'MON! I'M IN THE MIDDLE OF A *JOB INTERVIEW*! I'M TRYING TO FIND EMPLOYMENT!
REALLY? YOU'RE HAVING MONEY ISSUES?
KINDA.
I DON'T GET PAID A SALARY FOR THE SUPERHERO THING. IT'S VOLUNTARY.
WOW. ...HUH. OH HEY, YOU KNOW WHAT *DOES* PAY?
CRIME!! MUAHAHA!
I'M REALLY SORRY ABOUT ALL THIS.

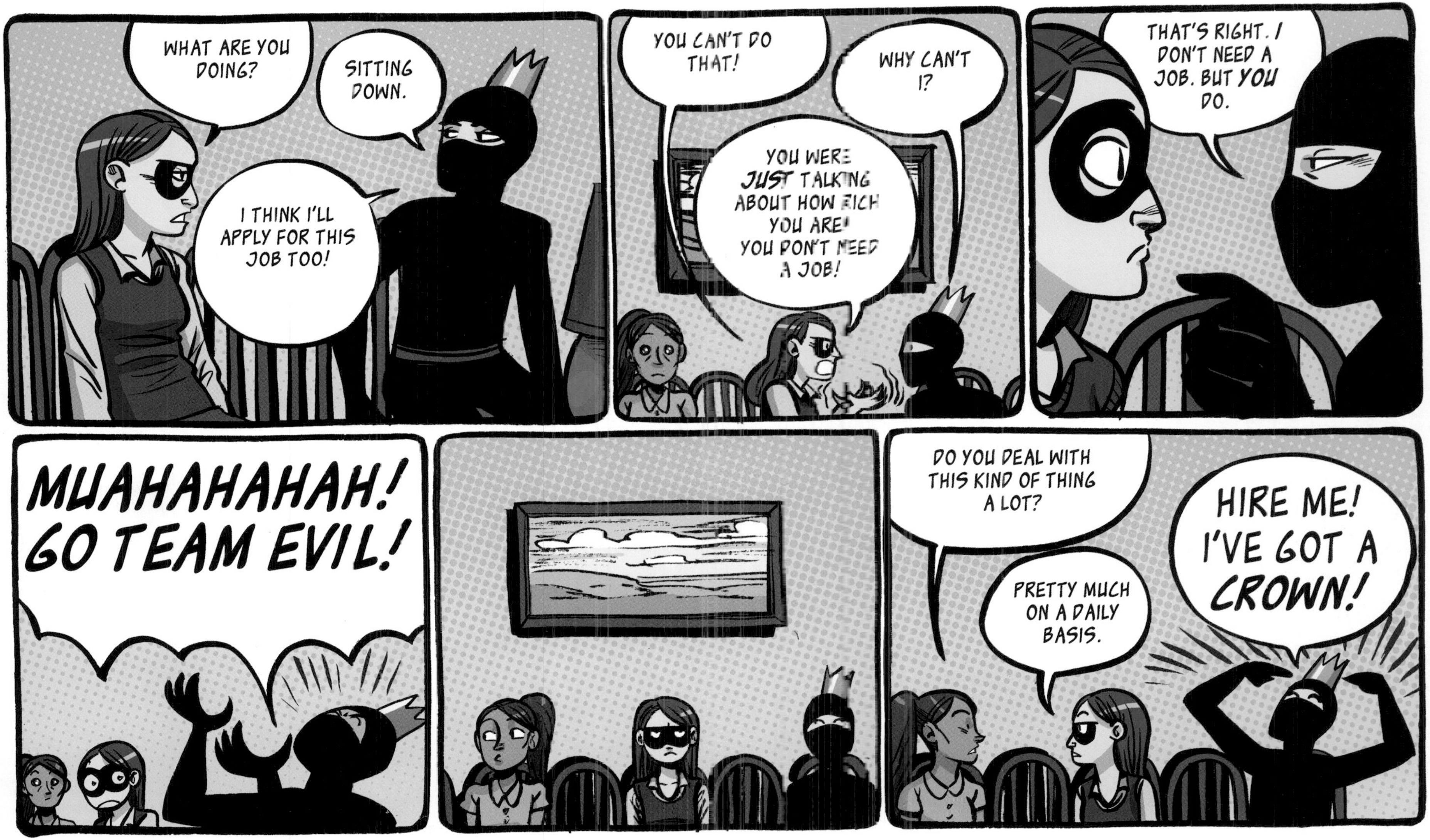
WHAT ARE YOU DOING?
SITTING DOWN.
I THINK I'LL APPLY FOR THIS JOB TOO!
YOU CAN'T DO THAT!
WHY CAN'T I?
YOU WERE JUST TALKING ABOUT HOW RICH YOU ARE! YOU DON'T NEED A JOB!
THAT'S RIGHT. I DON'T NEED A JOB. BUT YOU DO.
MUAHAHAHAH! GO TEAM EVIL!
DO YOU DEAL WITH THIS KIND OF THING A LOT?
PRETTY MUCH ON A DAILY BASIS.
HIRE ME! I'VE GOT A CROWN!

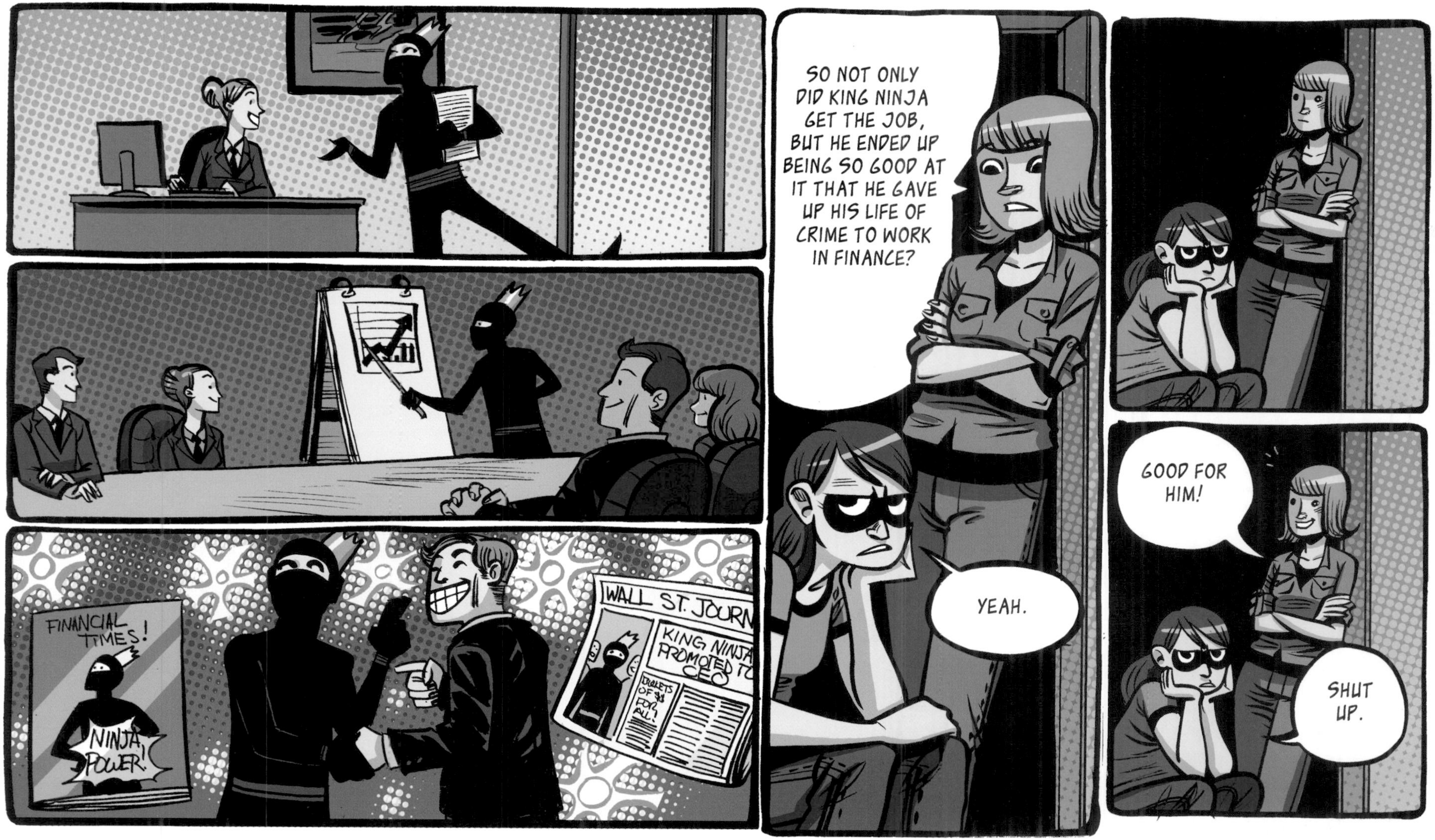
FINANCIAL TIMES!
NINJA POWER!
WALL ST. JOURN
KING NINJA PROMOTED T CEO
SO NOT ONLY DID KING NINJA GET THE JOB, BUT HE ENDED UP BEING SO GOOD AT IT THAT HE GAVE UP HIS LIFE OF CRIME TO WORK IN FINANCE?
YEAH.
GOOD FOR HIM!
SHUT UP.

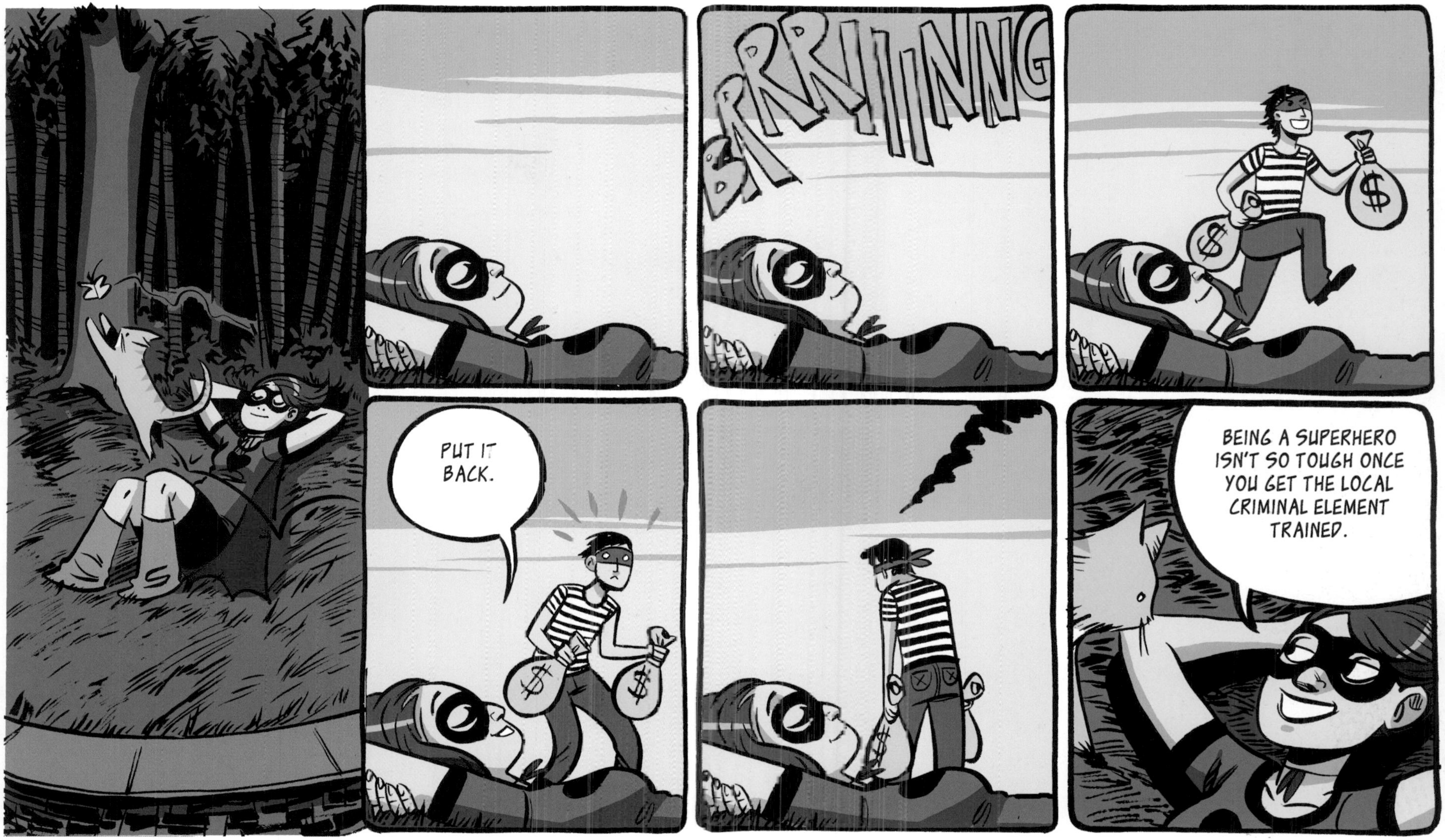
BRRRIIIINNG
PUT IT BACK.
BEING A SUPERHERO ISN'T SO TOUGH ONCE YOU GET THE LOCAL CRIMINAL ELEMENT TRAINED.

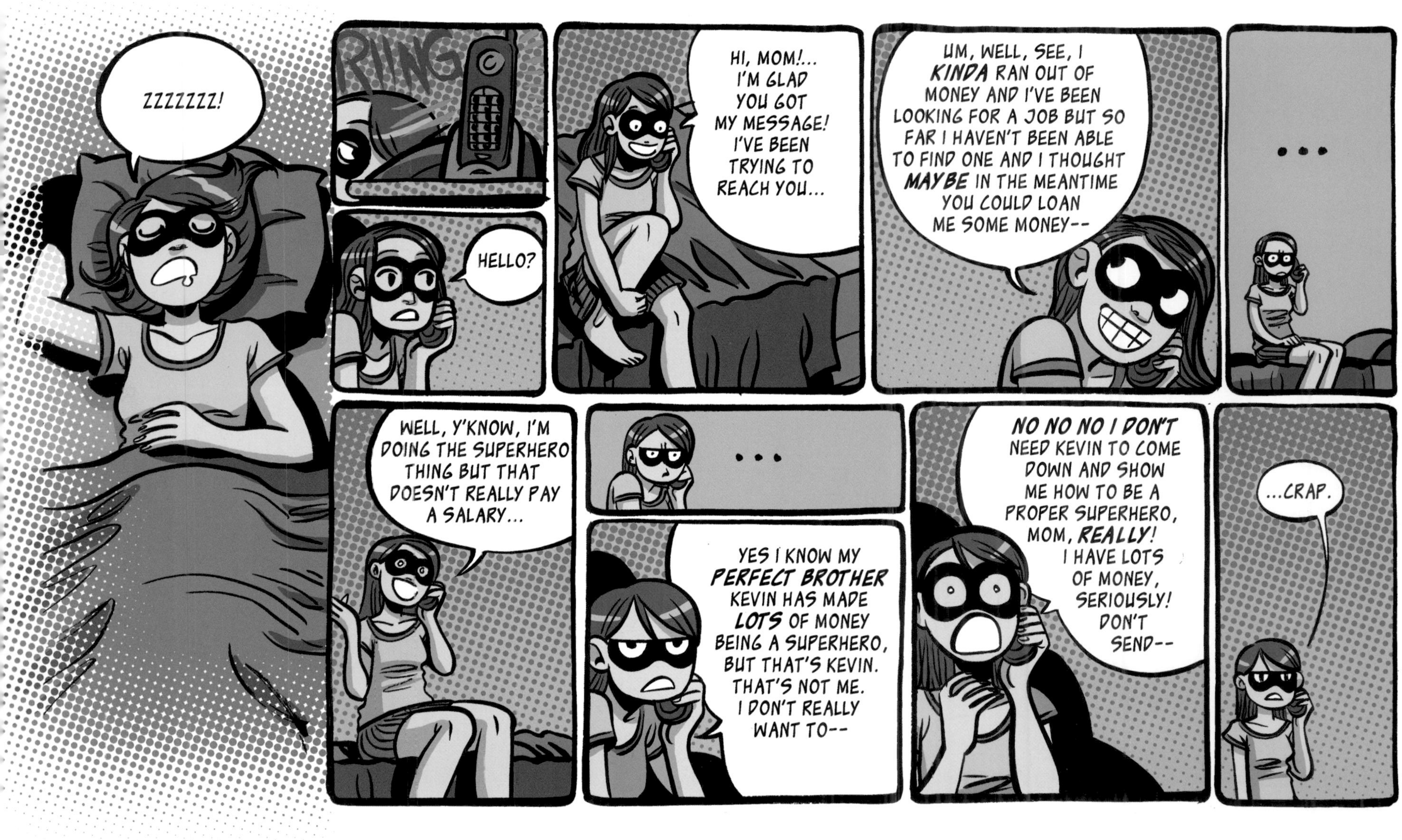
ZZZZZZZ!
RIIING
HELLO?
HI, MOM!... I'M GLAD YOU GOT MY MESSAGE! I'VE BEEN TRYING TO REACH YOU...
UM, WELL, SEE, I *KINDA* RAN OUT OF MONEY AND I'VE BEEN LOOKING FOR A JOB BUT SO FAR I HAVEN'T BEEN ABLE TO FIND ONE AND I THOUGHT *MAYBE* IN THE MEANTIME YOU COULD LOAN ME SOME MONEY--
...
WELL, Y'KNOW, I'M DOING THE SUPERHERO THING BUT THAT DOESN'T REALLY PAY A SALARY...
...
YES I KNOW MY *PERFECT BROTHER* KEVIN HAS MADE *LOTS* OF MONEY BEING A SUPERHERO, BUT THAT'S KEVIN. THAT'S NOT ME. I DON'T REALLY WANT TO--
NO NO NO I DON'T NEED KEVIN TO COME DOWN AND SHOW ME HOW TO BE A PROPER SUPERHERO, MOM, *REALLY*! I HAVE LOTS OF MONEY, SERIOUSLY! DON'T SEND--
...CRAP.

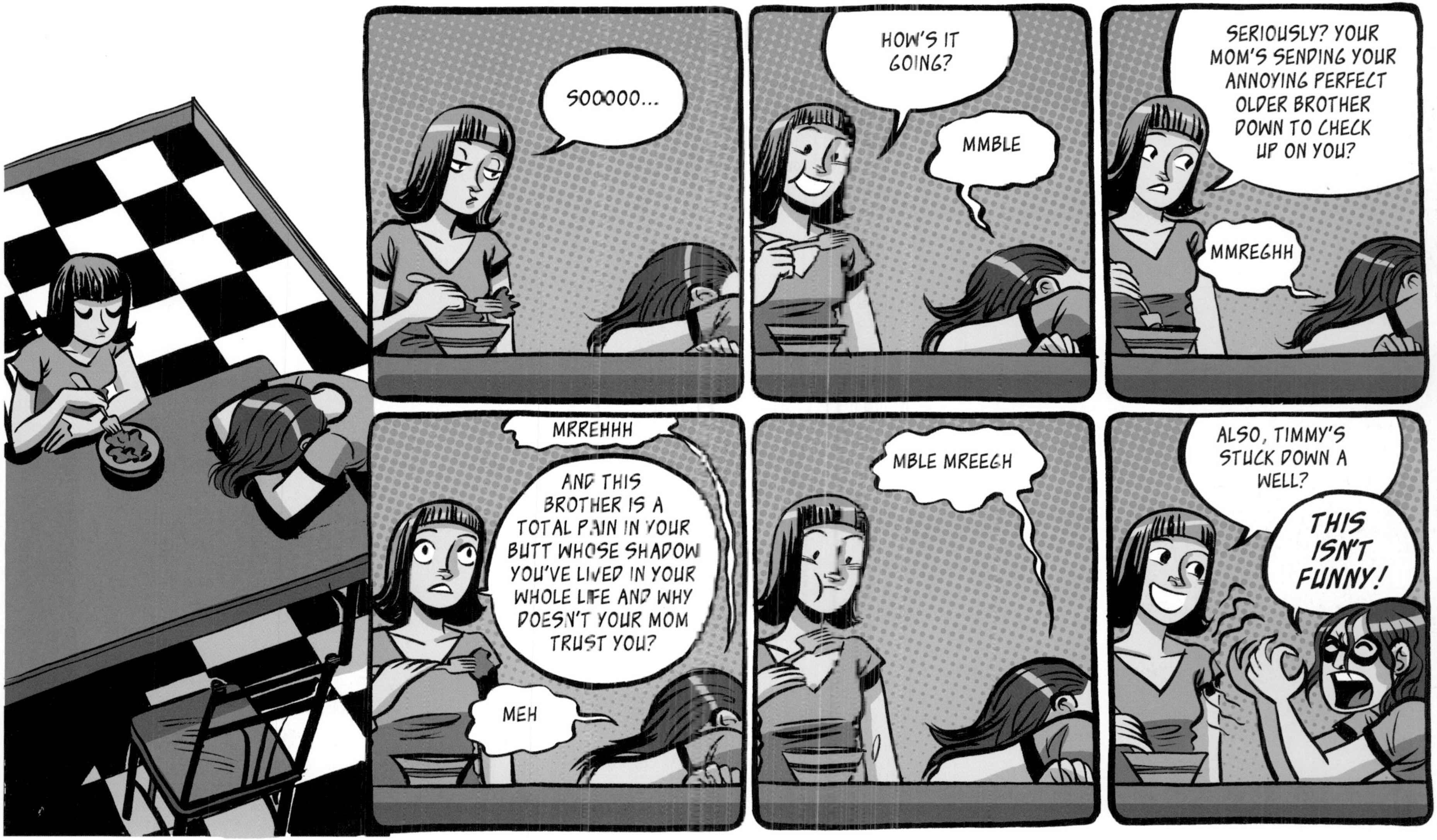
SOOOOO...
HOW'S IT GOING?
MMBLE
SERIOUSLY? YOUR MOM'S SENDING YOUR ANNOYING PERFECT OLDER BROTHER DOWN TO CHECK UP ON YOU?
MMREGHH
MRREHHH
AND THIS BROTHER IS A TOTAL PAIN IN YOUR BUTT WHOSE SHADOW YOU'VE LIVED IN YOUR WHOLE LIFE AND WHY DOESN'T YOUR MOM TRUST YOU?
MEH
MBLE MREEGH
ALSO, TIMMY'S STUCK DOWN A WELL?
THIS ISN'T FUNNY!

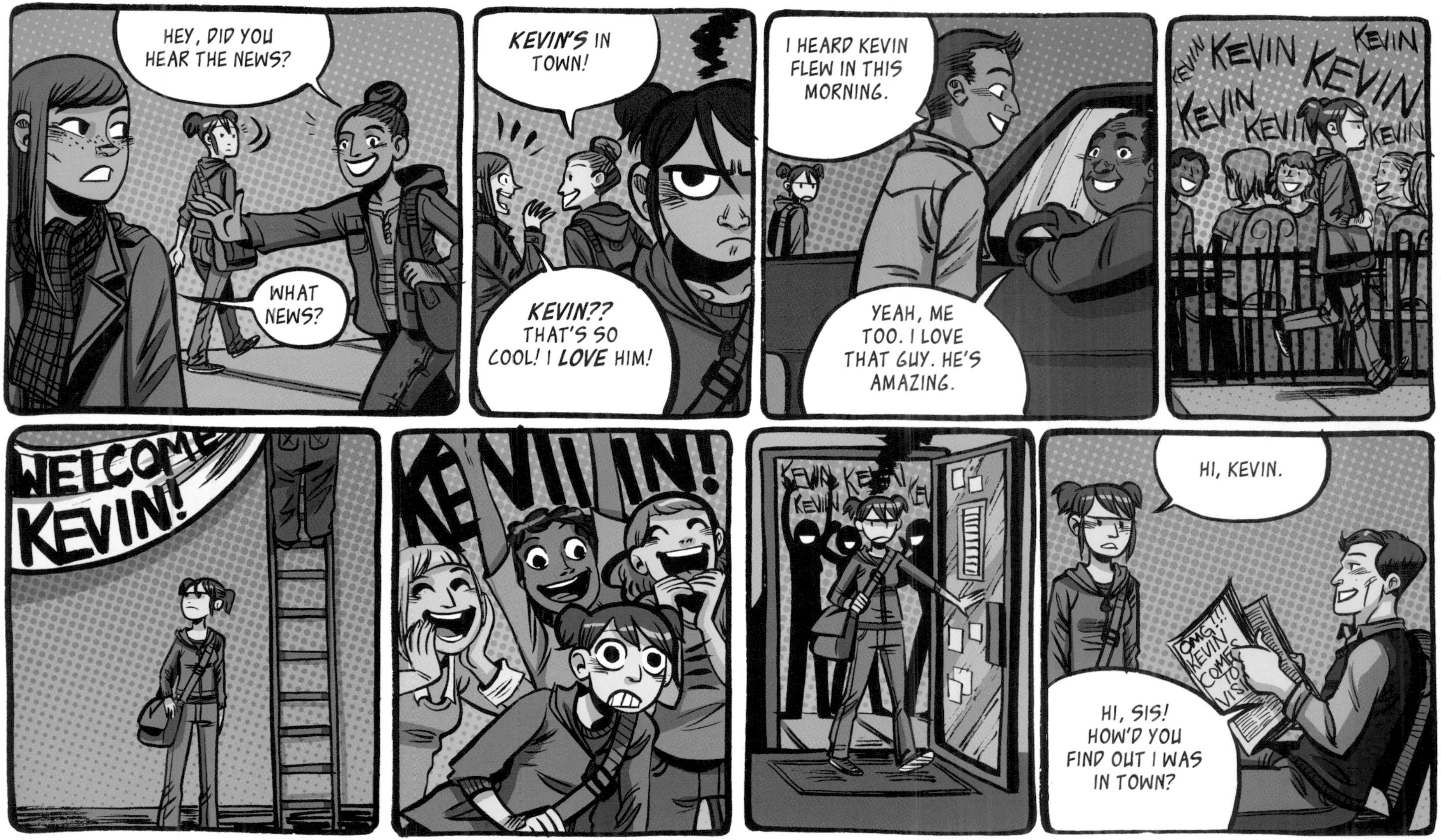
HEY, DID YOU HEAR THE NEWS?
WHAT NEWS?
KEVIN'S IN TOWN!
KEVIN?? THAT'S SO COOL! I LOVE HIM!
I HEARD KEVIN FLEW IN THIS MORNING.
YEAH, ME TOO. I LOVE THAT GUY. HE'S AMAZING.
KEVIN KEVIN KEVIN KEVIN KEVIN KEVIN KEVIN KEVIN
WELCOME KEVIN!
KEVIIIIN!
HI, KEVIN.
HI, SIS! HOW'D YOU FIND OUT I WAS IN TOWN?
OMG!!! KEVIN COMES TO VISIT

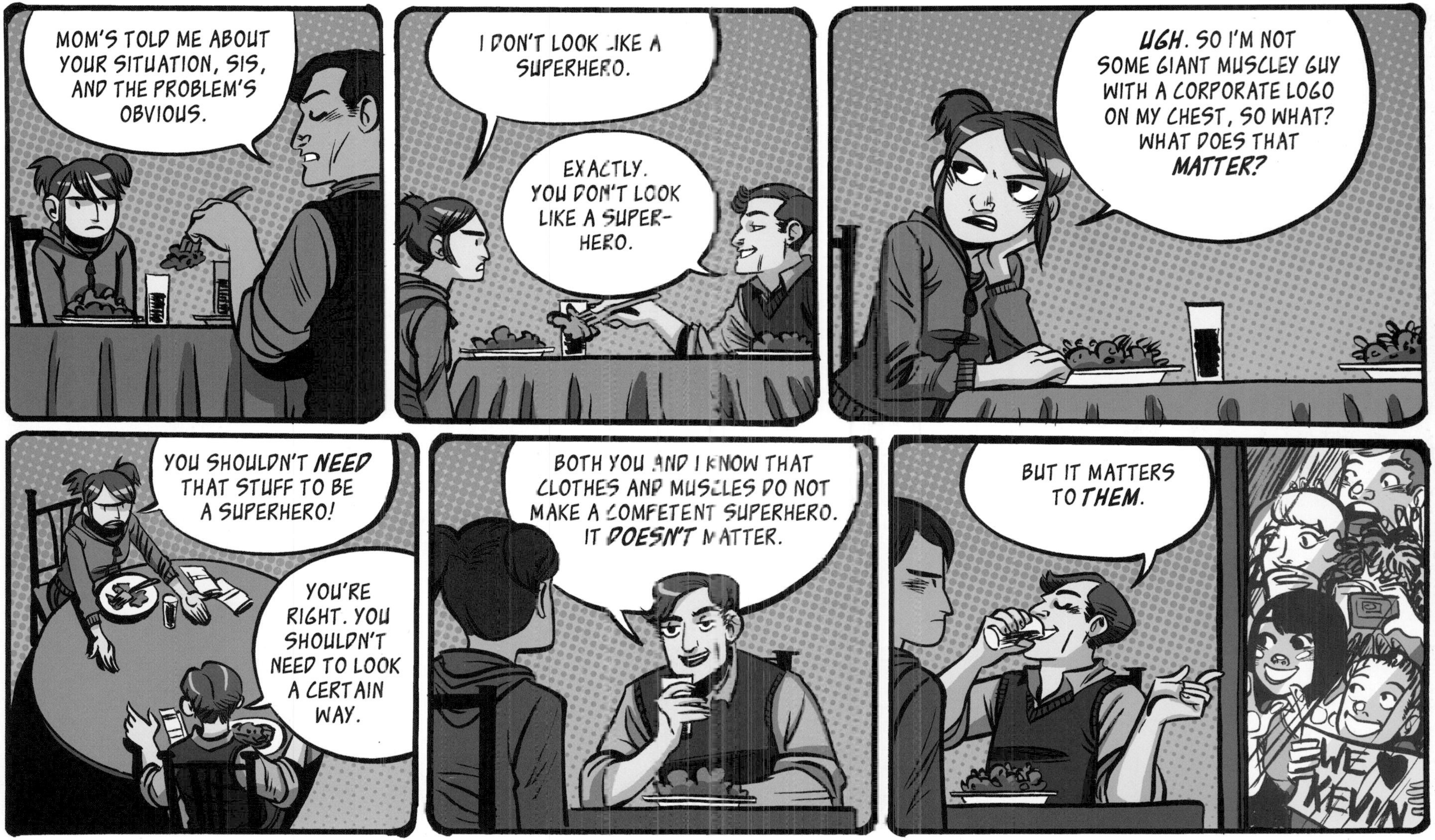
MOM'S TOLD ME ABOUT YOUR SITUATION, SIS, AND THE PROBLEM'S OBVIOUS.
I DON'T LOOK LIKE A SUPERHERO.
EXACTLY. YOU DON'T LOOK LIKE A SUPER-HERO.
UGH. SO I'M NOT SOME GIANT MUSCLEY GUY WITH A CORPORATE LOGO ON MY CHEST, SO WHAT? WHAT DOES THAT MATTER?
YOU SHOULDN'T NEED THAT STUFF TO BE A SUPERHERO!
YOU'RE RIGHT. YOU SHOULDN'T NEED TO LOOK A CERTAIN WAY.
BOTH YOU AND I KNOW THAT CLOTHES AND MUSCLES DO NOT MAKE A COMPETENT SUPERHERO. IT DOESN'T MATTER.
BUT IT MATTERS TO THEM.
WE ♥ KEVIN

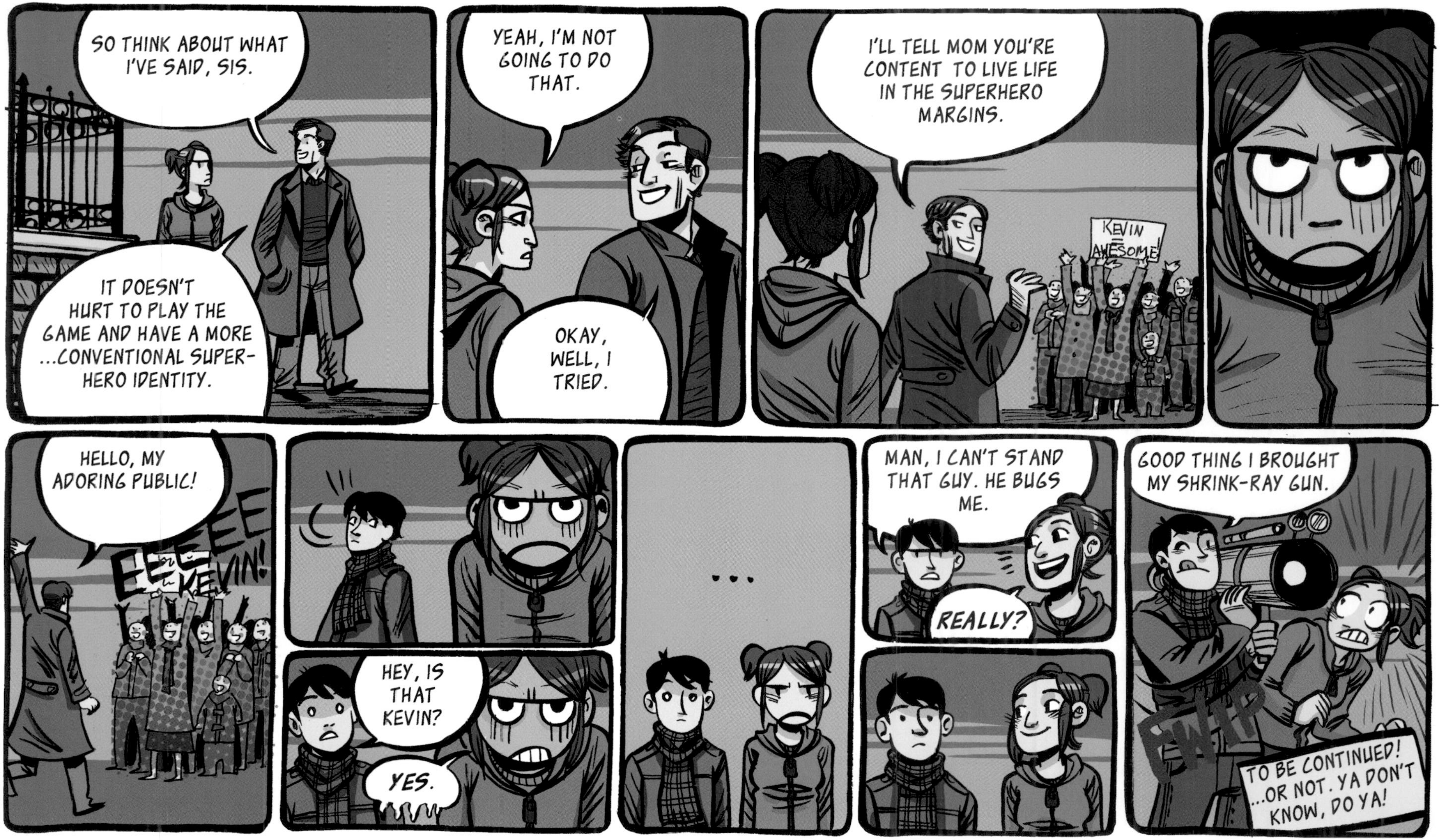
SO THINK ABOUT WHAT I'VE SAID, SIS.
IT DOESN'T HURT TO PLAY THE GAME AND HAVE A MORE ...CONVENTIONAL SUPER-HERO IDENTITY.
YEAH, I'M NOT GOING TO DO THAT.
OKAY, WELL, I TRIED.
I'LL TELL MOM YOU'RE CONTENT TO LIVE LIFE IN THE SUPERHERO MARGINS.
KEVIN = AWESOME!
HELLO, MY ADORING PUBLIC!
EEEEEE KEVIN!
HEY, IS THAT KEVIN?
YES.
...
MAN, I CAN'T STAND THAT GUY. HE BUGS ME.
REALLY?
GOOD THING I BROUGHT MY SHRINK-RAY GUN.
FWIP
TO BE CONTINUED! ...OR NOT. YA DON'T KNOW, DO YA!

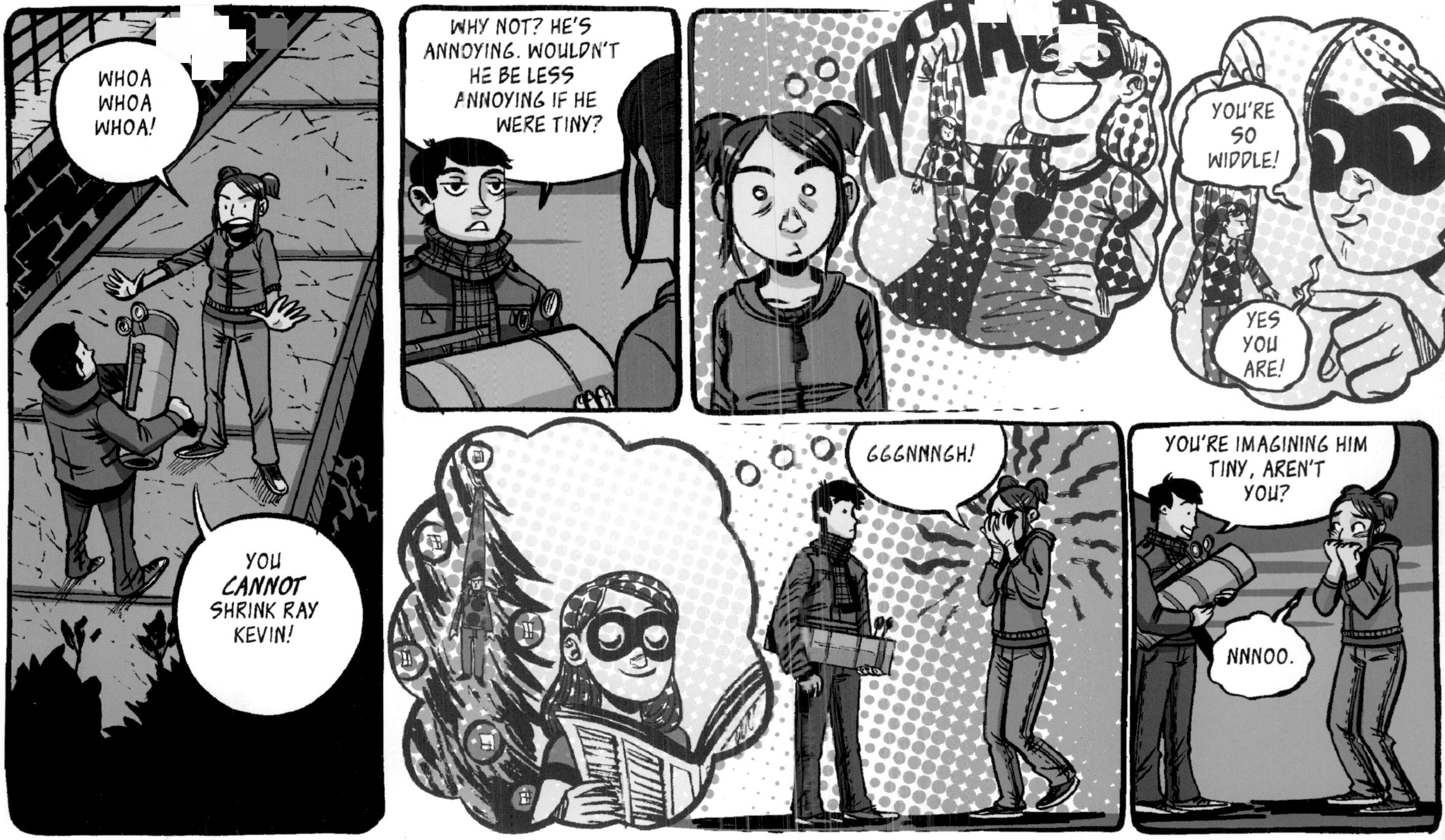
WHOA WHOA WHOA!
YOU CANNOT SHRINK RAY KEVIN!
WHY NOT? HE'S ANNOYING. WOULDN'T HE BE LESS ANNOYING IF HE WERE TINY?
YOU'RE SO WIDDLE!
YES YOU ARE!
GGGNNNGH!
YOU'RE IMAGINING HIM TINY, AREN'T YOU?
NNNOO.

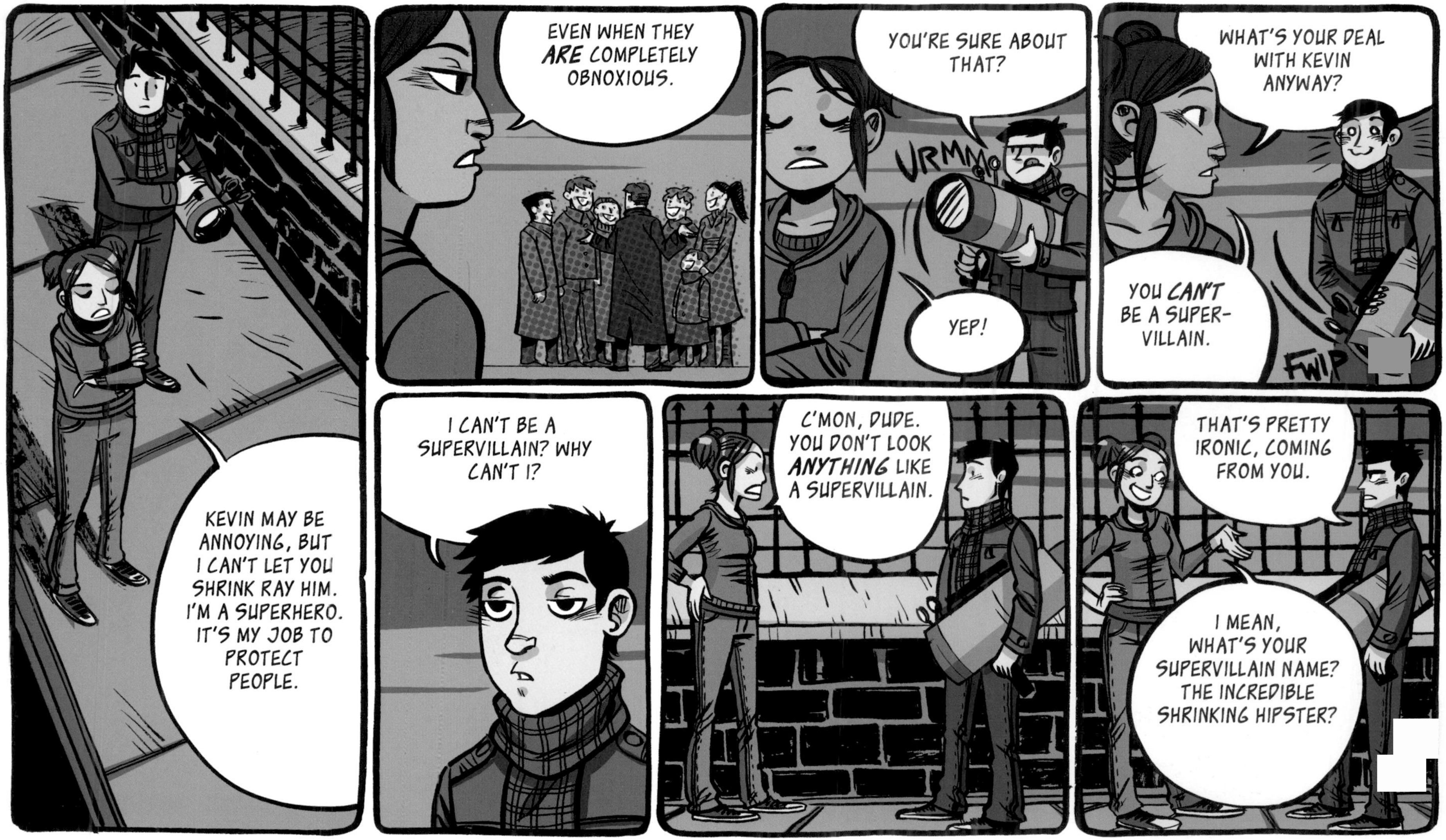
KEVIN MAY BE ANNOYING, BUT I CAN'T LET YOU SHRINK RAY HIM. I'M A SUPERHERO. IT'S MY JOB TO PROTECT PEOPLE.
EVEN WHEN THEY ARE COMPLETELY OBNOXIOUS.
YOU'RE SURE ABOUT THAT?
VRMMM
YEP!
WHAT'S YOUR DEAL WITH KEVIN ANYWAY?
YOU CAN'T BE A SUPER-VILLAIN.
FWIP
I CAN'T BE A SUPERVILLAIN? WHY CAN'T I?
C'MON, DUDE. YOU DON'T LOOK ANYTHING LIKE A SUPERVILLAIN.
THAT'S PRETTY IRONIC, COMING FROM YOU.
I MEAN, WHAT'S YOUR SUPERVILLAIN NAME? THE INCREDIBLE SHRINKING HIPSTER?

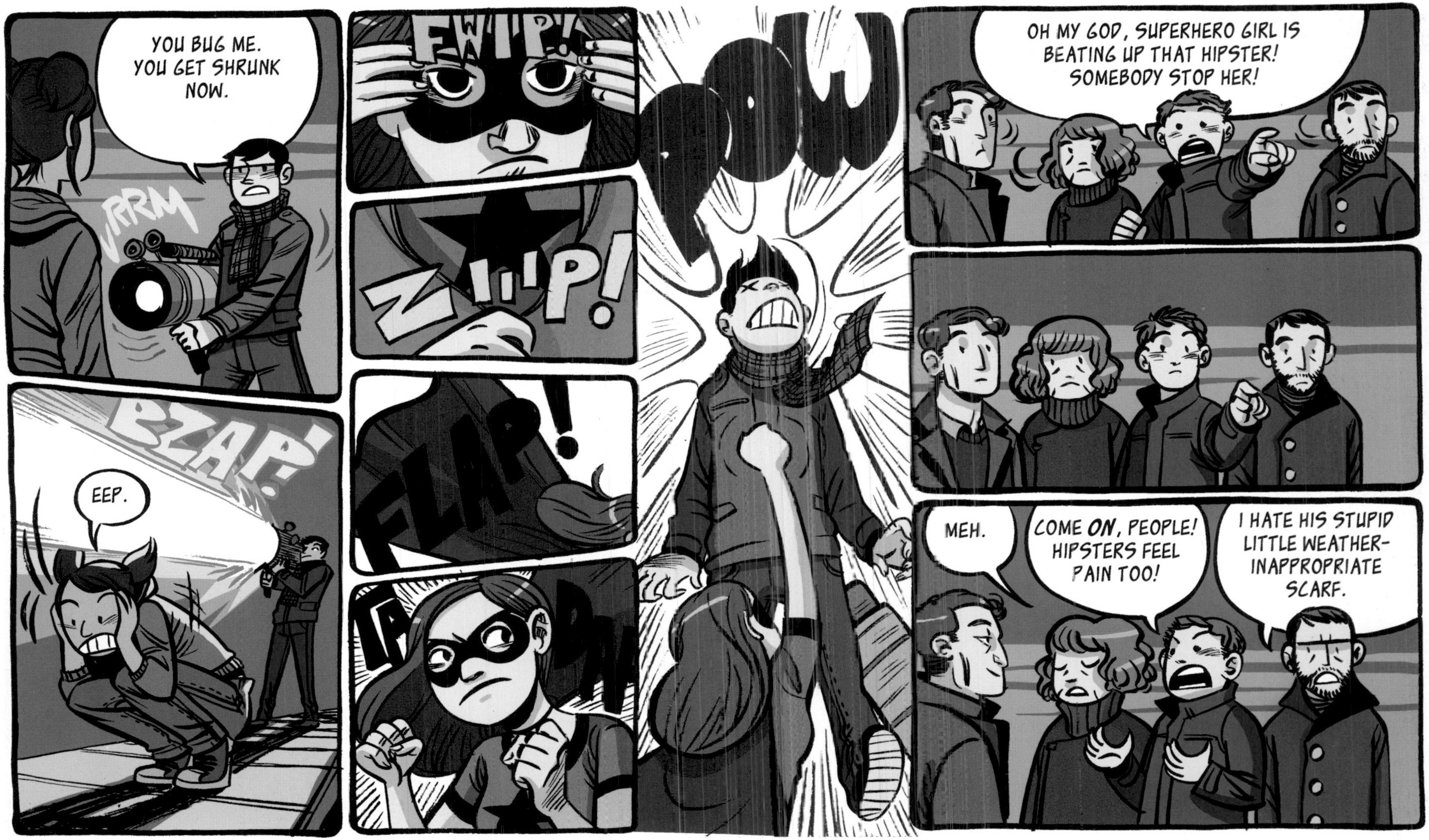
YOU BUG ME.
YOU GET SHRUNK
NOW.
VRRM
BZAP!
EEP.
FWIP!
ZIIIP!
FLAP!
TA-DA!
POW!
OH MY GOD, SUPERHERO GIRL IS
BEATING UP THAT HIPSTER!
SOMEBODY STOP HER!
MEH.
COME ON, PEOPLE!
HIPSTERS FEEL
PAIN TOO!
I HATE HIS STUPID
LITTLE WEATHER-
INAPPROPRIATE
SCARF.

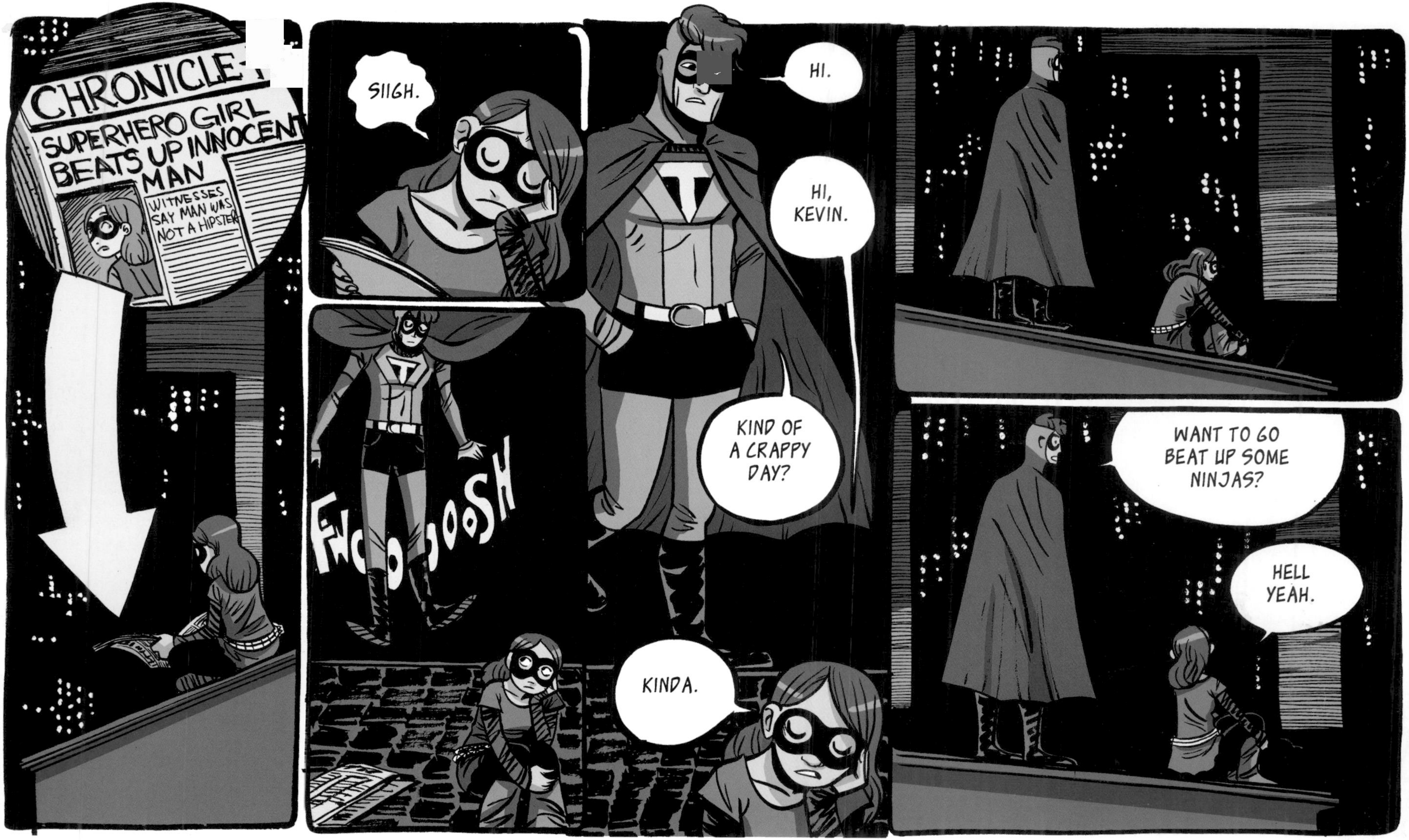
CHRONICLE
SUPERHERO GIRL BEATS UP INNOCENT MAN
WITNESSES SAY MAN WAS NOT A HIPSTER
SIIGH.
FWOOOOSH
HI.
HI, KEVIN.
KIND OF A CRAPPY DAY?
KINDA.
WANT TO GO BEAT UP SOME NINJAS?
HELL YEAH.

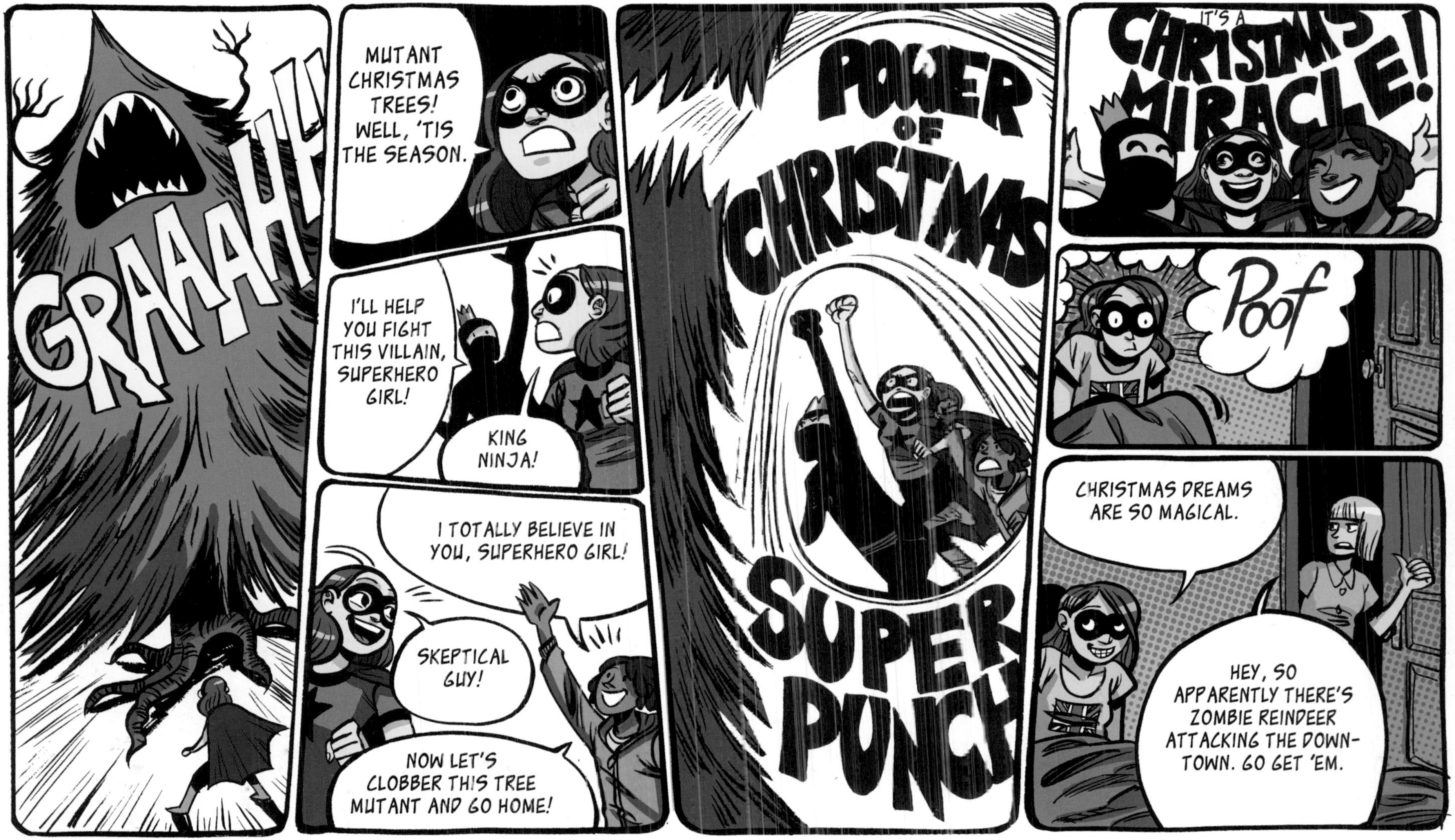
GRAAAHH
MUTANT CHRISTMAS TREES! WELL, 'TIS THE SEASON.
I'LL HELP YOU FIGHT THIS VILLAIN, SUPERHERO GIRL!
KING NINJA!
I TOTALLY BELIEVE IN YOU, SUPERHERO GIRL!
SKEPTICAL GUY!
NOW LET'S CLOBBER THIS TREE MUTANT AND GO HOME!
POWER OF CHRISTMAS SUPER PUNCH
IT'S A CHRISTMAS MIRACLE!
Poof
CHRISTMAS DREAMS ARE SO MAGICAL.
HEY, SO APPARENTLY THERE'S ZOMBIE REINDEER ATTACKING THE DOWN-TOWN. GO GET 'EM.

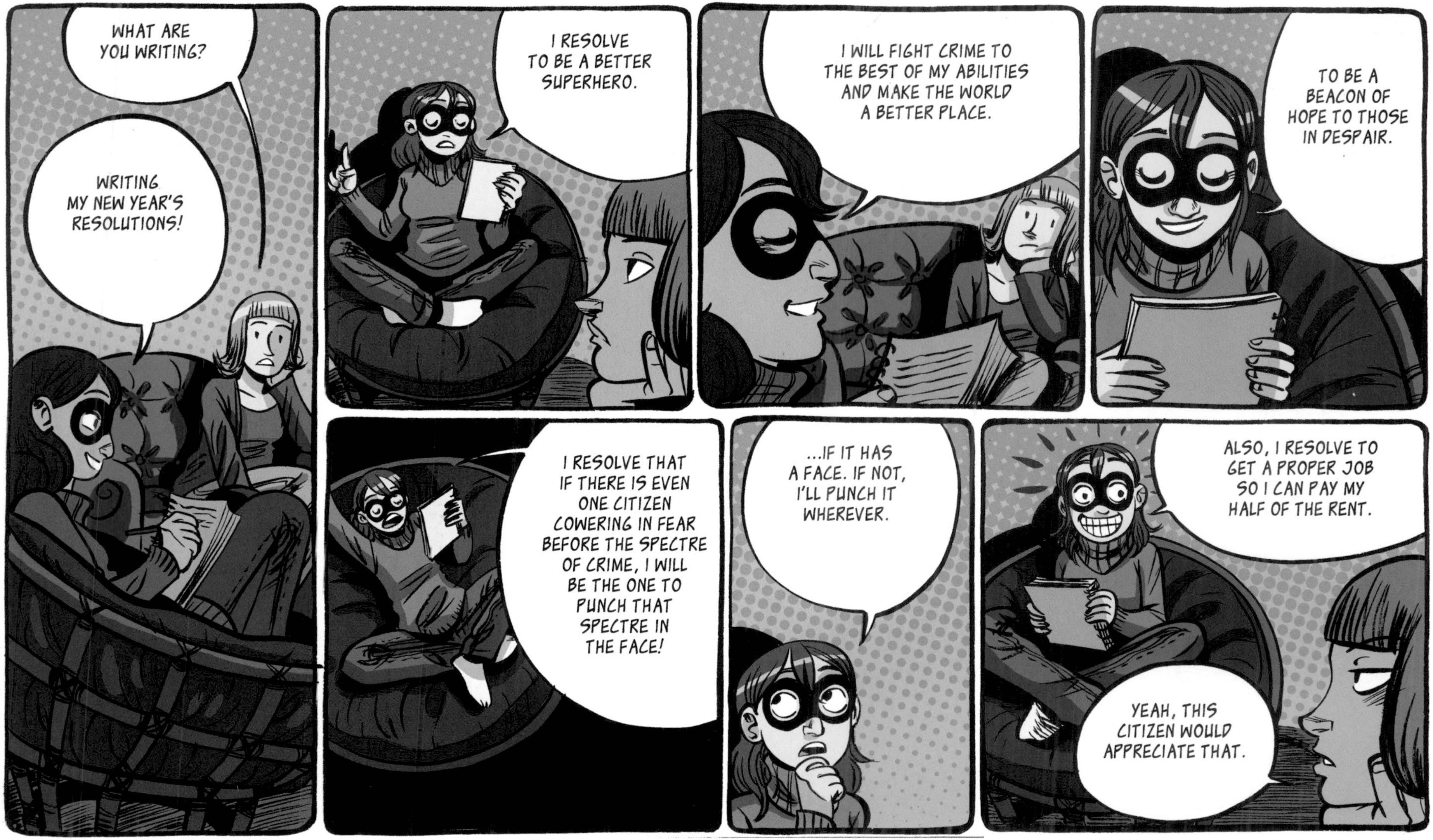
WHAT ARE YOU WRITING?
WRITING MY NEW YEAR'S RESOLUTIONS!
I RESOLVE TO BE A BETTER SUPERHERO.
I WILL FIGHT CRIME TO THE BEST OF MY ABILITIES AND MAKE THE WORLD A BETTER PLACE.
TO BE A BEACON OF HOPE TO THOSE IN DESPAIR.
I RESOLVE THAT IF THERE IS EVEN ONE CITIZEN COWERING IN FEAR BEFORE THE SPECTRE OF CRIME, I WILL BE THE ONE TO PUNCH THAT SPECTRE IN THE FACE!
...IF IT HAS A FACE. IF NOT, I'LL PUNCH IT WHEREVER.
ALSO, I RESOLVE TO GET A PROPER JOB SO I CAN PAY MY HALF OF THE RENT.
YEAH, THIS CITIZEN WOULD APPRECIATE THAT.

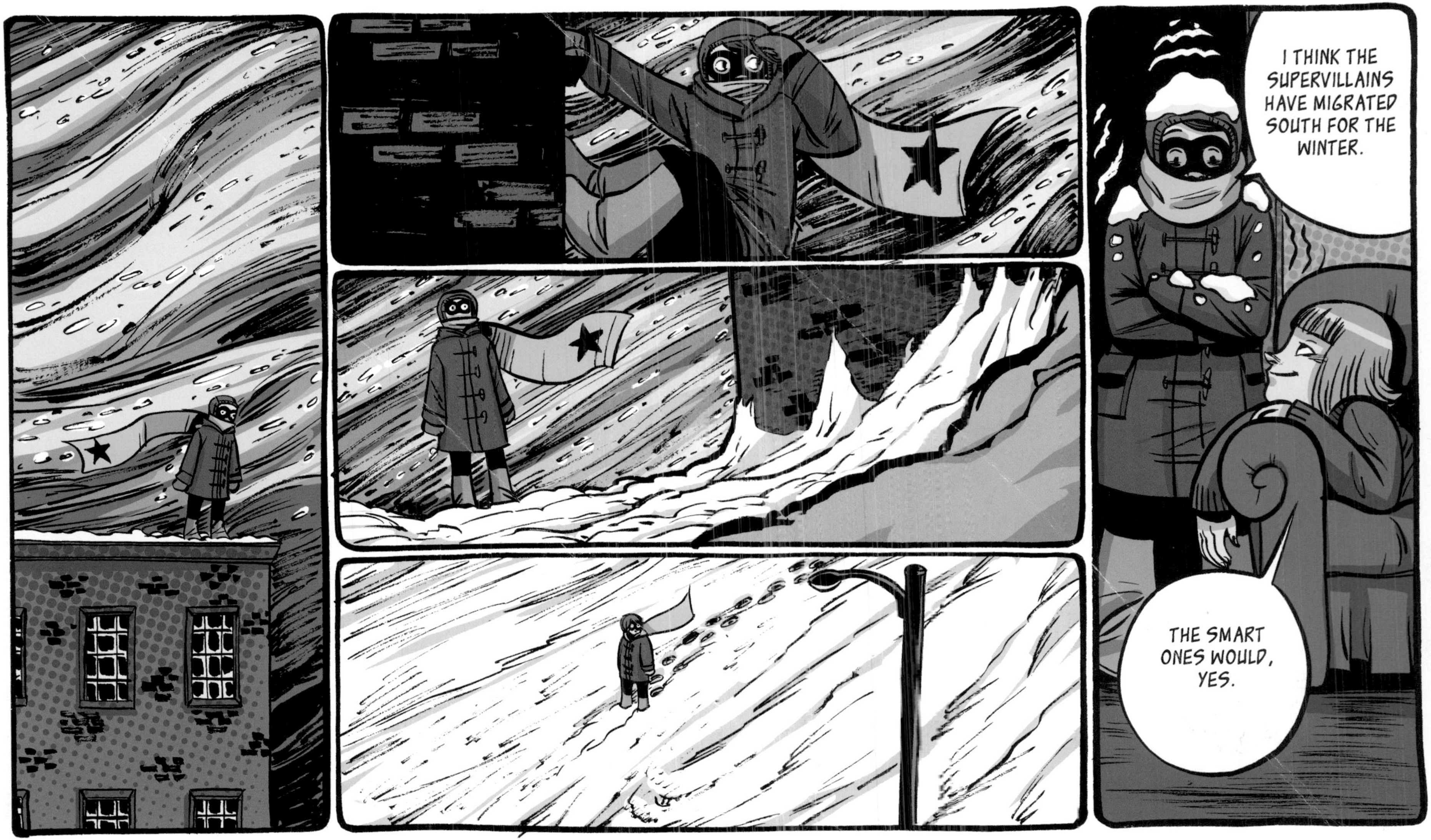
I THINK THE SUPERVILLAINS HAVE MIGRATED SOUTH FOR THE WINTER.
THE SMART ONES WOULD, YES.

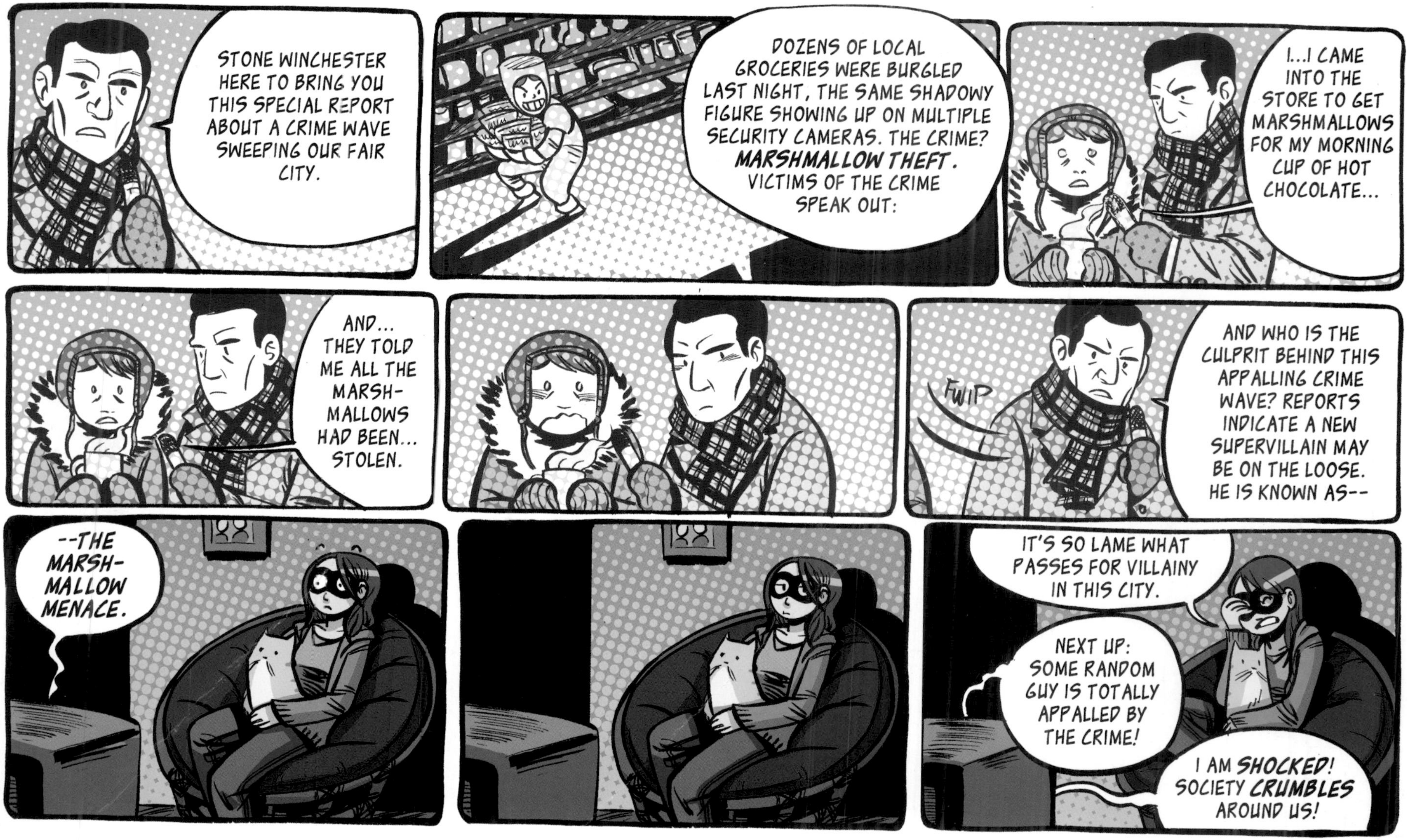
STONE WINCHESTER HERE TO BRING YOU THIS SPECIAL REPORT ABOUT A CRIME WAVE SWEEPING OUR FAIR CITY.
DOZENS OF LOCAL GROCERIES WERE BURGLED LAST NIGHT, THE SAME SHADOWY FIGURE SHOWING UP ON MULTIPLE SECURITY CAMERAS. THE CRIME? MARSHMALLOW THEFT. VICTIMS OF THE CRIME SPEAK OUT:
I...I CAME INTO THE STORE TO GET MARSHMALLOWS FOR MY MORNING CUP OF HOT CHOCOLATE...
AND... THEY TOLD ME ALL THE MARSH-MALLOWS HAD BEEN... STOLEN.
FWIP
AND WHO IS THE CULPRIT BEHIND THIS APPALLING CRIME WAVE? REPORTS INDICATE A NEW SUPERVILLAIN MAY BE ON THE LOOSE. HE IS KNOWN AS--
--THE MARSH-MALLOW MENACE.
IT'S SO LAME WHAT PASSES FOR VILLAINY IN THIS CITY.
NEXT UP: SOME RANDOM GUY IS TOTALLY APPALLED BY THE CRIME!
I AM SHOCKED! SOCIETY CRUMBLES AROUND US!

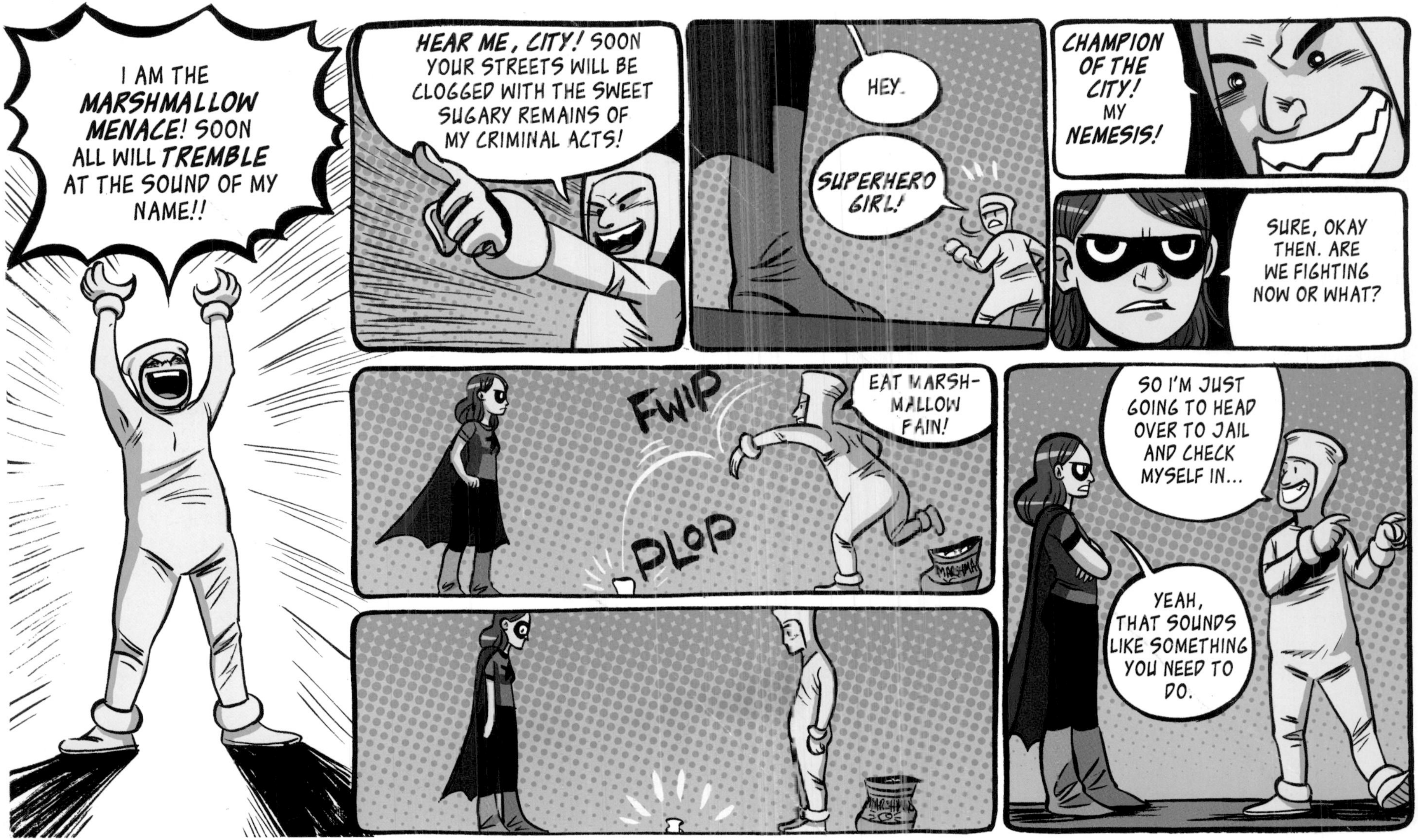
I AM THE MARSHMALLOW MENACE! SOON ALL WILL TREMBLE AT THE SOUND OF MY NAME!!
HEAR ME, CITY! SOON YOUR STREETS WILL BE CLOGGED WITH THE SWEET SUGARY REMAINS OF MY CRIMINAL ACTS!
HEY.
SUPERHERO GIRL!
CHAMPION OF THE CITY! MY NEMESIS!
SURE, OKAY THEN. ARE WE FIGHTING NOW OR WHAT?
FWIP
EAT MARSH-MALLOW PAIN!
PLOP
MARSHMA
SO I'M JUST GOING TO HEAD OVER TO JAIL AND CHECK MYSELF IN...
YEAH, THAT SOUNDS LIKE SOMETHING YOU NEED TO DO.

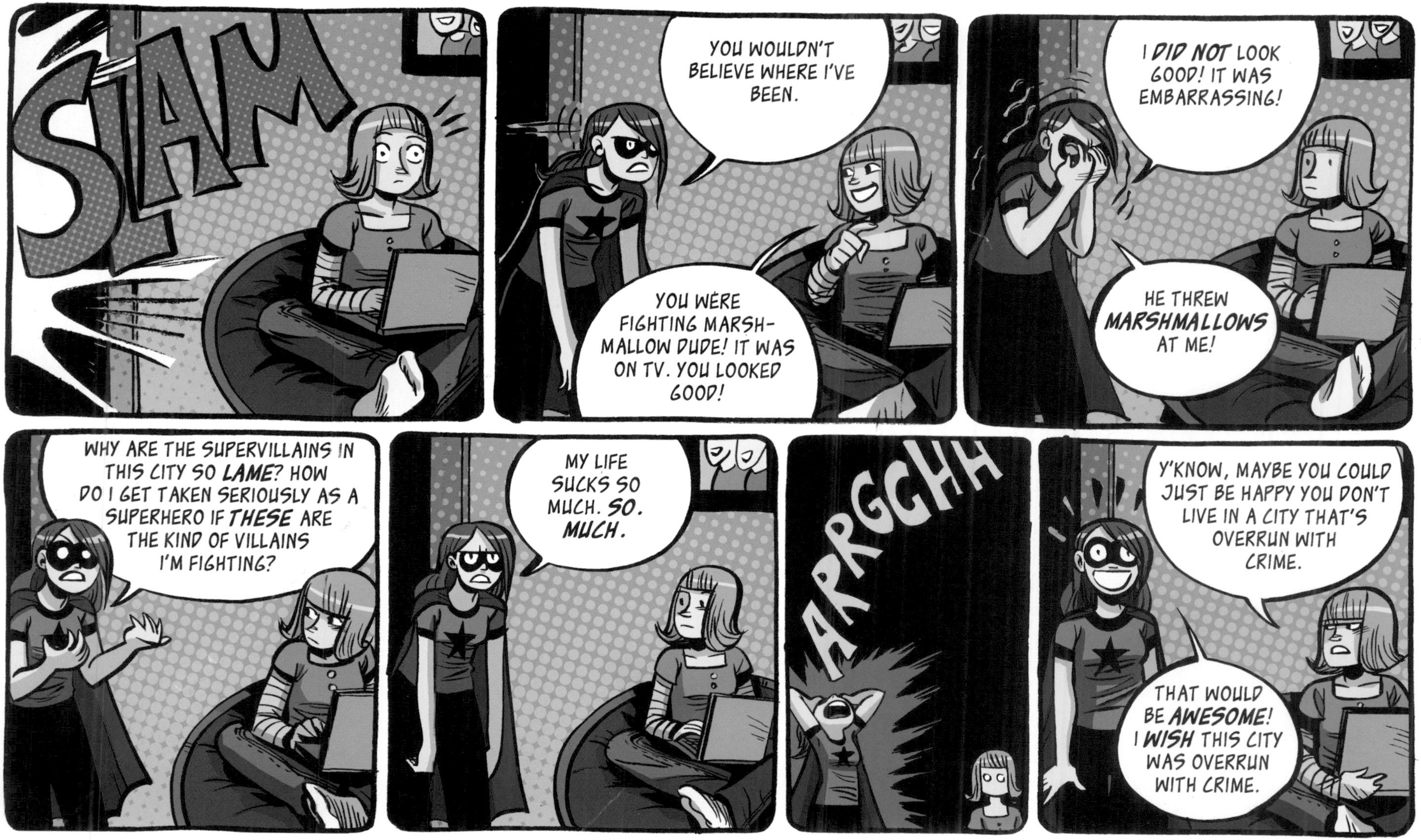
SLAM
YOU WOULDN'T BELIEVE WHERE I'VE BEEN.
YOU WERE FIGHTING MARSH-MALLOW DUDE! IT WAS ON TV. YOU LOOKED GOOD!
I DID NOT LOOK GOOD! IT WAS EMBARRASSING!
HE THREW MARSHMALLOWS AT ME!
WHY ARE THE SUPERVILLAINS IN THIS CITY SO LAME? HOW DO I GET TAKEN SERIOUSLY AS A SUPERHERO IF THESE ARE THE KIND OF VILLAINS I'M FIGHTING?
MY LIFE SUCKS SO MUCH. SO. MUCH.
ARRGGHH
Y'KNOW, MAYBE YOU COULD JUST BE HAPPY YOU DON'T LIVE IN A CITY THAT'S OVERRUN WITH CRIME.
THAT WOULD BE AWESOME! I WISH THIS CITY WAS OVERRUN WITH CRIME.

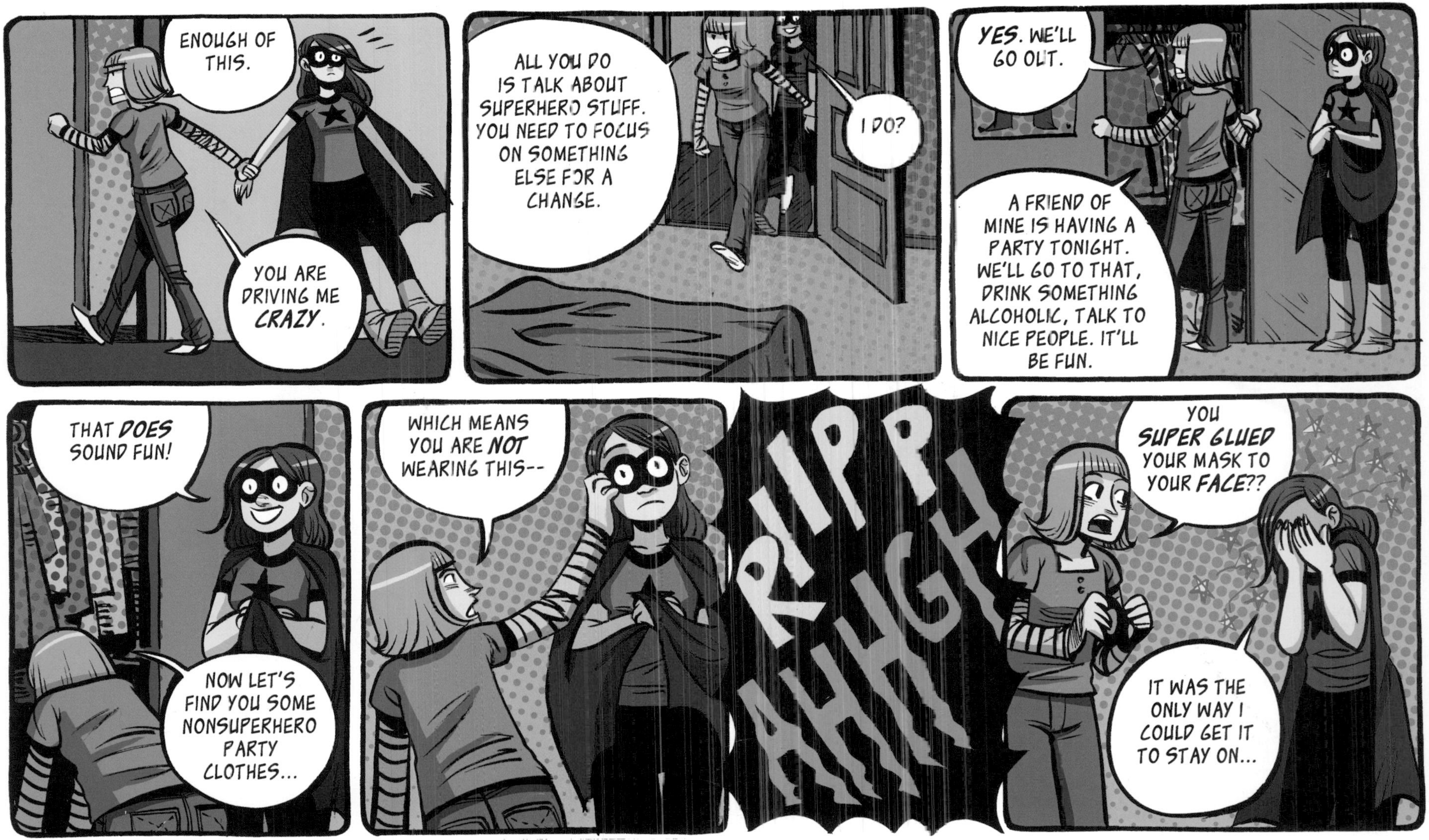
ENOUGH OF THIS.
YOU ARE DRIVING ME *CRAZY*.
ALL YOU DO IS TALK ABOUT SUPERHERO STUFF. YOU NEED TO FOCUS ON SOMETHING ELSE FOR A CHANGE.
I DO?
YES. WE'LL GO OUT.
A FRIEND OF MINE IS HAVING A PARTY TONIGHT. WE'LL GO TO THAT, DRINK SOMETHING ALCOHOLIC, TALK TO NICE PEOPLE. IT'LL BE FUN.
THAT *DOES* SOUND FUN!
NOW LET'S FIND YOU SOME NONSUPERHERO PARTY CLOTHES...
WHICH MEANS YOU ARE *NOT* WEARING THIS--
RIIPP
AHHGH
YOU *SUPER GLUED* YOUR MASK TO YOUR *FACE*??
IT WAS THE ONLY WAY I COULD GET IT TO STAY ON...

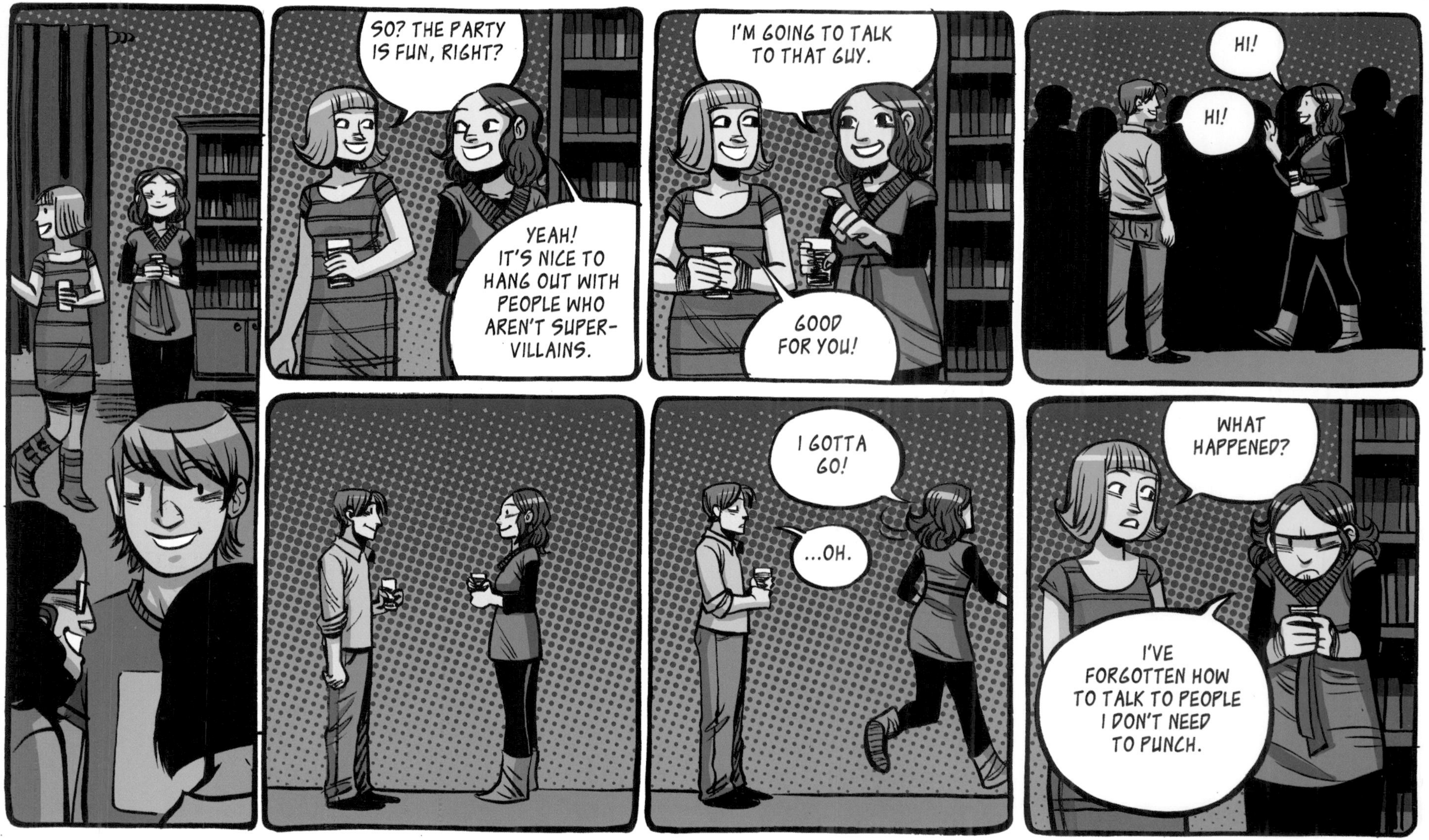

SO? THE PARTY IS FUN, RIGHT?
YEAH! IT'S NICE TO HANG OUT WITH PEOPLE WHO AREN'T SUPER-VILLAINS.
I'M GOING TO TALK TO THAT GUY.
GOOD FOR YOU!
HI!
HI!
I GOTTA GO!
...OH.
WHAT HAPPENED?
I'VE FORGOTTEN HOW TO TALK TO PEOPLE I DON'T NEED TO PUNCH.

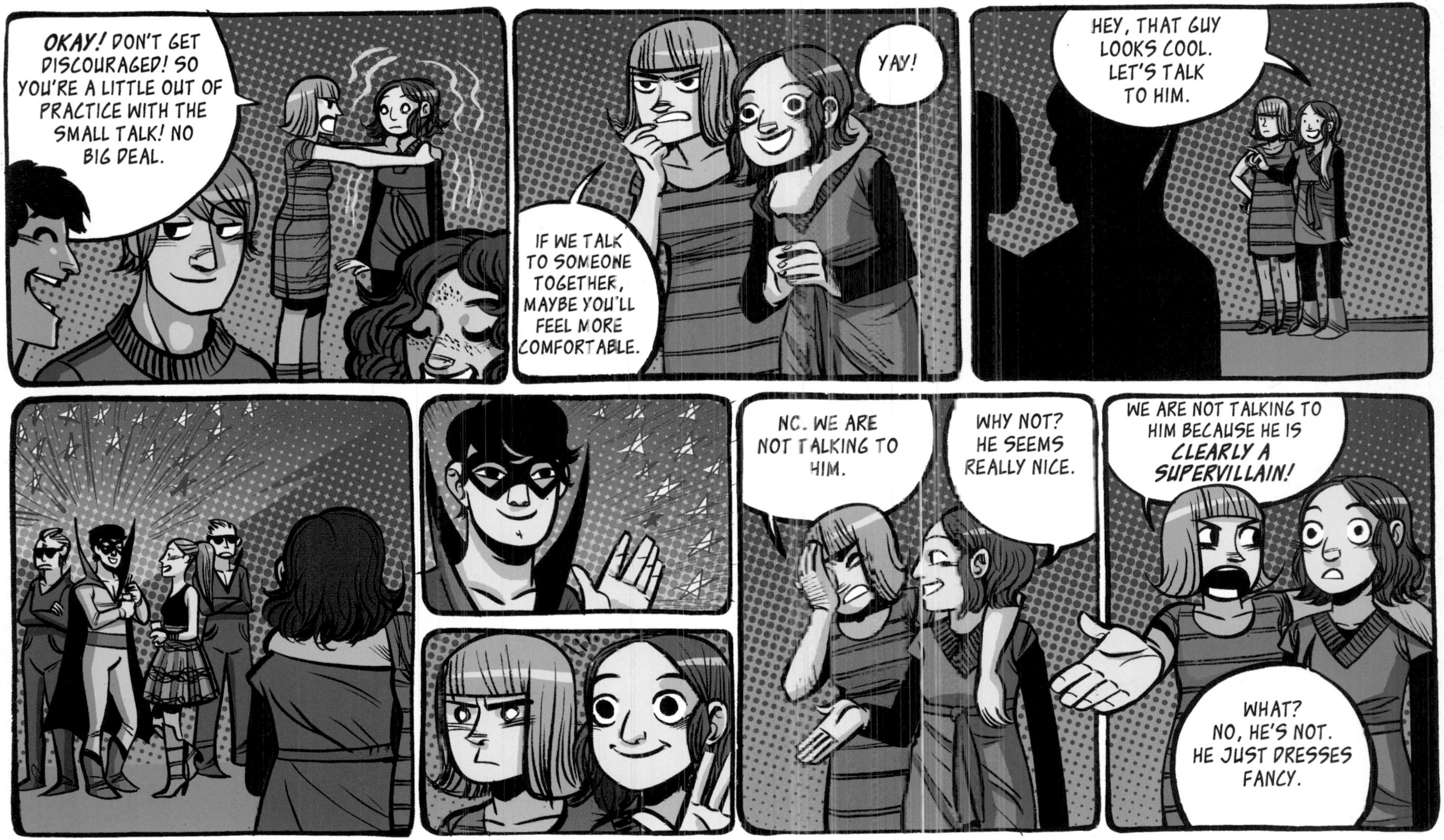
OKAY! DON'T GET DISCOURAGED! SO YOU'RE A LITTLE OUT OF PRACTICE WITH THE SMALL TALK! NO BIG DEAL.
IF WE TALK TO SOMEONE TOGETHER, MAYBE YOU'LL FEEL MORE COMFORTABLE.
YAY!
HEY, THAT GUY LOOKS COOL. LET'S TALK TO HIM.
NO. WE ARE NOT TALKING TO HIM.
WHY NOT? HE SEEMS REALLY NICE.
WE ARE NOT TALKING TO HIM BECAUSE HE IS *CLEARLY A SUPERVILLAIN!*
WHAT? NO, HE'S NOT. HE JUST DRESSES FANCY.

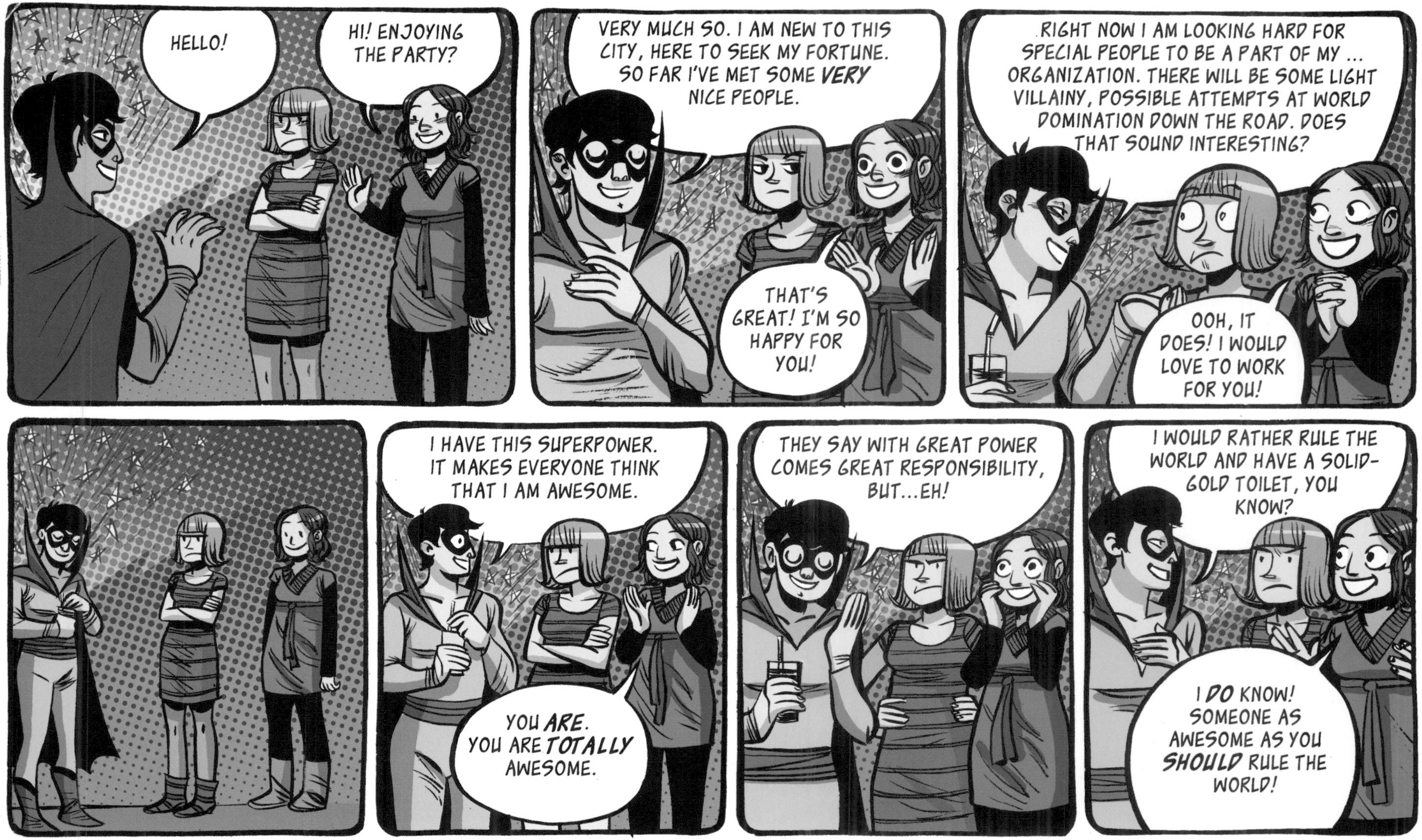
HELLO!
HI! ENJOYING THE PARTY?
VERY MUCH SO. I AM NEW TO THIS CITY, HERE TO SEEK MY FORTUNE. SO FAR I'VE MET SOME *VERY* NICE PEOPLE.
THAT'S GREAT! I'M SO HAPPY FOR YOU!
RIGHT NOW I AM LOOKING HARD FOR SPECIAL PEOPLE TO BE A PART OF MY ... ORGANIZATION. THERE WILL BE SOME LIGHT VILLAINY, POSSIBLE ATTEMPTS AT WORLD DOMINATION DOWN THE ROAD. DOES THAT SOUND INTERESTING?
OOH, IT DOES! I WOULD LOVE TO WORK FOR YOU!
I HAVE THIS SUPERPOWER. IT MAKES EVERYONE THINK THAT I AM AWESOME.
YOU *ARE*. YOU ARE *TOTALLY* AWESOME.
THEY SAY WITH GREAT POWER COMES GREAT RESPONSIBILITY, BUT...EH!
I WOULD RATHER RULE THE WORLD AND HAVE A SOLID-GOLD TOILET, YOU KNOW?
I *DO* KNOW! SOMEONE AS AWESOME AS YOU *SHOULD* RULE THE WORLD!

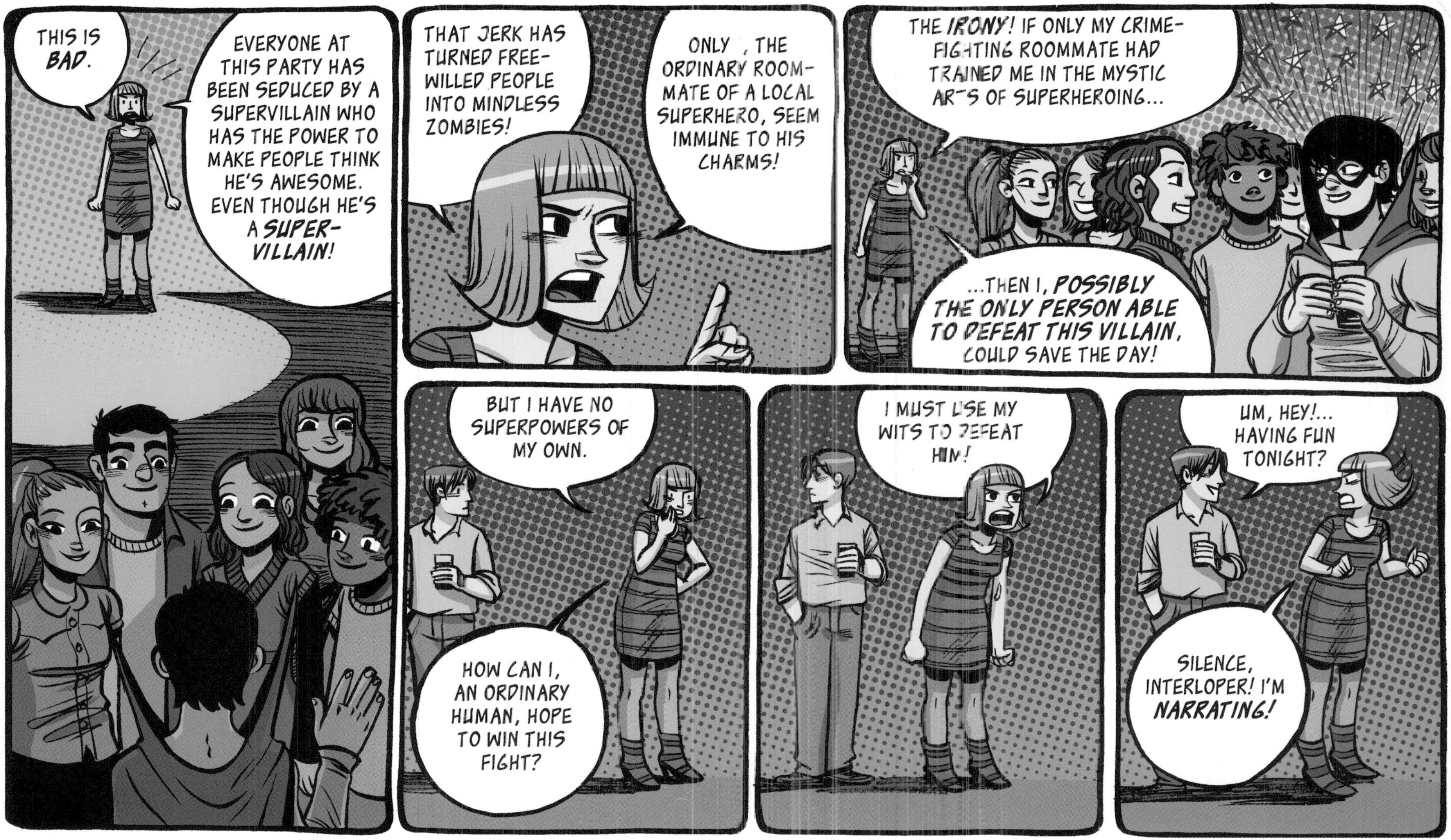

THIS IS *BAD*.
EVERYONE AT THIS PARTY HAS BEEN SEDUCED BY A SUPERVILLAIN WHO HAS THE POWER TO MAKE PEOPLE THINK HE'S AWESOME. EVEN THOUGH HE'S A ***SUPER-VILLAIN***!
THAT JERK HAS TURNED FREE-WILLED PEOPLE INTO MINDLESS ZOMBIES!
ONLY , THE ORDINARY ROOM-MATE OF A LOCAL SUPERHERO, SEEM IMMUNE TO HIS CHARMS!
THE *IRONY*! IF ONLY MY CRIME-FIGHTING ROOMMATE HAD TRAINED ME IN THE MYSTIC ARTS OF SUPERHEROING...
...THEN I, ***POSSIBLY THE ONLY PERSON ABLE TO DEFEAT THIS VILLAIN***, COULD SAVE THE DAY!
BUT I HAVE NO SUPERPOWERS OF MY OWN.
HOW CAN I, AN ORDINARY HUMAN, HOPE TO WIN THIS FIGHT?
I MUST USE MY WITS TO DEFEAT HIM!
UM, HEY!... HAVING FUN TONIGHT?
SILENCE, INTERLOPER! I'M ***NARRATING***!

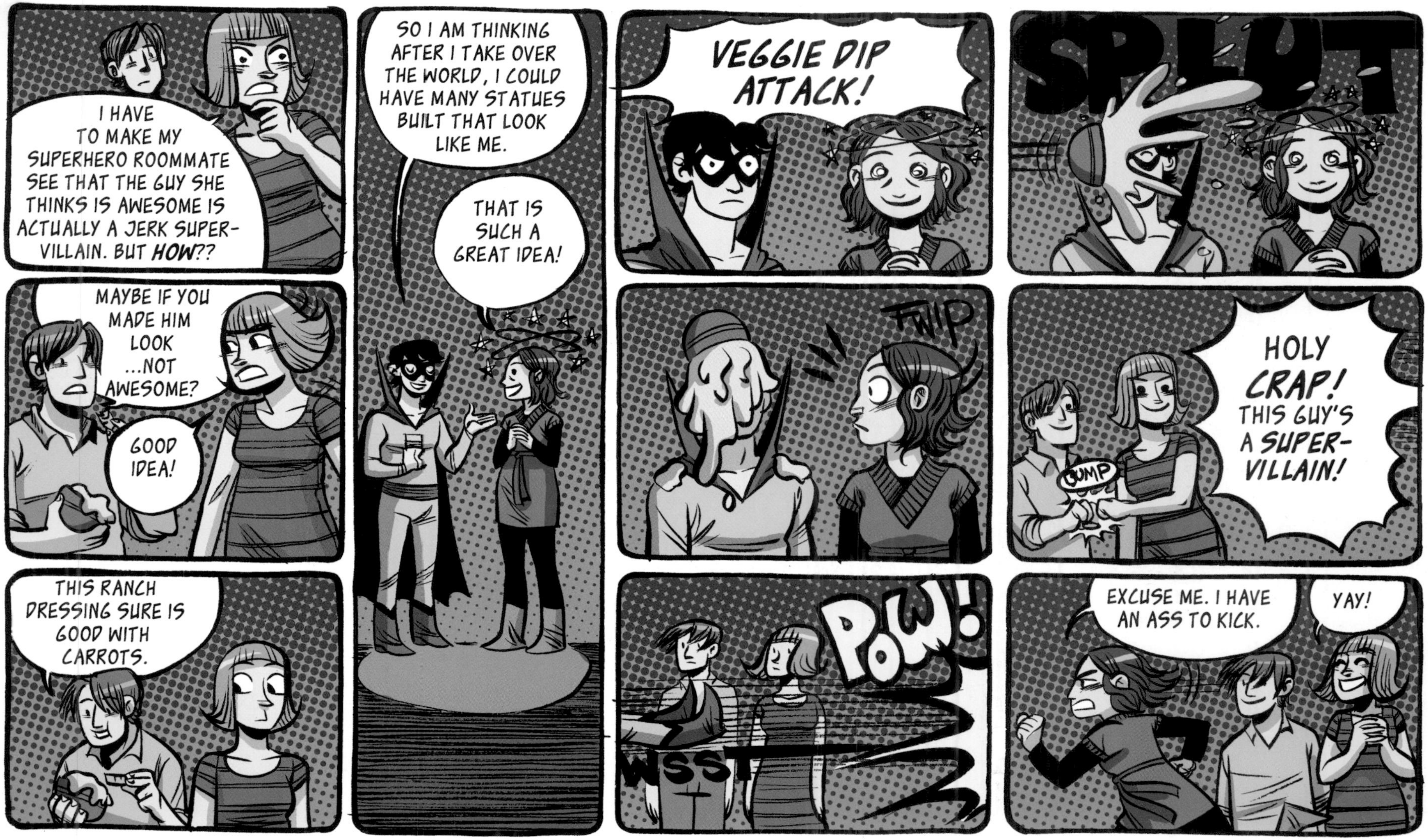
I HAVE TO MAKE MY SUPERHERO ROOMMATE SEE THAT THE GUY SHE THINKS IS AWESOME IS ACTUALLY A JERK SUPER-VILLAIN. BUT HOW??
MAYBE IF YOU MADE HIM LOOK ...NOT AWESOME?
GOOD IDEA!
THIS RANCH DRESSING SURE IS GOOD WITH CARROTS.
SO I AM THINKING AFTER I TAKE OVER THE WORLD, I COULD HAVE MANY STATUES BUILT THAT LOOK LIKE ME.
THAT IS SUCH A GREAT IDEA!
VEGGIE DIP ATTACK!
FWIP
WSST
POW!
SPLUT
HOLY CRAP! THIS GUY'S A SUPER-VILLAIN!
BUMP
EXCUSE ME. I HAVE AN ASS TO KICK.
YAY!

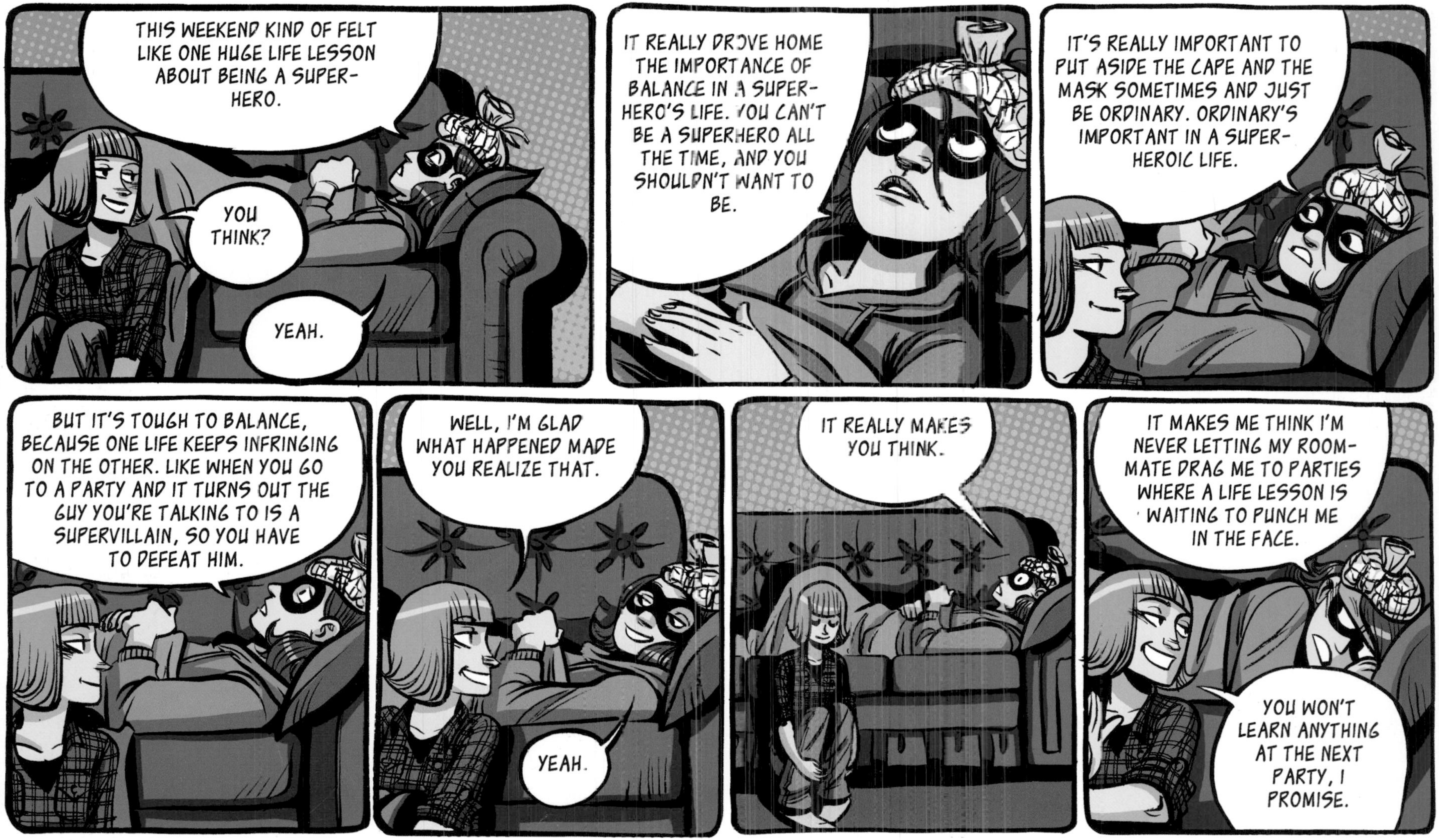
THIS WEEKEND KIND OF FELT LIKE ONE HUGE LIFE LESSON ABOUT BEING A SUPER-HERO.
YOU THINK?
YEAH.
IT REALLY DROVE HOME THE IMPORTANCE OF BALANCE IN A SUPER-HERO'S LIFE. YOU CAN'T BE A SUPERHERO ALL THE TIME, AND YOU SHOULDN'T WANT TO BE.
IT'S REALLY IMPORTANT TO PUT ASIDE THE CAPE AND THE MASK SOMETIMES AND JUST BE ORDINARY. ORDINARY'S IMPORTANT IN A SUPER-HEROIC LIFE.
BUT IT'S TOUGH TO BALANCE, BECAUSE ONE LIFE KEEPS INFRINGING ON THE OTHER. LIKE WHEN YOU GO TO A PARTY AND IT TURNS OUT THE GUY YOU'RE TALKING TO IS A SUPERVILLAIN, SO YOU HAVE TO DEFEAT HIM.
WELL, I'M GLAD WHAT HAPPENED MADE YOU REALIZE THAT.
YEAH.
IT REALLY MAKES YOU THINK.
IT MAKES ME THINK I'M NEVER LETTING MY ROOM-MATE DRAG ME TO PARTIES WHERE A LIFE LESSON IS WAITING TO PUNCH ME IN THE FACE.
YOU WON'T LEARN ANYTHING AT THE NEXT PARTY, I PROMISE.

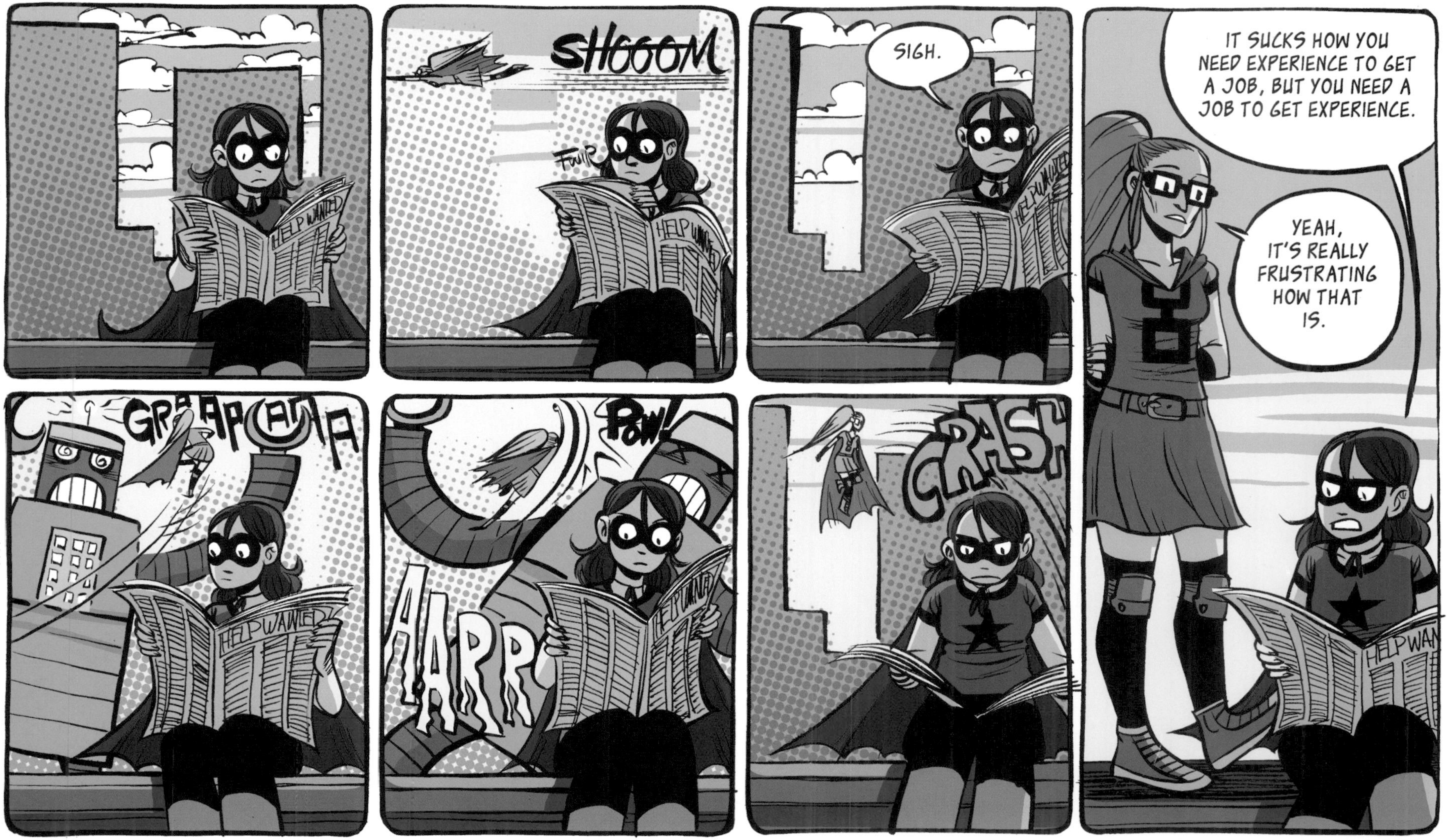

HELP WANTED
SHOOOM
SIGH.
POW!
AARR
CRASH
IT SUCKS HOW YOU NEED EXPERIENCE TO GET A JOB, BUT YOU NEED A JOB TO GET EXPERIENCE.
YEAH, IT'S REALLY FRUSTRATING HOW THAT IS.

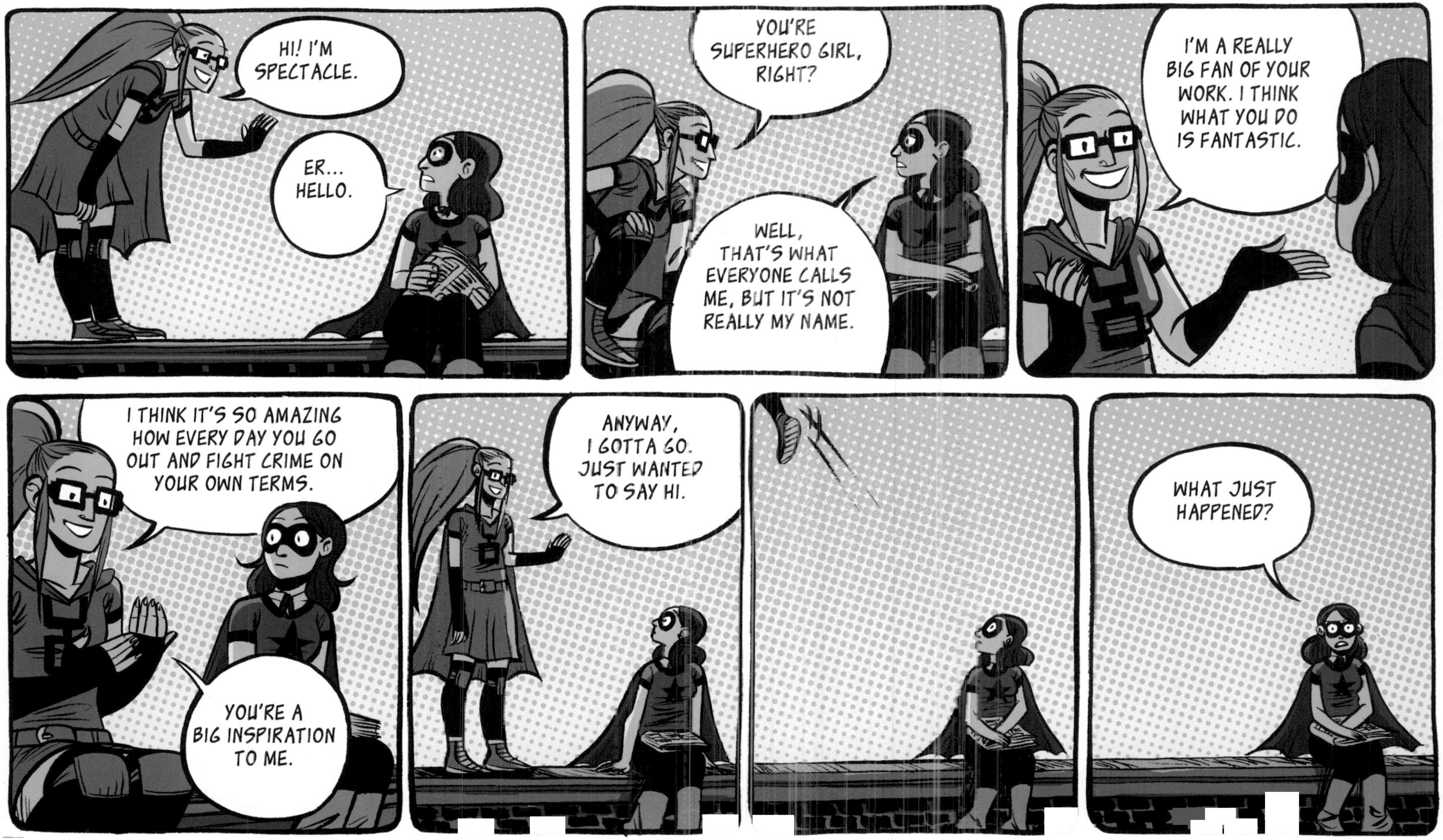
HI! I'M SPECTACLE.
ER... HELLO.
YOU'RE SUPERHERO GIRL, RIGHT?
WELL, THAT'S WHAT EVERYONE CALLS ME, BUT IT'S NOT REALLY MY NAME.
I'M A REALLY BIG FAN OF YOUR WORK. I THINK WHAT YOU DO IS FANTASTIC.
I THINK IT'S SO AMAZING HOW EVERY DAY YOU GO OUT AND FIGHT CRIME ON YOUR OWN TERMS.
YOU'RE A BIG INSPIRATION TO ME.
ANYWAY, I GOTTA GO. JUST WANTED TO SAY HI.
WHAT JUST HAPPENED?

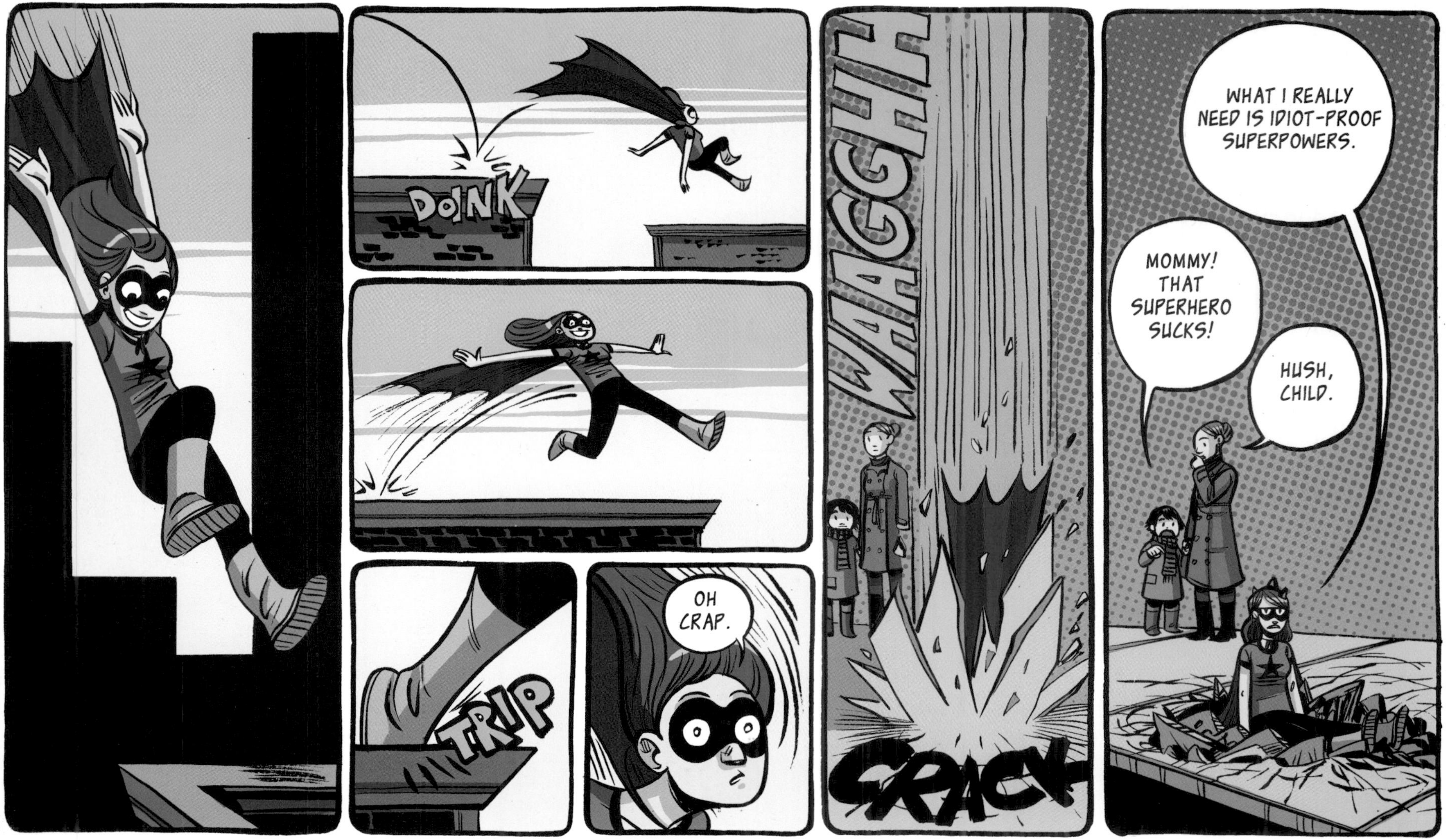
DOINK
TRIP
OH CRAP.
WAAGGHH
CRACK
WHAT I REALLY NEED IS IDIOT-PROOF SUPERPOWERS.
MOMMY! THAT SUPERHERO SUCKS!
HUSH, CHILD.

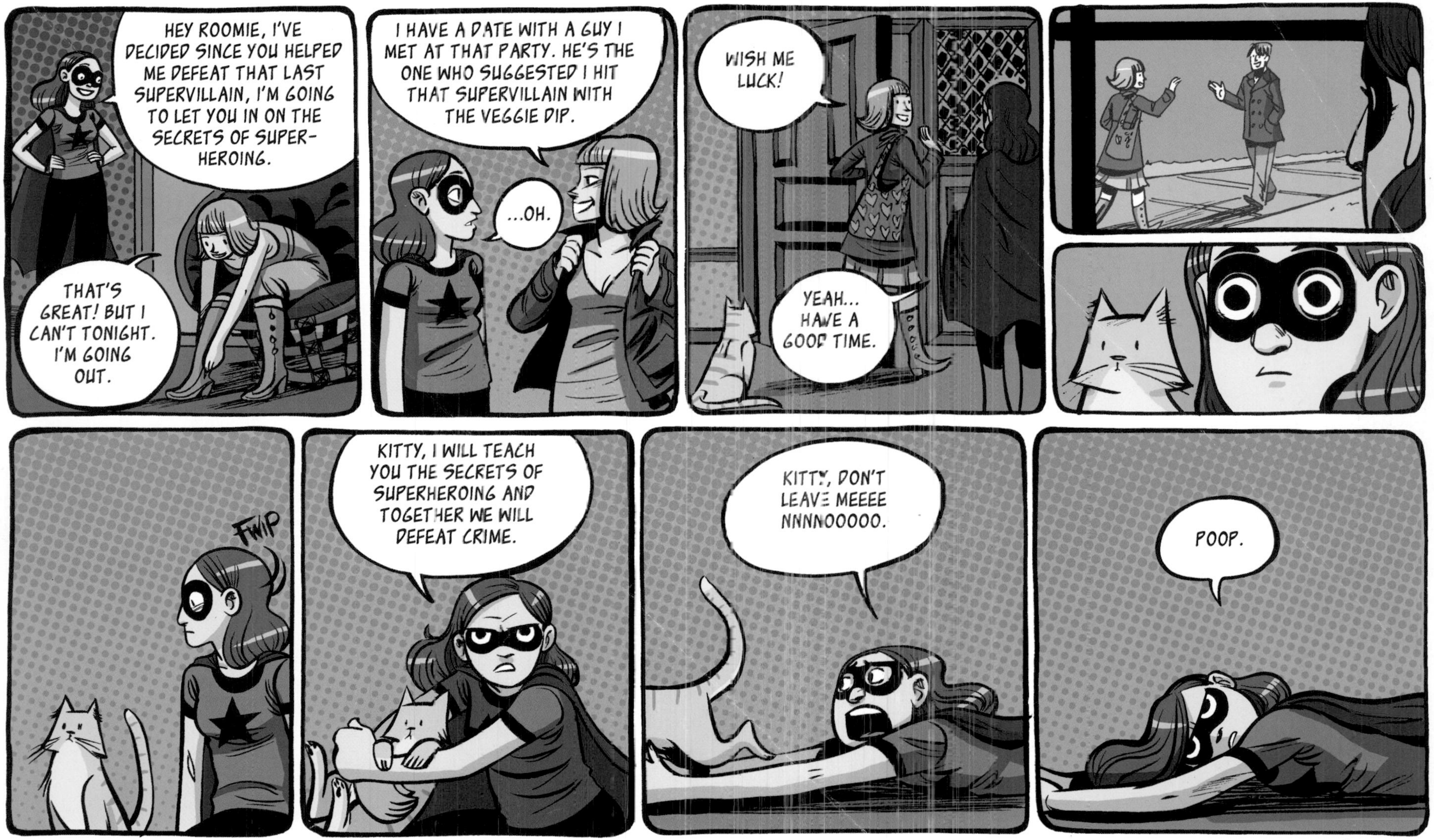
HEY ROOMIE, I'VE DECIDED SINCE YOU HELPED ME DEFEAT THAT LAST SUPERVILLAIN, I'M GOING TO LET YOU IN ON THE SECRETS OF SUPER-HEROING.
THAT'S GREAT! BUT I CAN'T TONIGHT. I'M GOING OUT.
I HAVE A DATE WITH A GUY I MET AT THAT PARTY. HE'S THE ONE WHO SUGGESTED I HIT THAT SUPERVILLAIN WITH THE VEGGIE DIP.
...OH.
WISH ME LUCK!
YEAH... HAVE A GOOD TIME.
FWIP
KITTY, I WILL TEACH YOU THE SECRETS OF SUPERHEROING AND TOGETHER WE WILL DEFEAT CRIME.
KITTY, DON'T LEAVE MEEEE NNNNOOOOO.
POOP.

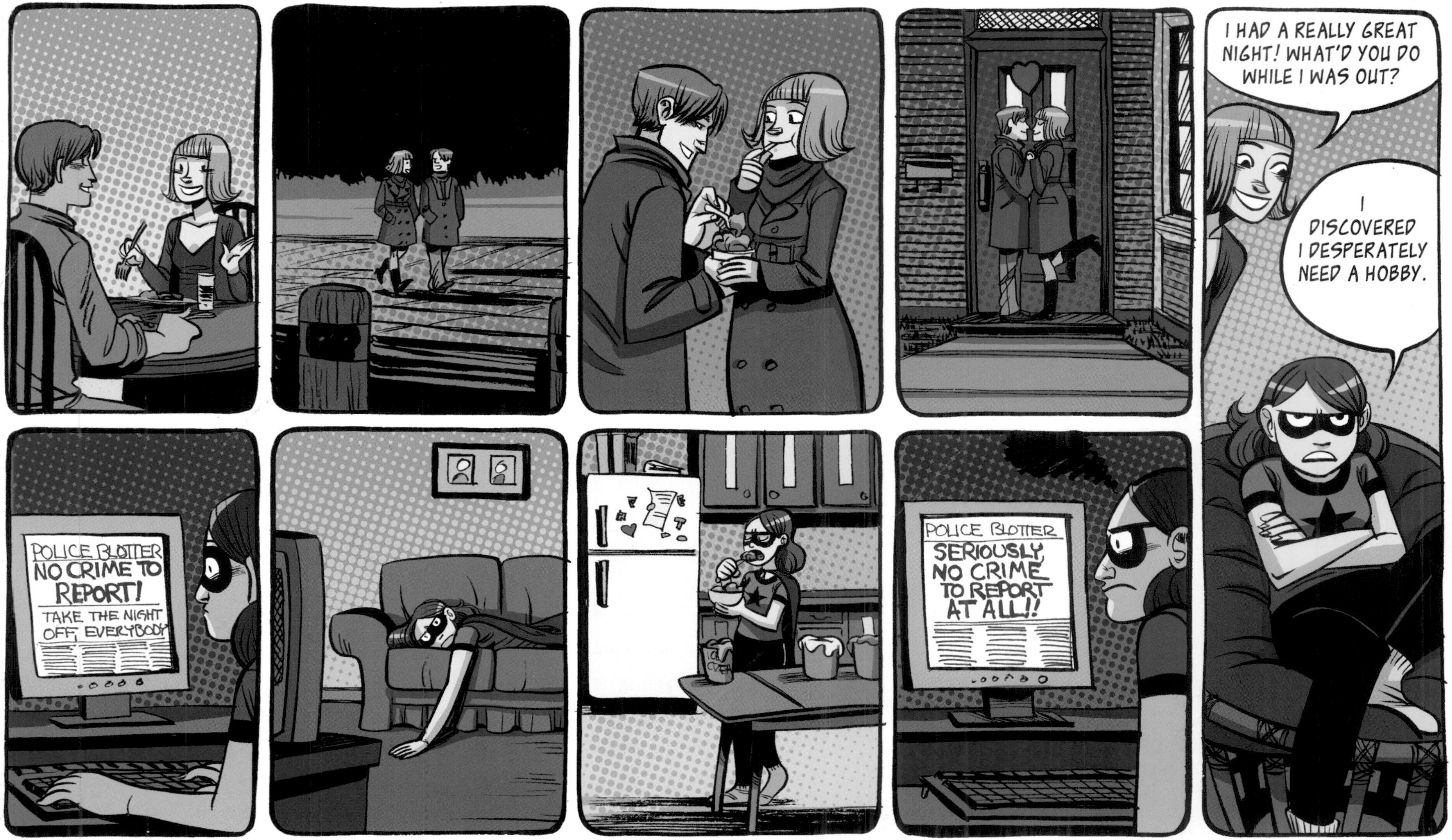
POLICE BLOTTER
NO CRIME TO REPORT!
TAKE THE NIGHT OFF, EVERYBODY!
POLICE BLOTTER
SERIOUSLY, NO CRIME TO REPORT AT ALL!!
I HAD A REALLY GREAT NIGHT! WHAT'D YOU DO WHILE I WAS OUT?
I DISCOVERED I DESPERATELY NEED A HOBBY.

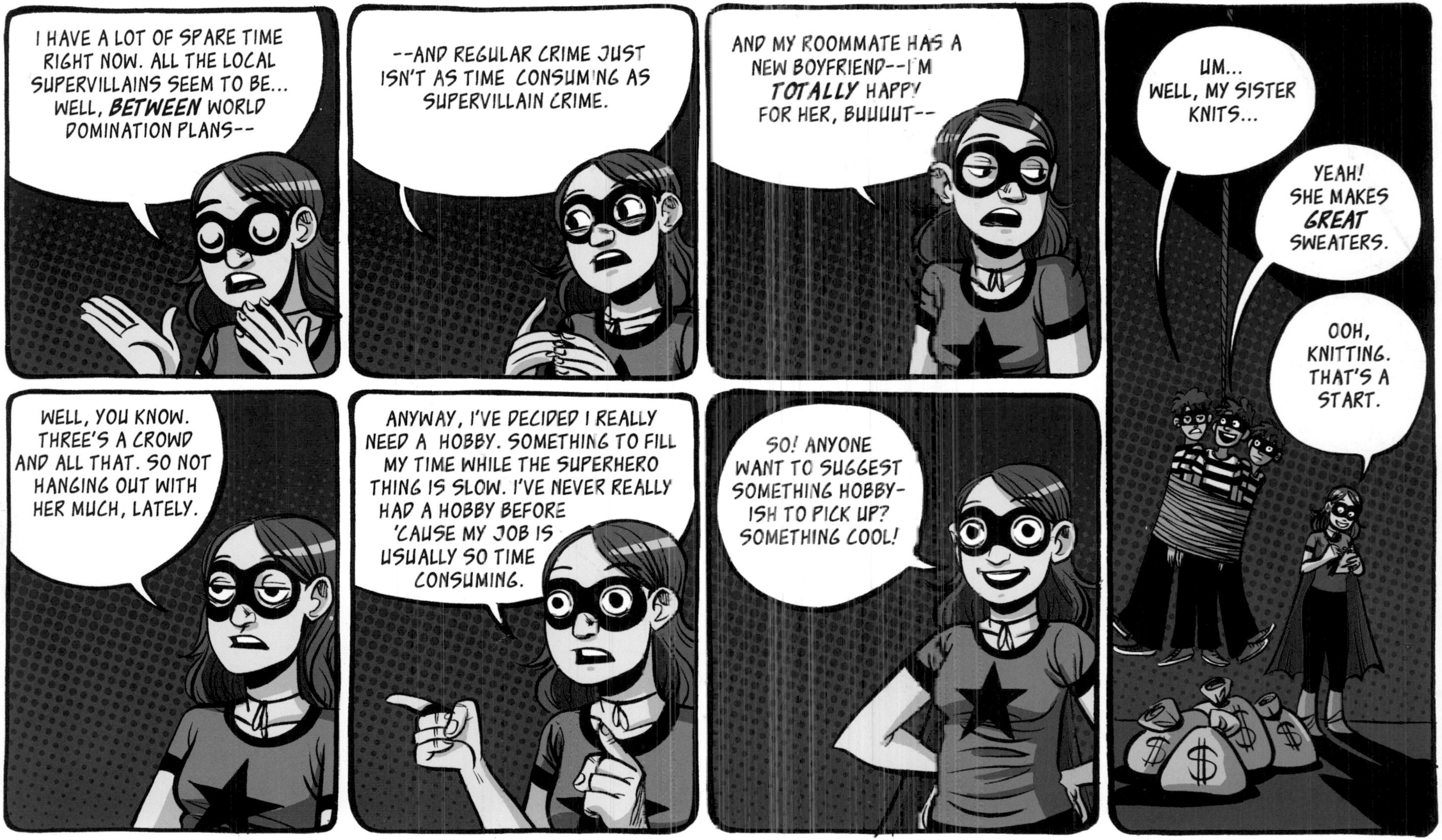
I HAVE A LOT OF SPARE TIME RIGHT NOW. ALL THE LOCAL SUPERVILLAINS SEEM TO BE... WELL, **BETWEEN** WORLD DOMINATION PLANS--
--AND REGULAR CRIME JUST ISN'T AS TIME CONSUMING AS SUPERVILLAIN CRIME.
AND MY ROOMMATE HAS A NEW BOYFRIEND--I'M **TOTALLY** HAPPY FOR HER, BUUUUT--
WELL, YOU KNOW. THREE'S A CROWD AND ALL THAT. SO NOT HANGING OUT WITH HER MUCH, LATELY.
ANYWAY, I'VE DECIDED I REALLY NEED A HOBBY. SOMETHING TO FILL MY TIME WHILE THE SUPERHERO THING IS SLOW. I'VE NEVER REALLY HAD A HOBBY BEFORE 'CAUSE MY JOB IS USUALLY SO TIME CONSUMING.
SO! ANYONE WANT TO SUGGEST SOMETHING HOBBY-ISH TO PICK UP? SOMETHING COOL!
UM... WELL, MY SISTER KNITS...
YEAH! SHE MAKES **GREAT** SWEATERS.
OOH, KNITTING. THAT'S A START.

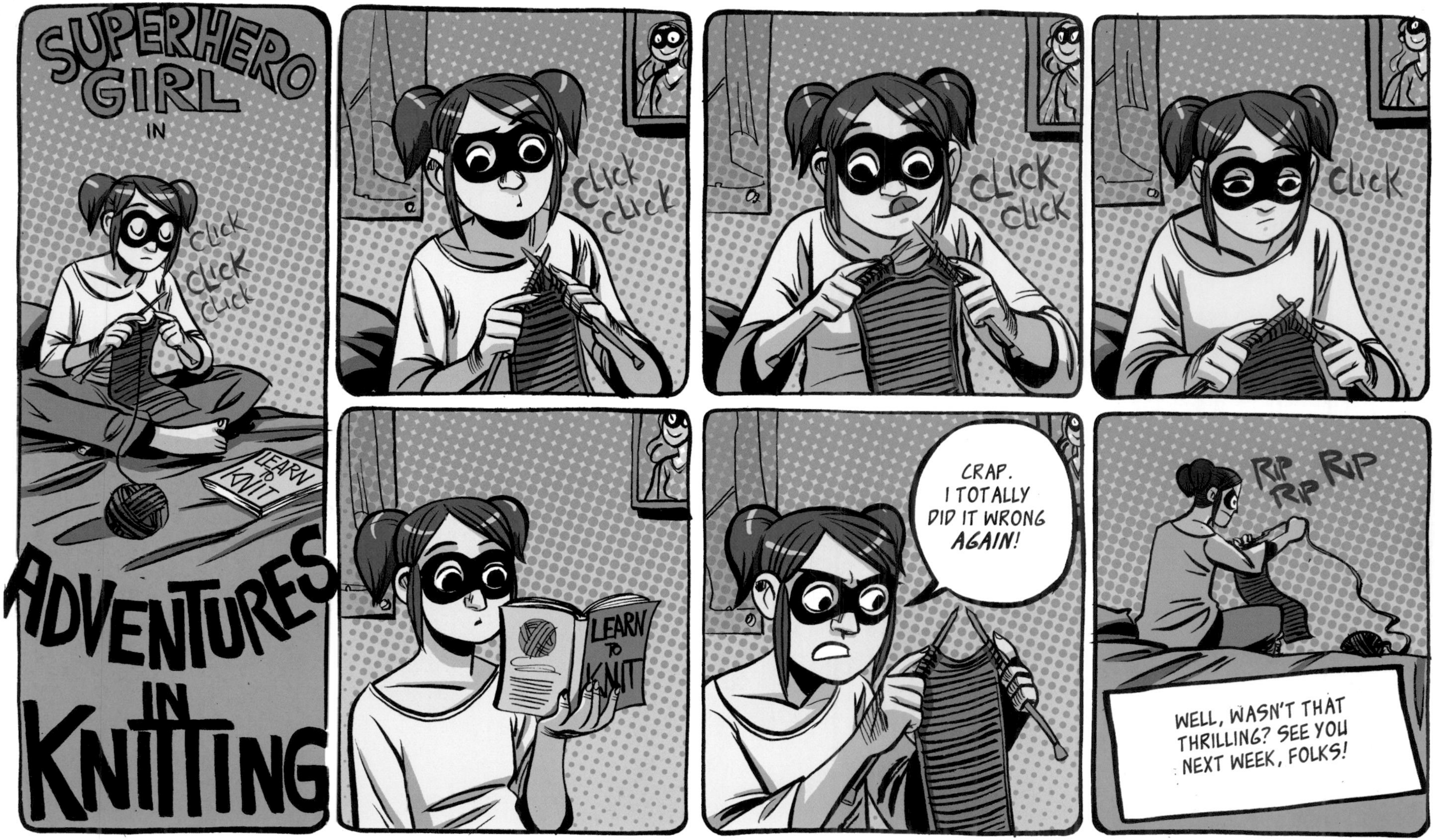
SUPERHERO GIRL
IN
CLICK CLICK CLICK
LEARN TO KNIT
ADVENTURES IN KNITTING
CLICK CLICK
CLICK CLICK
CLICK
LEARN TO KNIT
CRAP. I TOTALLY DID IT WRONG AGAIN!
RIP RIP RIP
WELL, WASN'T THAT THRILLING? SEE YOU NEXT WEEK, FOLKS!

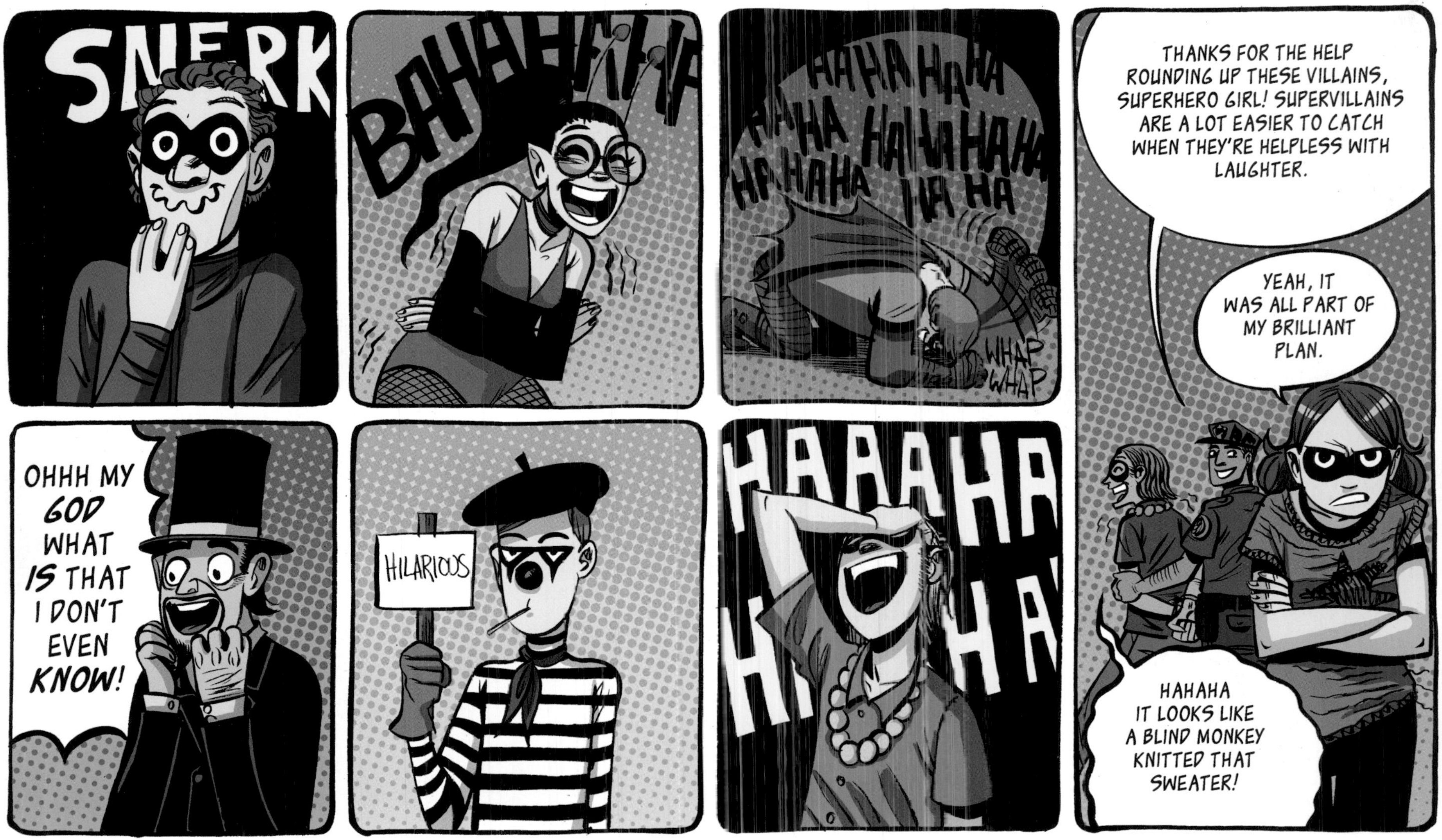
SNERK
WHAP WHAP
OHHH MY GOD WHAT IS THAT I DON'T EVEN KNOW!
HILARIOUS
THANKS FOR THE HELP ROUNDING UP THESE VILLAINS, SUPERHERO GIRL! SUPERVILLAINS ARE A LOT EASIER TO CATCH WHEN THEY'RE HELPLESS WITH LAUGHTER.
YEAH, IT WAS ALL PART OF MY BRILLIANT PLAN.
HAHAHA IT LOOKS LIKE A BLIND MONKEY KNITTED THAT SWEATER!

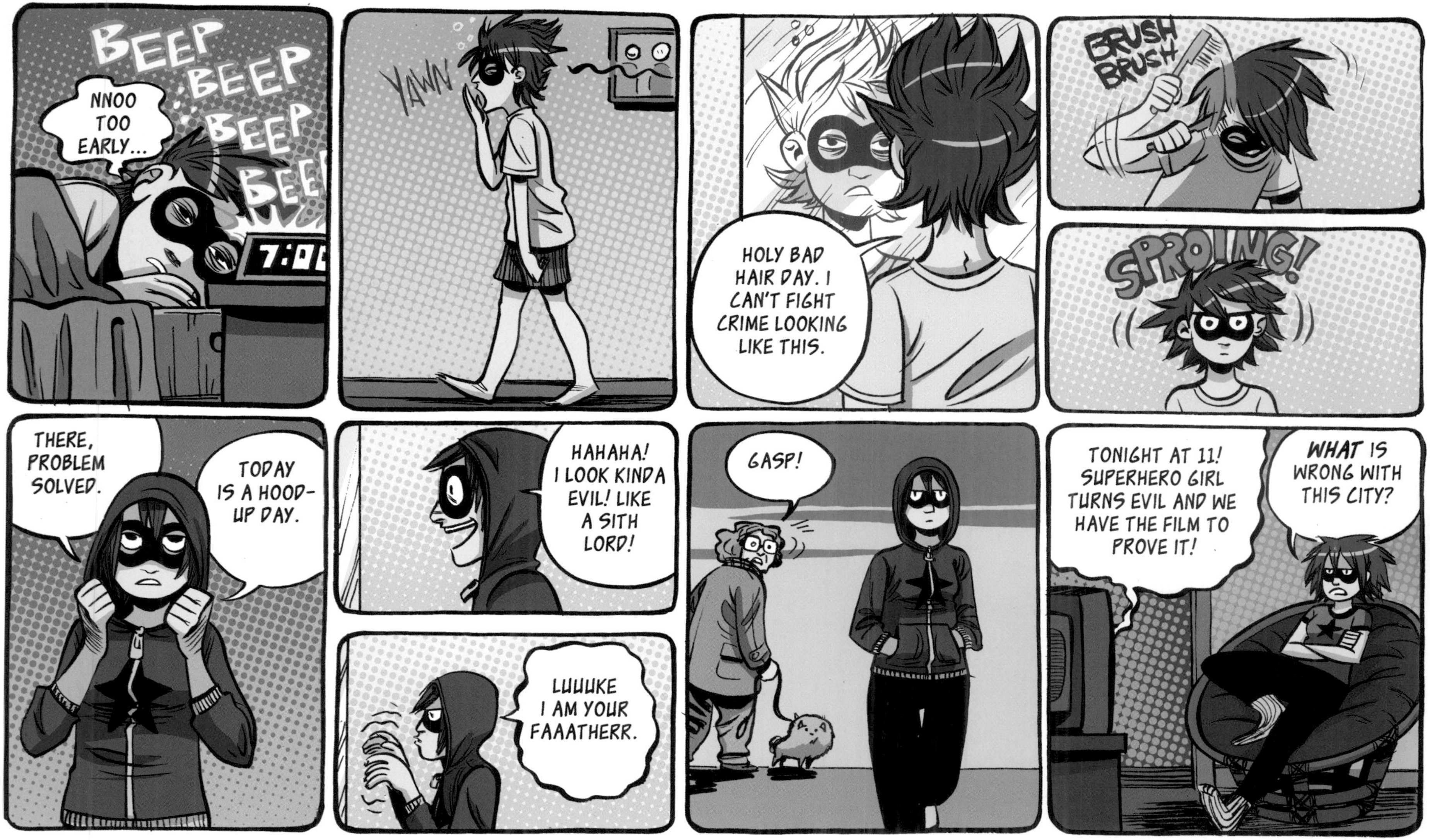
BEEP BEEP BEEP BEEP
NNOO TOO EARLY...
7:00
YAWN
HOLY BAD HAIR DAY. I CAN'T FIGHT CRIME LOOKING LIKE THIS.
BRUSH BRUSH
SPROING!
THERE, PROBLEM SOLVED.
TODAY IS A HOOD-UP DAY.
HAHAHA! I LOOK KINDA EVIL! LIKE A SITH LORD!
LUUUKE I AM YOUR FAAATHERR.
GASP!
TONIGHT AT 11! SUPERHERO GIRL TURNS EVIL AND WE HAVE THE FILM TO PROVE IT!
WHAT IS WRONG WITH THIS CITY?

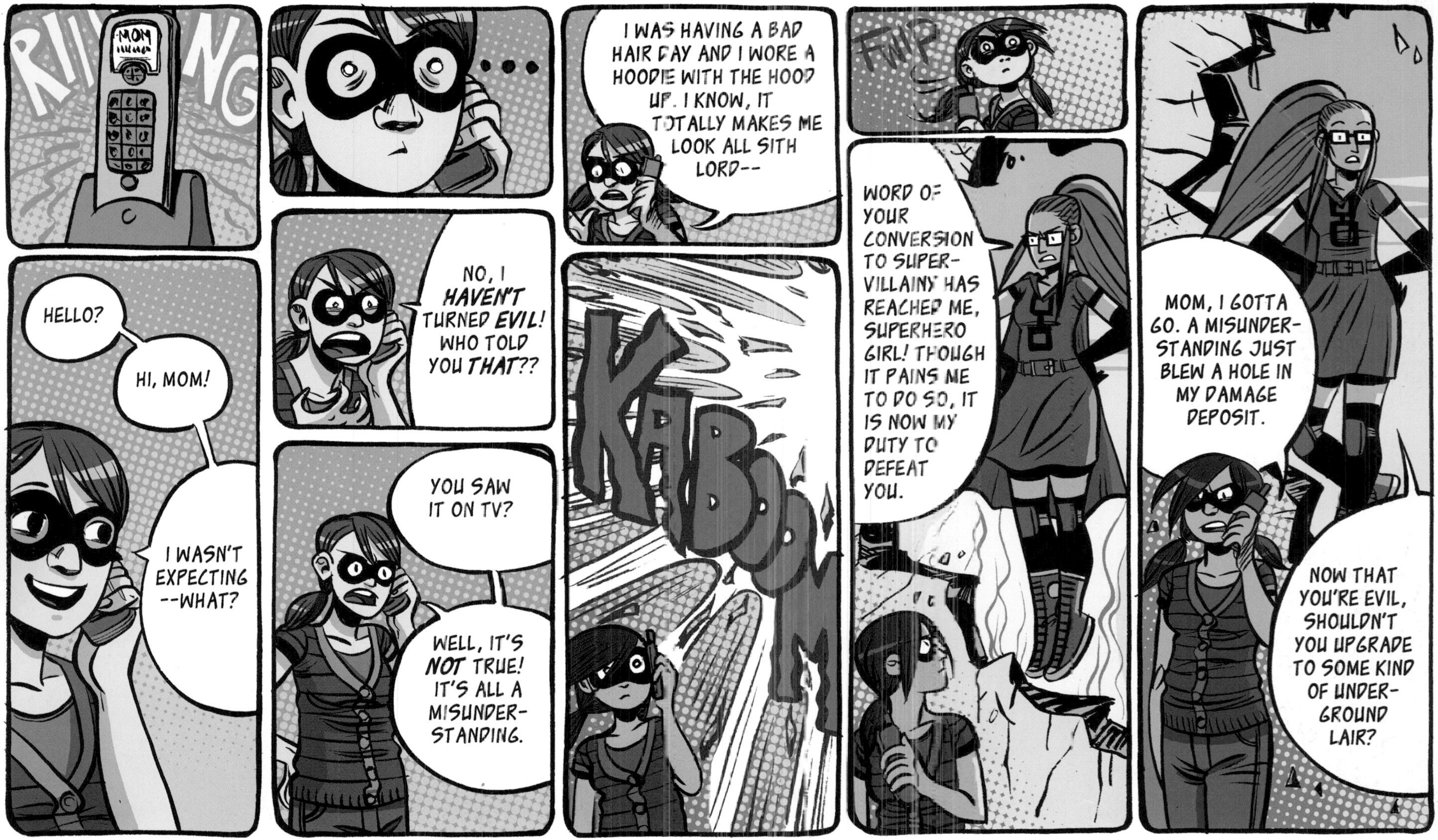
RIIING
MOM
HELLO?
HI, MOM!
I WASN'T EXPECTING --WHAT?
...
NO, I *HAVEN'T* TURNED *EVIL*! WHO TOLD YOU *THAT*??
YOU SAW IT ON TV?
WELL, IT'S *NOT* TRUE! IT'S ALL A MISUNDER-STANDING.
I WAS HAVING A BAD HAIR DAY AND I WORE A HOODIE WITH THE HOOD UP. I KNOW, IT TOTALLY MAKES ME LOOK ALL SITH LORD--
KABOOM
FWIP
WORD OF YOUR CONVERSION TO SUPER-VILLAINY HAS REACHED ME, SUPERHERO GIRL! THOUGH IT PAINS ME TO DO SO, IT IS NOW MY DUTY TO DEFEAT YOU.
MOM, I GOTTA GO. A MISUNDER-STANDING JUST BLEW A HOLE IN MY DAMAGE DEPOSIT.
NOW THAT YOU'RE EVIL, SHOULDN'T YOU UPGRADE TO SOME KIND OF UNDER-GROUND LAIR?

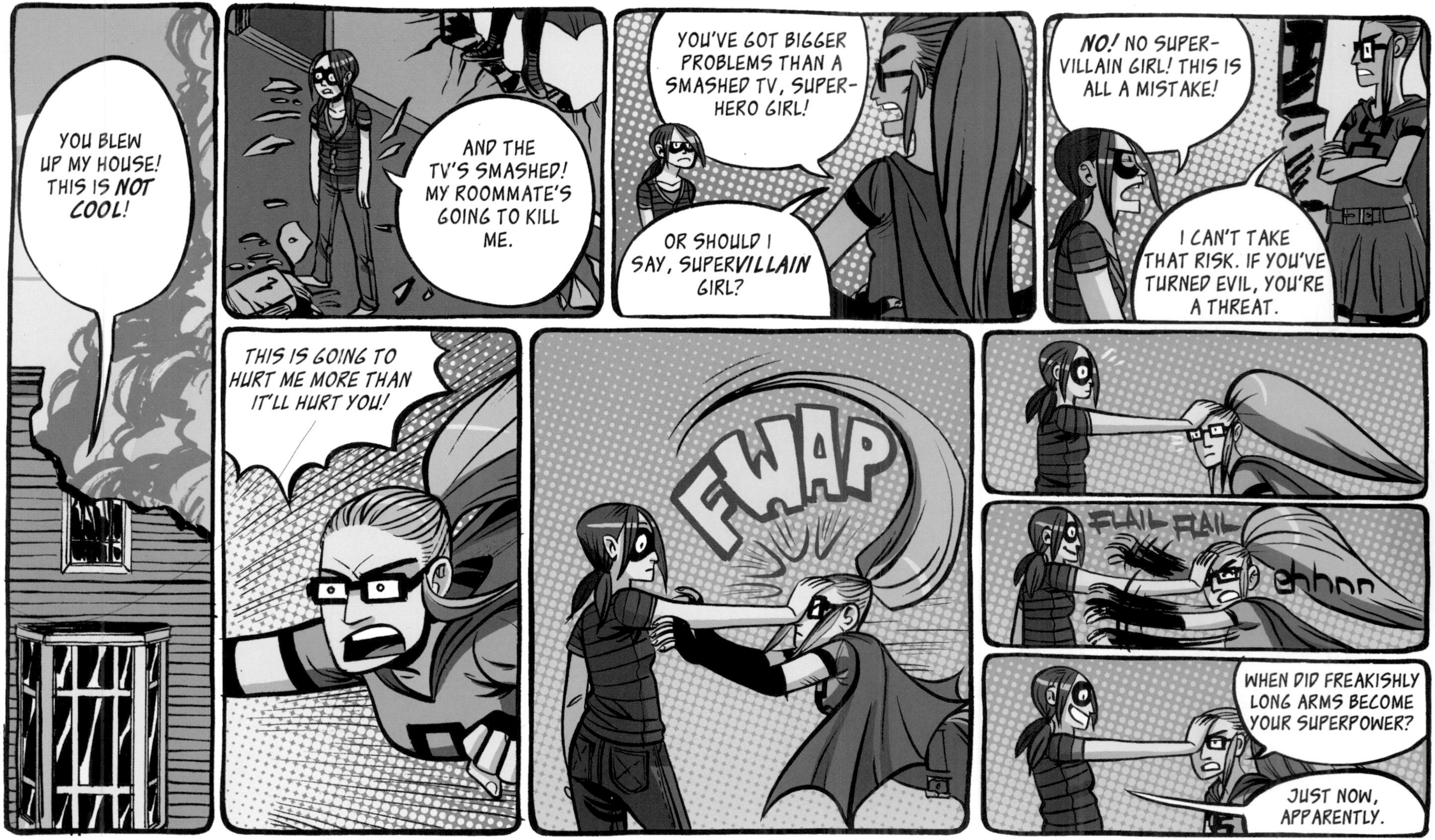
YOU BLEW UP MY HOUSE! THIS IS NOT COOL!
AND THE TV'S SMASHED! MY ROOMMATE'S GOING TO KILL ME.
YOU'VE GOT BIGGER PROBLEMS THAN A SMASHED TV, SUPER-HERO GIRL!
OR SHOULD I SAY, SUPERVILLAIN GIRL?
NO! NO SUPER-VILLAIN GIRL! THIS IS ALL A MISTAKE!
I CAN'T TAKE THAT RISK. IF YOU'VE TURNED EVIL, YOU'RE A THREAT.
THIS IS GOING TO HURT ME MORE THAN IT'LL HURT YOU!
FWAP
FLAIL FLAIL
nhhnn
WHEN DID FREAKISHLY LONG ARMS BECOME YOUR SUPERPOWER?
JUST NOW, APPARENTLY.

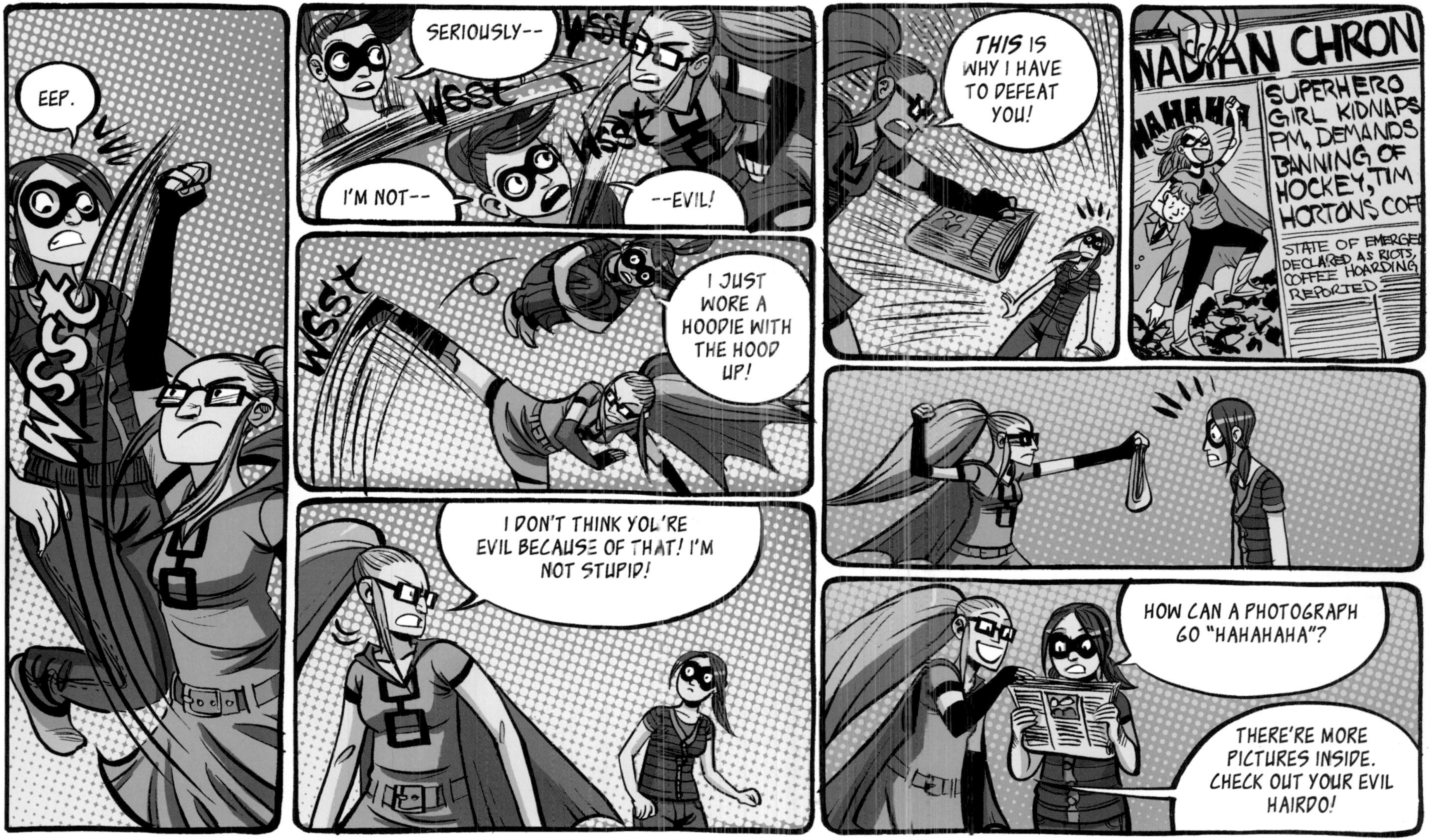
EEP.
WSST
SERIOUSLY--
WSST
WSST
WSST
I'M NOT--
--EVIL!
WSST
I JUST WORE A HOODIE WITH THE HOOD UP!
I DON'T THINK YOU'RE EVIL BECAUSE OF THAT! I'M NOT STUPID!
THIS IS WHY I HAVE TO DEFEAT YOU!
NADIAN CHRON
HAHAHA
SUPERHERO GIRL KIDNAPS PM, DEMANDS BANNING OF HOCKEY, TIM HORTONS COFF
STATE OF EMERGE DECLARED AS RIOTS, COFFEE HOARDING REPORTED
HOW CAN A PHOTOGRAPH GO "HAHAHAHA"?
THERE'RE MORE PICTURES INSIDE. CHECK OUT YOUR EVIL HAIRDO!

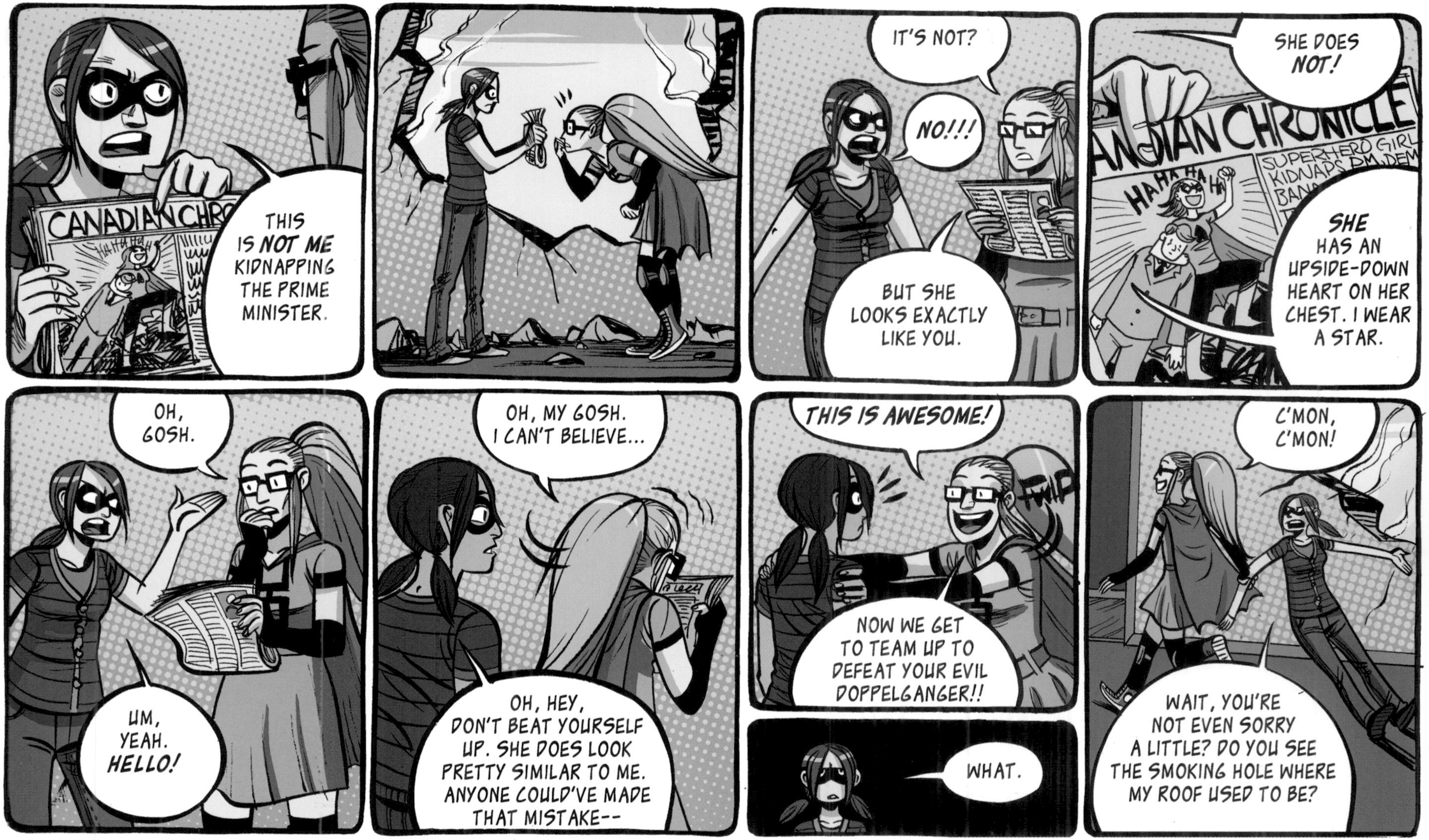
CANADIAN CHRO
THIS IS NOT ME KIDNAPPING THE PRIME MINISTER.
IT'S NOT?
NO!!!
BUT SHE LOOKS EXACTLY LIKE YOU.
SHE DOES NOT!
ANADIAN CHRONICLE
SUPERHERO GIRL KIDNAPS PM, DEM
HA HA HA HA
SHE HAS AN UPSIDE-DOWN HEART ON HER CHEST. I WEAR A STAR.
OH, GOSH.
UM, YEAH. HELLO!
OH, MY GOSH. I CAN'T BELIEVE...
OH, HEY, DON'T BEAT YOURSELF UP. SHE DOES LOOK PRETTY SIMILAR TO ME. ANYONE COULD'VE MADE THAT MISTAKE--
THIS IS AWESOME!
FWIP
NOW WE GET TO TEAM UP TO DEFEAT YOUR EVIL DOPPELGANGER!!
WHAT.
C'MON, C'MON!
WAIT, YOU'RE NOT EVEN SORRY A LITTLE? DO YOU SEE THE SMOKING HOLE WHERE MY ROOF USED TO BE?

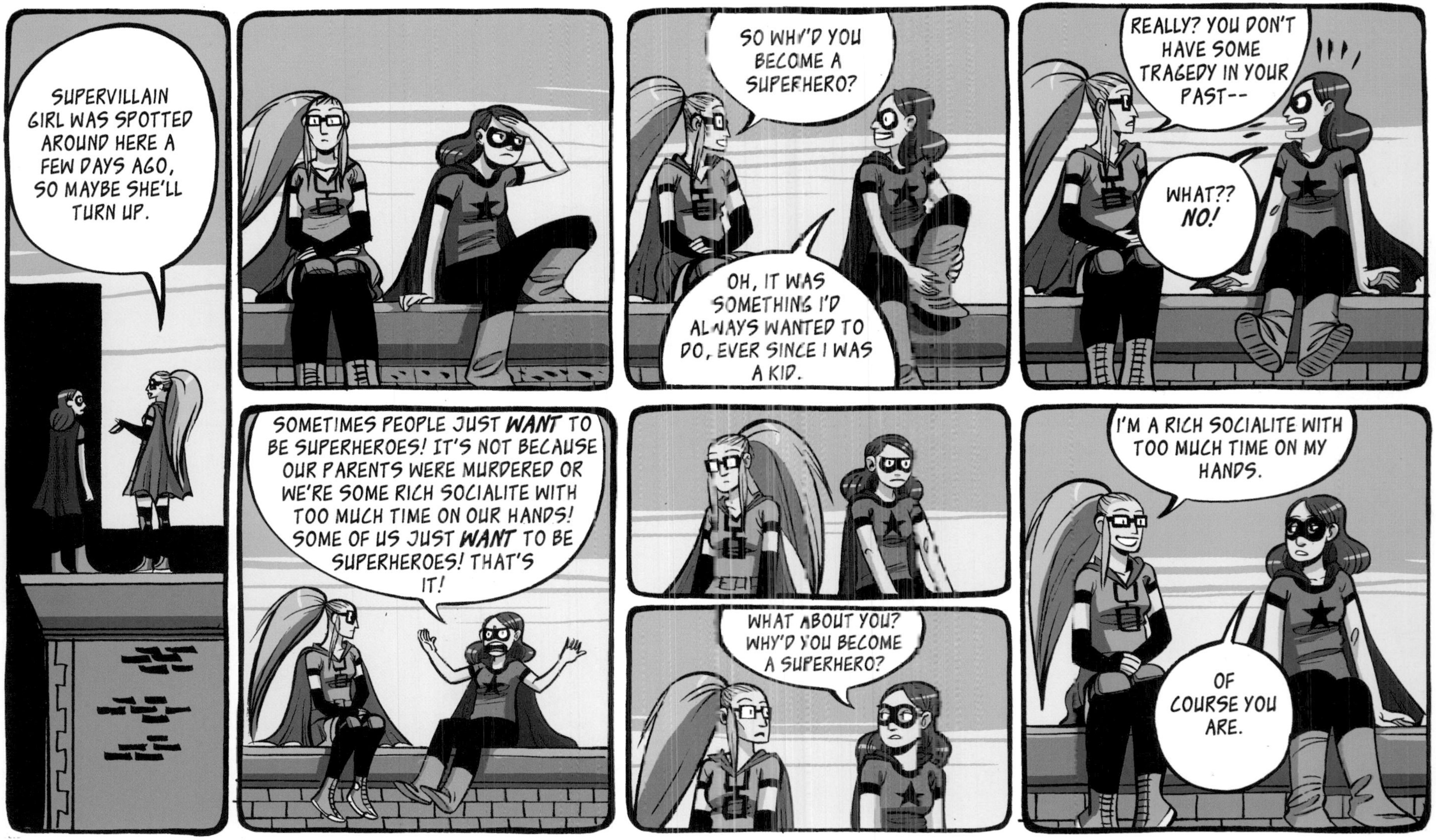
SUPERVILLAIN GIRL WAS SPOTTED AROUND HERE A FEW DAYS AGO, SO MAYBE SHE'LL TURN UP.
SO WHY'D YOU BECOME A SUPERHERO?
OH, IT WAS SOMETHING I'D ALWAYS WANTED TO DO, EVER SINCE I WAS A KID.
REALLY? YOU DON'T HAVE SOME TRAGEDY IN YOUR PAST--
WHAT?? NO!
SOMETIMES PEOPLE JUST WANT TO BE SUPERHEROES! IT'S NOT BECAUSE OUR PARENTS WERE MURDERED OR WE'RE SOME RICH SOCIALITE WITH TOO MUCH TIME ON OUR HANDS! SOME OF US JUST WANT TO BE SUPERHEROES! THAT'S IT!
WHAT ABOUT YOU? WHY'D YOU BECOME A SUPERHERO?
I'M A RICH SOCIALITE WITH TOO MUCH TIME ON MY HANDS.
OF COURSE YOU ARE.

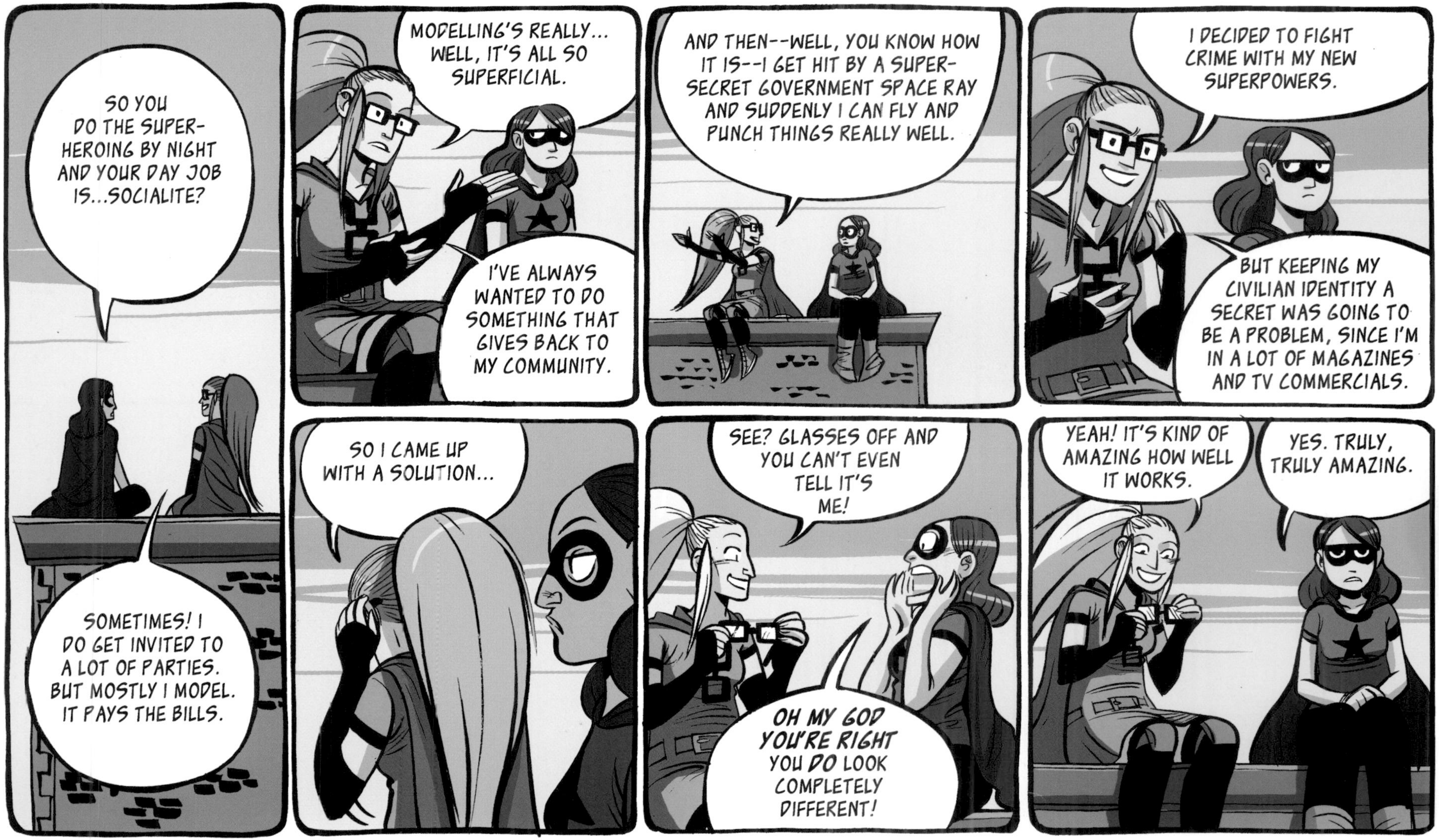
SO YOU DO THE SUPER-HEROING BY NIGHT AND YOUR DAY JOB IS...SOCIALITE?
SOMETIMES! I DO GET INVITED TO A LOT OF PARTIES. BUT MOSTLY I MODEL. IT PAYS THE BILLS.
MODELLING'S REALLY... WELL, IT'S ALL SO SUPERFICIAL.
I'VE ALWAYS WANTED TO DO SOMETHING THAT GIVES BACK TO MY COMMUNITY.
AND THEN--WELL, YOU KNOW HOW IT IS--I GET HIT BY A SUPER-SECRET GOVERNMENT SPACE RAY AND SUDDENLY I CAN FLY AND PUNCH THINGS REALLY WELL.
I DECIDED TO FIGHT CRIME WITH MY NEW SUPERPOWERS.
BUT KEEPING MY CIVILIAN IDENTITY A SECRET WAS GOING TO BE A PROBLEM, SINCE I'M IN A LOT OF MAGAZINES AND TV COMMERCIALS.
SO I CAME UP WITH A SOLUTION...
SEE? GLASSES OFF AND YOU CAN'T EVEN TELL IT'S ME!
OH MY GOD YOU'RE RIGHT YOU DO LOOK COMPLETELY DIFFERENT!
YEAH! IT'S KIND OF AMAZING HOW WELL IT WORKS.
YES. TRULY, TRULY AMAZING.

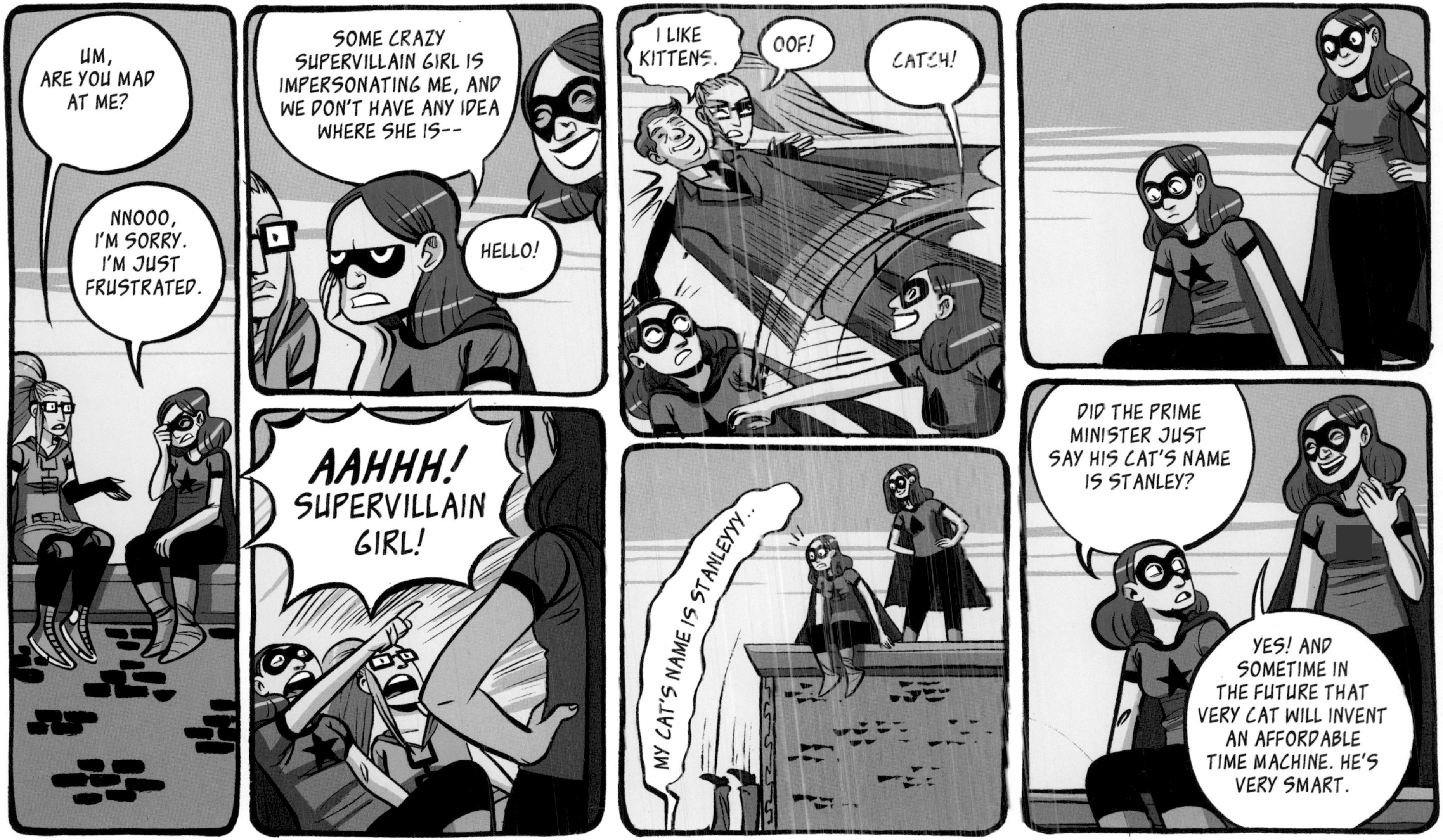
UM, ARE YOU MAD AT ME?
NNOOO, I'M SORRY. I'M JUST FRUSTRATED.
SOME CRAZY SUPERVILLAIN GIRL IS IMPERSONATING ME, AND WE DON'T HAVE ANY IDEA WHERE SHE IS--
HELLO!
AAHHH! SUPERVILLAIN GIRL!
I LIKE KITTENS.
OOF!
CATCH!
MY CAT'S NAME IS STANLEYYY...
DID THE PRIME MINISTER JUST SAY HIS CAT'S NAME IS STANLEY?
YES! AND SOMETIME IN THE FUTURE THAT VERY CAT WILL INVENT AN AFFORDABLE TIME MACHINE. HE'S VERY SMART.

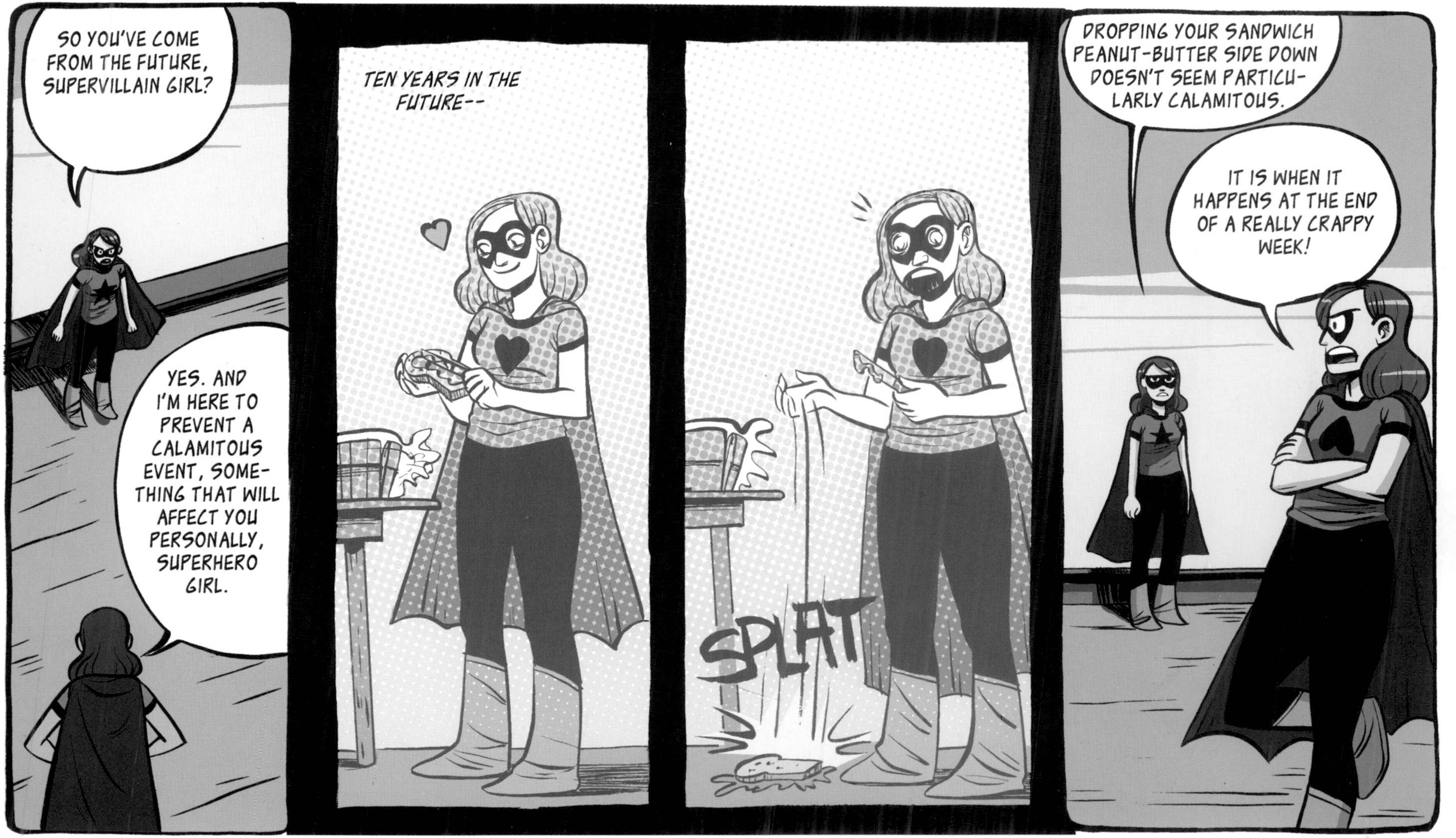
SO YOU'VE COME FROM THE FUTURE, SUPERVILLAIN GIRL?
YES. AND I'M HERE TO PREVENT A CALAMITOUS EVENT, SOME-THING THAT WILL AFFECT YOU PERSONALLY, SUPERHERO GIRL.
TEN YEARS IN THE FUTURE--
SPLAT
DROPPING YOUR SANDWICH PEANUT-BUTTER SIDE DOWN DOESN'T SEEM PARTICU-LARLY CALAMITOUS.
IT IS WHEN IT HAPPENS AT THE END OF A REALLY CRAPPY WEEK!

I CAN'T BELIEVE I BECAME A *SUPERVILLAIN* TEN YEARS IN THE FUTURE JUST BECAUSE I HAD A CRAPPY WEEK!

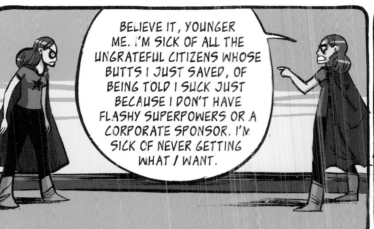

BELIEVE IT, YOUNGER ME. I'M SICK OF ALL THE UNGRATEFUL CITIZENS WHOSE BUTTS I JUST SAVED, OF BEING TOLD I SUCK JUST BECAUSE I DON'T HAVE FLASHY SUPERPOWERS OR A CORPORATE SPONSOR. I'M SICK OF NEVER GETTING WHAT *I* WANT.

ENOUGH OF THIS CRAPPY SUPERHERO LIFE! I WANT TO BE *RICH* AND *POWERFUL*, LIKE A SUPERVILLAIN!!

SINCE THE EASIEST WAY TO GET RICH IS TO STEAL A BUNCH OF DOUGH--

--I DECIDED TO TIME TRAVEL TO THE PAST WHEN I WAS A CRAPPY SUPERHERO WHO HAD NO CHANCE OF STOPPING AN OLDER, MORE AWESOME VERSION OF HERSELF.

SO LET'S FIGHT.

YOU'LL LOSE BECAUSE I'VE GOT TEN YEARS' EXPERIENCE ON YOU, AND I'LL STEAL ALL THE GOLD AND JEWELS THIS TIME PERIOD HAS ON HAND, AND TAKE THEM BACK WITH ME.

I CAN'T BELIEVE WHAT A BUTTHEAD I AM IN THE FUTURE.

YEAH, WELL, THAT'S HOW IT IS: YOU TURN THIRTY AND IT'S TIME FOR MAMA TO GET *PAID*.

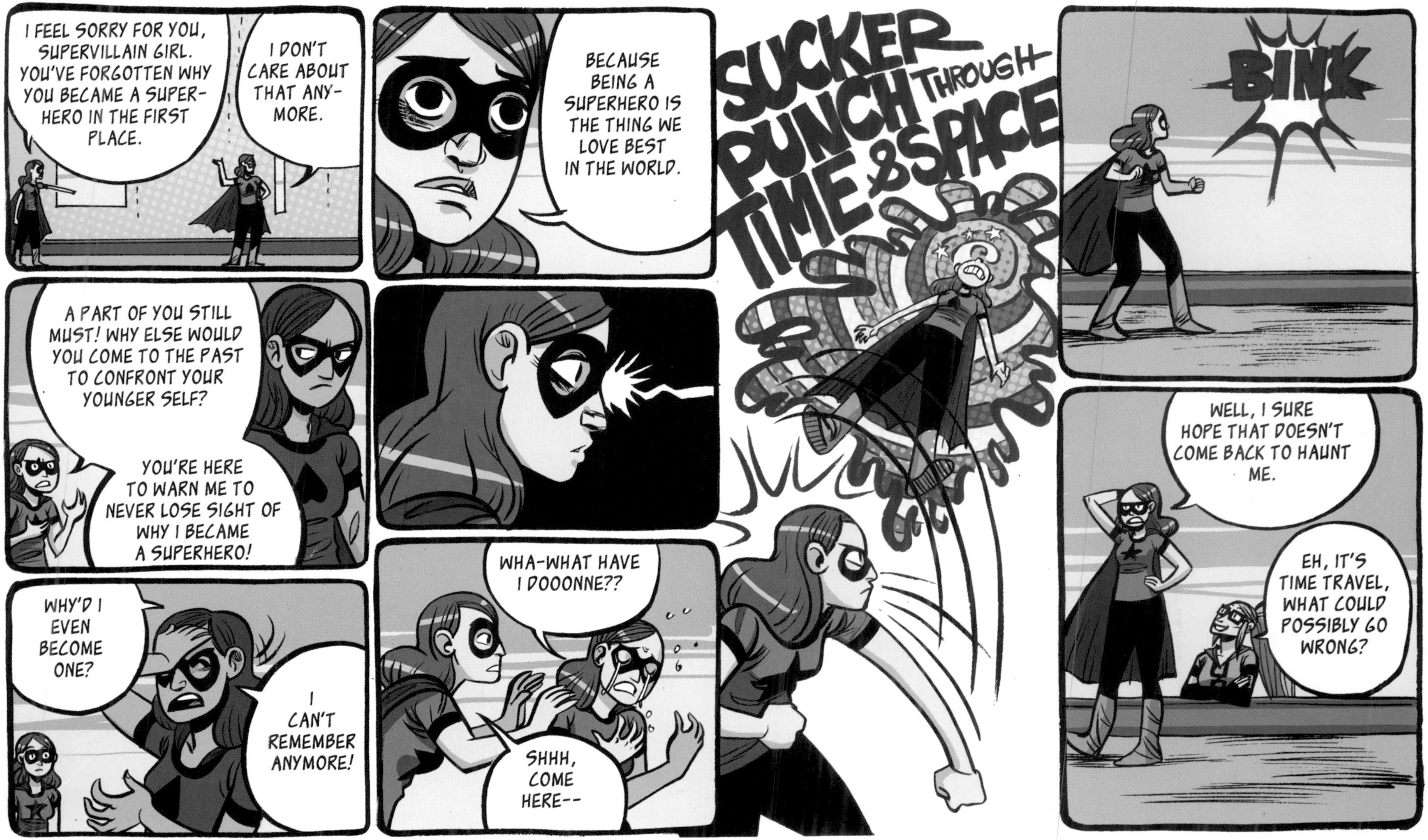

I FEEL SORRY FOR YOU, SUPERVILLAIN GIRL. YOU'VE FORGOTTEN WHY YOU BECAME A SUPER-HERO IN THE FIRST PLACE.
I DON'T CARE ABOUT THAT ANY-MORE.
BECAUSE BEING A SUPERHERO IS THE THING WE LOVE BEST IN THE WORLD.
A PART OF YOU STILL MUST! WHY ELSE WOULD YOU COME TO THE PAST TO CONFRONT YOUR YOUNGER SELF?
YOU'RE HERE TO WARN ME TO NEVER LOSE SIGHT OF WHY I BECAME A SUPERHERO!
WHY'D I EVEN BECOME ONE?
I CAN'T REMEMBER ANYMORE!
WHA-WHAT HAVE I DOOONNE??
SHHH, COME HERE--
SUCKER PUNCH THROUGH TIME & SPACE
BINK
WELL, I SURE HOPE THAT DOESN'T COME BACK TO HAUNT ME.
EH, IT'S TIME TRAVEL, WHAT COULD POSSIBLY GO WRONG?

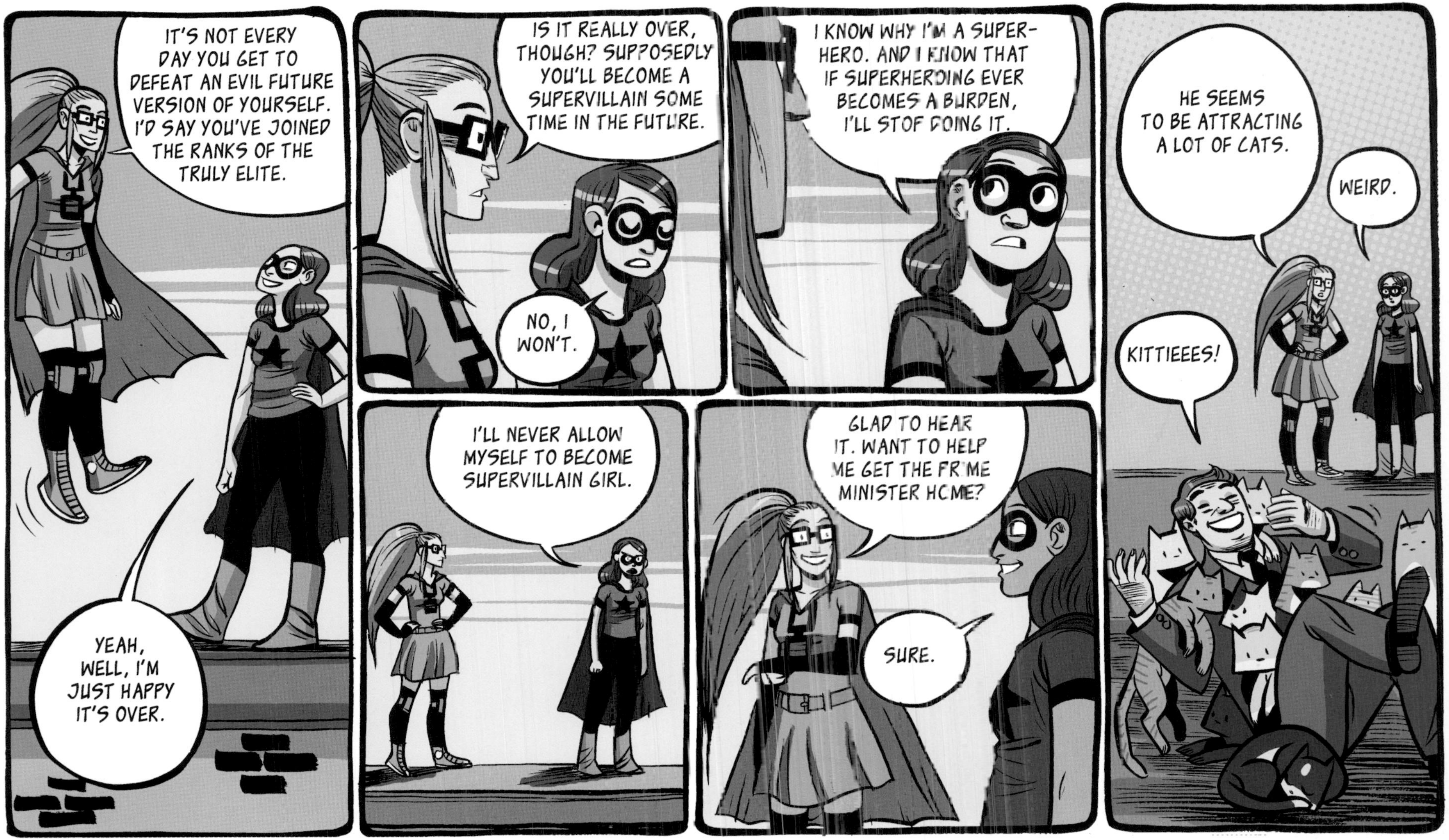
IT'S NOT EVERY DAY YOU GET TO DEFEAT AN EVIL FUTURE VERSION OF YOURSELF. I'D SAY YOU'VE JOINED THE RANKS OF THE TRULY ELITE.
YEAH, WELL, I'M JUST HAPPY IT'S OVER.
IS IT REALLY OVER, THOUGH? SUPPOSEDLY YOU'LL BECOME A SUPERVILLAIN SOME TIME IN THE FUTURE.
NO, I WON'T.
I KNOW WHY I'M A SUPERHERO. AND I KNOW THAT IF SUPERHEROING EVER BECOMES A BURDEN, I'LL STOP DOING IT.
I'LL NEVER ALLOW MYSELF TO BECOME SUPERVILLAIN GIRL.
GLAD TO HEAR IT. WANT TO HELP ME GET THE PRIME MINISTER HOME?
SURE.
HE SEEMS TO BE ATTRACTING A LOT OF CATS.
WEIRD.
KITTIEEES!

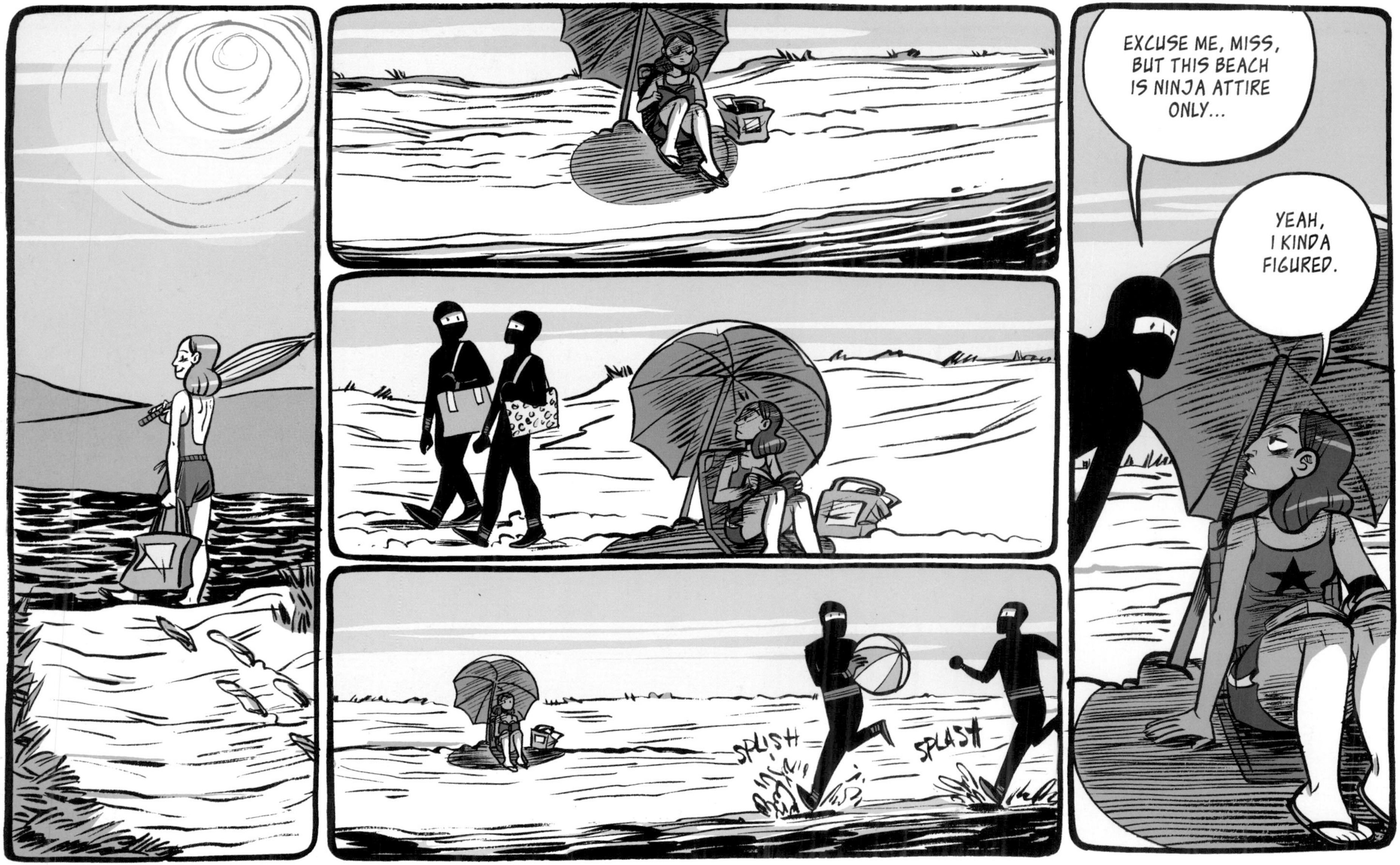
SPLISH
SPLASH
EXCUSE ME, MISS, BUT THIS BEACH IS NINJA ATTIRE ONLY...
YEAH, I KINDA FIGURED.

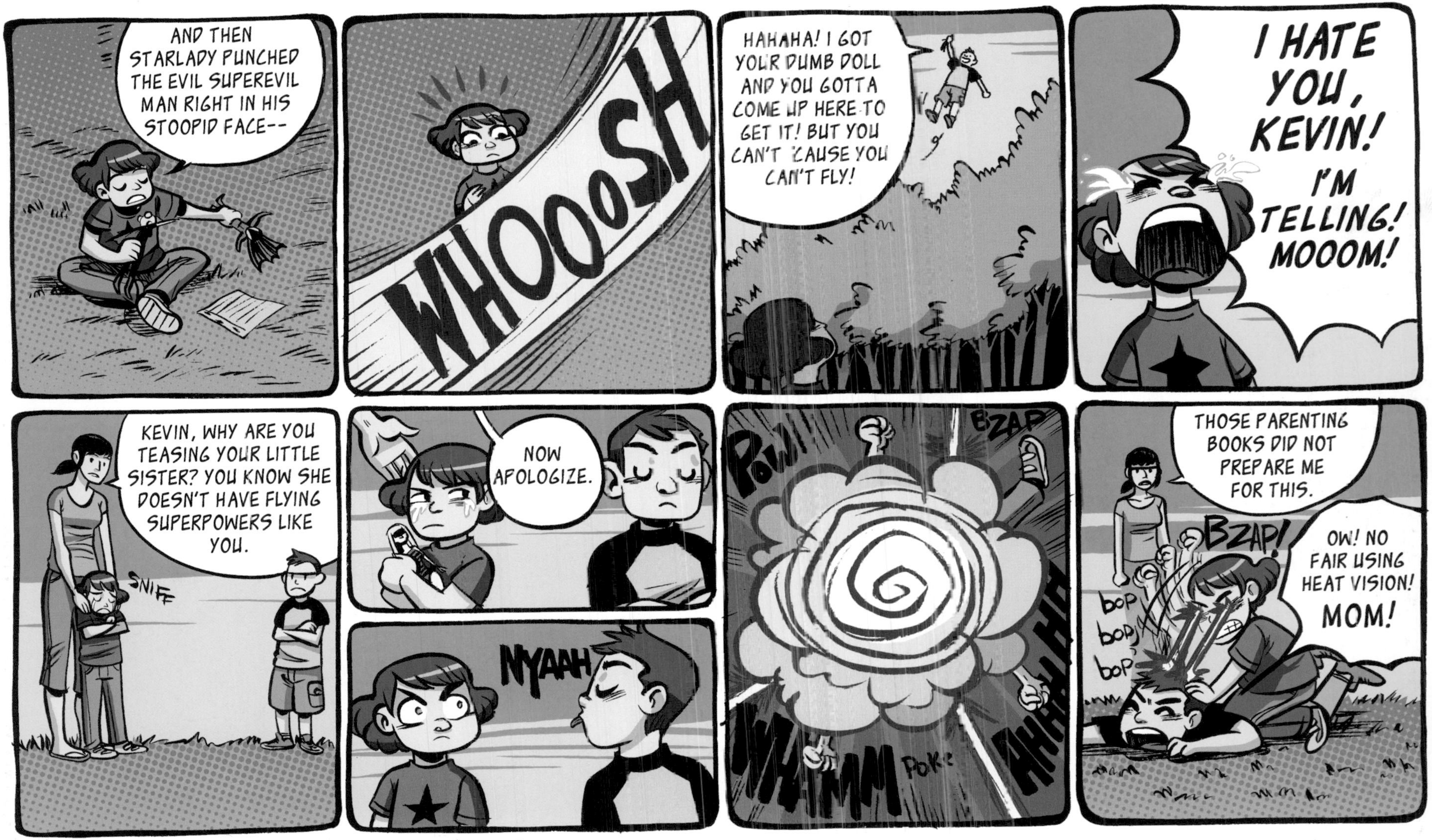
AND THEN STARLADY PUNCHED THE EVIL SUPEREVIL MAN RIGHT IN HIS STOOPID FACE--
WHOOOSH
HAHAHA! I GOT YOUR DUMB DOLL AND YOU GOTTA COME UP HERE TO GET IT! BUT YOU CAN'T 'CAUSE YOU CAN'T FLY!
I HATE YOU, KEVIN!
I'M TELLING! MOOOM!
KEVIN, WHY ARE YOU TEASING YOUR LITTLE SISTER? YOU KNOW SHE DOESN'T HAVE FLYING SUPERPOWERS LIKE YOU.
SNIFF
NOW APOLOGIZE.
NYAAH
BZAP
POKE
THOSE PARENTING BOOKS DID NOT PREPARE ME FOR THIS.
BZAP!
bop
bop
bop
OW! NO FAIR USING HEAT VISION! MOM!

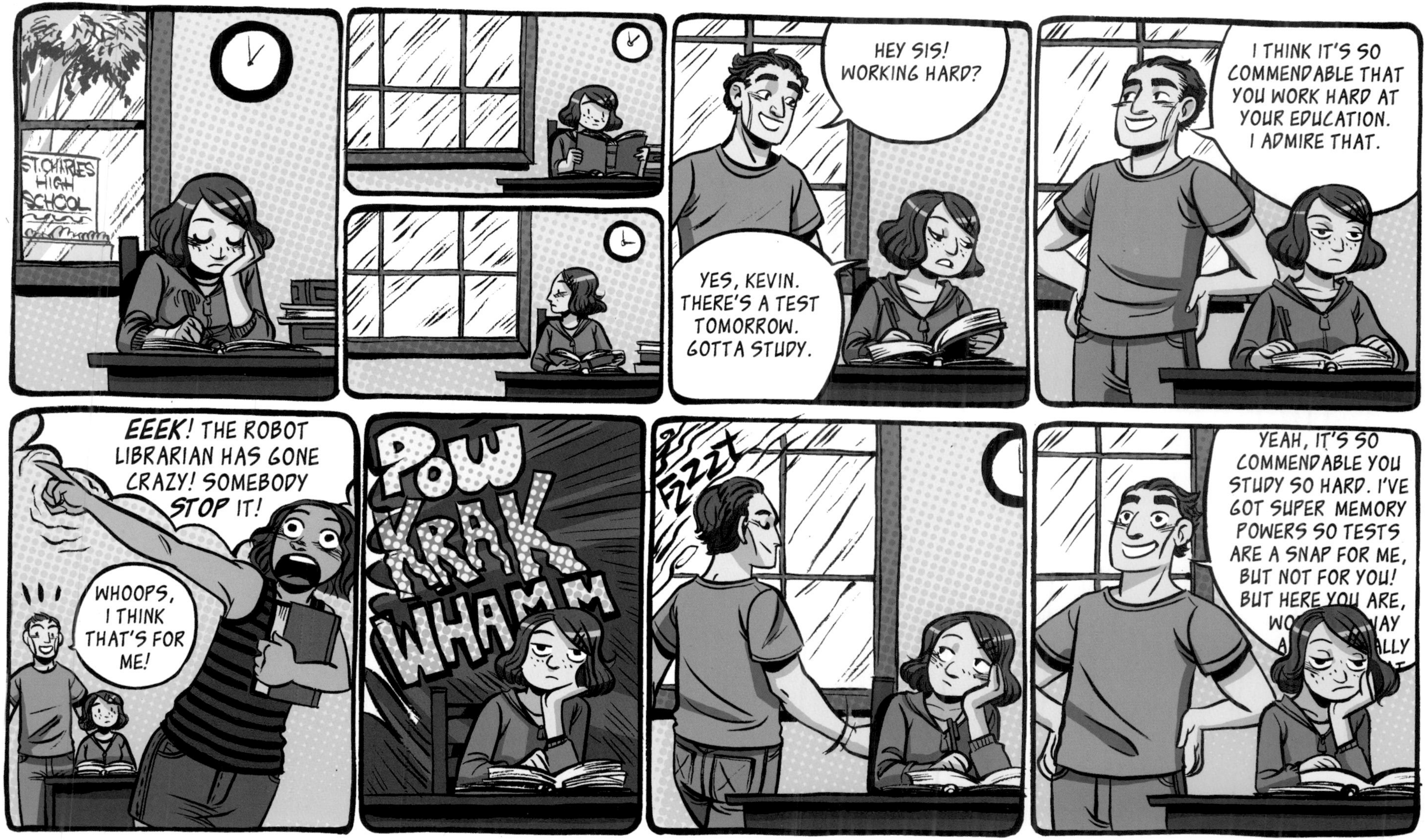

ST. CHARLES HIGH SCHOOL
HEY SIS! WORKING HARD?
YES, KEVIN. THERE'S A TEST TOMORROW. GOTTA STUDY.
I THINK IT'S SO COMMENDABLE THAT YOU WORK HARD AT YOUR EDUCATION. I ADMIRE THAT.
EEEK! THE ROBOT LIBRARIAN HAS GONE CRAZY! SOMEBODY STOP IT!
WHOOPS, I THINK THAT'S FOR ME!
POW
KRAK
WHAMM
FZZZT
YEAH, IT'S SO COMMENDABLE YOU STUDY SO HARD. I'VE GOT SUPER MEMORY POWERS SO TESTS ARE A SNAP FOR ME, BUT NOT FOR YOU! BUT HERE YOU ARE,

blurrghh BLAHHGG Ick

SPloorch

THE BLOB FAMILY! THIS IS GOING TO BE...*GROSS.*

WHAP BLOSSH WHAP OOF SPLIT EWW! GLURP bloop blurg blurp

NEVER FEAR, KEVIN'S HERE!

WAIT, I CAN HANDLE--

ick blek Blurg blorp

KER-POW

HAH *HAH!* LOOK AT THEM RUN!

HEY, I HAD IT UNDER CONTROL.

SURE YOU DID. NOW WAVE!

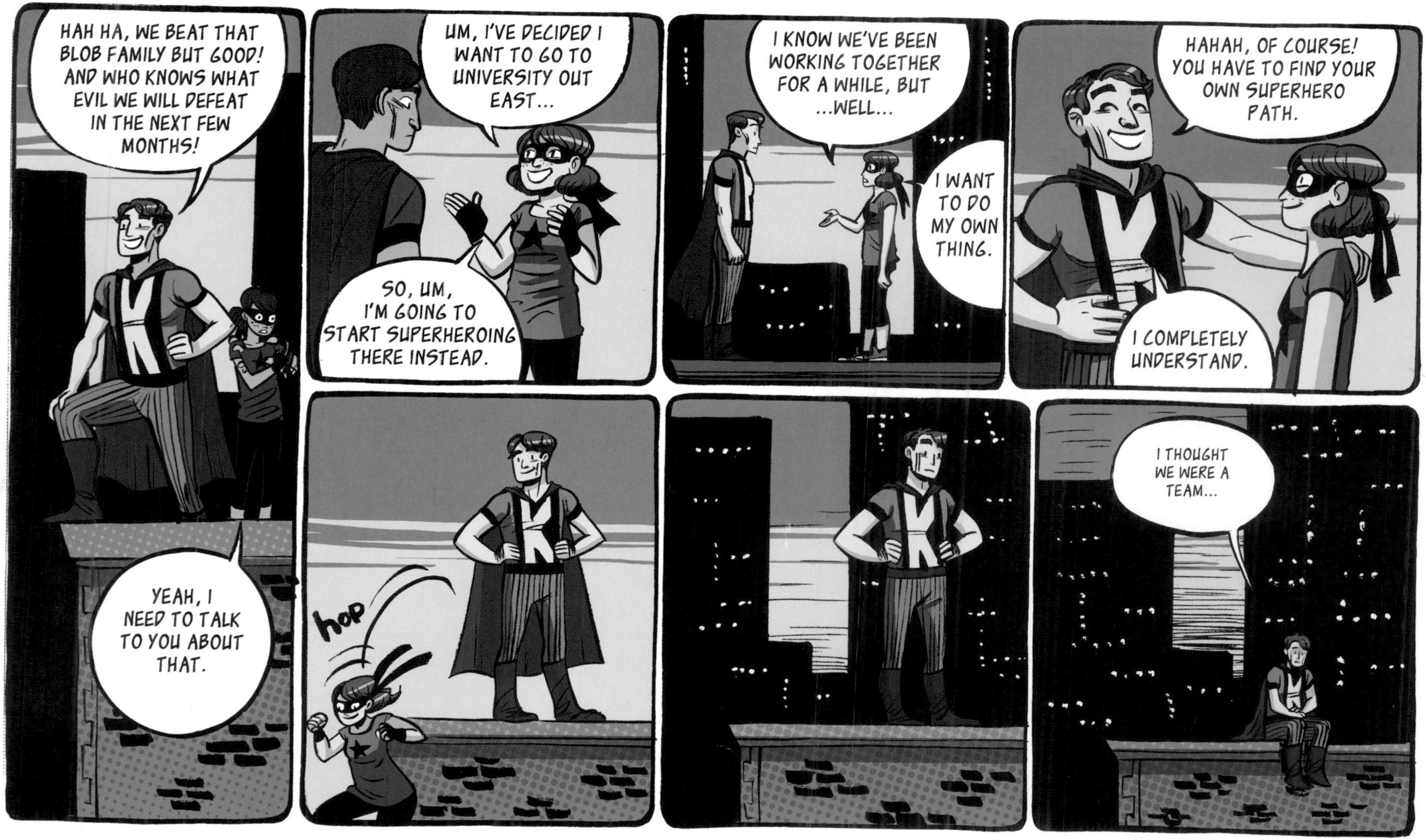
HAH HA, WE BEAT THAT BLOB FAMILY BUT GOOD! AND WHO KNOWS WHAT EVIL WE WILL DEFEAT IN THE NEXT FEW MONTHS!
YEAH, I NEED TO TALK TO YOU ABOUT THAT.
UM, I'VE DECIDED I WANT TO GO TO UNIVERSITY OUT EAST...
SO, UM, I'M GOING TO START SUPERHEROING THERE INSTEAD.
I KNOW WE'VE BEEN WORKING TOGETHER FOR A WHILE, BUT ...WELL...
I WANT TO DO MY OWN THING.
HAHAH, OF COURSE! YOU HAVE TO FIND YOUR OWN SUPERHERO PATH.
I COMPLETELY UNDERSTAND.
hop
I THOUGHT WE WERE A TEAM...

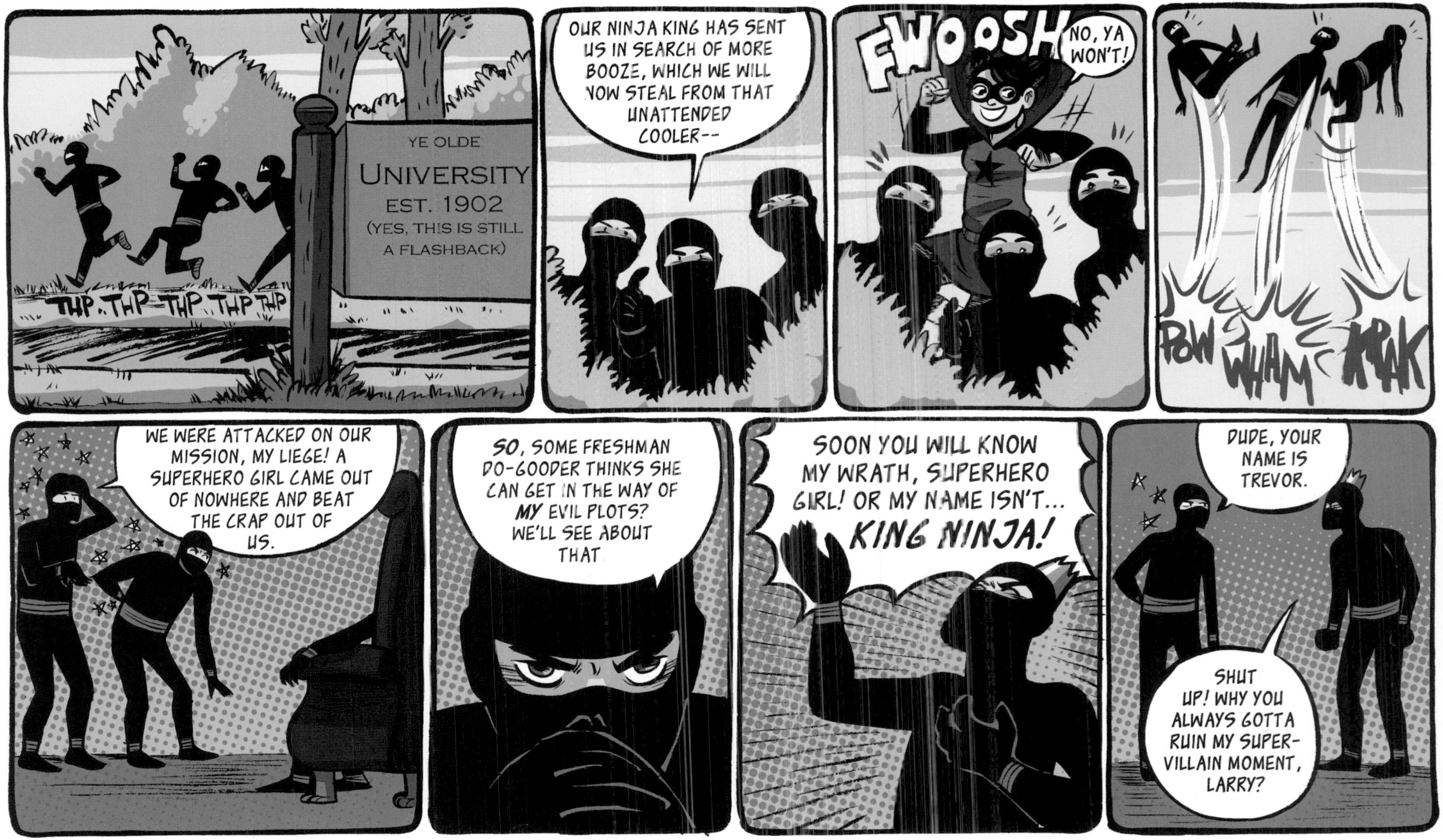
YE OLDE
UNIVERSITY
EST. 1902
(YES, THIS IS STILL A FLASHBACK)
THP THP THP THP THP
OUR NINJA KING HAS SENT US IN SEARCH OF MORE BOOZE, WHICH WE WILL NOW STEAL FROM THAT UNATTENDED COOLER--
FWOOSH
NO, YA WON'T!
POW
WHAM
KRAK
WE WERE ATTACKED ON OUR MISSION, MY LIEGE! A SUPERHERO GIRL CAME OUT OF NOWHERE AND BEAT THE CRAP OUT OF US.
SO, SOME FRESHMAN DO-GOODER THINKS SHE CAN GET IN THE WAY OF MY EVIL PLOTS? WE'LL SEE ABOUT THAT.
SOON YOU WILL KNOW MY WRATH, SUPERHERO GIRL! OR MY NAME ISN'T... KING NINJA!
DUDE, YOUR NAME IS TREVOR.
SHUT UP! WHY YOU ALWAYS GOTTA RUIN MY SUPER-VILLAIN MOMENT, LARRY?

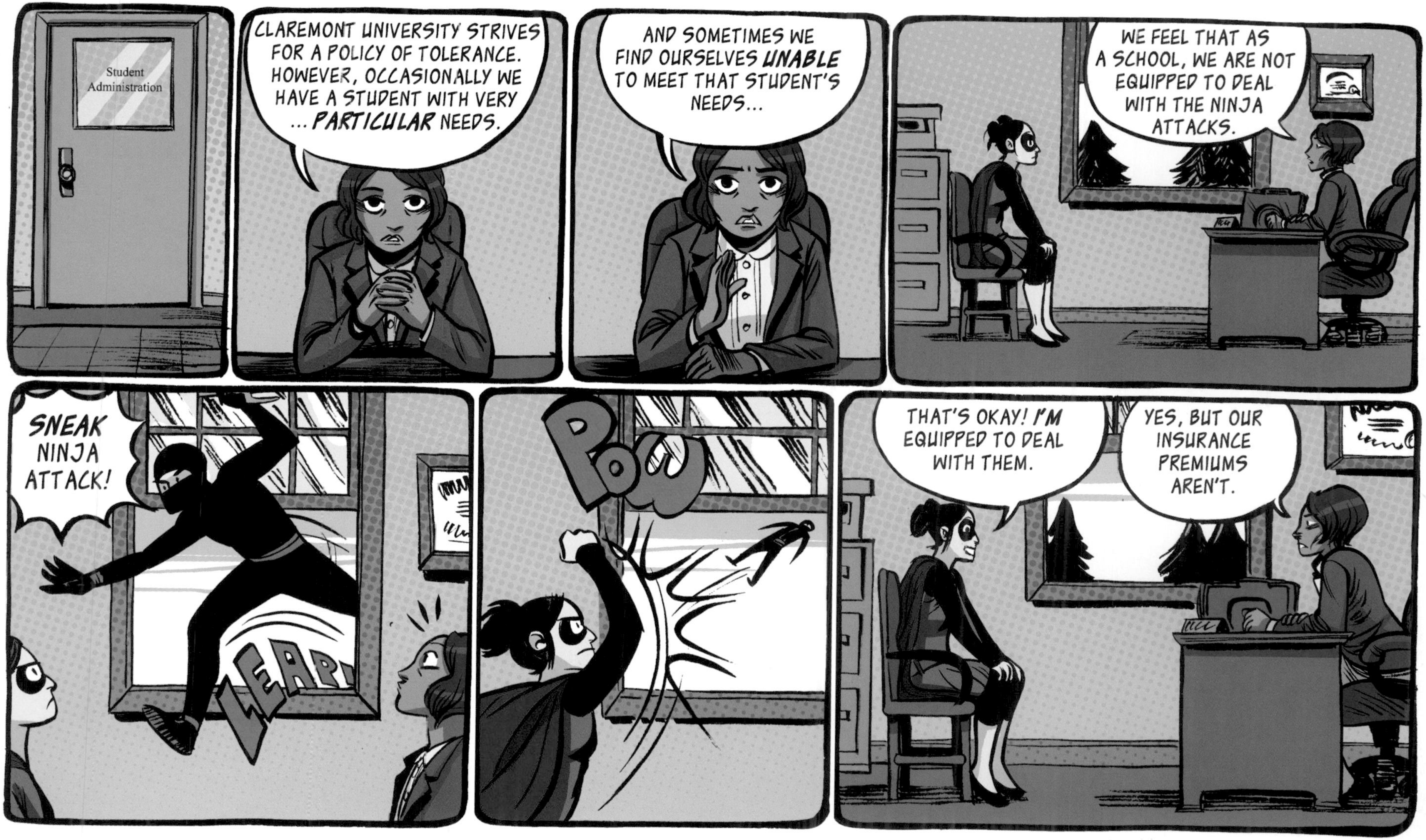

Student Administration
CLAREMONT UNIVERSITY STRIVES FOR A POLICY OF TOLERANCE. HOWEVER, OCCASIONALLY WE HAVE A STUDENT WITH VERY ...PARTICULAR NEEDS.
AND SOMETIMES WE FIND OURSELVES UNABLE TO MEET THAT STUDENT'S NEEDS...
WE FEEL THAT AS A SCHOOL, WE ARE NOT EQUIPPED TO DEAL WITH THE NINJA ATTACKS.
SNEAK NINJA ATTACK!
POW
THAT'S OKAY! I'M EQUIPPED TO DEAL WITH THEM.
YES, BUT OUR INSURANCE PREMIUMS AREN'T.

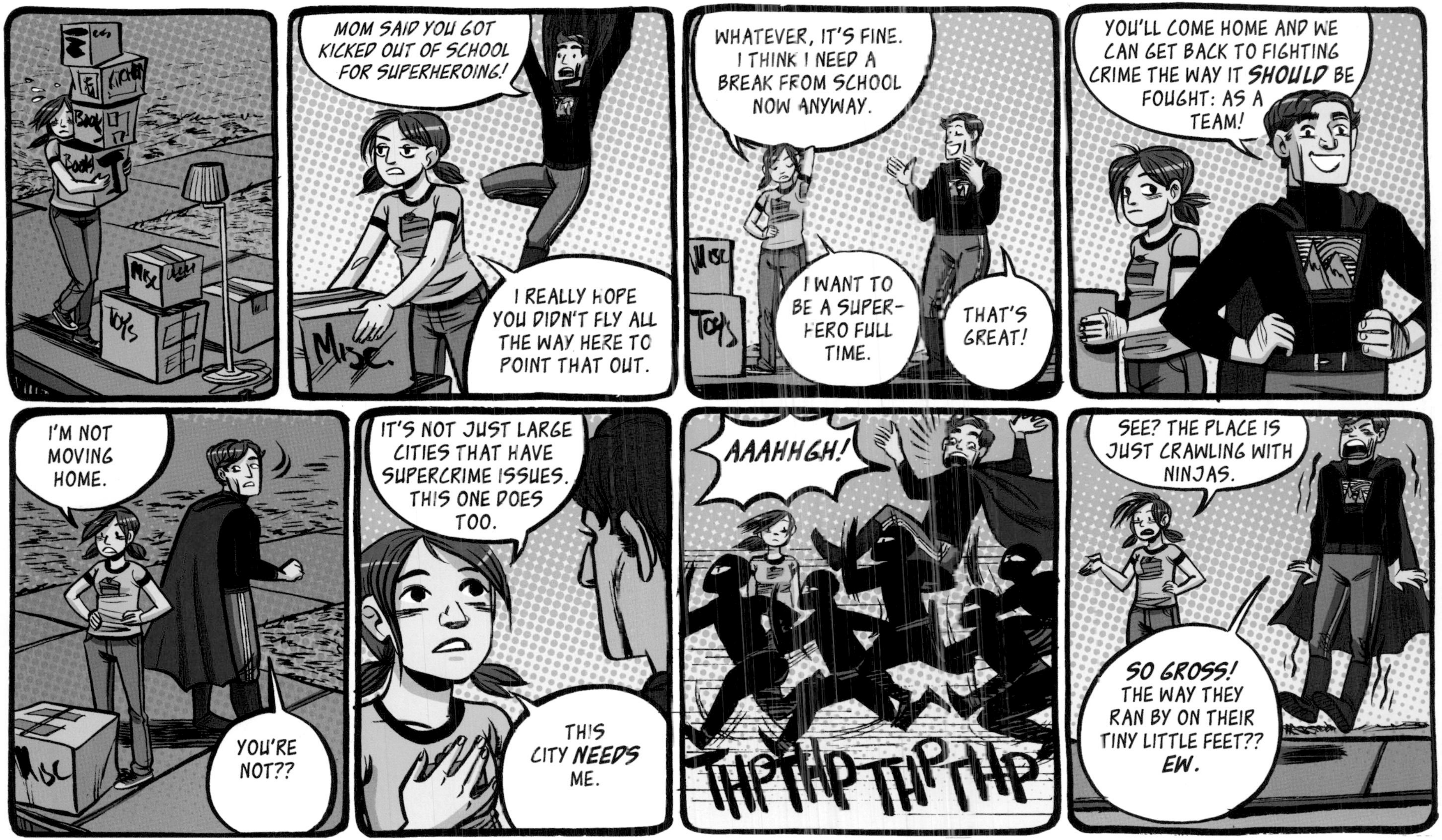
MOM SAID YOU GOT KICKED OUT OF SCHOOL FOR SUPERHEROING!
I REALLY HOPE YOU DIDN'T FLY ALL THE WAY HERE TO POINT THAT OUT.
WHATEVER, IT'S FINE. I THINK I NEED A BREAK FROM SCHOOL NOW ANYWAY.
I WANT TO BE A SUPER-HERO FULL TIME.
THAT'S GREAT!
YOU'LL COME HOME AND WE CAN GET BACK TO FIGHTING CRIME THE WAY IT SHOULD BE FOUGHT: AS A TEAM!
I'M NOT MOVING HOME.
YOU'RE NOT??
IT'S NOT JUST LARGE CITIES THAT HAVE SUPERCRIME ISSUES. THIS ONE DOES TOO.
THIS CITY NEEDS ME.
AAAHHGH!
THPTHPTHPTHP
SEE? THE PLACE IS JUST CRAWLING WITH NINJAS.
SO GROSS! THE WAY THEY RAN BY ON THEIR TINY LITTLE FEET?? EW.

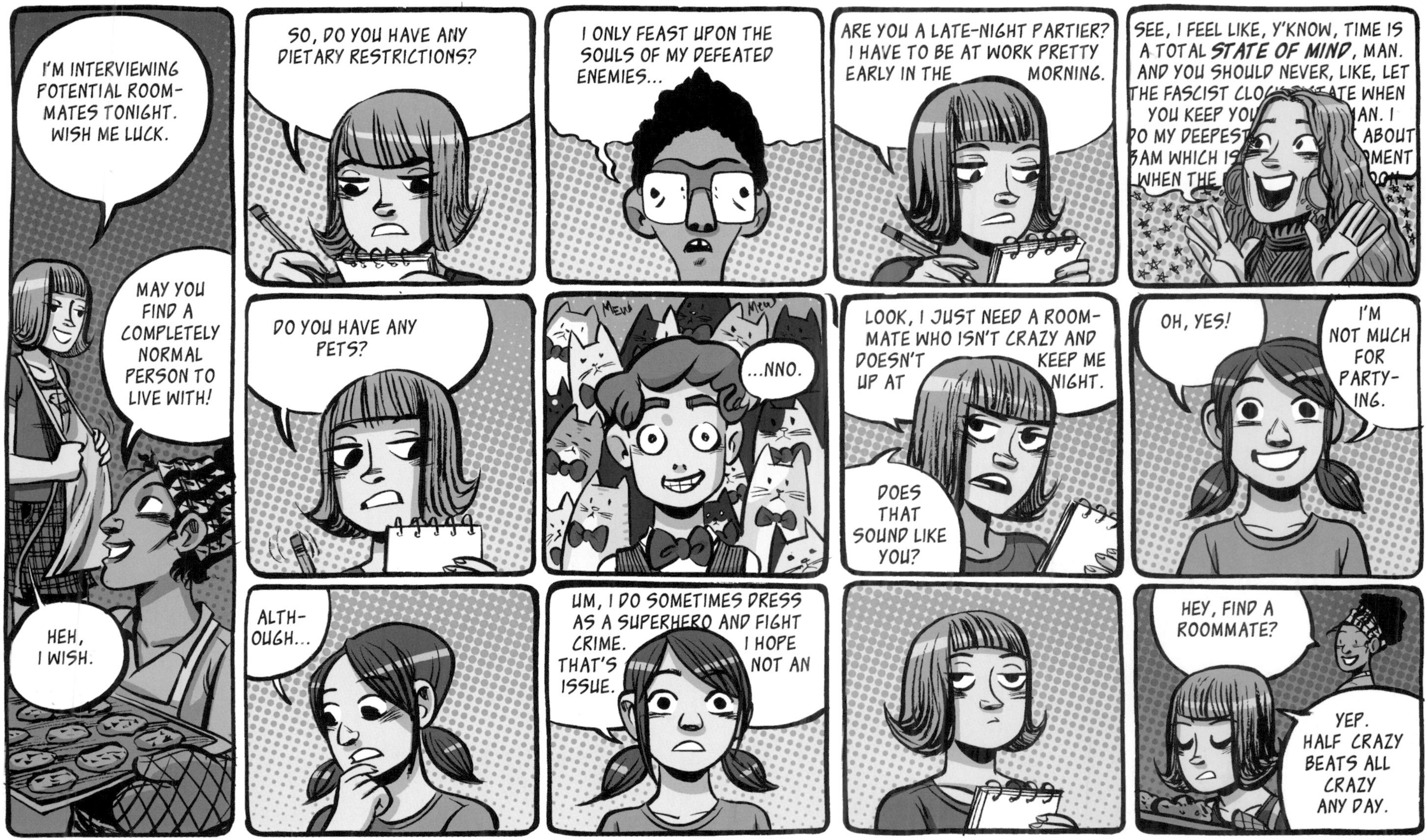

I'M INTERVIEWING POTENTIAL ROOM-MATES TONIGHT. WISH ME LUCK.
MAY YOU FIND A COMPLETELY NORMAL PERSON TO LIVE WITH!
HEH, I WISH.
SO, DO YOU HAVE ANY DIETARY RESTRICTIONS?
I ONLY FEAST UPON THE SOULS OF MY DEFEATED ENEMIES...
ARE YOU A LATE-NIGHT PARTIER? I HAVE TO BE AT WORK PRETTY EARLY IN THE MORNING.
SEE, I FEEL LIKE, Y'KNOW, TIME IS A TOTAL STATE OF MIND, MAN. AND YOU SHOULD NEVER, LIKE, LET THE FASCIST CLOC ATE WHEN YOU KEEP YOU MAN. I DO MY DEEPEST ABOUT 3AM WHICH IS MENT WHEN THE
DO YOU HAVE ANY PETS?
MEW
MEW
...NNO.
LOOK, I JUST NEED A ROOM-MATE WHO ISN'T CRAZY AND DOESN'T KEEP ME UP AT NIGHT.
DOES THAT SOUND LIKE YOU?
OH, YES!
I'M NOT MUCH FOR PARTY-ING.
ALTH-OUGH...
UM, I DO SOMETIMES DRESS AS A SUPERHERO AND FIGHT CRIME. I HOPE THAT'S NOT AN ISSUE.
HEY, FIND A ROOMMATE?
YEP. HALF CRAZY BEATS ALL CRAZY ANY DAY.

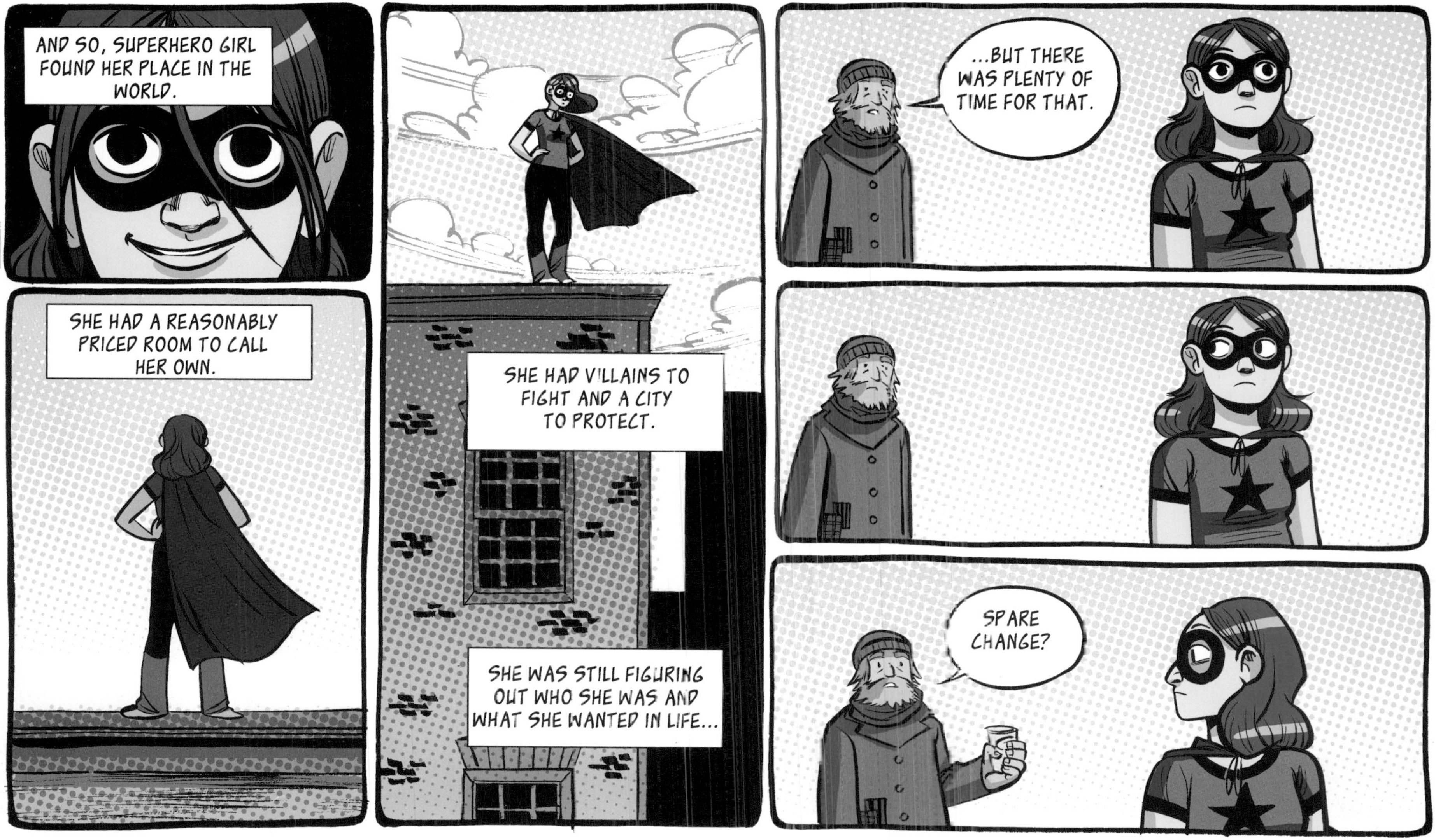
AND SO, SUPERHERO GIRL FOUND HER PLACE IN THE WORLD.
SHE HAD A REASONABLY PRICED ROOM TO CALL HER OWN.
SHE HAD VILLAINS TO FIGHT AND A CITY TO PROTECT.
SHE WAS STILL FIGURING OUT WHO SHE WAS AND WHAT SHE WANTED IN LIFE...
...BUT THERE WAS PLENTY OF TIME FOR THAT.
SPARE CHANGE?

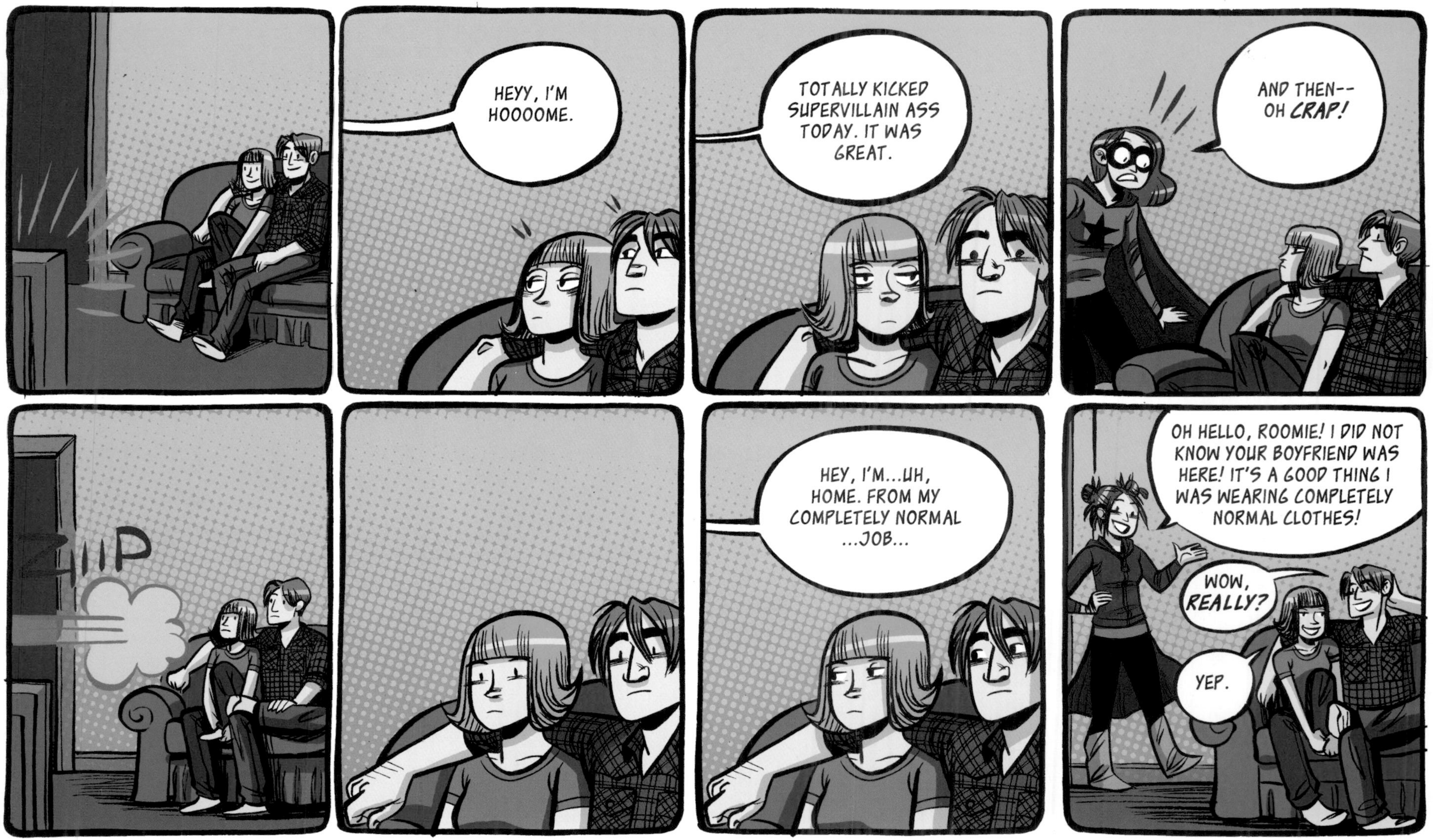
HEYY, I'M HOOOOME.
TOTALLY KICKED SUPERVILLAIN ASS TODAY. IT WAS GREAT.
AND THEN--OH *CRAP!*
ZIIIP
HEY, I'M...UH, HOME. FROM MY COMPLETELY NORMAL ...JOB...
OH HELLO, ROOMIE! I DID NOT KNOW YOUR BOYFRIEND WAS HERE! IT'S A GOOD THING I WAS WEARING COMPLETELY NORMAL CLOTHES!
WOW, *REALLY?*
YEP.

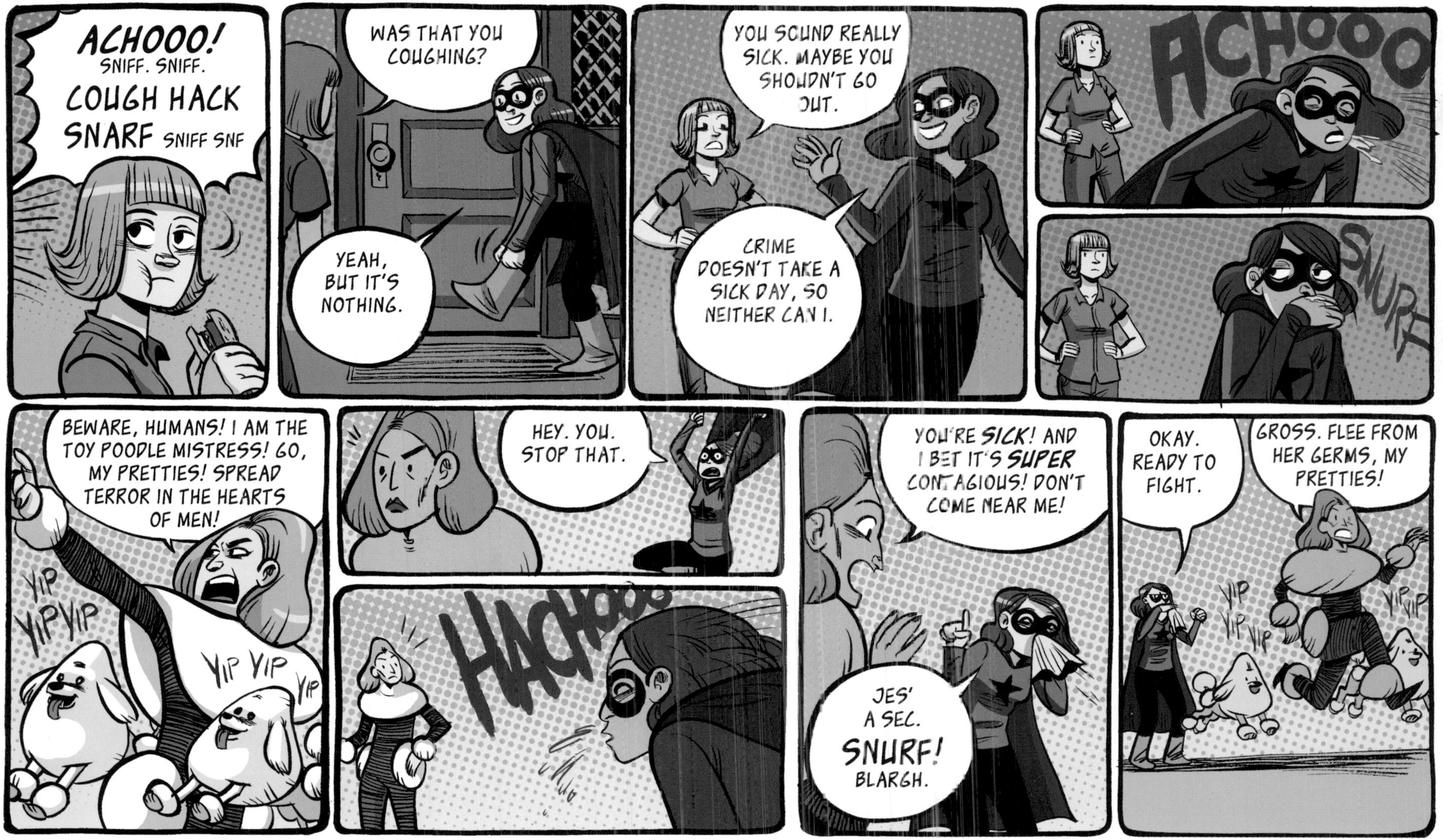
ACHOOO!
SNIFF. SNIFF.
COUGH HACK
SNARF SNIFF SNF
WAS THAT YOU COUGHING?
YEAH, BUT IT'S NOTHING.
YOU SOUND REALLY SICK. MAYBE YOU SHOUDN'T GO OUT.
CRIME DOESN'T TAKE A SICK DAY, SO NEITHER CAN I.
ACHOOO
SNURF
BEWARE, HUMANS! I AM THE TOY POODLE MISTRESS! GO, MY PRETTIES! SPREAD TERROR IN THE HEARTS OF MEN!
YIP YIP YIP
YIP YIP
YIP
HEY. YOU. STOP THAT.
HACHOOO
YOU'RE SICK! AND I BET IT'S SUPER CONTAGIOUS! DON'T COME NEAR ME!
JES' A SEC.
SNURF!
BLARGH.
OKAY. READY TO FIGHT.
GROSS. FLEE FROM HER GERMS, MY PRETTIES!
YIP YIP YIP
YIP YIP

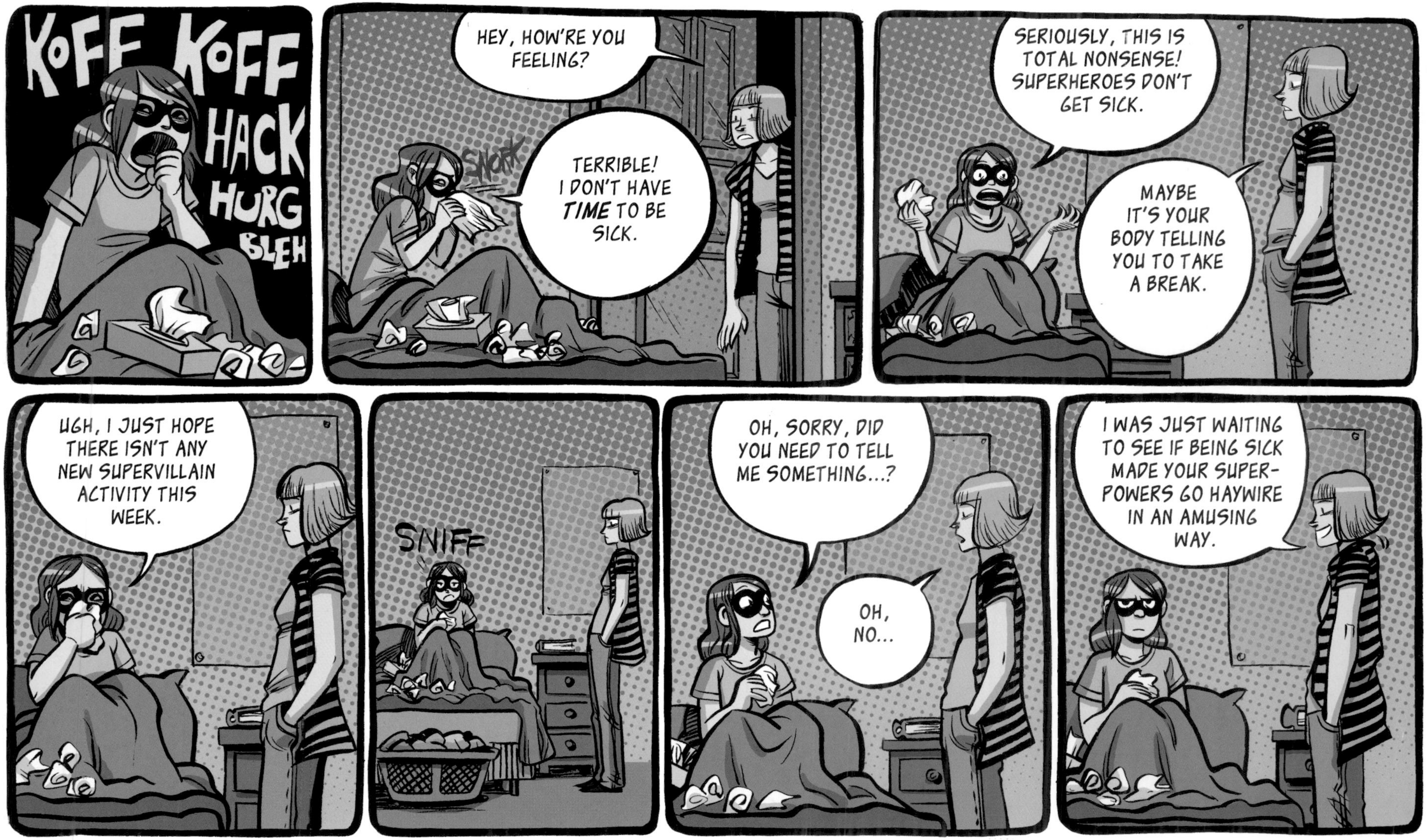
KOFF KOFF
HACK
HURG
BLEH
HEY, HOW'RE YOU FEELING?
SNORK
TERRIBLE! I DON'T HAVE *TIME* TO BE SICK.
SERIOUSLY, THIS IS TOTAL NONSENSE! SUPERHEROES DON'T GET SICK.
MAYBE IT'S YOUR BODY TELLING YOU TO TAKE A BREAK.
UGH, I JUST HOPE THERE ISN'T ANY NEW SUPERVILLAIN ACTIVITY THIS WEEK.
SNIFF
OH, SORRY, DID YOU NEED TO TELL ME SOMETHING...?
OH, NO...
I WAS JUST WAITING TO SEE IF BEING SICK MADE YOUR SUPER-POWERS GO HAYWIRE IN AN AMUSING WAY.

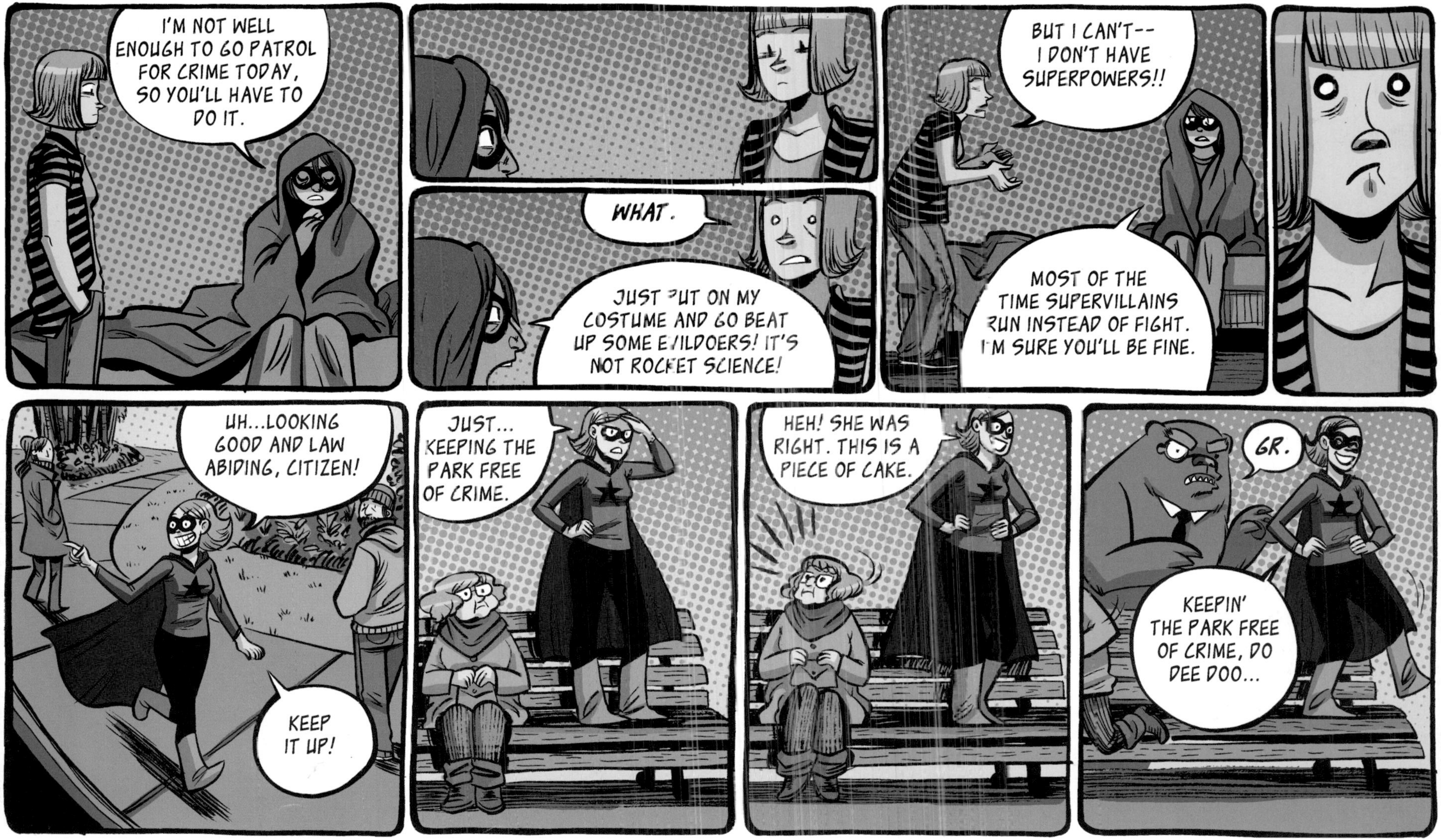
I'M NOT WELL ENOUGH TO GO PATROL FOR CRIME TODAY, SO YOU'LL HAVE TO DO IT.
WHAT.
JUST PUT ON MY COSTUME AND GO BEAT UP SOME EVILDOERS! IT'S NOT ROCKET SCIENCE!
BUT I CAN'T-- I DON'T HAVE SUPERPOWERS!!
MOST OF THE TIME SUPERVILLAINS RUN INSTEAD OF FIGHT. I'M SURE YOU'LL BE FINE.
UH...LOOKING GOOD AND LAW ABIDING, CITIZEN!
KEEP IT UP!
JUST... KEEPING THE PARK FREE OF CRIME.
HEH! SHE WAS RIGHT. THIS IS A PIECE OF CAKE.
GR.
KEEPIN' THE PARK FREE OF CRIME, DO DEE DOO...

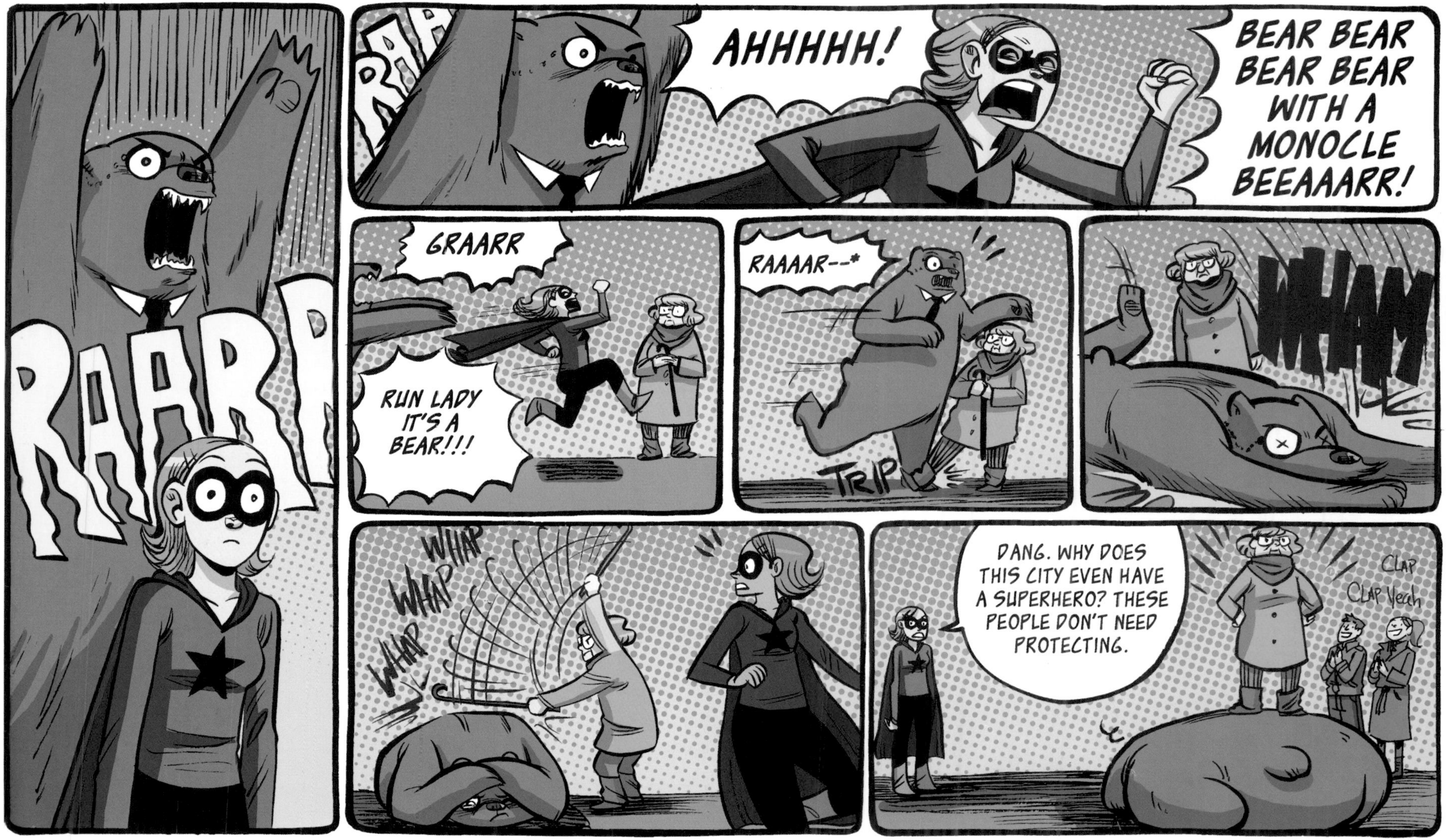
RAARR
AHHHHH!
BEAR BEAR BEAR BEAR WITH A MONOCLE BEEAAARR!
GRAARR
RUN LADY IT'S A BEAR!!!
RAAAAR--*
TRIP
WHAM
WHAP WHAP WHAP
DANG. WHY DOES THIS CITY EVEN HAVE A SUPERHERO? THESE PEOPLE DON'T NEED PROTECTING.
CLAP CLAP Yeah

SNFF

BEAR, ARE YOU CRYING?

OH, I'M SO SORRY, SUPERHERO GIRL. I DIDN'T MEAN TO CAUSE YOU PROBLEMS.

I'M NOT A REGULAR BEAR. A SCIENTIST GAVE ME SUPER-INTELLIGENCE, THEN ABANDONED ME WHEN HIS FUNDING WAS CUT. RATHER THAN WALLOW IN DESPAIR, I MADE SOMETHING OF MYSELF.

EDUCATION SEEMED THE BEST WAY TO FURTHER MY SITUATION, SO I WENT TO UNIVERSITY. GOT MY BA, THEN MY MASTERS AND DOCTORATE. NOW I'M A PROFESSOR AT CLAREMONT UNIVERSITY...AND MOST OF THE TIME I'M NO THREAT TO CIVILIZED SOCIETY...

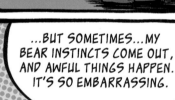

...BUT SOMETIMES...MY BEAR INSTINCTS COME OUT, AND AWFUL THINGS HAPPEN. IT'S SO EMBARRASSING.

HEY, IT'S OKAY. WE ALL HAVE BAD DAYS.

SO...I GUESS YOU COULD SAY YOU'RE **SMARTER THAN THE AVERAGE BEAR,** HUH?

HAHAHA!

GRAARR

AHHHHH

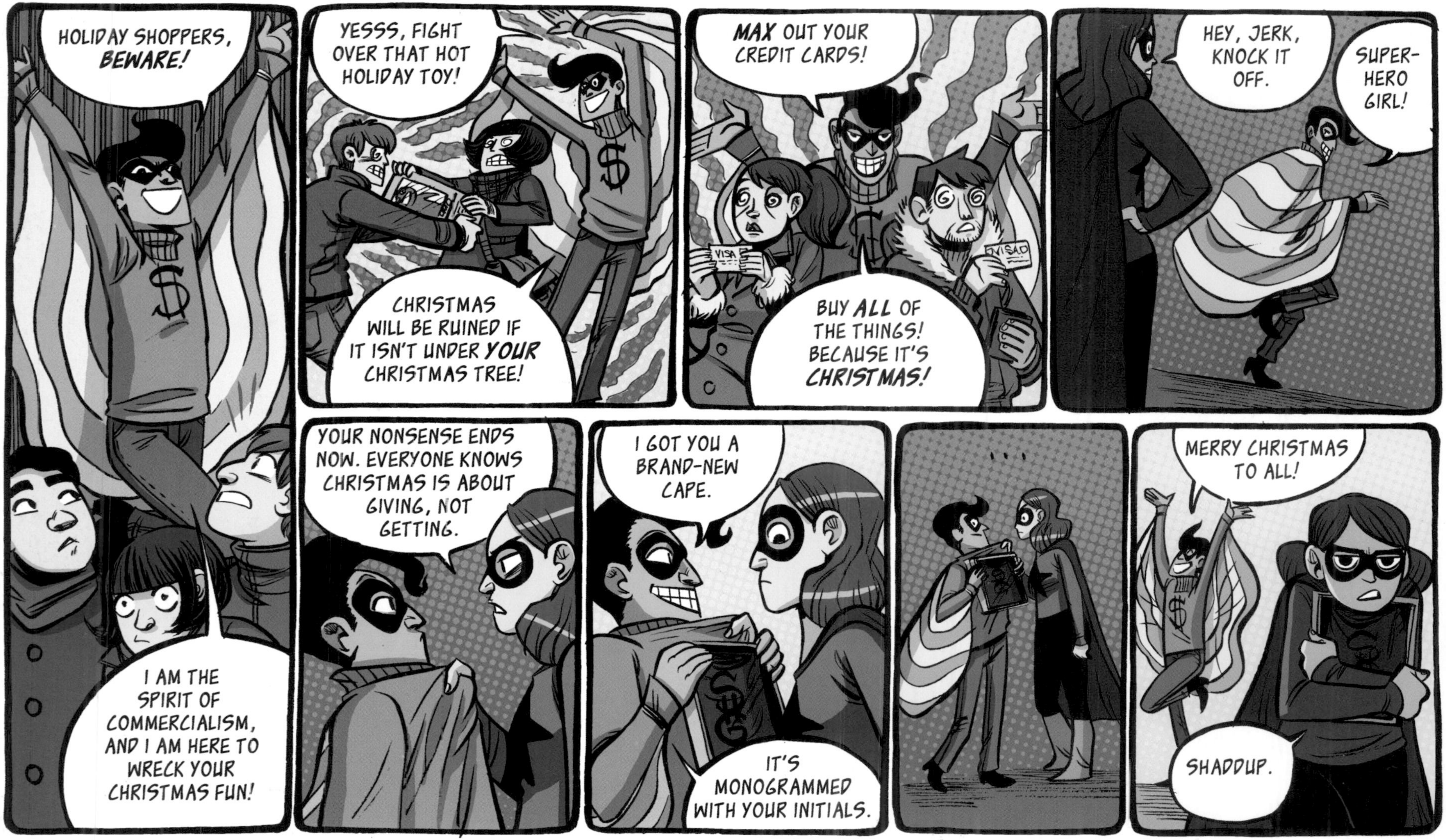
HOLIDAY SHOPPERS, BEWARE!
I AM THE SPIRIT OF COMMERCIALISM, AND I AM HERE TO WRECK YOUR CHRISTMAS FUN!
YESSS, FIGHT OVER THAT HOT HOLIDAY TOY!
CHRISTMAS WILL BE RUINED IF IT ISN'T UNDER YOUR CHRISTMAS TREE!
MAX OUT YOUR CREDIT CARDS!
VISA
VISA
BUY ALL OF THE THINGS! BECAUSE IT'S CHRISTMAS!
HEY, JERK, KNOCK IT OFF.
SUPER-HERO GIRL!
YOUR NONSENSE ENDS NOW. EVERYONE KNOWS CHRISTMAS IS ABOUT GIVING, NOT GETTING.
I GOT YOU A BRAND-NEW CAPE.
IT'S MONOGRAMMED WITH YOUR INITIALS.
...
MERRY CHRISTMAS TO ALL!
SHADDUP.

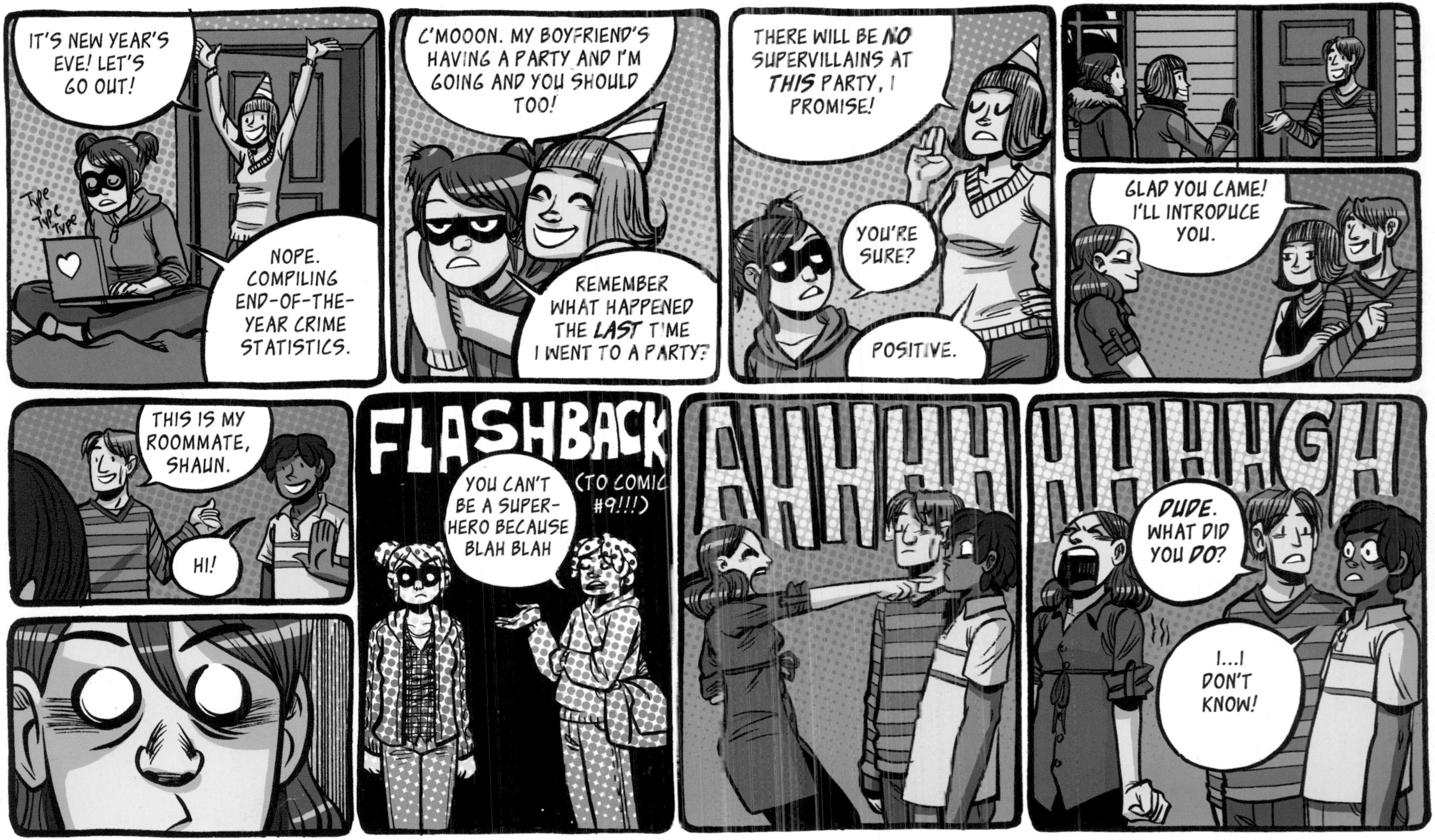
IT'S NEW YEAR'S EVE! LET'S GO OUT!
TYPE TYPE TYPE
NOPE. COMPILING END-OF-THE-YEAR CRIME STATISTICS.
C'MOOON. MY BOYFRIEND'S HAVING A PARTY AND I'M GOING AND YOU SHOULD TOO!
REMEMBER WHAT HAPPENED THE LAST TIME I WENT TO A PARTY?
THERE WILL BE NO SUPERVILLAINS AT THIS PARTY, I PROMISE!
YOU'RE SURE?
POSITIVE.
GLAD YOU CAME! I'LL INTRODUCE YOU.
THIS IS MY ROOMMATE, SHAUN.
HI!
FLASHBACK
(TO COMIC #9!!!)
YOU CAN'T BE A SUPER-HERO BECAUSE BLAH BLAH
AHHHHHHHHHHGH
DUDE. WHAT DID YOU DO?
I...I DON'T KNOW!

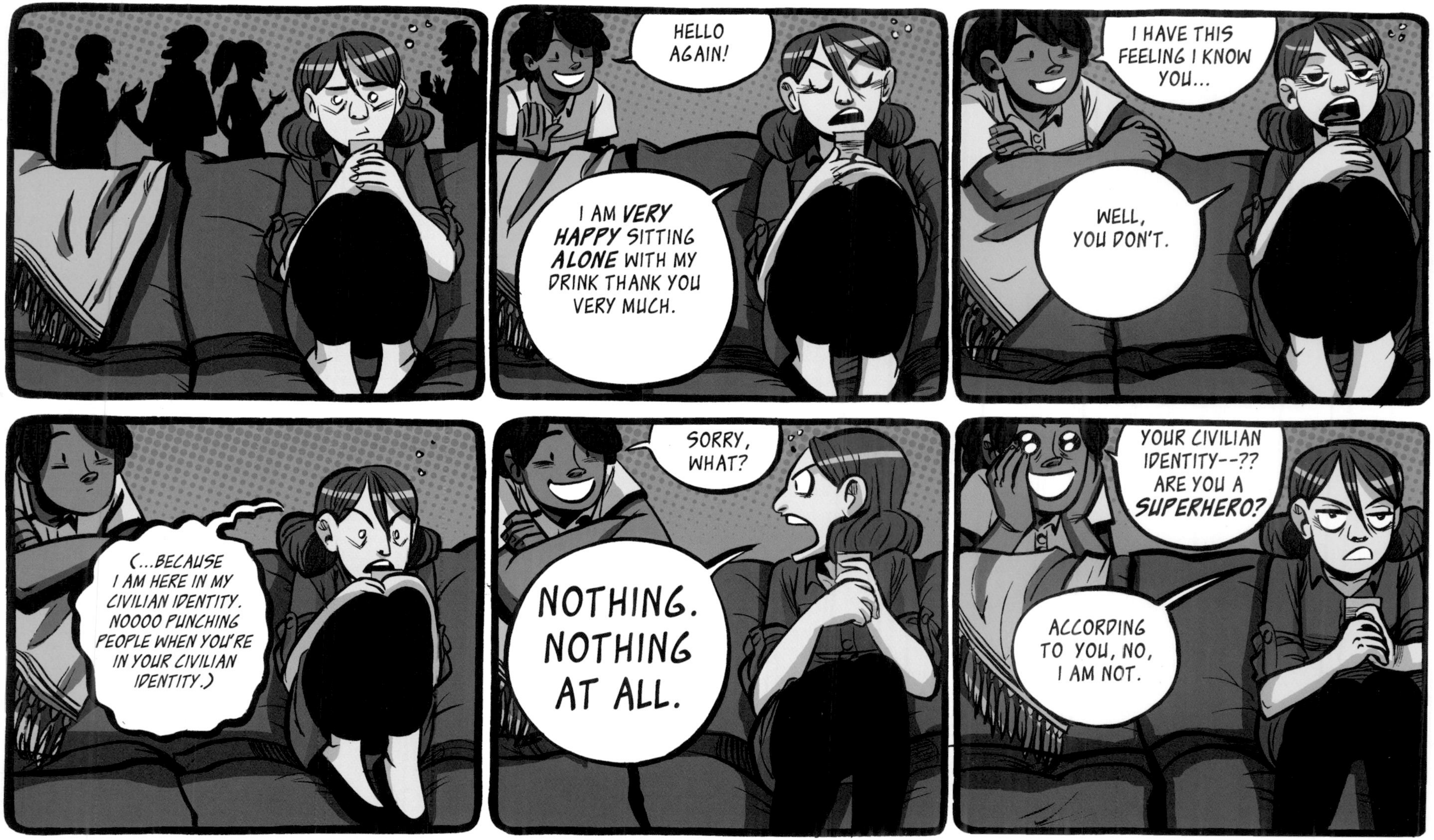
HELLO AGAIN!
I AM VERY HAPPY SITTING ALONE WITH MY DRINK THANK YOU VERY MUCH.
I HAVE THIS FEELING I KNOW YOU...
WELL, YOU DON'T.
(...BECAUSE I AM HERE IN MY CIVILIAN IDENTITY. NOOOO PUNCHING PEOPLE WHEN YOU'RE IN YOUR CIVILIAN IDENTITY.)
SORRY, WHAT?
NOTHING. NOTHING AT ALL.
YOUR CIVILIAN IDENTITY--?? ARE YOU A SUPERHERO?
ACCORDING TO YOU, NO, I AM NOT.

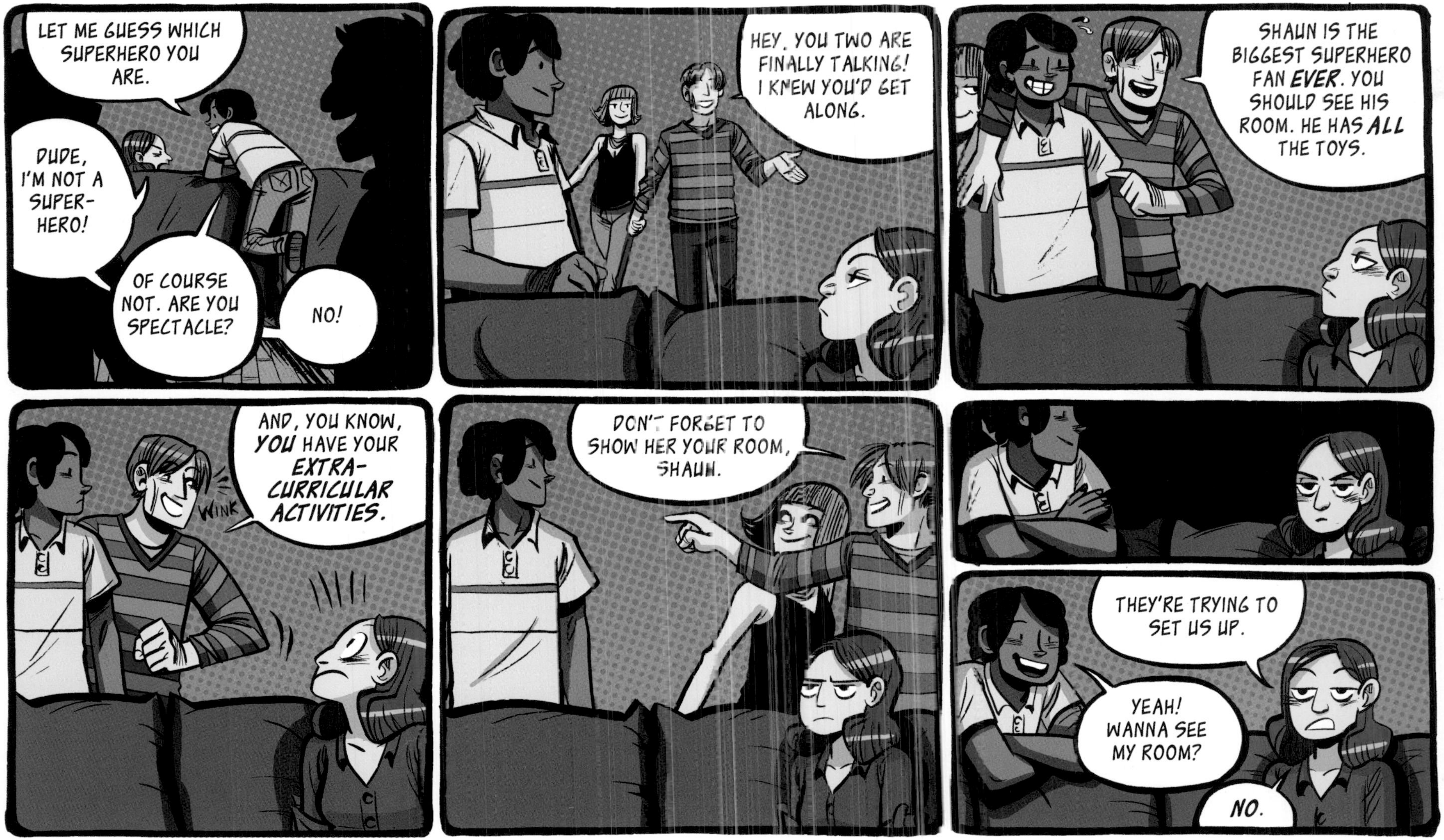
LET ME GUESS WHICH SUPERHERO YOU ARE.
DUDE, I'M NOT A SUPER-HERO!
OF COURSE NOT. ARE YOU SPECTACLE?
NO!
HEY, YOU TWO ARE FINALLY TALKING! I KNEW YOU'D GET ALONG.
SHAUN IS THE BIGGEST SUPERHERO FAN EVER. YOU SHOULD SEE HIS ROOM. HE HAS ALL THE TOYS.
AND, YOU KNOW, YOU HAVE YOUR EXTRA-CURRICULAR ACTIVITIES.
WINK
DON'T FORGET TO SHOW HER YOUR ROOM, SHAUN.
THEY'RE TRYING TO SET US UP.
YEAH! WANNA SEE MY ROOM?
NO.

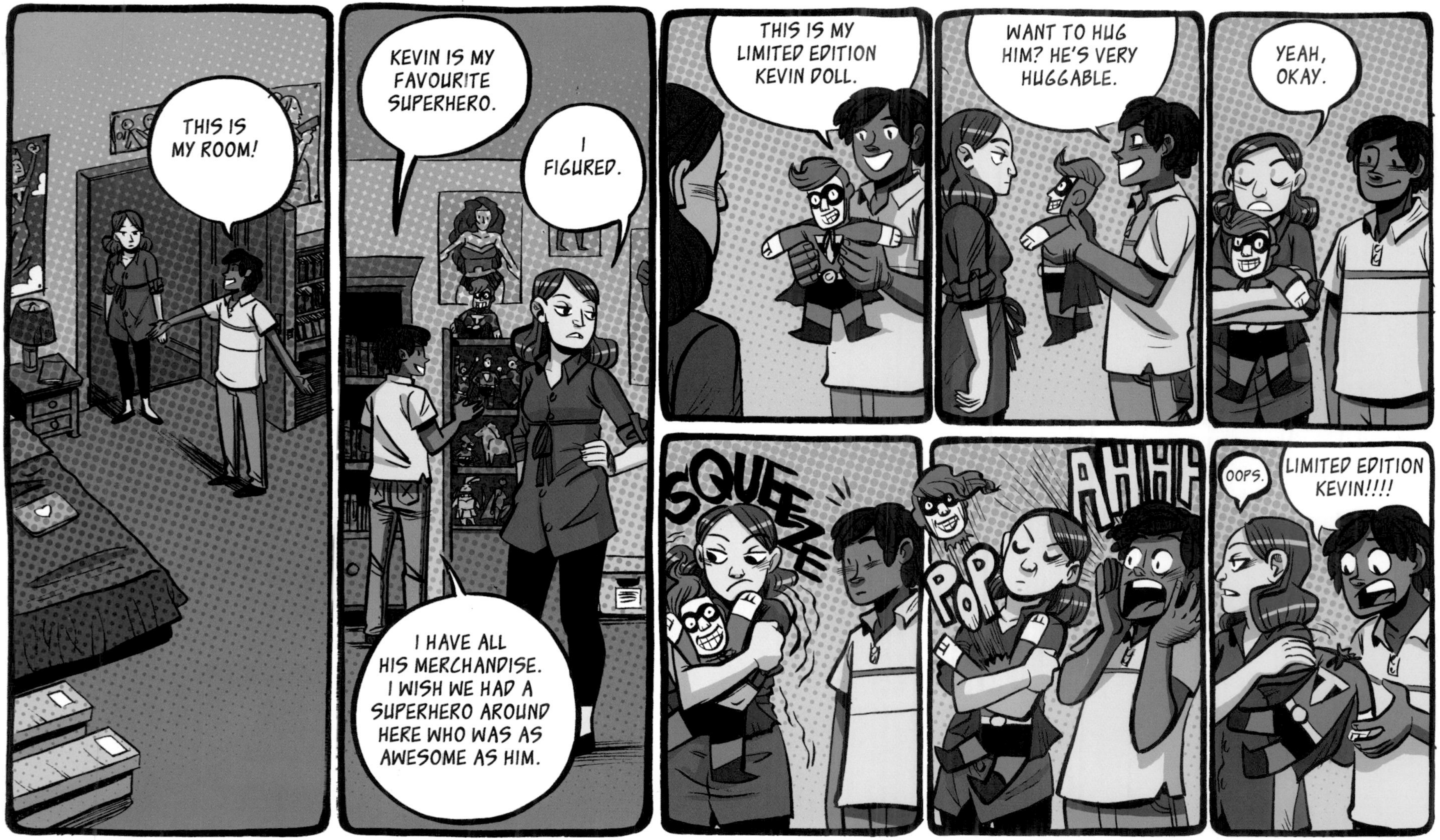
THIS IS MY ROOM!
KEVIN IS MY FAVOURITE SUPERHERO.
I FIGURED.
I HAVE ALL HIS MERCHANDISE. I WISH WE HAD A SUPERHERO AROUND HERE WHO WAS AS AWESOME AS HIM.
THIS IS MY LIMITED EDITION KEVIN DOLL.
WANT TO HUG HIM? HE'S VERY HUGGABLE.
YEAH, OKAY.
SQUEEZE
POP
AHHH
OOPS.
LIMITED EDITION KEVIN!!!!

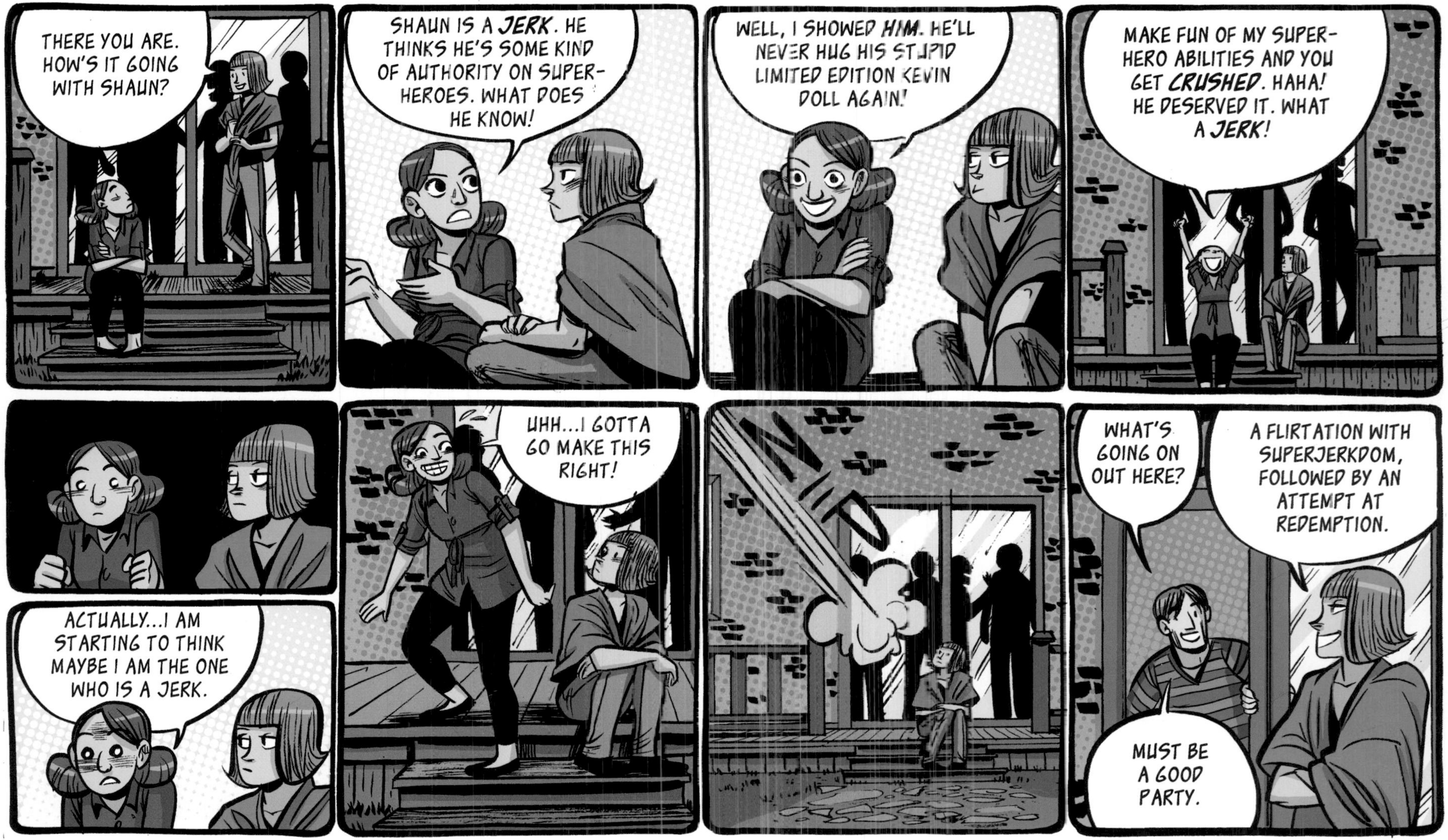
THERE YOU ARE. HOW'S IT GOING WITH SHAUN?
SHAUN IS A JERK. HE THINKS HE'S SOME KIND OF AUTHORITY ON SUPER-HEROES. WHAT DOES HE KNOW!
WELL, I SHOWED HIM. HE'LL NEVER HUG HIS STUPID LIMITED EDITION KEVIN DOLL AGAIN!
MAKE FUN OF MY SUPER-HERO ABILITIES AND YOU GET CRUSHED. HAHA! HE DESERVED IT. WHAT A JERK!
ACTUALLY...I AM STARTING TO THINK MAYBE I AM THE ONE WHO IS A JERK.
UHH...I GOTTA GO MAKE THIS RIGHT!
WHAT'S GOING ON OUT HERE?
A FLIRTATION WITH SUPERJERKDOM, FOLLOWED BY AN ATTEMPT AT REDEMPTION.
MUST BE A GOOD PARTY.

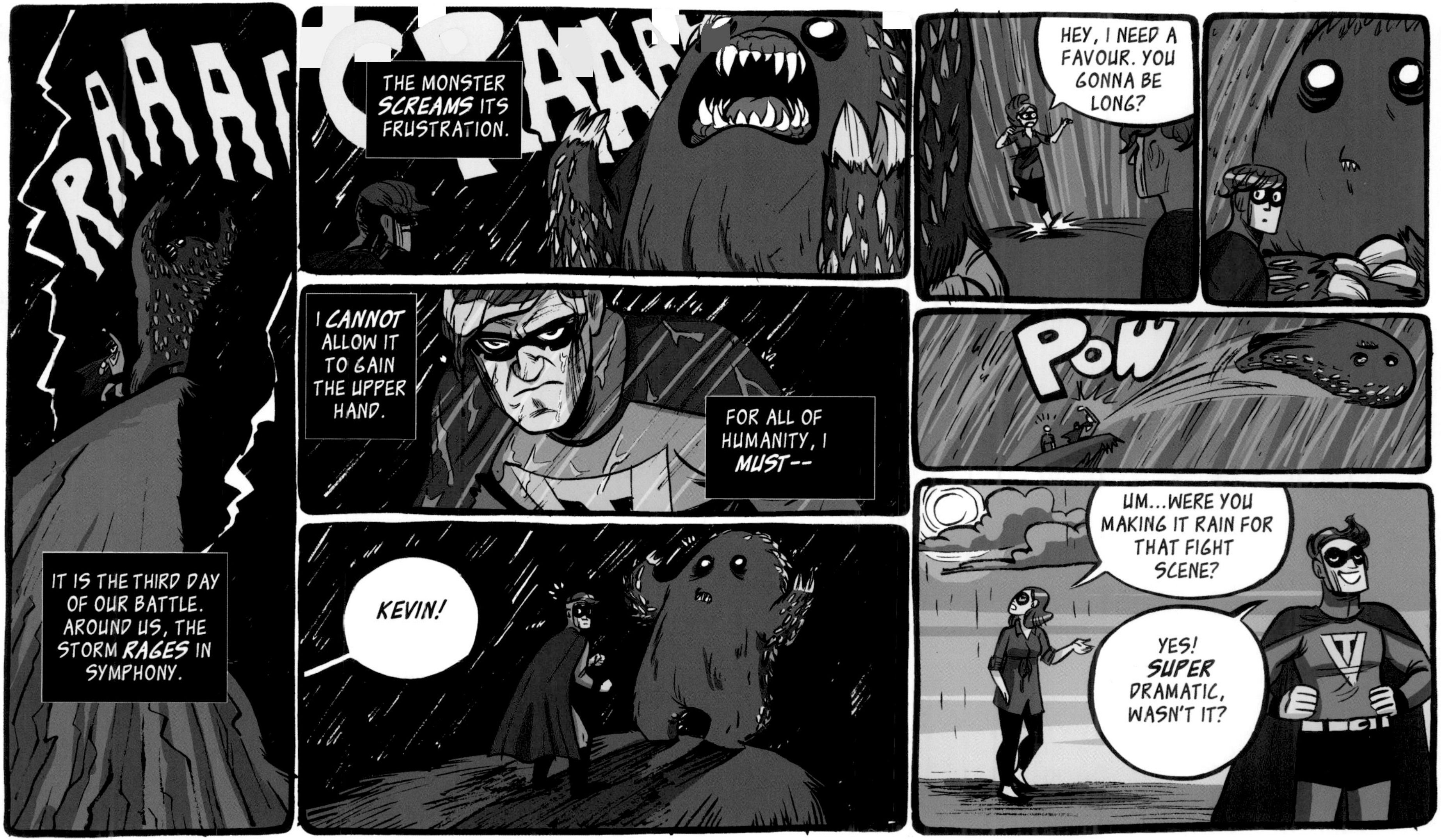

IT IS THE THIRD DAY OF OUR BATTLE. AROUND US, THE STORM RAGES IN SYMPHONY.
THE MONSTER SCREAMS ITS FRUSTRATION.
I CANNOT ALLOW IT TO GAIN THE UPPER HAND.
FOR ALL OF HUMANITY, I MUST--
KEVIN!
HEY, I NEED A FAVOUR. YOU GONNA BE LONG?
POW
UM...WERE YOU MAKING IT RAIN FOR THAT FIGHT SCENE?
YES! SUPER DRAMATIC, WASN'T IT?

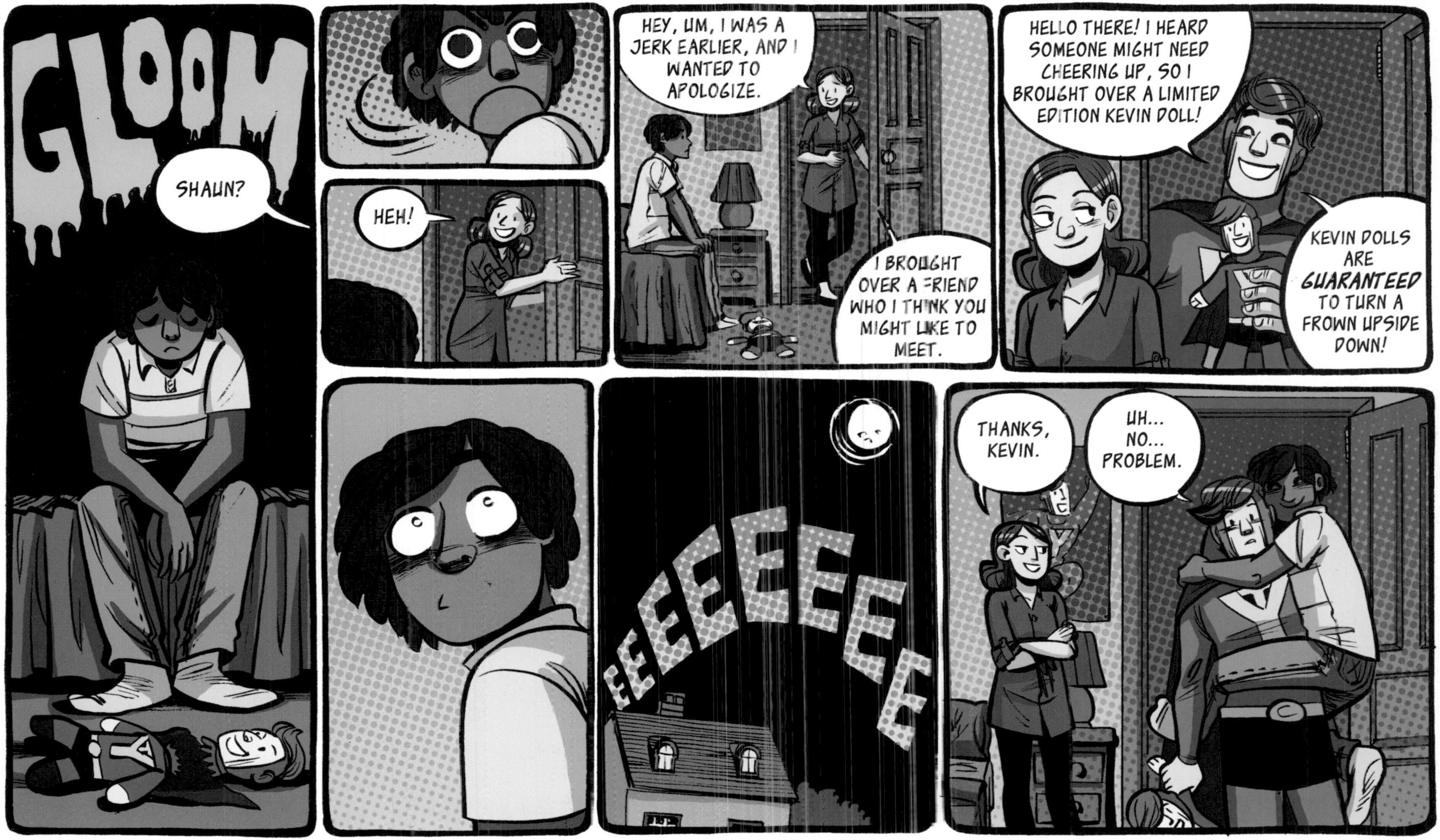
GLOOM
SHAUN?
HEH!
HEY, UM, I WAS A JERK EARLIER, AND I WANTED TO APOLOGIZE.
I BROUGHT OVER A FRIEND WHO I THINK YOU MIGHT LIKE TO MEET.
HELLO THERE! I HEARD SOMEONE MIGHT NEED CHEERING UP, SO I BROUGHT OVER A LIMITED EDITION KEVIN DOLL!
KEVIN DOLLS ARE GUARANTEED TO TURN A FROWN UPSIDE DOWN!
EEEEEEEEE
THANKS, KEVIN.
UH... NO... PROBLEM.

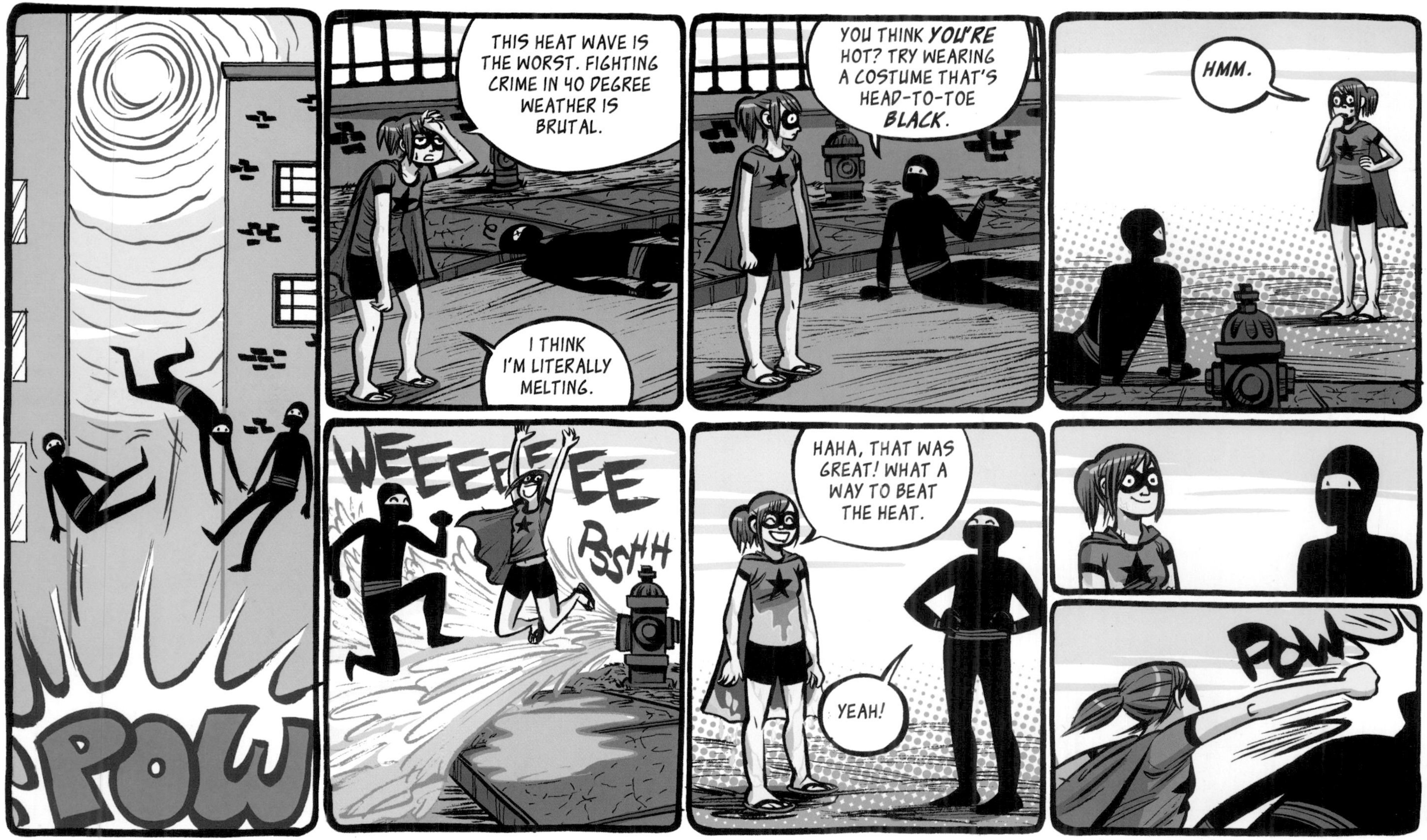
POW
THIS HEAT WAVE IS THE WORST. FIGHTING CRIME IN 40 DEGREE WEATHER IS BRUTAL.
I THINK I'M LITERALLY MELTING.
YOU THINK *YOU'RE* HOT? TRY WEARING A COSTUME THAT'S HEAD-TO-TOE *BLACK*.
HMM.
WEEEEEEEE
PSSHH
HAHA, THAT WAS GREAT! WHAT A WAY TO BEAT THE HEAT.
YEAH!
POW

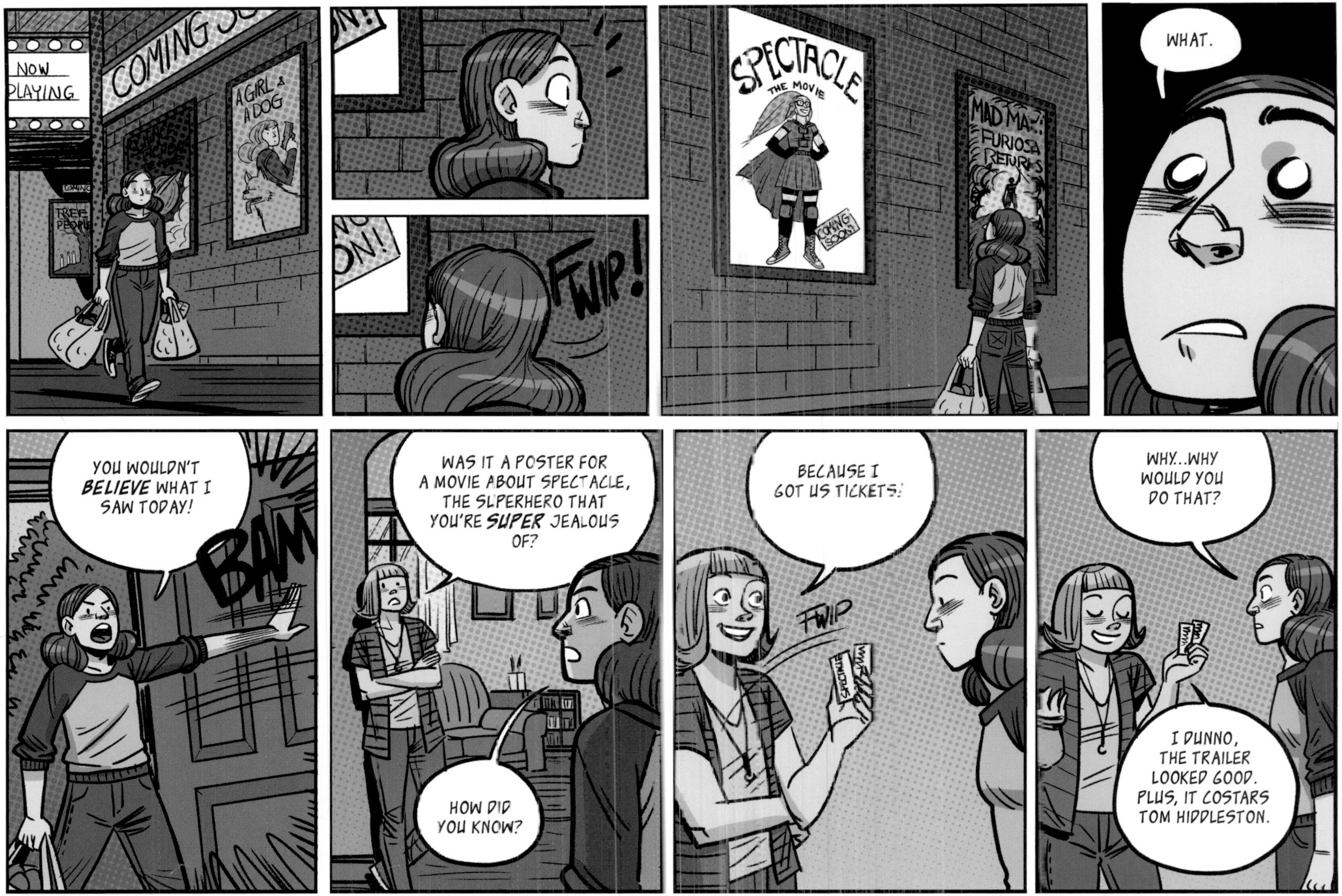
NOW PLAYING
COMING SO
A GIRL & A DOG
FWIP!
SPECTACLE THE MOVIE
COMING SOON!
MAD MAX: FURIOSA RETURNS
WHAT.
BAM
YOU WOULDN'T **BELIEVE** WHAT I SAW TODAY!
WAS IT A POSTER FOR A MOVIE ABOUT SPECTACLE, THE SUPERHERO THAT YOU'RE **SUPER** JEALOUS OF?
HOW DID YOU KNOW?
BECAUSE I GOT US TICKETS!
FWIP
WHY...WHY WOULD YOU DO THAT?
I DUNNO, THE TRAILER LOOKED GOOD. PLUS, IT COSTARS TOM HIDDLESTON.

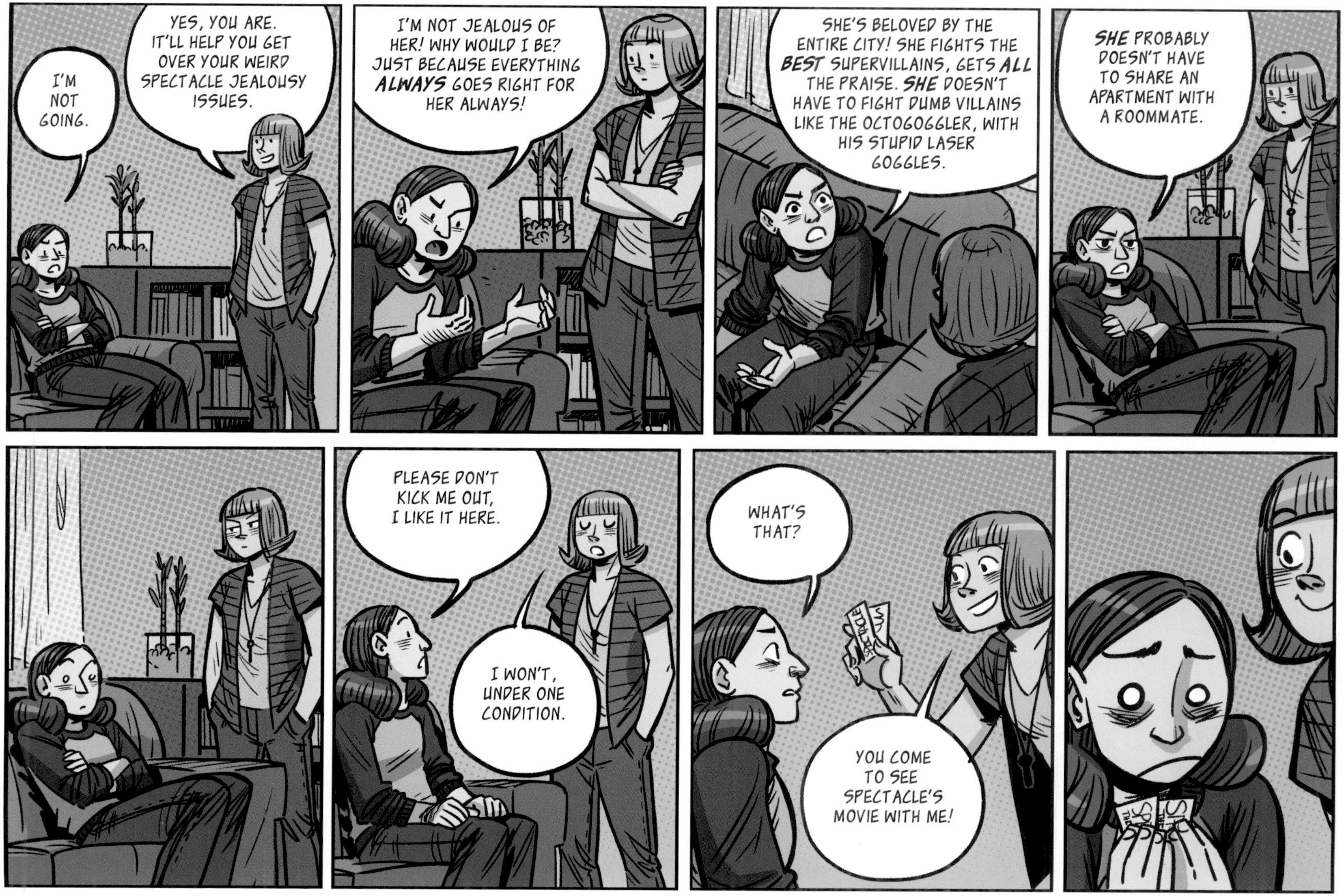
I'M NOT GOING.
YES, YOU ARE. IT'LL HELP YOU GET OVER YOUR WEIRD SPECTACLE JEALOUSY ISSUES.
I'M NOT JEALOUS OF HER! WHY WOULD I BE? JUST BECAUSE EVERYTHING ALWAYS GOES RIGHT FOR HER ALWAYS!
SHE'S BELOVED BY THE ENTIRE CITY! SHE FIGHTS THE BEST SUPERVILLAINS, GETS ALL THE PRAISE. SHE DOESN'T HAVE TO FIGHT DUMB VILLAINS LIKE THE OCTOGOGGLER, WITH HIS STUPID LASER GOGGLES.
SHE PROBABLY DOESN'T HAVE TO SHARE AN APARTMENT WITH A ROOMMATE.
PLEASE DON'T KICK ME OUT, I LIKE IT HERE.
I WON'T, UNDER ONE CONDITION.
WHAT'S THAT?
YOU COME TO SEE SPECTACLE'S MOVIE WITH ME!

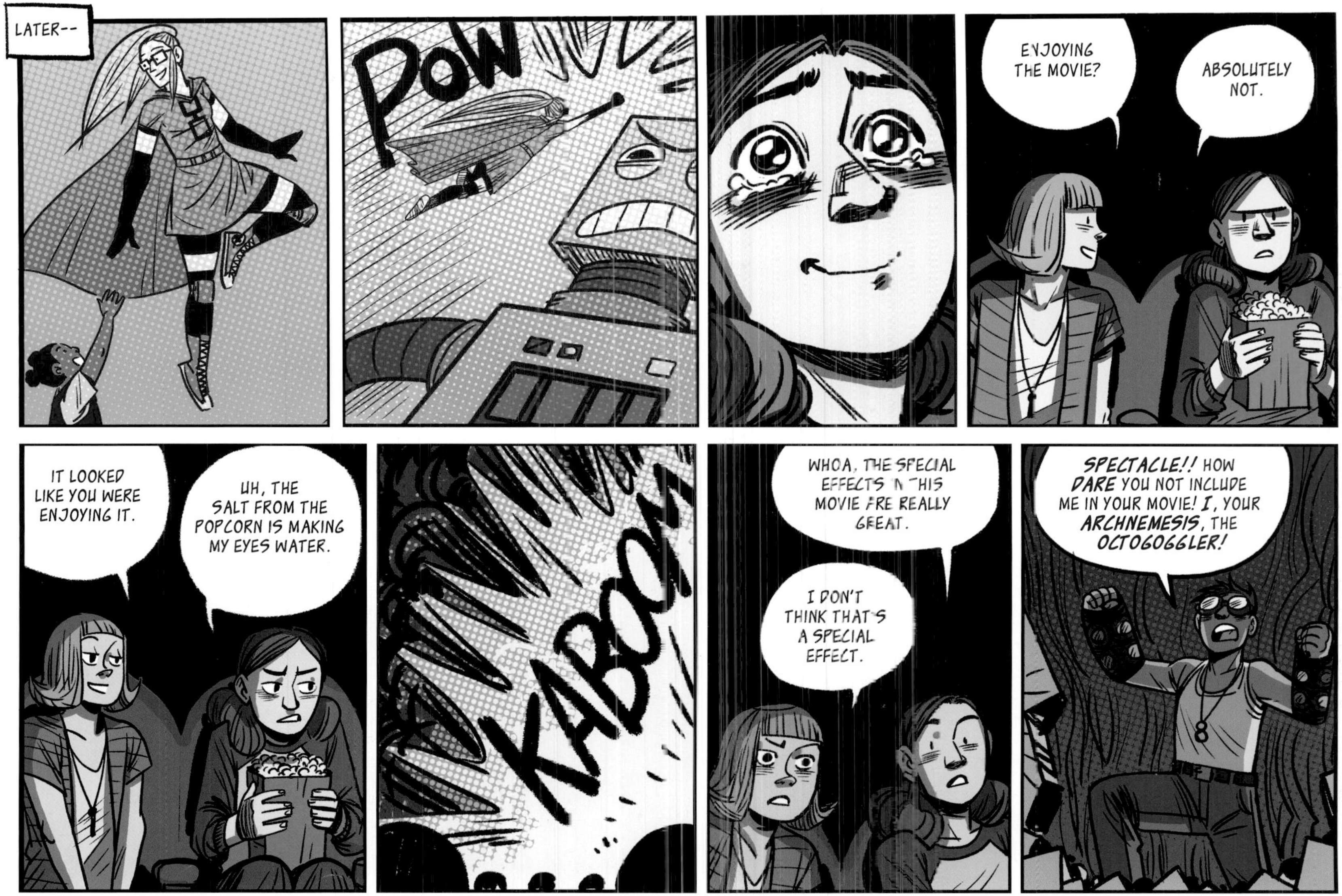
LATER--
POW
ENJOYING THE MOVIE?
ABSOLUTELY NOT.
IT LOOKED LIKE YOU WERE ENJOYING IT.
UH, THE SALT FROM THE POPCORN IS MAKING MY EYES WATER.
KABOOM
WHOA, THE SPECIAL EFFECTS IN THIS MOVIE ARE REALLY GREAT.
I DON'T THINK THAT'S A SPECIAL EFFECT.
SPECTACLE!! HOW DARE YOU NOT INCLUDE ME IN YOUR MOVIE! I, YOUR ARCHNEMESIS, THE OCTOGOGGLER!

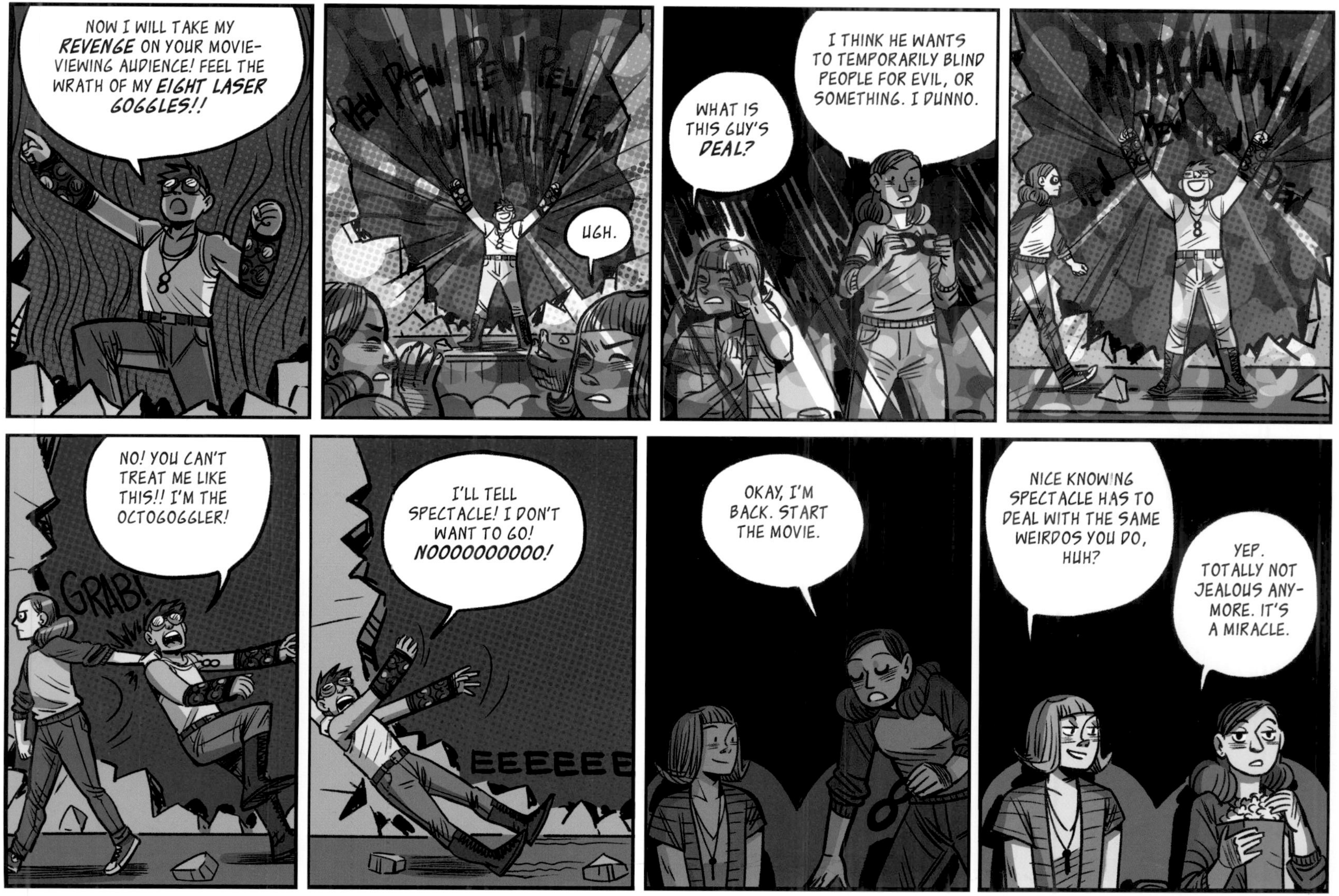
NOW I WILL TAKE MY REVENGE ON YOUR MOVIE-VIEWING AUDIENCE! FEEL THE WRATH OF MY EIGHT LASER GOGGLES!!
PEW PEW PEW PEW
MUHAHAHAHA
PEW
UGH.
WHAT IS THIS GUY'S DEAL?
I THINK HE WANTS TO TEMPORARILY BLIND PEOPLE FOR EVIL, OR SOMETHING. I DUNNO.
MUHAHAHA
PEW PEW PEW PEW
NO! YOU CAN'T TREAT ME LIKE THIS!! I'M THE OCTOGOGGLER!
GRAB!
I'LL TELL SPECTACLE! I DON'T WANT TO GO! NOOOOOOOOOO!
EEEEEEE
OKAY, I'M BACK. START THE MOVIE.
NICE KNOWING SPECTACLE HAS TO DEAL WITH THE SAME WEIRDOS YOU DO, HUH?
YEP. TOTALLY NOT JEALOUS ANY-MORE. IT'S A MIRACLE.

HI, READERS! THE COMICS IN THIS BOOK ARE NORMALLY DRAWN IN HORIZONTAL FORMAT, SO THE BOOK READS LIKE THIS:
THE ADVENTURES OF SUPERHERO GIRL
HOWEVER, THE NEXT TWO SUPERHERO GIRL SHORT STORIES WERE DRAWN IN VERTICAL FORMAT, SO PLEASE TURN THE BOOK LIKE THIS TO READ THEM. THANKS!
THE ADVENTURES OF SUPERHERO GIRL

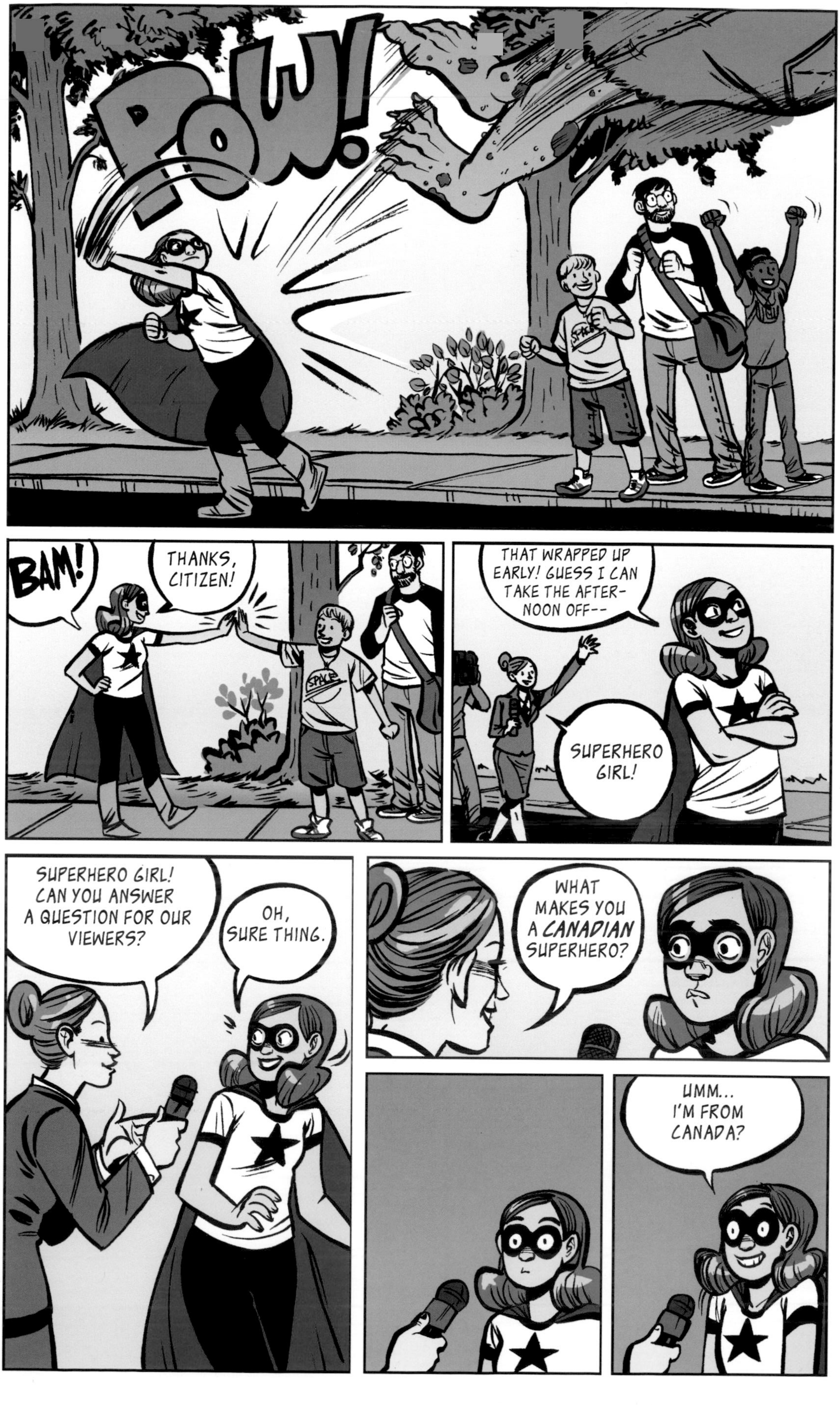
POW!
BAM!
THANKS, CITIZEN!
THAT WRAPPED UP EARLY! GUESS I CAN TAKE THE AFTER-NOON OFF--
SUPERHERO GIRL!
SUPERHERO GIRL! CAN YOU ANSWER A QUESTION FOR OUR VIEWERS?
OH, SURE THING.
WHAT MAKES YOU A *CANADIAN* SUPERHERO?
UMM... I'M FROM CANADA?

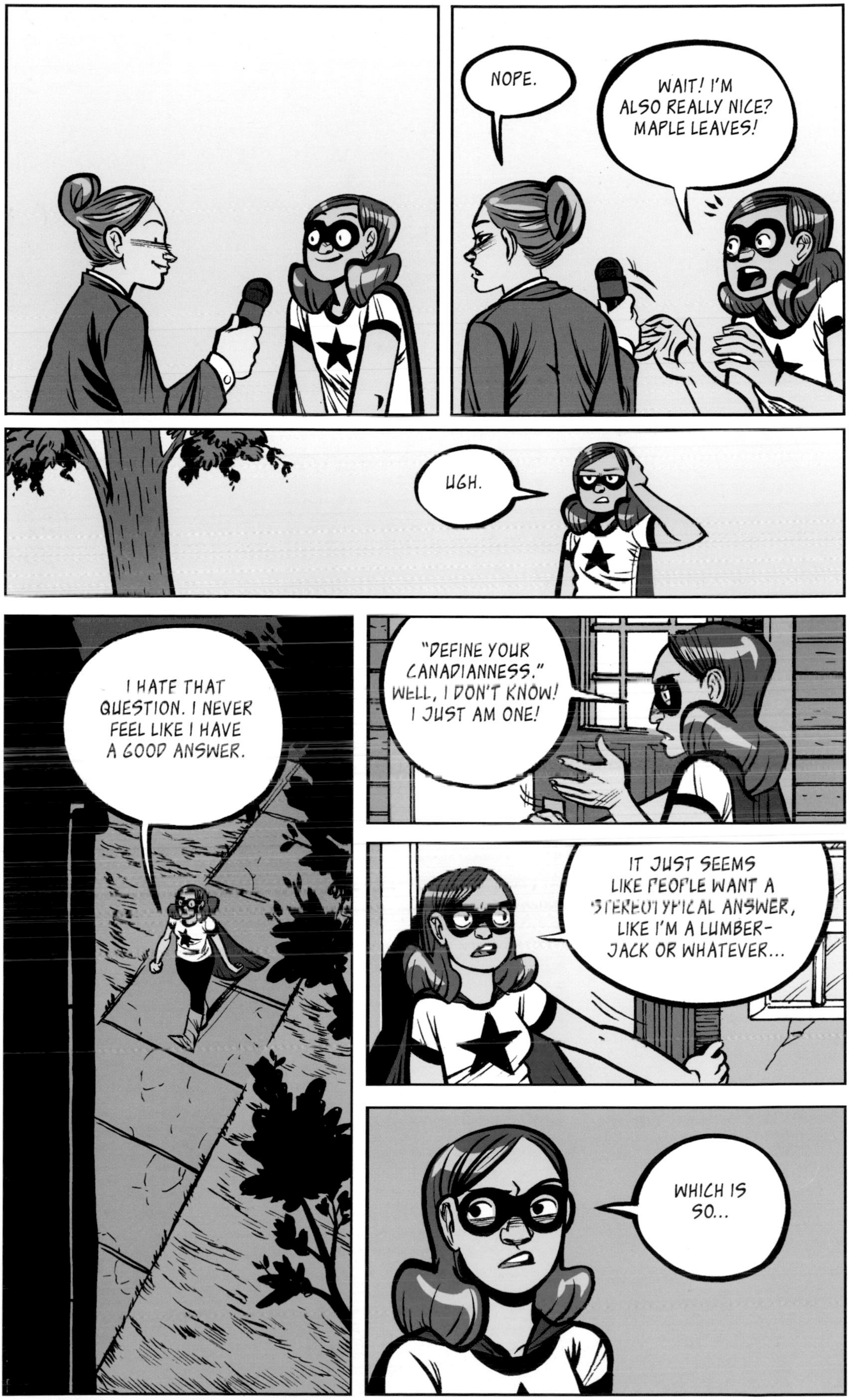
NOPE.
WAIT! I'M ALSO REALLY NICE? MAPLE LEAVES!
UGH.
I HATE THAT QUESTION. I NEVER FEEL LIKE I HAVE A GOOD ANSWER.
"DEFINE YOUR CANADIANNESS." WELL, I DON'T KNOW! I JUST AM ONE!
IT JUST SEEMS LIKE PEOPLE WANT A STEREOTYPICAL ANSWER, LIKE I'M A LUMBER-JACK OR WHATEVER...
WHICH IS SO...

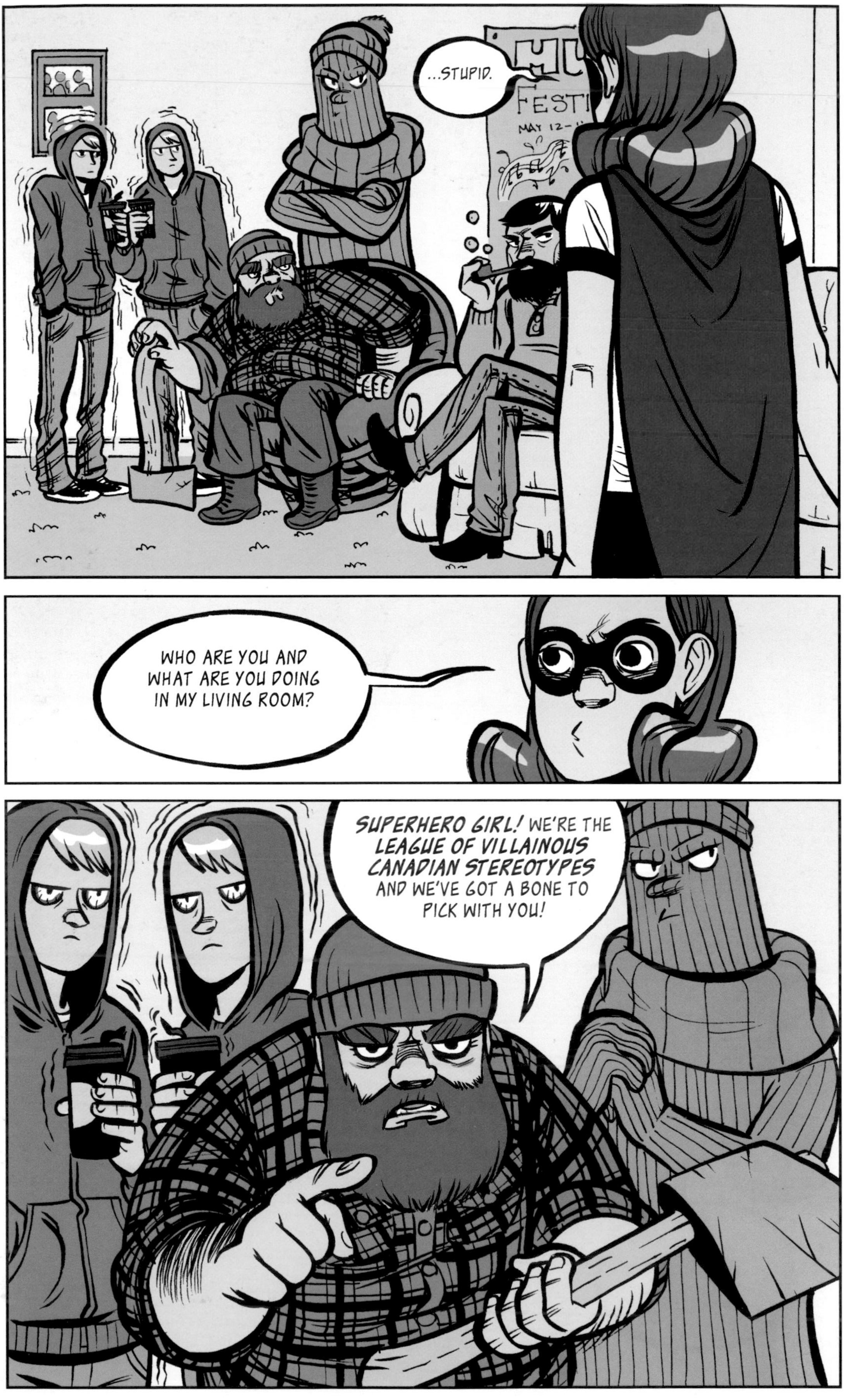
...STUPID.
WHO ARE YOU AND WHAT ARE YOU DOING IN MY LIVING ROOM?
SUPERHERO GIRL! WE'RE THE LEAGUE OF VILLAINOUS CANADIAN STEREOTYPES AND WE'VE GOT A BONE TO PICK WITH YOU!

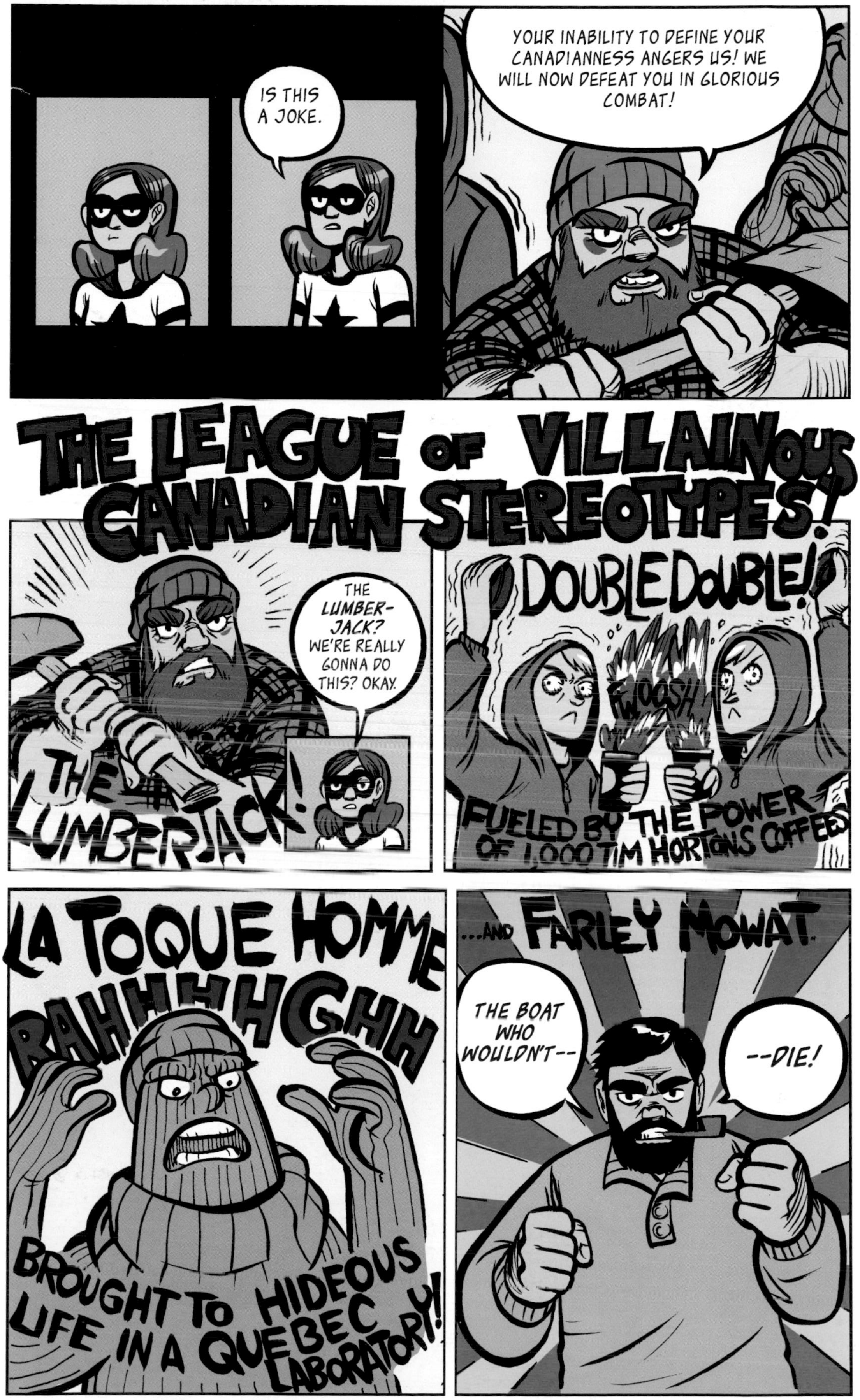
IS THIS A JOKE.
YOUR INABILITY TO DEFINE YOUR CANADIANNESS ANGERS US! WE WILL NOW DEFEAT YOU IN GLORIOUS COMBAT!
THE LEAGUE OF VILLAINOUS CANADIAN STEREOTYPES!
THE LUMBERJACK? WE'RE REALLY GONNA DO THIS? OKAY.
THE LUMBERJACK!
DOUBLE DOUBLE!
FWOOSH
FUELED BY THE POWER OF 1,000 TIM HORTONS COFFEES
LA TOQUE HOMME
RAHHHHGHH
BROUGHT TO HIDEOUS LIFE IN A QUEBEC LABORATORY!
...AND FARLEY MOWAT.
THE BOAT WHO WOULDN'T--
--DIE!

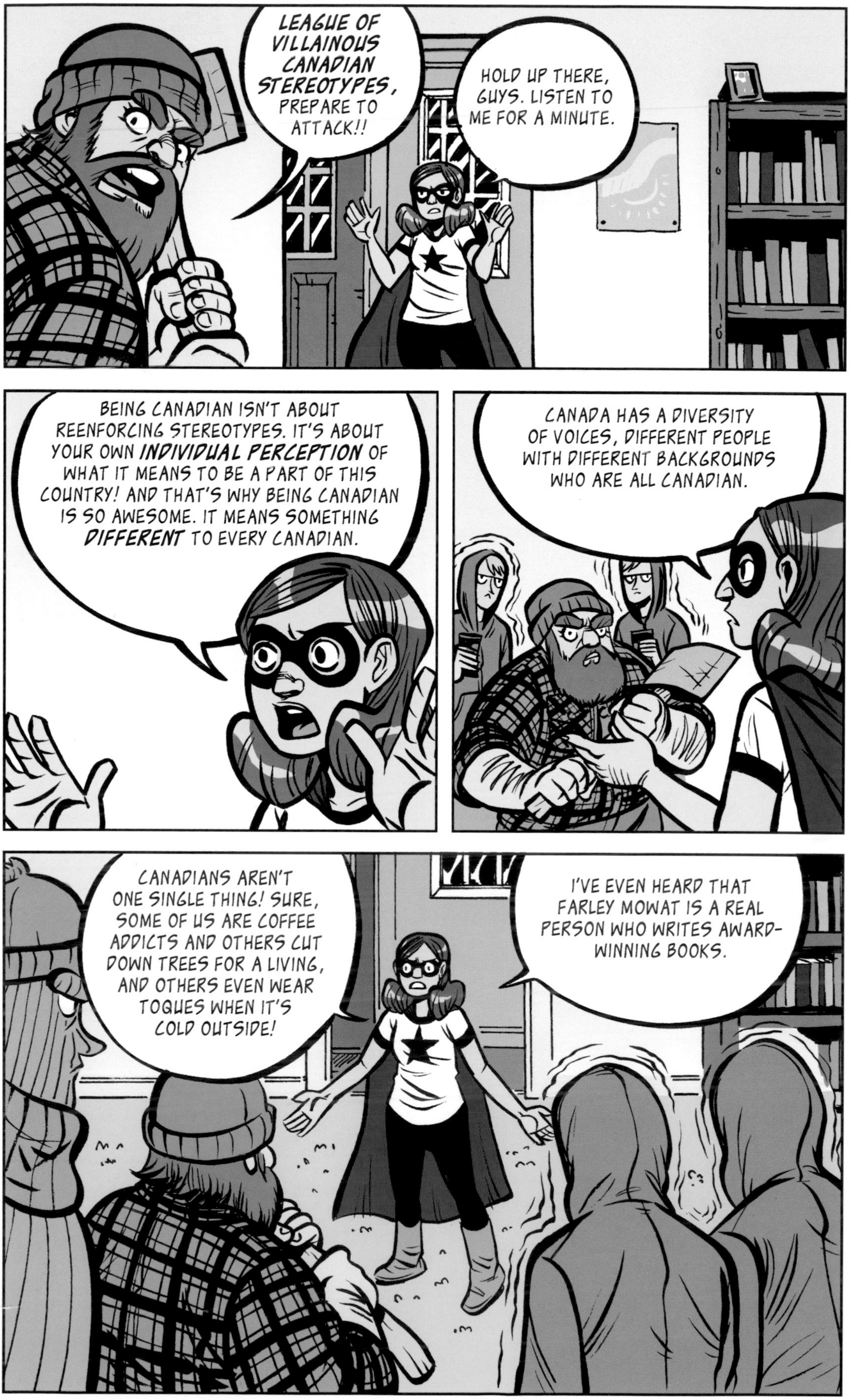
LEAGUE OF VILLAINOUS CANADIAN STEREOTYPES, PREPARE TO ATTACK!!
HOLD UP THERE, GUYS. LISTEN TO ME FOR A MINUTE.
BEING CANADIAN ISN'T ABOUT REENFORCING STEREOTYPES. IT'S ABOUT YOUR OWN INDIVIDUAL PERCEPTION OF WHAT IT MEANS TO BE A PART OF THIS COUNTRY! AND THAT'S WHY BEING CANADIAN IS SO AWESOME. IT MEANS SOMETHING DIFFERENT TO EVERY CANADIAN.
CANADA HAS A DIVERSITY OF VOICES, DIFFERENT PEOPLE WITH DIFFERENT BACKGROUNDS WHO ARE ALL CANADIAN.
CANADIANS AREN'T ONE SINGLE THING! SURE, SOME OF US ARE COFFEE ADDICTS AND OTHERS CUT DOWN TREES FOR A LIVING, AND OTHERS EVEN WEAR TOQUES WHEN IT'S COLD OUTSIDE!
I'VE EVEN HEARD THAT FARLEY MOWAT IS A REAL PERSON WHO WRITES AWARD-WINNING BOOKS.

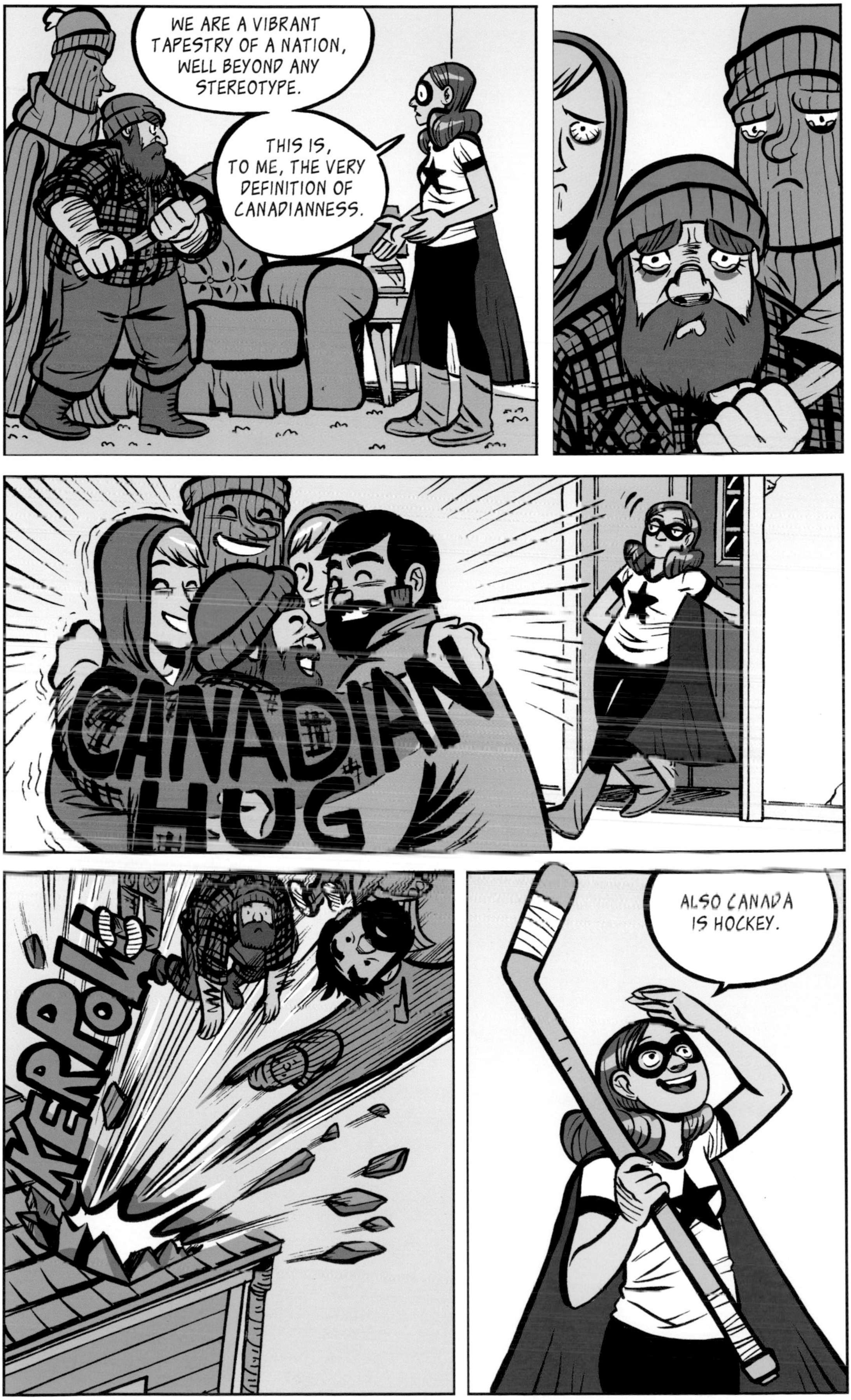
WE ARE A VIBRANT TAPESTRY OF A NATION, WELL BEYOND ANY STEREOTYPE.
THIS IS, TO ME, THE VERY DEFINITION OF CANADIANNESS.
CANADIAN HUG
KERPOW!
ALSO CANADA IS HOCKEY.

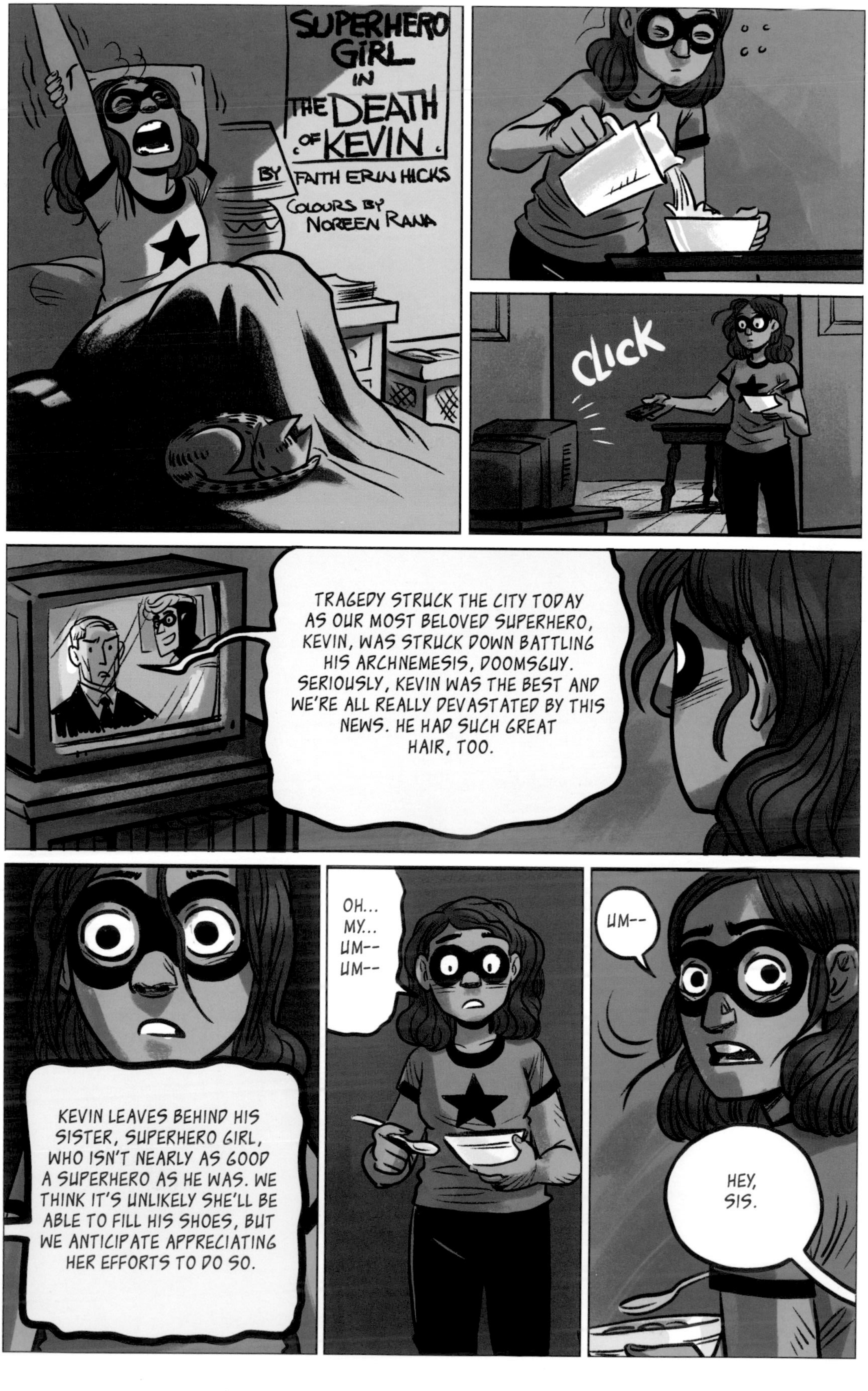
SUPERHERO GIRL IN THE DEATH OF KEVIN
BY FAITH ERIN HICKS
COLOURS BY NOREEN RANA
CLICK
TRAGEDY STRUCK THE CITY TODAY AS OUR MOST BELOVED SUPERHERO, KEVIN, WAS STRUCK DOWN BATTLING HIS ARCHNEMESIS, DOOMSGUY. SERIOUSLY, KEVIN WAS THE BEST AND WE'RE ALL REALLY DEVASTATED BY THIS NEWS. HE HAD SUCH GREAT HAIR, TOO.
KEVIN LEAVES BEHIND HIS SISTER, SUPERHERO GIRL, WHO ISN'T NEARLY AS GOOD A SUPERHERO AS HE WAS. WE THINK IT'S UNLIKELY SHE'LL BE ABLE TO FILL HIS SHOES, BUT WE ANTICIPATE APPRECIATING HER EFFORTS TO DO SO.
OH... MY... UM-- UM--
UM--
HEY, SIS.

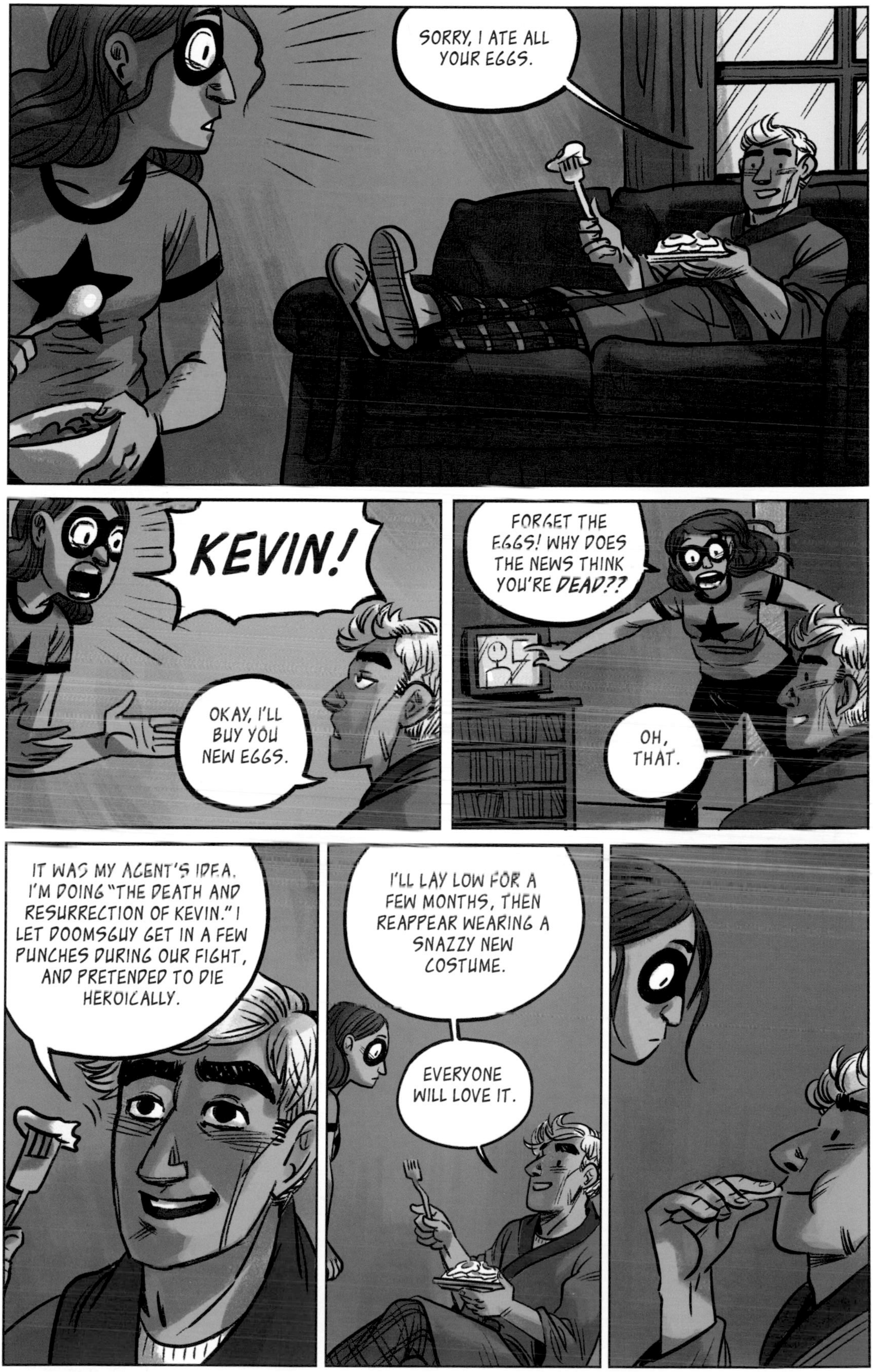
SORRY, I ATE ALL YOUR EGGS.
KEVIN!
OKAY, I'LL BUY YOU NEW EGGS.
FORGET THE EGGS! WHY DOES THE NEWS THINK YOU'RE *DEAD??*
OH, THAT.
IT WAS MY AGENT'S IDEA. I'M DOING "THE DEATH AND RESURRECTION OF KEVIN." I LET DOOMSGUY GET IN A FEW PUNCHES DURING OUR FIGHT, AND PRETENDED TO DIE HEROICALLY.
I'LL LAY LOW FOR A FEW MONTHS, THEN REAPPEAR WEARING A SNAZZY NEW COSTUME.
EVERYONE WILL LOVE IT.

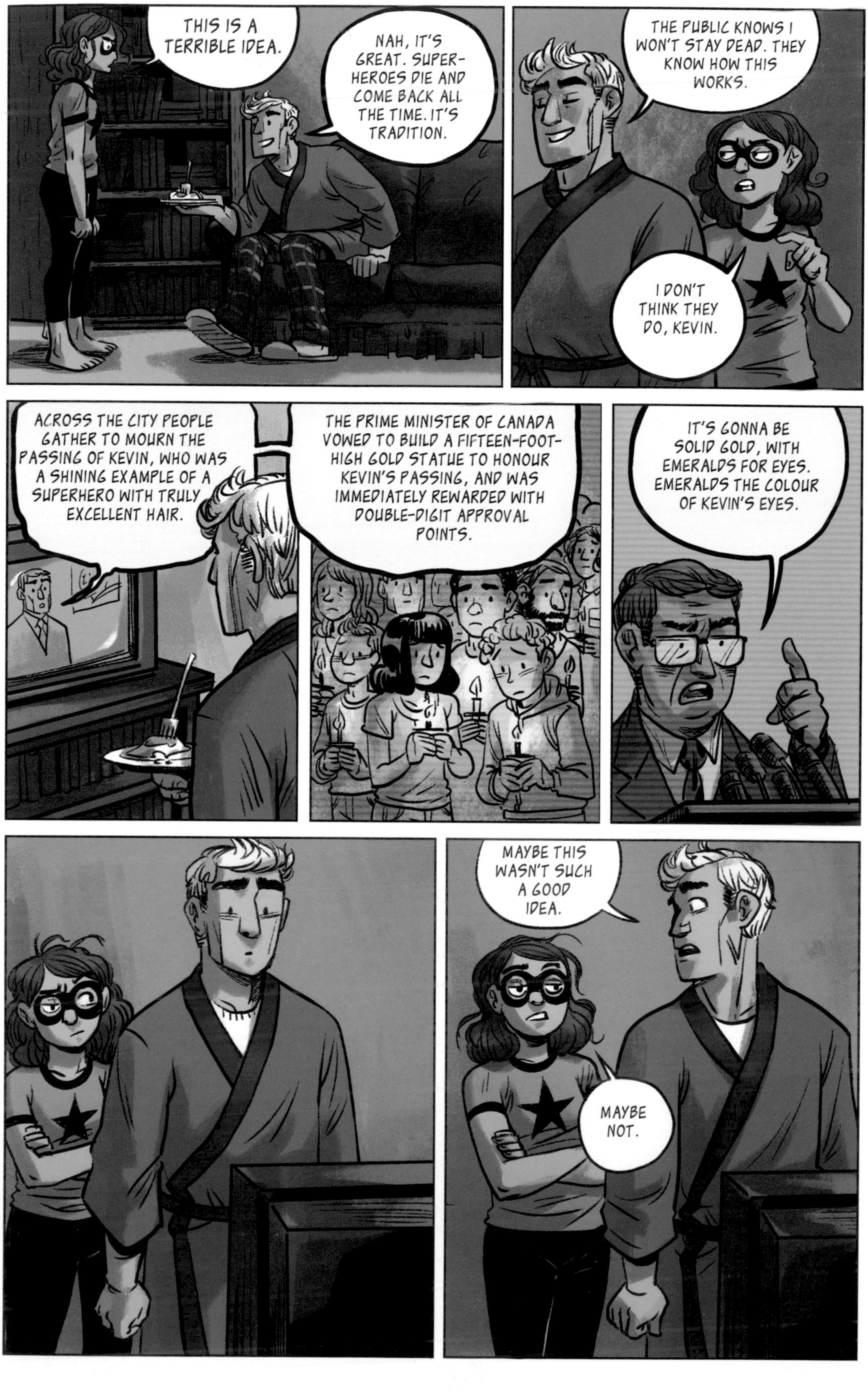
THIS IS A TERRIBLE IDEA.
NAH, IT'S GREAT. SUPER-HEROES DIE AND COME BACK ALL THE TIME. IT'S TRADITION.
THE PUBLIC KNOWS I WON'T STAY DEAD. THEY KNOW HOW THIS WORKS.
I DON'T THINK THEY DO, KEVIN.
ACROSS THE CITY PEOPLE GATHER TO MOURN THE PASSING OF KEVIN, WHO WAS A SHINING EXAMPLE OF A SUPERHERO WITH TRULY EXCELLENT HAIR.
THE PRIME MINISTER OF CANADA VOWED TO BUILD A FIFTEEN-FOOT-HIGH GOLD STATUE TO HONOUR KEVIN'S PASSING, AND WAS IMMEDIATELY REWARDED WITH DOUBLE-DIGIT APPROVAL POINTS.
IT'S GONNA BE SOLID GOLD, WITH EMERALDS FOR EYES. EMERALDS THE COLOUR OF KEVIN'S EYES.
MAYBE THIS WASN'T SUCH A GOOD IDEA.
MAYBE NOT.

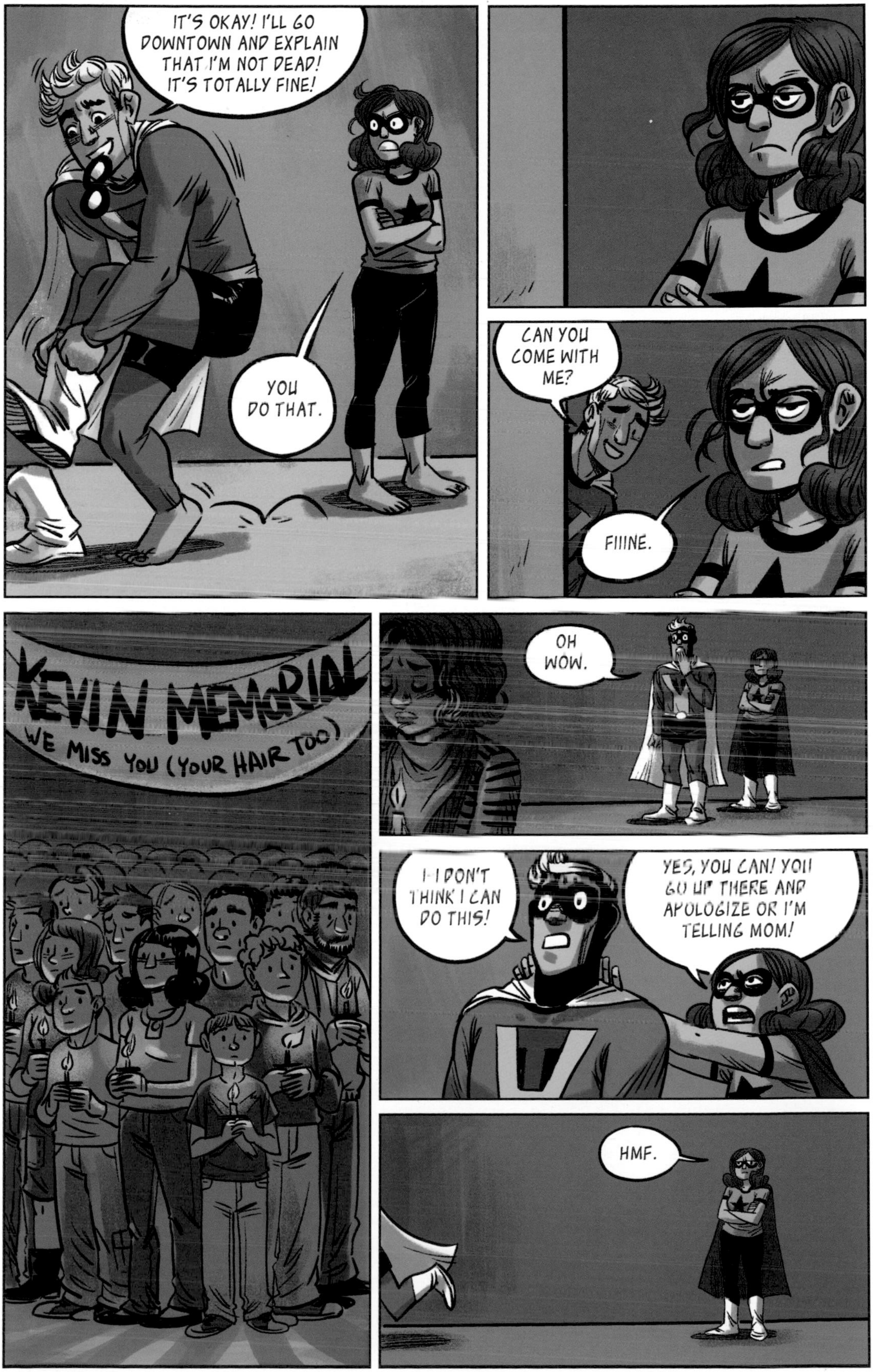

IT'S OKAY! I'LL GO DOWNTOWN AND EXPLAIN THAT I'M NOT DEAD! IT'S TOTALLY FINE!
YOU DO THAT.
CAN YOU COME WITH ME?
FIIINE.
KEVIN MEMORIAL
WE MISS YOU (YOUR HAIR TOO)
OH WOW.
I-I DON'T THINK I CAN DO THIS!
YES, YOU CAN! YOU GO UP THERE AND APOLOGIZE OR I'M TELLING MOM!
HMF.

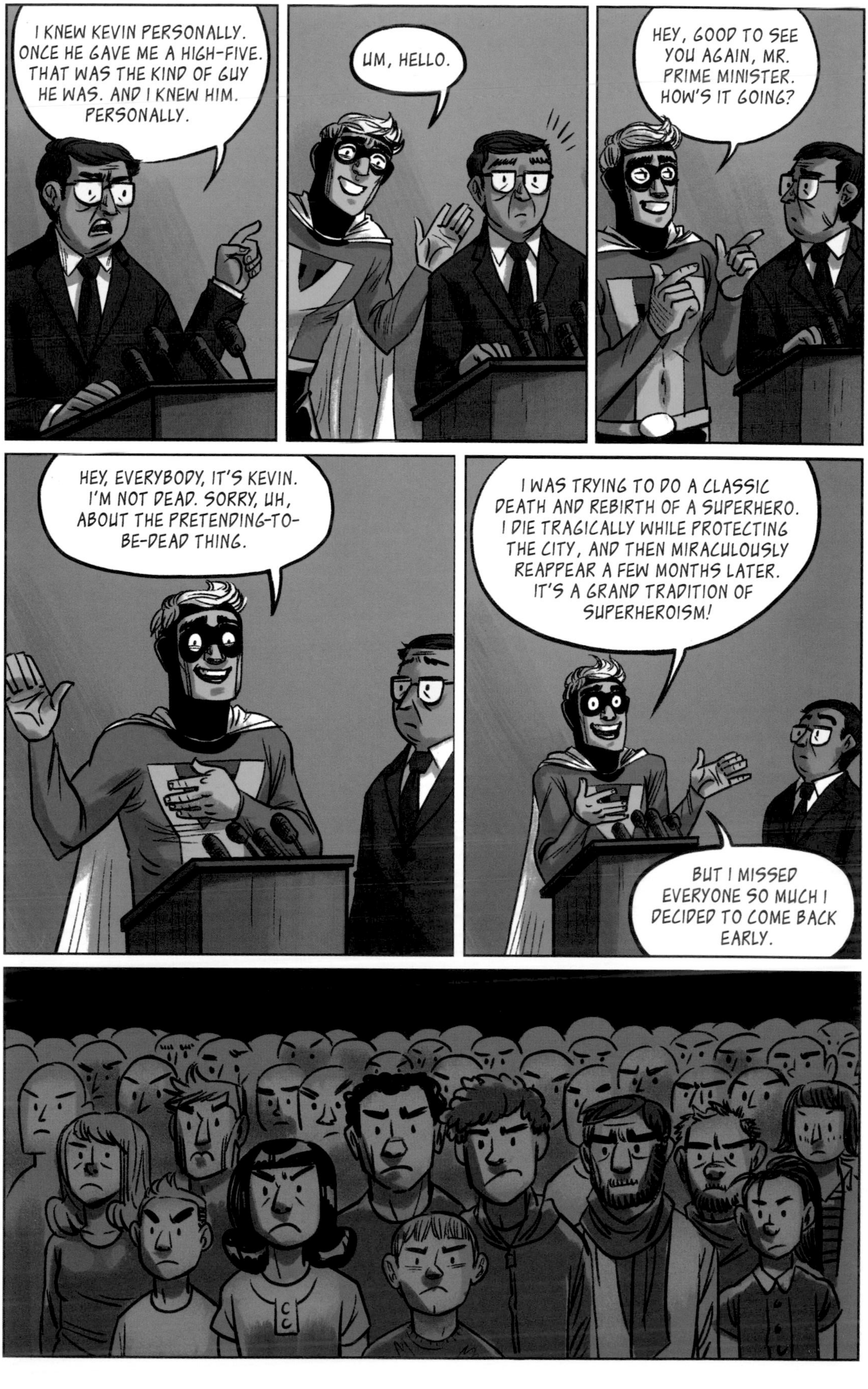
I KNEW KEVIN PERSONALLY. ONCE HE GAVE ME A HIGH-FIVE. THAT WAS THE KIND OF GUY HE WAS. AND I KNEW HIM. PERSONALLY.
UM, HELLO.
HEY, GOOD TO SEE YOU AGAIN, MR. PRIME MINISTER. HOW'S IT GOING?
HEY, EVERYBODY, IT'S KEVIN. I'M NOT DEAD. SORRY, UH, ABOUT THE PRETENDING-TO-BE-DEAD THING.
I WAS TRYING TO DO A CLASSIC DEATH AND REBIRTH OF A SUPERHERO. I DIE TRAGICALLY WHILE PROTECTING THE CITY, AND THEN MIRACULOUSLY REAPPEAR A FEW MONTHS LATER. IT'S A GRAND TRADITION OF SUPERHEROISM!
BUT I MISSED EVERYONE SO MUCH I DECIDED TO COME BACK EARLY.

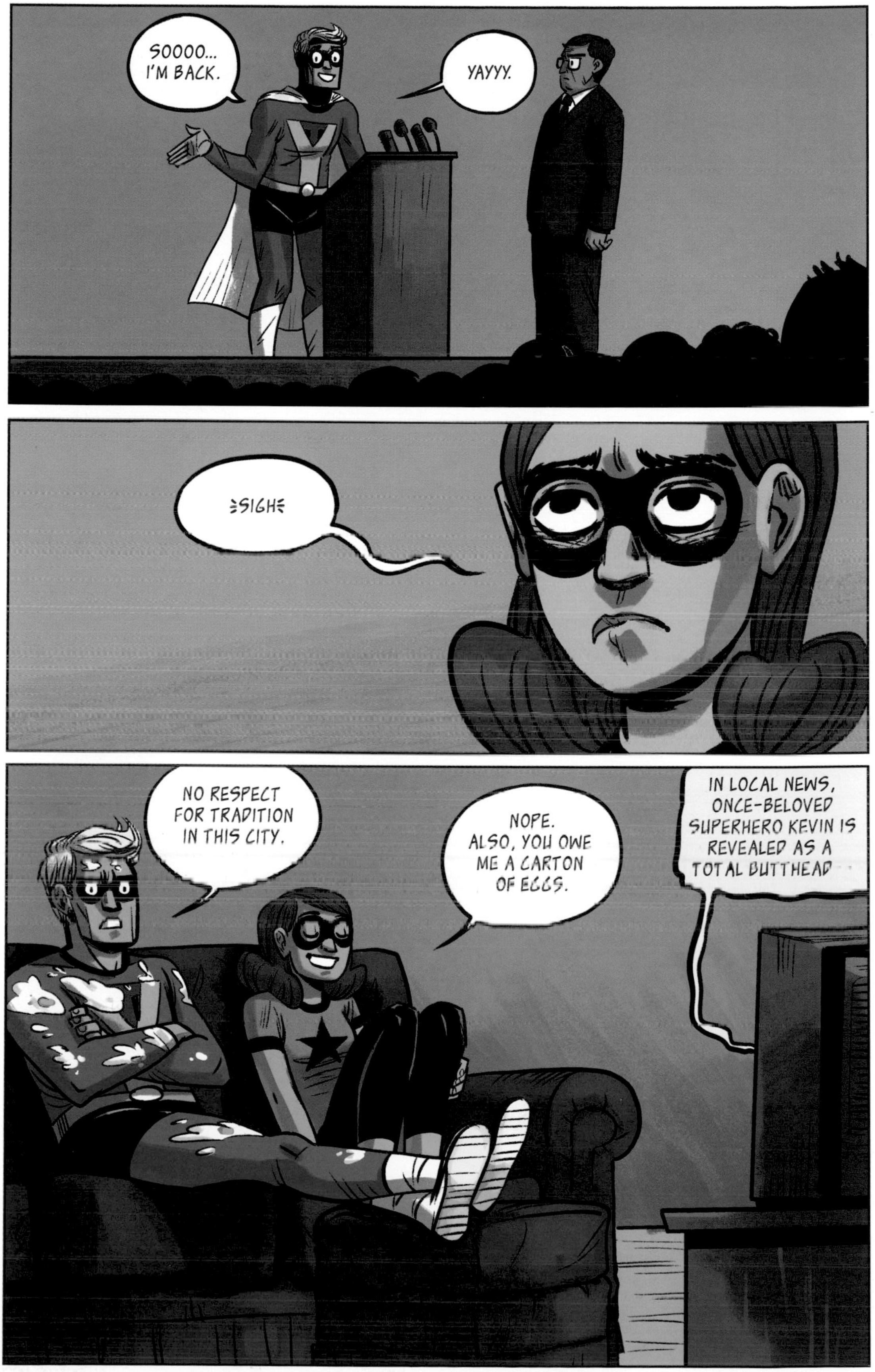
SOOOO... I'M BACK.
YAYYY.
SIGH
NO RESPECT FOR TRADITION IN THIS CITY.
NOPE. ALSO, YOU OWE ME A CARTON OF EGGS.
IN LOCAL NEWS, ONCE-BELOVED SUPERHERO KEVIN IS REVEALED AS A TOTAL BUTTHEAD

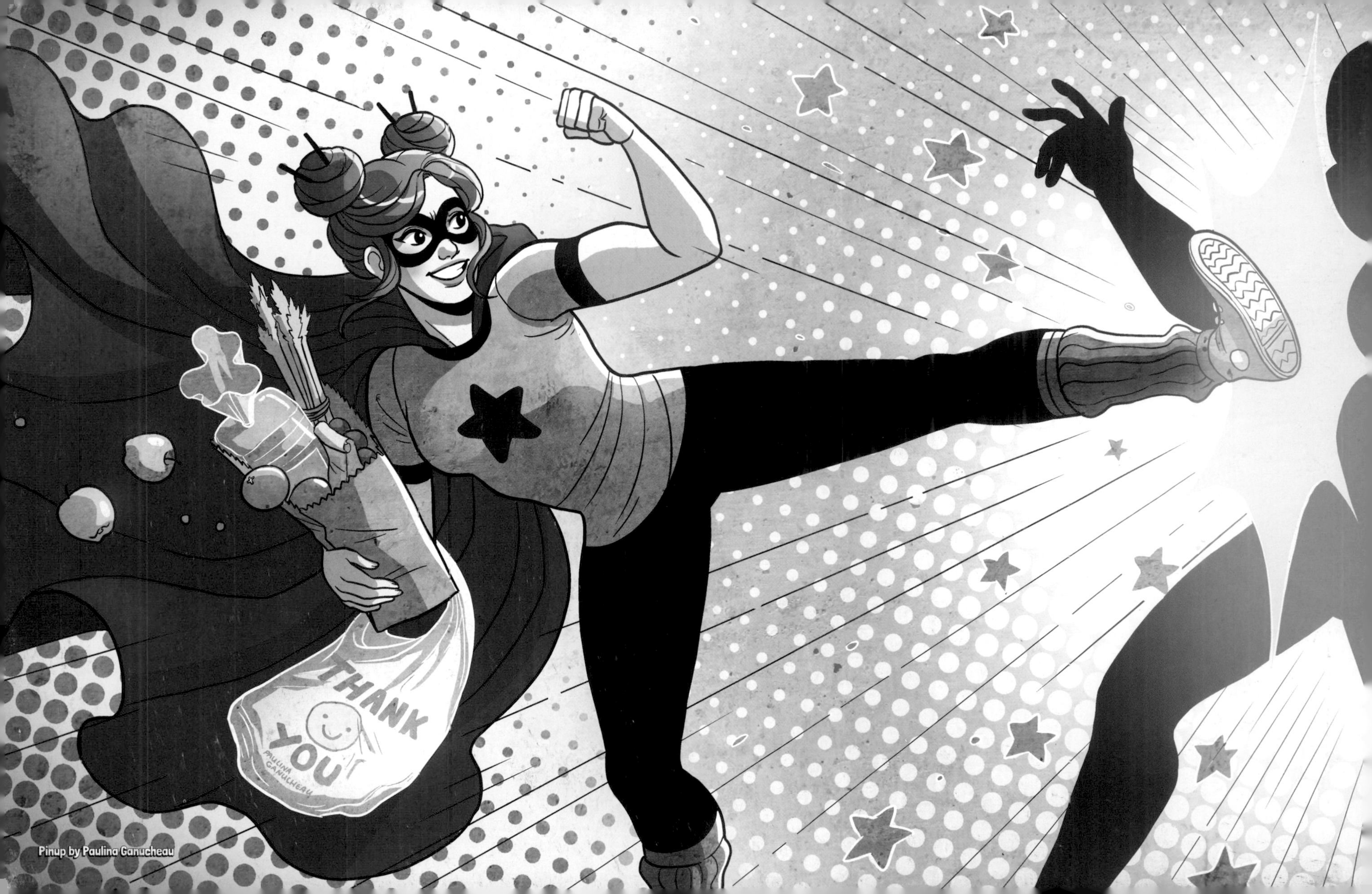

THANK
YOU
PAULINA
GANUCHEAU

Pinup by Paulina Ganucheau

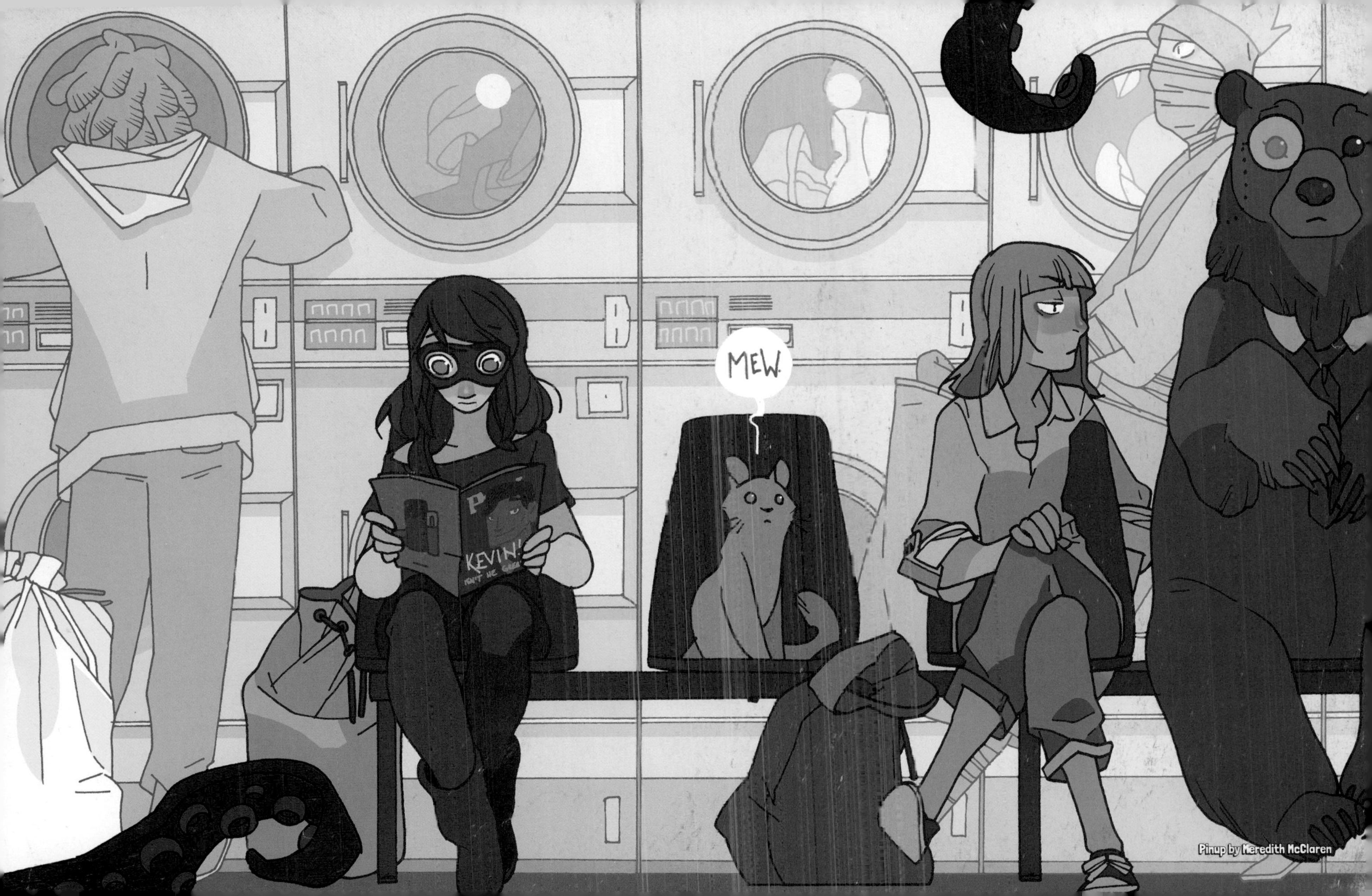
MEW.
KEVIN!
Pinup by Meredith McClaren

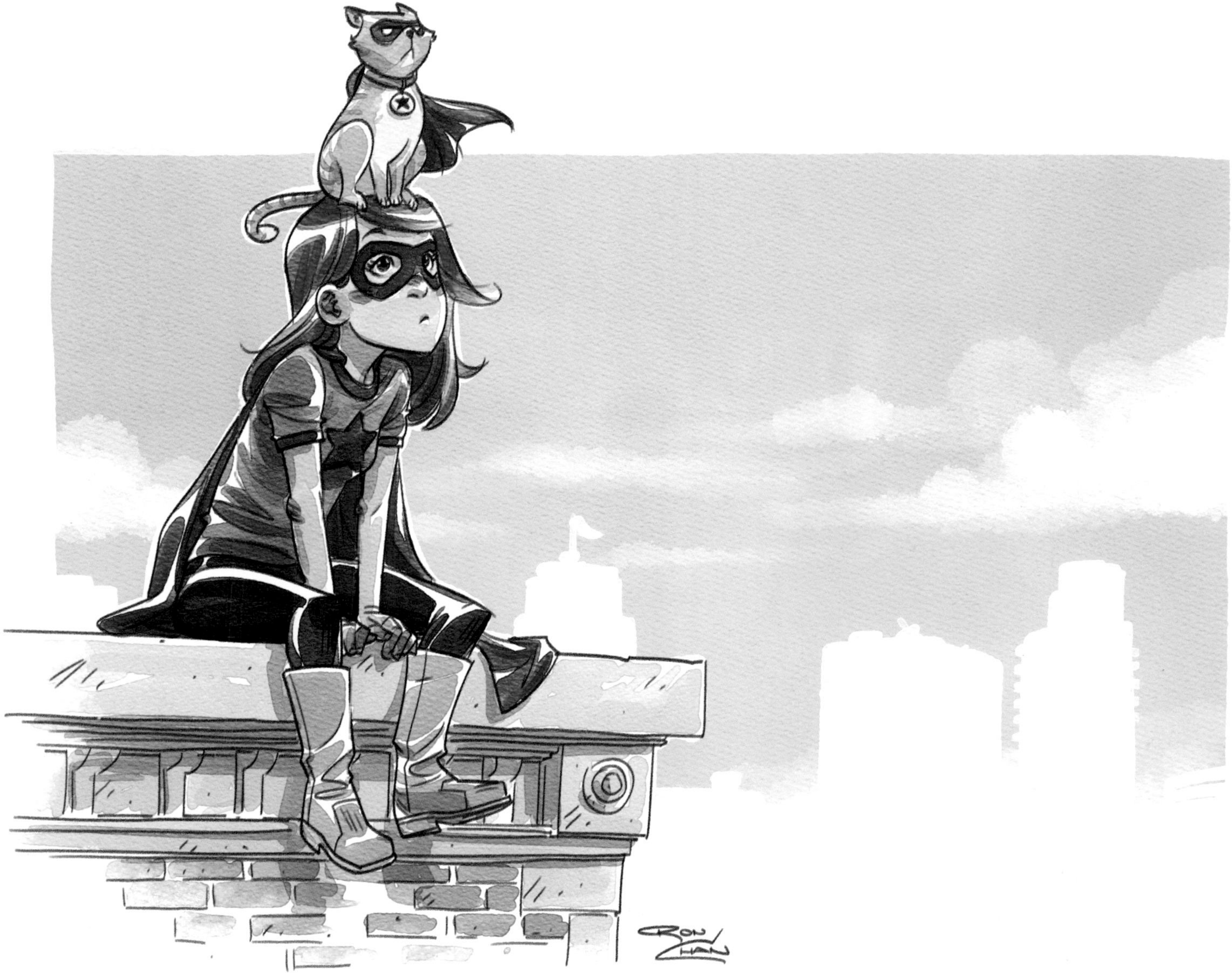
RON CHAN

Pinup by Ron Chan

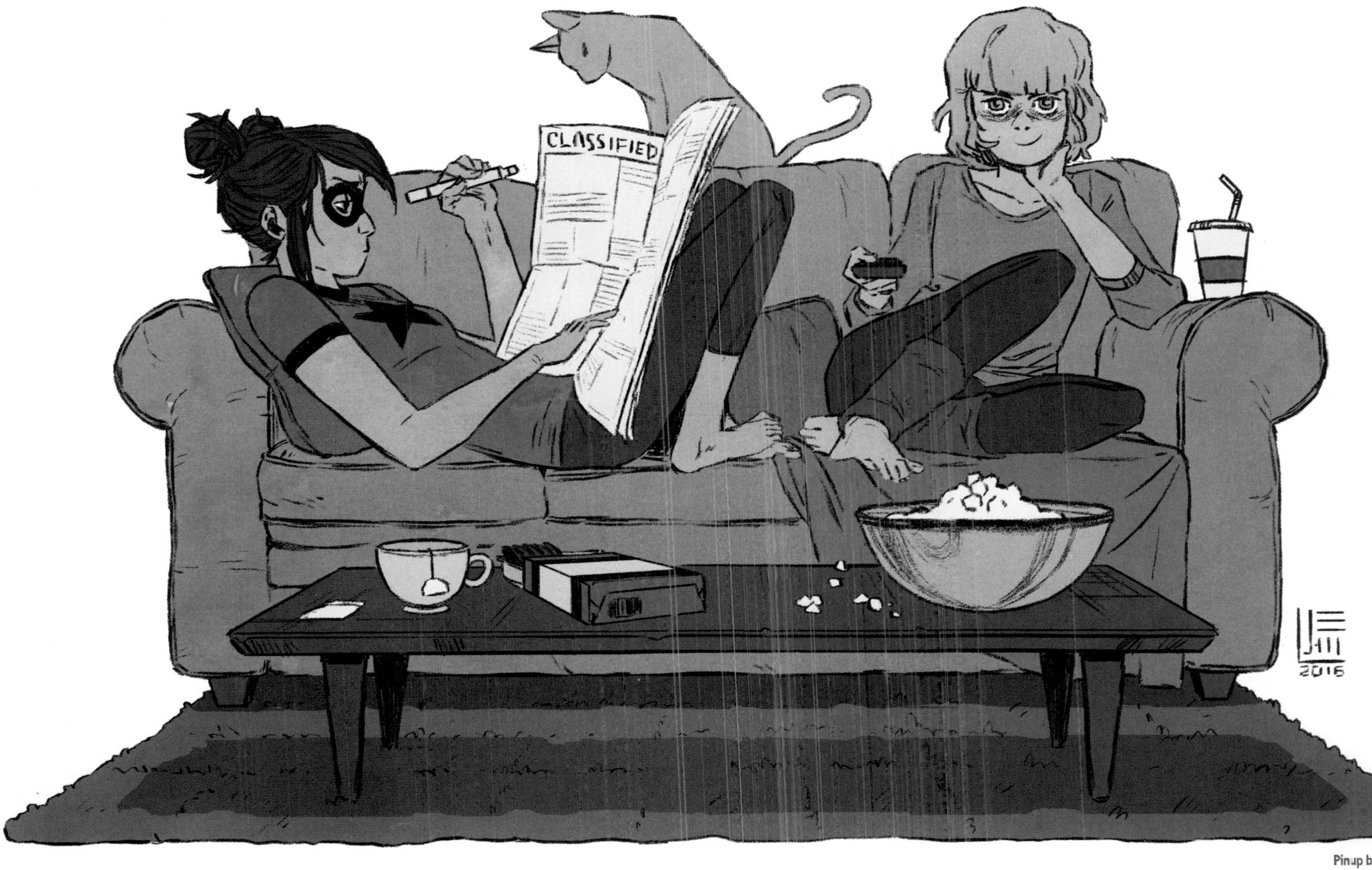
CLASSIFIED
2016

Pinup by Jake Wyatt

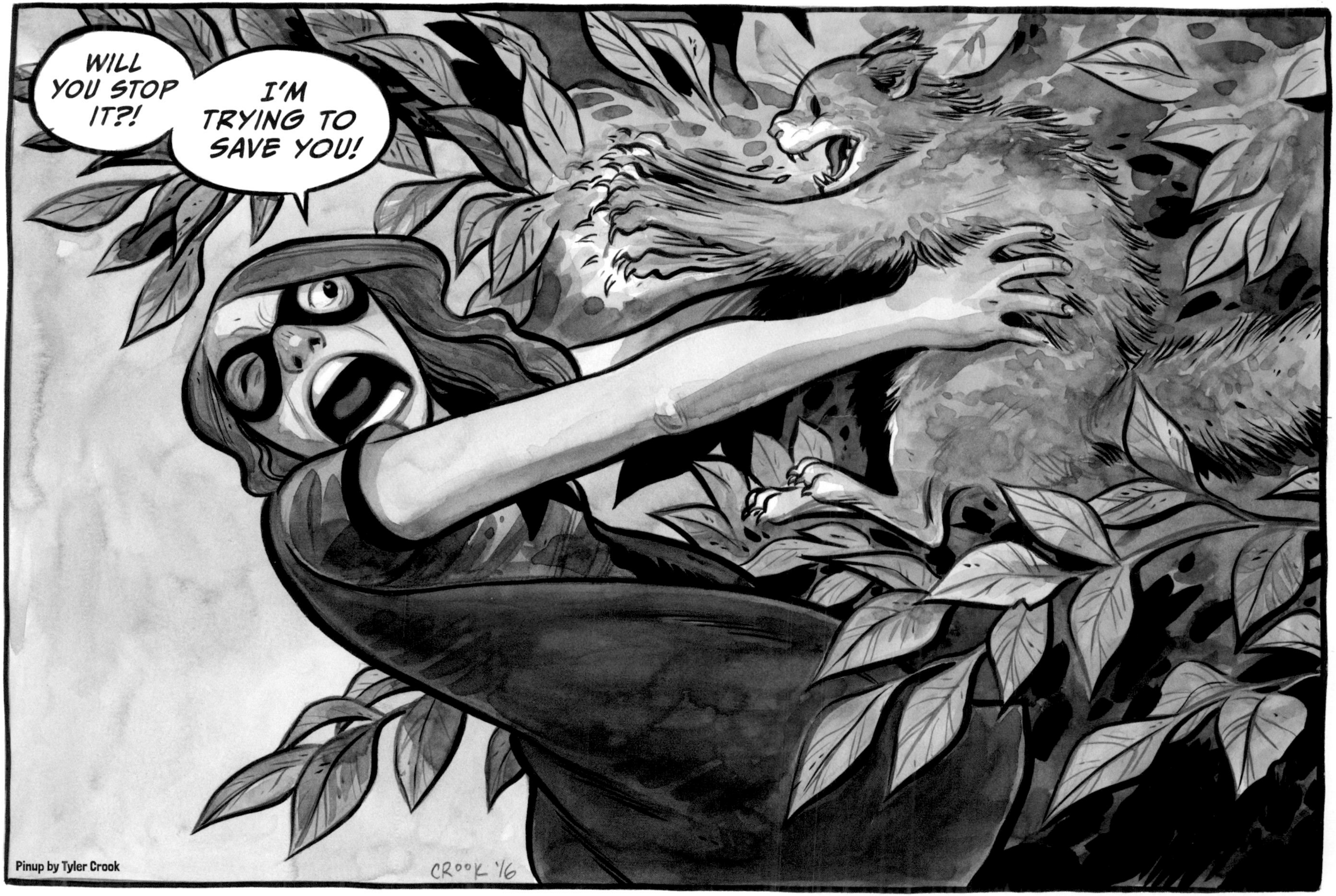
WILL YOU STOP IT?!
I'M TRYING TO SAVE YOU!
CROOK '16

Pinup by Tyler Crook